THE *DREAM HUNTERS*

BEVAN KNIGHT

is the final of the *Seeds of Time* trilogy,
following *The Wishing Tree*
and *Earthlight*

Print ISBN: 979-8-35098-962-5
eBook ISBN: 979-8-35098-963-2

Printed in the United States of America

O the mind, mind has mountains; cliffs of fall

Frightful, sheer, no-man-fathomed.

Gerard Manley Hopkins

CONTENTS

PROLOGUE

It was always the same. He was waiting on a crowded station platform, the people milling around as the train pulled in. Maria. Maria would surely come this time. Surely now. The passengers spilled out. The amorphous crowd resolved itself into little chattering groups, people embracing, people running to greet, people laughing, people crying. He willed the people to stay. As long as there was someone, some group, Maria would surely emerge, would be there.

The platform emptied. The station was bare.

And there was Belzic, not three feet away.

"Belzic, I've had that dream again."

"You are waiting for Maria? You know that is impossible, Andrew."

"Of course I know it's impossible!"

Stout little Belzic made his pronouncements like a judge. Belzic, not much taller than the Croans themselves, the only person he could really talk to, the only fellow human.

They were ninety days away from Planet Earth.

They were side by side, cocooned in what the Croans were pleased to call pods. Safe, if the unimaginable happened? Andrew would sooner not know. Now, he wriggled around, and listened. There was always sound, noises he could identify, and many more he could not. At the moment, voices. Belzic, of course, and the Croans, talking for once in English.

"Passengers, stay in your pods and ensure they are locked." That slightly raspy voice belonged to Schyl, the captain. "Leaving hyperdrive in five. All crew, at your stations."

Andrew braced himself. The jolt, the falling, falling ... the nausea ... the wish to be anywhere else, to be dead.

"Entering Groob's atmosphere in another twenty. Passengers, remain in your pods. Nice work, Erg."

"Thank you, captain." Erg, the navigation officer, a clipped voice, with a slight lisp, suggesting to Andrew an English admiral.

"Graviton now disconnecting. Grice, check manual in-flight functions." The captain again.

The ship was trembling. Very light, slight tremors. Andrew's fear returned. *And what use can I be anyway? More of a liability.*

"Lights! Lights! There are artificial lights below us." That had to be Grice, the engineer.

"Get a still image on the monitor, please, Grice." And that more mellifluous voice had to be Euse, their mission leader. "Fly cloaked now, captain. Extinguish all external lights."

"There's the image, Euse. Looks like a coastal settlement. Probably a town, or even a small city. Do you want to drop nearby? In that desert?"

"Yes, we'll take her down. Keep her cloaked all the way, captain."

The shaking increased as the ship dived.

Heat shield running at ninety-five percent capacity ... ninety-six percent. The metallic voice of the ship itself.

The ship dived lower.

Caution! Heat shield at ninety-seven percent. Please extinguish all unnecessary power usage.

The slowing craft shuddered along like a boat in a choppy sea.

"What are we looking for, Euse?"

"Captain, I'll know it when I see it. Something interesting, something other than sand. It may take some time."

"My God, look at that!"

"Yes, land right here, captain."

Andrew braced himself as the ship shook, and tipped and pranced like a slowing racehorse. Then when it came, the stillness felt unreal.

"Grice, I want heat sensors to cover a radius of sixty feet, in all directions. We'll see if anything is moving," said Schyl. "Passengers, you may leave your pods. Number one, please take the first watch."

Groose, first mate of the Duvra, settled down for a long vigil. His desk was ringed with monitors: three acting as heat detectors while two were visual. For Groose this planet was his last mission, or at least the last one on a government contract. It was definitely the last one he was going on while Euse was mission controller. Groose had problems with the science officer. Now, he put such thoughts from his head as he relaxed, his chair tilted backwards, one eye shut while the other roved from monitor to monitor. One of the visuals looked out over an ancient ruin: two towers inside a crenellated wall. It shone faintly, ghostlike, against the blackness of the Groobian night. A microphone placed by Groose's head registered the faint stirring of wind and the occasional crying of some desert animal. There were also internal sounds: talking and splashing as most of the remaining crew discarded their exoskeletons and dropped fishlike into the restoration tanks.

Groose dropped into a slumber, although his one open eye continued to rove over the monitors. Much later, he became fully awake. Outdoors there was something moving. It flitted across the visuals as scarcely more than a shadow, but it barely registered on the heat screens. A spirit being? A machine? Groose thought about alerting the mission controller, but decided against it. He can wait. Euse can wait, he thought. I get enough of him during daylight hours.

A few short steps away, Andrew stirred fitfully on the narrow shelf that passed, among Croans, for a bed. His unexpected weight gain after the landing had shocked him, and it was the sturdy Belzic who had helped him out of his pod.

"Yes, we're on a bigger planet than Earth. We need to take things slowly," Belzic had intoned, and Andrew had thought of the Croans in their exoskeletons. They came out of the sea aeons ago, so they said. Andrew tried to imagine the crude walking machines they must have started out with.

"They get an operation early in life, so they can be fully land based," Belzic had told him. Belzic was now sitting upright. "I can't sleep either," he said.

"Ninety days in a tin can, breathing canned air, and now nothing to see, nothing to hear."

"Yet," said Belzic.

A moment later a long, mournful animal howl penetrated their tin can, and echoed ghostlike through the cabins.

From the ship's database:

The Groob solar system has nine planets and fourteen moons. Five of the planets and two moons might support life. The fourth planet (Groob 4) is associated with the belief that it was once home to a very advanced civilization that destroyed itself. This may be no more than a folk tale.

The crew of the Duvra:

> *Mission leader: Science Officer P.B. Euse*
>
> *Captain: J.G. Schyl*
>
> *First Mate: R.G. Groose*
>
> *Navigator: M.Q. Erg*

Engineer: L.L. Grice

Comms.: Technician S. Cherg

Support: Technician A. Ess

Passengers:

Andrew Conway, Belzic Lebeau

WATER

On Groob the season of water begins the year,

offering great hope, great promise,

great possibilities, but also illusions,

fantasies, and insubstantial dreams.

That which is planted

may indeed thrive,

but whether as a blessing or a curse

none can say

CHAPTER 1

Aleb's house, Hilltop Road, City of Kraab

The evening of that momentous arrival was like any other evening for most in the city, although perhaps not for Aleb Foulkes. He had been busy most of the day, excitedly sorting and organising his few possessions in his little house on the edge of the desert, thinking all the while about how wonderful it was to have his own place, along with his new dream job. Now, he raised his eyes from the paper he had been reading and looked out over the desert. The day had darkened appreciably in the last half hour while his head was down, and his pen busy jotting notes for his first article. There were bands of green and orange rising halfway up the sky, and the various objects he had previously observed on the sand had taken on a mystical significance. Things that had blown there, or been uncovered by the shifting dunes, absorbing or reflecting the light, were throwing down their own curious shadows from Nubilus, the rising moon. Aleb watched them for a while, enjoying the way the darkness was stealing their identities, transforming them into incomprehensible features of the desert night.

To the east, the sea had taken on a gleam like molten metal, and Kraab was lighting up for the evening. Aleb's house sat at the very top of the city, which descended in a series of giant steps, or terraces, as far as the shoreline, and the coastal road that at present was being traced out by numerous flickering lights from the vehicles upon it. Aleb was now examining this place that was to become his home and livelihood. About halfway up the slope the City Hall building boasted a multitude of lights, all the more distinct for the dark expanse (the central park) that surrounded them. Aleb took his field glasses and trained them over the hall, and then over some of the main streets. All those little twinkling lights, any one of which might mark the place for a story worth my while, he thought. Aleb had just gained a contract with the Kraab Monitor to produce weekly articles. He was feeling pleased with himself, pleased with his newly acquired house, pleased with the way his career was going (albeit against his father's wishes), pleased with Kraab itself.

He was tired though. He yawned, stretched, thought about going to bed, but instead dozed off in his chair. When he woke again the sky was fully dark, and now riding high above Kraab, Rubilis, Groob's second moon, moon of illusions, cast down its bluish purple glow. Aleb focussed on it briefly, picking out that suggestion of a face which stared out at him, as it always did. Next, he looked up through the skylight, noting the familiar constellations: the Candle and the Fountain, with the Serpent encircling them both and attempting (as it eternally did) to insinuate itself between them. And the familiar stars beyond, with the pink Krumus, nearest of the planetary neighbours, almost at the zenith. He was about to put his glasses away when he saw something odd: a bright light, brighter than the stars, moving swiftly across the Serpent's tail. Too slow for a meteor, too fast for anything else, he thought. Briefly, it dimmed as it went behind a smudge of cloud, and then shone brightly once more. Too high for a balloon surely? And going now in the direction of the desert? A moment later it disappeared entirely, although the sky here was clear. Aleb thought about that, and went to the telephone.

CHAPTER 2

The Great Desert

The new day announced itself with the calling of birds, a cacophony of honks, clicks, tweets and whistles. Andrew, roused, slid off the bench that passed for his bed and fell to his knees. He was still shocked by his unexpected weight gain.

"Oh damn!" said Andrew. "No thanks, Belzic, I'll manage."

"It's a bigger planet than poor old Earth."

"At least we'll get to see it today."

"More than that, they're bound to want you in the first little sortie out the door."

A face looked into the passenger cabin. "You two are slow. You missed the birds, hundreds of them. Euse thinks they're off to nest somewhere. We've got wonderful photos." It was Erg, with the unmistakable lisp. "We want you, Andrew, right away."

Andrew was a head taller than Groose, the tallest of the Croans, and indeed Belzic's prediction came true. Andrew was second out the door, behind Euse and ahead of Ess the technician and Cherg of communications.

"Open your helmets for no more than a minute, and take shallow breaths. The air is rich in oxygen and I don't want anyone falling over." The voice came into their headphones from Groose, who was to lead the rescue party, should such a thing be needed.

All four of the landing party were armed, heavily padded and laden with various recording and sampling devices.

Ω

Aleb was up and busy the moment the sun reached through his bedroom windows. His first day of work, he had an interview, and he was reading up on the person involved when Ormond arrived, puffing a little, with the Kraab Monitor. Ormond was an old friend.

"I ought to charge you more for having to come all this way."

"Nonsense! It's good for you. Besides, there are five households along this street. Why don't you get them to subscribe?"

"You talk to them then." Ormond shook his head. "It's in your interest more than mine."

"The exercise will keep you young."

Aleb finished his breakfast while checking through the lead stories. Gratifyingly, the strange light he had spotted in the sky occupied the front page.

ARE WE BEING SPIED ON? MYSTERY BALLOON FLIGHT. Six Kraab residents reported seeing an object, thought to be a balloon, fly over the city at 10.30 yesterday evening, headed for the desert. No night time flights have been reported, and no balloons reported missing …

And below that, the editor had printed, word for word, an opinion piece he had put together from rather flimsy data.

IS SOMEBODY READING YOUR THOUGHTS? A new company, calling itself Dream Hunters, had been set up to peddle those gadgets that supposedly interpret your dreams and delve into the workings of your mind. These objects were, as the Monitor previously reported, excavated from the desert and their true purpose is unknown. We advise readers to have great caution if they ever have dealings with this company …

Yes! said Aleb to himself. I must hunt down those dream hunters. They'll be good for at least one story.

Ω

The Croans' ship was caught in shade afforded by the stone walls of the partly collapsed ruin. Outside these long shadows the desert gleamed silvery white under the sunrise. It was a curiously forbidding, monotone landscape, and the dark ruin confronting the landing party loomed almost as a threat. Once on the sand, they formed a close circle, and went through the prosaic but reassuring routine of checking their equipment and their communication systems, working closely with the ship as they did so.

"Allow yourselves to breathe the air for no more than a minute," Groose reminded them over the ship's speakers.

A circuit of the Duvra followed. "To get you used to walking, and to look very carefully for any damage," said Schyl.

The party began their exploration with a walk through an archway in the wall and an inspection of the nearest of the two towers. The tower also had an entrance arch, and as they reached it a large, dark flying creature flew out, giving an indignant howling cry and swooping low over their heads. Euse excitedly put a call through to Schyl, while the others gathered round the entrance. The floor within was covered with layers of old sticks, some of which crumbled to dust as Ess tried to move them. Little crawling things ran from the light of their torches. In the dimness overhead was the suggestion of old nests and dangling beams.

"Ess, see if you can get one of those beasties into a sample bottle," said Euse.

Ess clipped his torch onto his helmet, took a bottle and clamped it over one of the creatures on the sand.

"Ouch! Something got me." He raised one hand to show blood streaming from a hole in his glove. In another moment he had collapsed. Euse crouched beside him and undid a segment of his sleeve and exoskeleton, revealing a portion of flesh that looked as silver-white as the sand. He jabbed a needle into Ess's arm.

"Help me, Andrew."

Andrew knelt, putting one hand to the ground as he bent over Ess. A stabbing pain shot through his index finger. He stifled a cry and kept following Euse's directions, so that soon the two stood one on each side of the supported Ess. Andrew swayed.

"Easy, Andrew, easy. We'll walk him to the ship."

But then, right in their way as they reached the wall, was the most extraordinary creature Andrew had ever seen. It appeared to be dressed in silver armour, with long, thin metallic arms and legs, and a very long flexible neck. The face was the oddest thing of all: triangular, with a narrow groove that might have been a mouth, and two large protruding eyes. Andrew, Euse and Ess stopped dead in their tracks, with Cherg close behind. Andrew's head meanwhile was feeling very strange. He wondered if he was hallucinating, especially since the alien creature remained absolutely still. In another moment he let go of Ess and pitched forward onto the sand.

CHAPTER 3

On the Duvra

Report from Senior Science Officer Euse to Area Commander Queyn concerning our arrival and first investigations on the planet Groob 4, star system QR620 (Date: 50988/519)

Dear Commander

Firstly, please accept the congratulations of myself and all the crew of the starship. We were thrilled to hear of your promotion and consider it well-deserved!

The Duvra las landed, and our scout has now completed a high altitude examination of the whole planet, analysis of atmospheric temperatures and chemistry, as well as prominent ground features being attached as supplementary to this report. We have been very surprised by a number of features, unknown in the literature and certainly not anticipated by us. Most prominent would be:

- *the amount of surface water, which covers almost 85% of the planet*

- *the amount of desert, with the three largest land masses having dead centres*

- *the very extensive volcanic activity, much of it under water*

- *the relatively temperate climate*

We are working on the assumption that the volcanic vents are largely due to gravitational pressures. In other words, the planet is slowly being broken apart. The results of tests, currently being undertaken, will be available shortly.

The warmth may be explained in part by the mediating influence of the surface water, and the extensive cloud cover. On the other hand there is the reflective capacity of the very white desert sand. The chemical constituents of the sand are detailed in the supplement.

Presently we are landed in one of the said deserts, near a stone ruin, a kind of fort (image attached in the appendix) There is no sign of life here other than some small bug-like creatures (see images) and some kind of flying creature that was unfortunately too quick for us to capture. A pile of sticks in one of the towers suggests an old nest. There is certainly no intelligent life nearby, although we spotted artificial lighting, suggestive of a civilised community, when we arrived. There are also intelligent machines, since one confronted us when we left the ruin. Cherg and I both attempted to communicate with it, to no effect. Then Cherg simply shouted 'shoo' and the thing made off. We are having a rest day right now, while we run checks on the ship, but will be doing some low altitude exploring soon.. As you can see, our first objective (evidence of advanced technology) is already achieved. All our crew are well, and we are doing fine. We will keep you posted.

Sent by PB Euse, Senior Science Officer.

"There," said Euse. "Send that for me please, mister communications officer. How are our patients, by the way?"

"Your assistant is doing well. Andrew is struggling a bit, but Belzic is attending him. However did we manage to have two casualties?"

"Bad luck, Cherg. You saw how Ess was bitten. As for Andrew, I think that human is accident prone."

In the first aid room Belzic had strapped a protesting Andrew onto a board alongside Ess. Cherg had provided a syringe which he assured Belzic 'could do no harm'. However as Belzic ministered to him Andrew gave a cry of alarm. He had the sensation of his arm expanding to a vast size.

"I feel as though there is an enormous river running through me," he complained.

Nonetheless when Belzic inspected the swollen discolored hand he gave a cheery whistle.

"You're doing fine, old chap. Just relax and let that river run."

"Heaven knows how this will end, Belzic."

"I certainly don't, and right now I'm hungry. And it's my turn in the galley. What do you want for breakfast Andrew?"

CHAPTER 4

Aleb's house, Hilltop Road

Aleb lingered just a little over his breakfast, savouring the moment: his own column in the Monitor, and ability to work his own hours. Finally, he cleared the table, collected his bicycle and freewheeled down through the main streets of the city. He had a busy morning: first to call in at the office, and then on to his interview for the day. He was on the trail of a young woman who had made the news some six years earlier, but had since been largely forgotten by the media, and certainly by the public. Aleb was on a contract to write stories about such people, to be featured weekly under the heading, 'Whatever happened to—'. Jelani Therim was the next one on his list. He had read her story the day before. How she had traveled to the little island of Skerron on vacation …

Feeling indisposed one day, she left the tour group to their more strenuous activities and wandered off on her own. She walked out to the coast, and was standing under the giant marker rock, thinking about her father, when a stabbing pain struck her between the eyes. In another moment she was on her back, gasping for breath. In the invisible air, it seemed that some malevolent force was pushing her down. With a desperate effort she struggled to her feet, steadied herself against the great stone beside her, and screamed out to the empty ocean: "Help me! Somebody help me!"

Her father's body was washed up on a beach eight days later. He had been struck between the eyes, knocked down in his boat, pushed overboard and held forcibly beneath the surface until he drowned. His cargo was unloaded and the boat sunk by pirates, who made their way into one of the myriad mazes of islands that adorned the great Southern Ocean.

At least, that was the reconstruction of the crime that the investigators delivered in the weeks that followed, working from his last known position, and finally coming upon the wreck.

After a period of mourning Jelani made a vow: I experienced what my father went through, but how was this possible? I will devote my life to finding out.

Her early investigations were not encouraging: *You could not have known what happened: therefore you did not know. What you thought you experienced was a false memory, or perhaps just a dizzy spell. You must understand, my dear, that the brain is very clever at playing these tricks on us.* That was what one member of the Groob Institute of Science told her, condescendingly, and his words, or at least sentiments, were echoed by most of those she consulted over the next two years. After that she gave up asking.

Other interests took over her life. She married, gave birth to twins, and later separated, finding too late that her husband opposed her psychic interests.

"I won't have you delving into things that don't concern us. You have two lovely children—what more do you want?"

Jelani is a suub, and as such speaks the wrong way, dresses the wrong way, has the wrong education, and once lived in one of the worst parts of Kraab. It was all the more remarkable that she was awarded one of the first female scholarships to study in the great city, or that in four years she should be invited to speak to the prestigious Council of Light. She had just turned twenty.

As Aleb read the notes on her file that previous evening he turned to observe her photograph: large resolute eyes, finely boned face, and dark, swept back hair. He pictured her, walking onto the stage in that hallowed hall, to be confronted by a sombre row of men in formal attire. Perhaps she felt an uneasy moment as she introduced her topic with an impassioned voice:

"I shall begin with the tragic death of my father. Like you, he was, in his way, a scientist. He taught me never to take things for granted, to question everything, and above all to think, think. Apart from my life, I owe him so very much. For example, I owe it to him that I am standing here today, talking to you all ..."

About now she would have stepped forward a little more, gripped the microphone stem a little harder, and stared out over the sea of faces. As she spoke, she would have lost all sense of time...

"It is a truism that information is never totally lost, and this I submit is true of articulated information, such as is carried by words, and informed by images, sounds, smells, along with the things we taste, and touch. We attend, we remember, we think, and all these impressions are given out to the world. And we develop sensitivities. We know that there are places where we feel comfortable, locations we love to visit, and other places we try to avoid. How do we know? It is not always obvious. It may be no more than a feeling, a hunch, an intuition that directs our footsteps. What then guides us? Something in the air? Could the brain itself transmit a message: a wave perhaps on a frequency that is beyond our technology to register? Ladies and gentlemen, I have with me over a hundred case studies that call for an explanation. I also have a number of hypotheses to share. Please bear with me."

As she pinned up her charts she would have been dimly aware of her audience's responses: interest, puzzlement, excitement and indignation among others.

"I speak of thoughts, but I should make it clear that for me 'mind' is not a place: it is a process. Each one of us is an information hub. We are receiving, processing and transmitting information every living moment of our lives, whether we are aware or not, and it is this hive of activity we call mind. We send out and we receive through our feelings, moods, posture, expressions, the tone of our voices, the scent from our breath and sweat, even, I would say, through our very thoughts. We are 'mind' from the tops of our heads to the tips of our toes …"

At the end, the applause was polite, and the speeches following were kind. The media reaction ran on predictable lines:

A keen young scientist, Jelani Therim, enthused over her 'discovery' that the unaided brain can receive and transmit information, but provided only limited data, wrote the Science Observer. *Considering no clinical tests support her efforts we consider her excitement to be premature.*

An exciting new advance in neuroscience, said the Psychic Messenger. *A brave young woman takes on the Council of Light.*

There were other reports, many of them, but no further information was forthcoming in the six following years. Jelani applied to various institutions for funding to continue her work, but was always met with polite, regretful words of refusal: Perhaps later …. The demand for research is very great at present …. Perhaps if you were to find a sponsor …

Jelani was not too concerned, since she had discovered, at least to her own satisfaction, what happened to her when her father died; and she was convinced that sooner or later somebody would take up her work at the point where she left off. This indeed happened, but not at all in the way she expected; not at any rate by a commercial company with the fanciful name *Dream Hunters*.

Ω

As Aleb approached the house he was astonished by its opulence. It sat on a little rise above the beach, in an upmarket part of Kraab. Grassy terraces led down to the sea; that expanse of thermal water which the natives called, with considerable understatement, *the pond*. He wondered if the Therim family were wealthy; that would be unusual for suubs, although not unheard of. Aleb felt a little tense; he was early, and Jelani was reputed to be rather short with interviewers. He rang the bell, and waited, half expecting a servant to open the door.

"Is that you Aleb? Come in, come in! The voice came over a speaker, and continued as he opened the door. "Mind where you step. I'm getting rid of the past. Take the first door on your right."

Aleb negotiated through piles of assorted papers, carry bags, and clutter. Jelani, kneeling beside a pile of books, looked up as he entered the room. The first thing he noticed were her eyes; there was something compelling, some pain, behind those beautiful eyes. She spoke again,

"Hello. You are Aleb?"

"Yes, I am. Is there somewhere we can sit down?"

"Yes, sorry." She arose lightly from the floor, cleared a couple of chairs, and gestured for him to be seated.

"You are a suub?" she asked when the two were sitting.

"Yes, I think so. My mother said I came out of a porthole, whatever that means." Aleb gave a false laugh. "Do you mind if I switch on my recorder?"

"Could it be a portal?"

"Sorry?"

"You said porthole. Could she have meant portal?"

Later when Aleb left his head was spinning, and he was barely able to remember a single word of the interview. But after some hours, as he sat in his own house and watched the evening sky darken, it occurred to him that he had been thinking continuously, unceasingly, about Jelani, in a way that had nothing to do with her research. He wondered then what was happening to him—to his mind, in fact. Finally, he wrote the article, taking it through several revisions, and going to bed late. Jelani Therim, he thought, oh Jelani Therim, what have you done to me?

CHAPTER 5

On the Duvra

The Duvra crew intermittently worked and rested through their long first day. They took measurements of the ruined fortress, studied its construction and speculated about its purpose. They searched without success for any artefacts that might have belonged to it. They kept a constant watch for the strange creature that had confronted them, or in fact any creatures at all. The desert remained stubbornly empty, vast and featureless to its horizon. The Duvra lifted off with the last rays of the sun, while two moons rose, one following close upon the other.

There was nothing more to see in this dead centre. In the navigation room time dragged with the slow monotony of the desert sand itself, and Schyl's head was nodding towards his console as the night wore on.

"Ship, let me know if you spot anything interesting," he said, and uttered a huge yawn.

Please define what is interesting, the ship responded.

"That's the trouble with artificial intelligence," said Grice. "It never understands what you mean."

However, a moment later the engineer's voice voice rang out.

"Whoa! Whoa! Slow! Ship, tight circle!" An image came up, bright and clear on the screen. Strange creatures were moving across the sand.

Things like giraffes in metallic silver glinted in the moonlight. They strode on broad paddle legs, while black, shorter creatures like giant toads maintained pace with giant hops. A trail of fine dust followed them.

"Drop a thousand feet, Erg. We must follow this."

From the air the creatures were easily located by their long dust trails. The ship now passed by several groups, and then hovered over a large column, some eighty or more that were moving fast, clearly in a hurry. The ship floated overhead, keeping pace, and recording. Its lights reflected back off the column in a myriad of dazzling colors. The troop came to an amphitheater formed by a semicircular outcrop of rocks. The sand had banked up behind, leaving a long shallow scoop in front. Here the creatures swarmed, firstly into the little valley in the sand and then mounting as high as they could onto the rocks above it.

"What are they, Grice? Machines? Attention crew, watch your monitors."

"The ship doesn't sense any life in them, Schyl."

Now a second column, larger than the first, reached the hollow, and what happened next brought exclamations of amazement from the crew. The groups clashed together in violent combat. Projectiles in the form of spears and discs flew, projections in the form of snapping jaws with huge teeth lunged out on sinuous snake-like necks. The newcomers soon proved themselves more effective. Gradually the first group were pulled away or beaten off the rocks and systematically torn apart. A small number escaped. The captured ones were broken up into small pieces, which were loaded into baskets, now evident on the backs of some of the victorious troops. Several robots in the victory group were also seriously damaged and prostrated on the sand, and these too were demolished, crushed, and taken away.

"What do you make of that, Euse?"

"Mostly that these damn things are brutal, captain, and we'd better keep clear of them."

"Ship, are the creatures below us alive?"

Machines are not considered life forms.

"There's your answer, Schyl. No doubt these things are just carrying on where the people left off."

"If there are any people left," said Schyl. "If those transmissions we keep picking up are not simply machine transmissions. We'll climb now, Euse, if you're happy with that. The night is over and I want to get a much wider view."

It was in the air on that second long day that the planet became beautiful to its visitors. Captain Schyl initially took them to a great height, so that the ruined structure where they had spent the night became a mere black dot in a white wilderness, and they saw that there were other dots, mostly scattered miles apart, and, (as was apparent when the viewer enlarged a few) all roughly similar, with towers, turrets, and walls, and all in black or white stone. There were many natural examples of that stone now evident, peering out of the sand like reefs out of the sea; some almost entirely covered, while others reared up like wild creatures, according to the waywardness of the wind. No longer featureless, the desert was marked with dots, scars, gouges and the occasional larger hole formed by the protruding rocks. The ground no longer appeared a uniform white. There were orange tints where dunes rose and dipped, with darker streaks too, grey-black or brown, and the hint of old river valleys with branching arteries. And in the very far distance a blue haze, which Euse called on the ship to explain.

Mountain range two hundred miles to the west, said the ship.

"We must investigate that later", said Euse. "And we need more sand samples. For now, turn north—no, north-east, if you please. Higher, Schyl, higher and faster."

The ship moved on. The land was changing, sand giving way to small shrubs and grasses. The horizon was now blotted out by clouds. The ship continued to rise.

In the control room the crew watched their monitors in anticipation.

Surface water detected, said the ship.

"This is what we expected," Euse said excitedly. "According to the scout the sea should be very close now."

Almost immediately the clouds gave way, and stretching ahead, vast, to the distant horizon, was the ocean. It was an ocean of many colours: browns, blues, emerald greens, all entwined, the colours flowing, mixing and diverging. And rising out of the ocean in many places, flowing into the sky, was steam. Little curlicues of coloured light flickered here and there amid the waves like roaming butterflies, and the whole sea's surface, it seemed to Andrew, quivered with an immense vitality.

"Yes! This is what I was looking for," said Euse. "According to the stories there is supposed to be an ocean with ten thousand islands, and this could be it. Ship, can you tell us the temperature of this water?"

Accurate data is not possible from this height. Surface temperature varies from approximately sixteen degrees to approximately sixty degrees.

From their great height the crew were able to observe a school of aquatic creatures racing across the wrinkled, colourful sea.

"Life," said Euse. "We have creatures in the sand and fish in the sea. Even if there are no intelligent beings here this is certainly not a dead planet."

"Navigator," said Schyl, "find us one of these ten thousand islands where we can land."

CHAPTER 6

The Dream Hunters

Aleb rode his bicycle through the big gateway arch, dismounted and gazed up at the six story structure built of black and white stone. A large sign on the tower announced 'Dream Hunters—we turn your dreams into reality.' Judging from the movement in the foyer, the company was not lacking in clients. Vehicles came and went. People carried strange items in, and out. Aleb whimsically considered that catching dreams and solidifying them must involve a lot of work. He took his time and watched the activity before working his way around obstacles to reach the front door. Two name plates announced, respectively, 'Dreamland Enterprises—Ground Floor' and 'Dream Hunters—Floor 6'. Aleb, stood pondering about the remaining four floors, until his contact, Hamul, came running out, apologetic about the wait.

"Aleb? Come in, come in! So sorry, so sorry ... no, not that, that's the goods lift ... this one ... here we are, top floor."

"It's like a fortress." Aleb looked down from where he'd come, scanned the courtyard, the opposite tower, the crenelated outer wall. "I've gone past it often enough, but never thought too much about it."

"It's very old." Hamul smiled. "Many were demolished, but fortunately not this one, because it's perfect for us."

"They demolished them? Yes, I do recall hearing something about that."

"The ones on prime land came down; new housing was desperately needed, and building material too. Then, the south road round the coast was another urgent matter."

"Just the same ..." Aleb retreated from the window, leaving his thoughts unfinished.

"Ask me anything you like. I notice you weren't very complimentary when you mentioned us in the Monitor. I'm hoping to turn that view around."

Aleb flushed. "I promise I'll keep an open mind." He took the offered seat at the table and set up his recording equipment. Sounds from below filtered upwards.

"You seem to be very busy."

"Oh, most of that is because new tenants are moving into the floor below us. Some kind of trading company I believe." Hamul paused, and listened to the muffled noises. "No modern building would be so well insulated, except maybe City Hall."

"So tell me, just how old is this building, and how did it survive?"

"Nobody can be sure. It's hard to date stone buildings, but this one here certainly goes back to the elder days. There are still plenty of them out in the desert, mostly in ruins, with some almost buried in the sand. More have been discovered recently, virtually unspoilt, and built to virtually the same design: two towers, a central courtyard, an outer wall. This is one of the larger ones. It came under the protection of Groob's Building Committee. We repaired the walls, added some steel reinforcement, the lifts, and of course plumbing, wiring, air conditioning—all the essential stuff. But, as you see, we've kept the walls looking as far as possible in their original state."

"What about the other tower?"

"That's in a worse state, and we're not sure whether to restore it or demolish it. We could use those big stone blocks for something more useful."

It was not hard for Aleb, surrounded by those heavy blocks, to imagine himself transported back in time. He closed his eyes, leaned a little sideways and ran his fingers over one of the dark, smooth surfaces. Then he sat up a little straighter and shook himself free of the illusion.

"Perhaps now you could tell me about the company, what you do, and so on."

"All right. I joined when we were part of Dreamland, which is a company that makes mostly beds, mattresses, pillows and quilts, along with a few gadgets that are designed to induce relaxation. I took over the technical side, and then I heard about the controversy that Jelani Therim had stirred up. I thought there just might be something there we could use. Never mind the science—I know a lot of scientists declare the idea is rubbish. Commercially, that doesn't really matter. We were intending in any case to use the image of a joyful young woman, contemplating all the wonders of the world, as a brand, and as a way to introduce some recently discovered neurotechnical devices from the desert. I had a few prototypes made, and then I chased up Jelani. She was hostile at first, but when I assured her I'd give her a big budget to play with, and she could experiment as much as she liked, she relented. Her name still attracts people, and apart from that she's a great looker. I just wanted her to be part of our advertising." Hamul paused and handed over a paper folder. Aleb frowned, opened it, and took out some glossy leaflets. The words Dream Hunters were displayed, the large capital 'D' forming a frame for Jelani's face. In the background was a view of a brightly coloured balloon sailing into the sky. "Dream Hunters," he said aloud.

"Yes. It seemed the obvious name to us. It even shows the link to the parent company, Dreamland Enterprises. Did you see the names in the foyer? Dreamland has the ground floor, we have the sixth."

"So I suppose you've found some means of recording people's dreams?"

"Not quite. The word is to be taken more in its other sense, the things we aspire to."

"And Jelani is part of your team?" Aleb felt a little betrayed. She had not mentioned the company by name, although she did say she had found 'an opening' but the details were still being worked out.

"She's better than we'd hoped. Her suggestions, along with the skill of my very capable technical team, have produced our number one product. Of course, it's all stuff that came out of the desert in the first place; that is, from their surviving documents and artefacts, adapted to our materials and more limited expertise. Here, have a look through this." Hamul handed over a headset, and Aleb rather gingerly put it on. It showed a large white screen in front of his gaze. This was featureless, but as he looked into it, it gave him the illusion of opening up a vista that stretched into the infinite distance.

"Now, push that little switch on the side. You should be looking at a red light, yes? That means you have to tune the device so it can read your brain ... Push the switch again ... No, don't worry, it can't hurt you. At most you might feel a slight tingling. Raise your hand when you see a green light."

Aleb was directed to look at a series of faces, some sad, some happy, some angry, some afraid. Eventually a green light winked on and off and the screen cleared once more. Aleb raised his hand.

"Good. Your machine is now tuned, ready for action. Just let your eyes rest on a figure that is about to appear.

Aleb saw a young woman in a tutu performing on a stage. "Classical ballet," he said under his breath.

"Now, push the switch again."

The woman became fully three-dimensional. She was on the white screen he had seen first of all, and was retreating away from him, dancing still, but moving off as if making her way down a long white corridor. Eventually she faded out of sight. Aleb took off the headset.

"Yes?"

"This is D1, our first product. As you saw, the visual construct that your brain creates is copied into the viewer giving that intensely real, almost surreal effect."

"Yes, hyper-real I would call it, but my brain didn't create it—it was already there."

"Not that last bit, where the dancer moves off into the distance. That was something you were doing yourself."

"I find that hard to believe. You are saying my brain is looking at the results of its own visual construction, when I look into your viewer?"

"Yes. Your first construct is fairly minimal, but the interaction with the screen image, which incidentally goes on, and on, builds it up in extraordinary vividness. In other words, you are looking at your own visual construct, and filling it in in greater and greater detail."

"How on earth did you manage it?"

"We didn't. We got lucky. A couple of archaeologists sold us a gadget they'd found in the desert. It was damaged, but our team did their own searching and found enough undamaged parts to make a complete device. We don't yet fully understand it, but what we do know is it reads the visual cortex and projects the result onto an external screen. What the elders did with such a thing we don't yet know."

"Amazing. Convince me this is not a trick, Hamul."

"Okay. Think about something, some memory perhaps, or I could provide you with a picture?"

Aleb thought about the moment when he had first met Jelani, in her room, with all her possessions, seemingly, scattered on the floor. He put on the headset.

There she was, and he could have sworn he could reach out and touch her, she looked so close. He gave a little exclamation of astonishment.

"Do you mind if I look in—if it isn't too private? These devices communicate with each other."

"Yes? Oh, sure."

"Oh, Jelani again. You've already met her?"

"I interviewed her," said Aleb. He removed the headset. Vaguely, he heard the lift in the passage open. There was a knock on the door, and then Jelani herself entered. Aleb jumped up in astonishment. She raised her hand in a sort of salute to Hamul and then looked at Aleb.

"I heard you were coming," she said, smiling.

CHAPTER 7

The ocean

The ship moved into a high, slow orbit. From here the planet displayed an expansive face of blue, dotted with flecks of grey, which the ship identified as steam. A carpet of clouds blotted out large portions of the ocean, but here and there were unmistakable islands, green smudges surrounded by white foam, and beyond the foam the sea shone with a soft blue sheen.

Schyl dropped the ship into a lower, faster orbit, and soon it was enveloped in darkness. The monitor, now in heat sensing mode, gave a spectral view of the planet beneath, with lighter patches appearing like scratches over the velvety black ocean. Occasionally faint ghost-like shapes flickered in and out of view.

"That looks like a good one, Erg. Euse?"

Euse looked at the captain, who had spoken, and then at Erg, the navigator.

"It could be a little too small, with not much prospect of intelligent life," said Euse, "but it does give us all a chance to inspect the sea. That sea interests me immensely."

"Land here, Erg," said Schyl.

The landing lights showed the island to be a swampy, barren arc of land, covered in rocks, bird droppings, and straggling grasses.

Warning, uneven ground, said the ship as it hovered low.

"Erg, do the best you can," said the captain. Euse and Groose, the number one, exchanged glances.

"The captain is tired. It's been a long day," said Groose.

The ship dropped lower, hovered, and then bounced slightly, before settling softly on its shock absorbers.

"There, a perfect landing," said Schyl.

A loud crackling sound arose from under the ship; It shook, then tipped so violently that both Schyl and Groose were thrown from their seats.

"You were saying?" said Euse. He was clinging to the side of his monitor screen. The others rose cautiously on the steeply sloping floor.

"Everybody out," the captain continued, against a background of indignant gasps and groans.

"We may need to blast away some of those rocks to get her even," said Grice later. He had crawled underneath, in the only gap available, to inspect the ship's own capacity, or rather lack of capacity, to dig down.

"Not if it damages my ship, you don't," said Schyl.

"All right, we'll have to move," said Grice sulkily.

"Ship, can you lift off from where you are?" asked Schyl.

Warning, very risky manoeuvre. Port side extension may become trapped.

"You'll have to move some rocks, then winch her, get her even so she can hover," said Grice, who was becoming interested in the technical aspects of the problem.

Schyl took a walk around the craft. There was a hatch that led directly to the hold, where all the ship's heavy equipment was housed, but that particular entry point was pressing hard against the ground.

"Take the digger up through the main cabins?" Erg suggested.

"No chance," said Grice. "I wouldn't want it taken to pieces."

Groose, arguably the most intelligent (as well as the most taciturn) of the crew, suddenly appeared alongside his captain and gave the rocks in question a kick.

"You'll have to dig down below those rocks, and roll them," he said. "It may take a full day, or longer."

"Euse, what have you got that would help?" Schyl asked.

"Nothing whatsoever," the science officer responded, rather snappishly.

"You wanted us to land here."

"I didn't ask you to wreck the ship!" Euse stretched full length on the ground and studied the situation more carefully.

"Grice, for a start, can you get the extensions up, please," Schyl continued. "If the rocks move any more we'll be trapped.

Andrew meanwhile, stood back and watched the altercation between Euse, Schyl, Grice and Groose. He had been thrown by the landing, his arm was in a sling, and his whole body felt shaken. He flexed his fingers, then looked nervously about the island. There was very little to see: some woody shrubs, one crushed by the landing, and stubby projecting rocks. Andrew looked sourly at some small creatures crawling near his feet. He turned his light on them and watched them scuttle away.

"We'll rest here until morning," Schyl decided. "Things will look better in daylight. Back on the ship, everyone!"

Andrew, too exhausted to care, staggered through the airlock and promptly fell asleep against a wall. He awoke in the morning, painfully sore, and desperate to move, but trapped by the tilt of the floor. However, help was at hand. Belzic, surprisingly strong for a short, stout man, lifted Andrew's lanky body and supported him out into the warm sunlight of a new day.

With his feet back on solid ground, Andrew noticed Groose, Grice, Schyl and Euse in animated conversation, while Erg and Ess stood nearby.

"Come on Ess, let's check out the shoreline." Erg, the youngest crew member suggested. Erg had won his place as navigator after being highly rated for a range of aptitudes, including logical reasoning. Ess, technical assistant mostly to Euse, was a little older than Erg and immensely talented—these two were natural companions. Ess had been liberated from the slant board where he had been strapped, and was itching to move about. His arm remained in a sling.

It was an immensely peaceful scene. Little sun-sparkled waves landed with a gentle hiss on the nearby beach. A wide, wide sea beneath a wide, wide sky, Andrew murmured to himself.

Cherg brought bowls of food down to the beach, and both earthlings realized they were indeed starving.

"There you are, entirely free of bugs," said Cherg. "Don't ask me how I managed to cook with everything almost on its side—I hardly know myself."

"Thanks for leaving out the bugs, but right now I could have eaten anything. But tell me more about this legend you're supposed to investigate." Andrew leaned back against a pile of driftwood, and looked expectantly at Cherg.

"Yes. The natives here were supposed to travel through space using a system of portals—that's really all the legend amounts to. Well, you know, legends grow over time, and whatever kernel of truth there was at the start gets grossly exaggerated." Cherg turned his attention to the soup, as did the other two, but after a while, perhaps feeling he had diminished the point of their journey, he turned to Andrew once more.

"The other main reason for being here is simply to find out what happened. There was supposed to be a very advanced civilisation on Groob, but we've never had any radio signals. Of course Groob is nearly three hundred light years from our home planet so we wouldn't know about anything recent." Cherg looked out over the sea, perhaps half hoping to see something that would resolve the issue.

"At least we know there is a civilisation of sorts, and they have robots," said Andrew. "Perhaps they just wanted to keep to themselves." He followed Cherg's example, and stared out over the empty horizon.

"So what else do you know about this legend?" said Belzic. He finished his soup, stood up and turned his back to the sea.

"Almost nothing, I'm afraid. Just what I said: the folk on Groob had developed a system of travel, enabling them to move very quickly around the galaxy. They called it travel by portal. Now, if they had such a system, and we could get hold of it, we'd be literally light years ahead of all our competitors."

"But you have a system of rapid travel," Andrew objected.

"Not the sort they were reputed to have. It would still take several months, traveling directly, to get to Groob from our home planet. That's why we stopped off at Trilfarne, and then your Earth, to make the journey worth the time. Now according to the portal system, you could travel many light years in just a few hours."

"Perhaps the present inhabitants of Groob know about these portals," said Belzic. "If they do, are you going to try and take it off them?"

"If there are any inhabitants we might arrange to share ownership," said Cherg cautiously. "In exchange, we'd help them develop their technology."

"If there really are people here," said Andrew. "All we've seen so far are intelligent machines."

"It is possible, then," said Belzic, voicing what the others were thinking, "that the entire planet is run by machines."

"And perhaps all the people were exterminated by them?" Andrew added. "That means we may all be in danger."

"And in any case, we may be just chasing a dream," said Cherg.

Suddenly, Ess and Erg came running back from their walk, shouting.

"Get your weapons, everyone, get your weapons!"

Belzic jumped up in an instant and ran in the direction the two were pointing. The others followed more slowly, traipsing across the island.

Moments later, Belzic reappeared.

"What do you think of that, Andrew, Cherg?"

A huge, rounded head arose from the water, brown and green like the sea, with wicked protruding jaws.

Everyone began to move slowly forward, Schyl and Euse together, and slightly ahead of the others. Euse simply walked, while Schyl had his laser pistol trained on the monster. Erg and Ess walked excitedly behind, exchanging glances, with the rest straggling along after. Andrew and Belzic stepped up onto a hummocky rock, where they remained to watch. The head shelved gently onto the edge of the beach. A crab crawled out of an empty eye socket and scuttled down to the shingle.

"Ha!" said Euse, and brought out his camera. Cherg also began filming.

The head was now almost fully beached, and it became apparent that the monster was entirely hollow.

"Note the smell," said Ess to Andrew. "Not a stink, but rather sweet and musty."

But Andrew, who had come down from the rock and walked up close, wrinkled his nose and shook his head.

Erg the young navigator was laughing. "Scared you all, didn't it? Come on, let's pull it right out."

"What a trophy!" said Cherg. "Euse, would you like this one in your collection?"

It was no more than a head, the rest of the creature having decomposed, or been devoured. Half lifted, and half dragged by Cherg and Belzic, it was taken up to the rocky eminence, and settled alongside the ship.

"Our guardian, to scare away any bad creatures," said Cherg.

"Except that there's absolutely nothing for miles and miles around," said Erg, who was waving his arms and jumping from rock to rock.

Schyl climbed up to the highest piece of land, raised his binoculars, and turned slowly round. The air was clear in almost all directions, allowing a view of an empty sea that stretched to the very remote horizon. Schyl turned his attention to a cloud of fog, or steam that was perhaps a half mile distant. Quite suddenly a most magnificent yacht emerged from within it. The tall masted vessel was heading directly towards their island.

CHAPTER 8

Kraab City Hall

Four days after their last meeting, Aleb took Jelani to Qu's presentation. The country's long time president, Anatolas, was about to retire, and had nominated Qu as his successor. Anatolas Chegaali himself had been an unlikely person to lead the dominion of Rangolia, belonging as he did to neither of the two dominant tribes that had settled the continent, but Qu's rise to fame was even stranger.

Qu had just turned four when her parents set out from their family island, leaving her in the care of an old servant. They were to return in two days at the most. They were never seen again. On the first day Qu wandered through the glades, told stories to herself, and went to bed early with her favourite picture books. On the second day she played hopscotch and fed the rabbits in their cage. On the third day she drew a picture of her parents waving goodbye. Nevala the servant prepared meals from their store every day, showed her how to forage in the forest, and how to find and prepare edible seaweed. Then came the day when she wouldn't wake up. Qu shook her periodically, called her name (at times pleadingly, at times as an order) and played for a long time beside the bed. Then she cried for a while, and finally heaped blankets over the bed, left the room and shut the door.

The strangers came a week later, pulling into the little landing bay, their voices booming through megaphones as they traipsed about the island. Terrified, Qu hid inside a hollow tree.

The strangers took away the servant's body.

Later, Qu took a pencil, and scribbled all over the picture of her parents. From that time on her island became an imaginary kingdom, watched over, in her mind, by the two robots her father had acquired. She began talking to them, and bringing them little gifts. The robots did not move, but their eyes sometimes appeared to shine with a secret intelligence.

More strangers came. This time they went through the house and took away a great many things. They did not touch the robots. Qu watched every-thing from her hiding place up in a bushy tree.

When she was five years old, she was found by a sniffer dog; a thin, po-faced child, dirty and disheveled. Along with other children, following the war and the pandemic, Qu was regarded as techno-feral (or simply TF). She was sent to a special school in Kraab, where, after three months, she attempted to kill the entire class by poisoning the drinking fountain. After an initial outrage, the teaching staff and resident psychiatrist became fascinated by Qu. Now viewed as 'a challenge', the school rose to the occasion, and gave her round-the-clock attention.

Two years later she was transferred to a school for the gifted.

Some twelve years past her school days she was on the Kraab board of councillors, and in a further six years she was head of Kraab International Enterprises; cold, ruthless, and frighteningly clever, according to those who worked with her. By the time the oil crisis struck she was part of the govern-ment, and her brutal decisiveness probably saved the mainland from eco-nomic catastrophe. A permit was required to drive an automobile, which was otherwise, strictly forbidden. Airships, previously limited in range, rivalled conventional shipping as businesses began to thrive again, and 'Qu' and 'Kraab' became almost synonymous.

Aleb and Jelani had taken their places near the back of the hall, and now Jelani looked critically over the front rows, noting the hairstyles of the women, the men's attire."

"Some of the men look quite shabby," she said indignantly.

"That's just an affectation. If you're rich you can get away with casual clothes. Now, look across on the far right, see the reporters in the gallery reserved for them. That's where I usually sit. It will be more interesting next year, since they'll be voting on Qu's performance, not just promises. Ah, the lights are dimming down."

The stage curtain rose, and the murmuring voices hushed. The lone figure stepped forward.

"Citizens, as most of you will know, my time as your president is over."

Jelani was jerked into alertness. She had been studying the rows of seats below her: the distinguished guests on the right, and on the left those whom she supposed would be doing the voting.

"I need hardly tell you about the momentous times we have been through, a war, a pandemic, and a long period of isolation which thankfully is now over. My policy has always been, stay safe, but don't be timid! I pass on the reins to one who has already proved herself able to handle the most difficult challenges we have ever had to face. Citizens, I present to you the future president of Rangolia!"

Chegaali gestured, and onto the stage stepped Qu. Jelani stared at her with interest. She was dressed, not as a business woman in the ubiquitous dark suit, but as a suubian peasant, with a simple cloth covering on her head, an embroidered bodice, and white linen trousers. Her voice belied her dress, since when she began to speak it was in the cultured dialect of the Groobian elite.

"Thank you, President Chegaali. I am greatly humbled to have been chosen as a candidate, but I will be proud if I can carry on the tradition of 'confidence with caution' which you have instilled in me. I now submit myself to the selectors."

Qu was joined by three others, all men. Jelani looked inquiringly at Aleb.

"They each have a say, and then that group on the left, who are supposed to be the experts, cast their votes."

"Oh? How do you get to be one of those?"

"You can get there by passing an exam, or winning a competition, but many nowadays have sponsors, and are there to represent the interests of various companies. Ah, they've voted. They will keep voting until one candidate gets more than half the votes cast."

In fact it took only one round for Qu to be declared the winner. Many in the hall stood on their feet to applaud, but Jelani was not impressed.

"She may be very capable, but I don't think she should dress like that. She's not a suub, not with that voice!"

Qu was bowing, smiling, waving.

"Thank you, thank you, ladies and gentlemen! Thank you for your confidence in me. I do have some experience in managing Kraab, and I will do my best to provide the same service for all of Rangolia."

At this there was a great deal of applause. Qu bowed some more.

"However, I could never have provided that service without having the very best of supporting staff. Please now welcome them as I call them to join me here."

Jelani watched for a time, and then turned again to Aleb.

"What do you think her problems will be?"

"Oil," said Aleb. "Our supplies remain erratic, so not much has changed. There is still very little trade, so you have to be rich to get much more than basic food."

Most of the inhabitants lived near the coasts of a land mass they knew as 'the mainland' although there was an old-fashioned word, Groob, which was incorporated into the names of various companies. Groob was a land that according to tradition was once fertile and forested, and was now mainly desert. Almost all the oil had to be imported.

"They don't say much about that," said Jelani. "I suppose," she added, voicing a common opinion, "I suppose there is oil somewhere in the desert."

"Yes, if only you knew where to look. Most of the local wells have dried up."

Jelani sighed.

"Here we are, sifting through the sands in search of scraps from a once great civilisation; trying to recreate all their marvellous technology."

Nobody knew what went wrong: an epidemic? A war? A famine? Like many before her, Jelani frowned, pondering the matter.

"Nobody knows what went wrong, but we're in a good position now," said Aleb.

"We're in a very strong position," said Qu from the stage. "We are opening up our trade and we are able to balance the competing interests of our rivals. And there are more and more exciting finds coming out of the desert." Qu was finishing her speech.

"Most of what people find is incomprehensible, won't work, or can't be copied," said Jelani. "It was all too long ago."

"For the next four years at least we can be optimistic," said Qu. "We now have telephones, radios, and even motor cars. My promise to you is that most people who want them will have them during my term in office."

By the time Aleb and Jelani left the hall there was a long queue waiting for the few remaining cabs.

"Let's walk anyway," said Jelani. "It's only half an hour if we stride out."

On the way, Aleb ventured to ask her how her custody battle was progressing.

"Oh, don't spoil my evening by making me think about that!"

An admiring throng remained in the hall, with doting followers queueing up to shake Qu's hand. Presently an official from the state security team pushed his way through it.

"Ma'am, excuse me, may I see you alone?" And later, in a private room: "We have reason to believe a group of spies have arrived on Pako three."

"Deval, what is Pako three?"

"It's one of our outlying islands, ma'am. An islet, actually, about two days' sail away."

"Very interesting," said Qu. "I assume your 'reason to believe' is that someone has actually seen them there. Let me know when you have them secure. I will be very interested to see these rascals that encroach on our territory. Who discovered them?"

"Blue Patrol, ma'am."

"Have them commended. And one more thing, Deval … I believe some company has discovered a device that can read people's thoughts? Dream Chaser, is it?"

"Dream Hunter, ma'am. And I understand the device reads feelings, not thoughts."

"Not much difference, Deval. Anyway, I want you to track down the boss of this dream hunting outfit. Get him here along with his gadget—we can try it on these spies. Deval, I want to know everything about them, from their shoe sizes to whatever goes on in their heads."

"Yes, ma'am. Certainly, ma'am."

CHAPTER 9

On Pako 3

"Ahoy there! Do you know you are trespassing? This is Rangolian territory."

The Croans watched as the little dinghy pulled into the shore, and they had their first view of intelligent natives. The language was guttural, the words rapidly articulated and seemingly blended together.

"Cherg, do we have anything that would match that?"

"Unlikely, Grice. Euse picked up something on a radio transmission, but unless you have a key, such as two languages in parallel, it's very hard to get anywhere."

There were four natives, all thick-set and at least a head taller than the Croans. Grice, Cherg and Ess were busy with their cameras, while Euse walked down to the edge of the sea. He raised his arms, palms outward, in a universal signal of incomprehension. As the dinghy grounded he stepped into the water and gave it a hefty tug. At once the leading native jumped out, touched his chest, pointed to the ground, pointed to Euse, and made a scrubbing motion with his hand.

"This, mine—yours, not!" said the leading native.

Euse responded by pointing to the front of his exoskeleton, and then to the spaceship in the background. The natives looked startled. The skeletal head of the sea monster had previously prevented them from seeing it.

They walked all round the ship, peered under it, struck it with their fists, and even tried to lift it, all four of them together. Then they turned back and stared once more at the Croans. Grice this time responded with elaborate hand signals to the effect: 'needs to get off rocks into water'. The natives suddenly began laughing. Two returned to the dinghy and began rapidly rowing towards their yacht. The other two continued to stare at the Croans, leaving off only to shake their heads.

"I feel as if I am some sort of strange animal, and they're wondering why I even exist," said Cherg. However Cherg was soon busy working with the remaining natives, exchanging personal names and quickly learning the words for island, sea, ship, rock, and other items of immediate concern. Then presently the two in the dinghy returned with assorted equipment, including metal bars, shovels, ropes and planks.

It took a long while, and much sweat, but the spaceship was eventually removed from the rocks and slid through a channel into the sea. By this time the crews of both ships had worked together for several hours, levering, hauling, digging trenches, chipping away rocks, and had learned a good many words from one another, including a number of profanities, and in particular the words for 'stupid', 'idiot', and 'crass insanity' were becoming understood by the Croans. They came to learn that, according to the natives' reconstruction of events, they had tried to sail their boat over the island, at a time when both moons were aligned, and the tide was running at its most full. Euse, normally not at all reticent in such matters, forbore to mention that once their ship was off its perilous position on the rocks it could very easily have moved itself down into the water. And while all the toil and sweat was continuing, another messenger came to Qu.

"It appears they may not be spies, ma'am. However, they have a very strange boat. We have taken ownership of it."

Ω

"What a great way to travel, Grice, don't you think? Far better than being in a spaceship, insulated from the world, whatever world it is, seeing everything through monitoring screens. Andrew, I suppose this is how you usually travel?"

"I have been on a sailboat," said Andrew cautiously. "Not recently, though."

Andrew, Grice, Euse, and Cherg, who had spoken first, were sitting in the main cabin of the substantial yacht, admiring the sparkling sea as it surged past. The island was fading into the distance behind them, while their own ship rocked jauntily along on the end of a tow rope.

"Where, by the way, is Belzic?" Andrew asked suddenly.

"Hopefully with the others in our own craft," said Grice. "Groose is working on a device that will enable us to control the ship remotely, while I run tests from this end."

"I'm impressed they can tow our ship," said Cherg. Grice laughed.

"They can't, actually, but don't tell them that. Schyl has the ship running of its own accord, obediently following on the end of the rope."

In the spaceship Groose stared sourly ahead at the tall masted vessel.

"How long are we going to keep this farce up, Schyl?"

"You'll have to talk to Euse," Schyl responded rather snappishly. "It's his expedition—of course I'll intervene if I think the ship is in danger."

"Then you'd better intervene. These folk will claim the ship as salvage, as according to the laws on most planets they're probably entitled to do."

Schyl laughed. "A fat lot of good it will do them."

"I'm serious. This is a dangerous planet. Remember those robots."

Schyl looked thoughtful. "I've been wondering about those. I doubt if they were made by the present civilisation. Why have we seen just sailboats, and nothing more advanced?" He nodded in the direction of the window, where, indeed, three ships were visible at or near the horizon, and all were carrying sail. "Besides, why no air traffic?" But here Ess suddenly pointed, and gave a delighted cry. The others followed his finger: a massive dirigible was floating through the air, a little way ahead and perhaps sixty meters above the sea.

"There you are," said Schyl. "They can use sails on the water, and they can get off the ground by filling bags with gas. And I gather we have another day of sailing, Groose, so you might as well relax and enjoy it."

Groose ignored the captain, and was once more intent on his work. Along with Schyl, Belzic, Ess and Erg he was in the navigation room, setting up the aforementioned controls, and intermittently talking to Grice in the yacht.

"Yes!" said Grice after one of these exchanges. "Euse, you will be pleased to know we can now call up the ship from anywhere and have it come to us—provided of course, that there are no obstacles to prevent it lifting up."

"And always provided it can get to wherever we are," Euse responded. He adjusted his position on the seat as the boat tilted, swinging from port tack to starboard. The wind was increasing.

Cherg, ensconced in a corner, continued to record and memorise more words with one of the crew. The Croans and natives had by now exchanged names: they had become acquainted with the burly Kit and Kel, the somewhat leaner Mootch, and the tall, muscular Fili. All the natives were immensely strong, having the thick bones that went with a large planet. They also had extremely long curly black hair, arranged in an assortment of pigtails and topknots, all of which fascinated the Croans. Euse, sitting apart from the others, was filling in time by creating an ongoing record of their travels, to be stored in their ship's memory, and later sent off to the Space Affairs office on Cronalink, the Croans' home planet. Meanwhile Fili came in to the cabin with four tankards of steaming liquid. "Tea," he said, using a word the others had just learnt. Cherg took a sip and gasped. A massive heat engulfed his tongue and lips, before hastening to share the sensation with various other parts of his anatomy. Inside his exoskeleton he writhed and suffered. "Lovely, lovely," he said, using another word just learned. "No thank you, that was enough!" However Andrew, to his surprise, found the liquid was warming, cheerful, and not particularly spicy. He watched the Croans struggling with it, surprise bordering on malicious glee. "Something troubling you?" he asked.

Euse surreptitiously tipped most of his tea overboard. Far from feeling threatened, he was enjoying the situation they were in, and wondering how he could exploit it.

CHAPTER 10

Dreamland factory, Folcorn

"Looks like we're getting the VIP treatment all right," said Jelani, who was looking out the window as the black automobile pulled up outside the Dreamland factory. "Damn, I wanted Aleb to be here as our press agent."

The two were in the nearby town of Folcorn where Dreamland Enterprises had first set up shop, and where many of their goods along with the reconstituted Dream Hunter gadgetry was made.

"They probably won't let him in," said Hamul. "I wouldn't."

"We can at least try! Hamul, see if you can delay the driver—or maybe we'll invite him in. Aleb did say he was going to meet us here."

Hamul stood up and lugged a large suitcase to the lift. Jelani put on a jacket and patted her hair. At the bottom she ran to talk to the driver.

"Take as many people as you like, lady. My brief was just to pick up the Dream folk."

Presently, Aleb arrived panting, handed his bicycle to the driver, and sat next to Hamul as the car pulled away. He was still breathing heavily as he stretched out his legs, leaned back, and gazed out the window. He had traveled over much of Rangolia, but this was only his second ever ride in a car. He watched out the window with great satisfaction as the driver pulled out into the priority/VIP lane, the preserve of diplomats, the very rich, and emergency vehicles. The two inner lanes were taken up with the usual flow of carts, horses, bicycles, and the occasional bus-cycle (twenty passengers maximum with the motive power provided in the main by the fitter, younger travellers). To his right a low wall partially obscured the view on this side: three lanes in the reverse direction followed by a waste-land of scrub and dunes that ended, some half mile distant, in the shore line. It was known, unofficially, as the storm plain, an enticing place, all the more so since it was officially prohibited to unaccompanied children, and was where Aleb had loved to wander as a small boy. To his left, a long line of palm trees, behind which were tall houses, built in the local black stone, overlooking a sea that was the lifeblood of the community, and was known, locally, as 'the Pond'.

"A lot of steam out there today," said the driver, jerking his thumb and disturbing Aleb's thoughts. "I reckon the Pond is heating up."

"It comes and goes," said Hamul dismissively.

Aleb, feeling the Pond was being slighted, was defensive. "It keeps the climate tropical and gives us the best gardens in Rangolia."

The driver glanced back, and deciding that his passengers were all suubs, regardless of their VIP status, felt free to speak his mind.

"Another thing," said the driver, jerking his thumb the other way, "those folk who're supposed to be running the country could do worse than put a bigger fence up against the desert. A mate of mine was almost attacked by one of them escaping frots" (referring to the 'feral robots' that roamed the interior of Groob), "so if you're going to see Qu you can tell her that from me—seeing that she welcomes the opinions of us ordinary folk, or says she does."

"Now why should there be a bigger fence?" said Hamul, interested.

"They have been known to move into housing areas, and tear pieces off cars," said Jelani.

"So they do, and not just pieces. They can wreck a car in a few min-utes, if they get hold of one," said the driver.

"I don't see that a fence would hold them, if they're that strong," said Hamul. "There are stone walls already behind Kraab, and a good way beyond, but you'd need to put up a stone wall that ran for miles and miles, and the cost of that doesn't bear thinking about."

The driver stuck to his guns. "All I can say is they've got to do something. They're getting dangerous, those frots. A friend of mine was nearly attacked by one the other day. He found one of the things in his yard, looking at him. Then he ran inside and locked the door."

"Did he have anything metallic on him? "

"That I don't know, sir. But I just think the government should do something. Shoot them, blow them up, anything."

"Well, for a start, they're protected. They're quite hard to kill, anyway. And then again, the scientists study them. They hope one day to understand how they work," Hamul continued.

The driver shook his head. "I can't see any good coming of that. It didn't help the old people now, did it? All gone they are, and nothing to show they were ever on the earth except those stupid machines."

"And most of Groob is a great desert, where before it was a rich, fertile land, so they say," said Jelani quietly.

"Ah, but we have lots of records," said Hamul. "We have experts working on them full time, with some of the languages already deciphered. "If it wasn't for those records, and a few artefacts, we wouldn't even have radio communications, or telephones, or a car like the one we're sitting in now."

"Eventually we could have the technology to turn the desert back to how it once was," put in Aleb.

The driver snorted. "The more you meddle, the worse things get."

"This car you're driving," Hamul continued. "It's given you a job, and all because we had enough ancient parts, along with instruction manuals to figure them out, to start manufacturing."

"And then you found there wasn't enough oil, so you had to stop making them!" The driver felt he had scored a point.

The conversation lapsed. The highway snaked around the tops of cliffs and climbed over the brows of hills. At one place they saw steam geysers; tight little whirlwinds which took water vapour to great heights, dancing sinuously, and occasionally colliding and converging, or ricocheting away. Always there were the swirling colours: muddy brown, green, grey, orange. Occasionally the fin of some large sea creature would rise above the surface, and once more plunge. Once the passengers caught the shadow of something really, really big moving just below the surface.

"One thing the old people did leave us," said Aleb thoughtfully, "the sea. I mean, look at the wealth that must be down there! All those minerals, all those nutrients."

"Thank God," said Hamul.

Rangolia lived chiefly off the sea, taking much of its food from the plants and animals in 'the Pond'. No profitable way had yet been found of extracting many of the needed elements from the water.

Jelani suddenly laughed. "Here we are, living on the fringe of a huge continent, sea monsters on one side, mechanical beasts on the other ..."

"You are implying?" Aleb prompted as Jelani's voice tailed away.

"Just that it doesn't say much for our abilities."

"We'll take back the desert, just give us time," said Hamul.

"Yeah? We'll find whatever destroyed the elders, and then we'll be destroyed as well," said the driver. "We should leave the desert alone."

Aleb looked at Hamul and grinned. 'Leaving the desert alone' was an opinion strongly held among a portion of the Rangolian population. The conversation lapsed once more.

The road turned inland, following a river valley. Here there was verdant bush right down to the river's edge, and a great many birds clustered around the river mouth.

"Ha!" said Hamul as the bridge crossed the river in a single giant span. "Now that was built following principles and old records we recovered just sixteen years ago."

"I always marvel at it, and the weight it can carry," said Aleb.

There was indeed a great deal of traffic on the bridge: horses, carts, bicycles, pedestrians, along with the occasional motor car. At the top of the span a banner bore the legend: Welcome to Kraab.

"Well, here you are," said the driver, "City Hall."

The building loomed up, eight stories of black stone and white painted woodwork.

"At least it has a lift," said Jelani.

A lift attendant whisked them up to the top floor. "Tallest building in Kraab," he said. "Please remember, you are entering Qu's private suite."

The lift opened on a room that seemed full of carpets, armchairs, and little occasional tables, but these were not what caught the travellers' attention. The bulk of Kraab, and the sea beyond, was spread out below them: the dark narrow jostling streets, red painted spires, tall transmitting aerials, glimpses of the grey green river they had crossed.

"Oh my gosh!" said Jelani.

An inner door opened, and Qu entered, smiling, glamorous. Behind her walked a smartly liveried attendant, and behind him came Euse, Schyl, Groose, Erg, Grice, Cherg, Ess, Andrew, and Belzic, and behind them two members of the Groose military.

"I recognise you, Jelani, and I think I can guess the names of your companions. Hamul and Aleb, are you not?" All three straightened up, and bowed to their hostess with murmured variants of 'so pleased to meet you, ma'am'. "Of course. Now I'd like to introduce you to nine folk who have taken the trouble to come all the way from beyond the sea to visit us."

It was Euse who stepped forward, beaming and bowing, to make the introductions, and make use of a good many of the words he was now able to master. He was, privately, noting the reactions of his own crew as well as the three from the DreamHunter Company. Schyl looked worried, Groose morose, Andrew dazed, Belzic … he wasn't sure about Belzic. Most of the others registered interest or excitement, Euse the most excited of the lot when he heard about the Dream Hunter company.

"Do sit down, everyone," said Qu, who was conducting her own experiment. "Refreshments will be brought in shortly."

There was silence for a time as food containers and large drinking vessels were delivered. Andrew was particularly interested in the food, and relieved to see that it looked innocuous: some kind of cooked fish served with spicy yellow cakes. Aleb, in between drinking and eating, looked curiously at the nine arrivals, noting the disparity in appearance between Andrew, Belzic and the others. "You people are from the outlands?" he said, combining sign language with the Rangolian dialect.

"Absolutely," said Euse, raising two thumbs.

"Since we closed our borders against the pandemic we of course see very little of you folk," said Qu. "I understand you somehow drifted into our territory, and got your ship trapped on rocks?" This was rather more difficult to convey by signs, but the liveried attendant managed it.

"Euse nodded enthusiastically.

"And your ship is apparently without oars or sails? Perhaps based on some design by the old people?"

Euse nodded.

"We will be very interested to examine it. Of course, according to our laws that ship is salvage, and belongs to us." This was easy to convey, and Qu managed it without help.

Groose banged his tankard noisily on the table, and glared at Euse. The latter ignored him, and continued to smile at Qu.

"I think you folk will need a little bit of assistance if you are to under-stand its workings." Euse did his best to convey the idea, but Qu merely made a scrubbing motion with her hand.

"There will be plenty of time for that, of course. Now you folk, along with the people from the Dream company, will be quarantined for the next week, so you will all have a chance to get to know one another." The assistant managed this rather well, while Hamul, Jelani and Aleb exchanged astonished glances.

"We need to know if you have any—er—condition that might infect our people. Also, Hamul and Jelani have very kindly brought along some exciting technology which I'm sure will interest you."

Euse beamed and nodded.

"Good. My servants will now conduct you to your rooms, which are just one floor below. Most of the things you will need are already provided, and of course my servants will fetch anything extra. Just tell them your requirements. Good day to you."

"And you, ma'am," said Euse, bowing for the last time. The rest were speechless.

CHAPTER 11

Kraab City Hall

Qu had a busy morning ahead of her: there were decisions to be made ahead of the release from quarantine of her visitors, along with planning for the festival, when her term would formally begin. Then there was that talk with her security chief, and the report from her Science and Technology minister to be discussed; not to mention a session with the minister for Energy. That most of all, since even with the rationing of oil that was still in place it would become unaffordable if no local discoveries were made. For her first day as president she decided on minimal make-up and a severe black suit.

The security chief was waiting when she entered her office, but she beckoned him impatiently to sit at the table, while she herself faced him on the other side with her notes spread out.

"Well, Guidon?"

"Nothing much new to report ma'am. That one called Euse has them all learning our language, after which we should get on better."

"I don't like it. Are you sure they haven't said where they come from? That tall one looks a bit like a Marehew, but the others—have you any idea where they are from?"

"No ma'am. At least, none of the suggestions we've made mean anything to them, and their word, Cronalink, means nothing to us. The best

I can get is 'a long way off' and that could mean anything. The Keyshae Islands are closest to where their boat was stranded, but our intelligence doesn't match them with any folk in that region. The Five Kingdoms region is more likely, but we don't seem to have many records to help us there."

"Well Guidon, I suggest you go search all your records."

"Until we find a match? Yes, ma'am. We've almost finished looking through our own, and we have a team standing by to search the Elder records, what there are of them."

"Get onto those at once Guidon, at once. When they know our language I don't want us to have to take their word for anything."

"Yes ma'am."

Qu thought of her own maps. Outside of Rangolia and the countries where Rangolia had traded, very little had survived. There were bits and pieces, the ink faded to vanishing and the words indecipherable.

"And what about those dream chaser folk? Are they interacting?"

"As I said, Euse is getting everyone to learn our language. The only other thing is that Hamul has produced a couple of the Dream Hunter gadgets which has them all excited."

"Good! We may get somewhere. Now, what about that ship of theirs? Where are we at with it?

"Nowhere much, I'm afraid. We can't get in without breaking the door—or what we presume is the door. I have a couple of naval scientists standing by, but we thought it best to wait a few days. When these folk have enough language we can interrogate them."

"I suppose you're right, though I hate the delay. That will be all then, thank you, Guidon."

"One more thing, ma'am."

"Yes?"

"The pandemic. Our medical folk think they can identify the virus from blood, now. It's just that, with none in the country, they haven't had a chance to test their knowledge."

Qu shuddered. "No, Guidon. I sincerely hope they never get that chance. I want Euse and the Dream folk to stay locked up for the full week. And that will be all. Just get back to me when you have some results."

"Yes, ma'am."

"And send in Jupella."

What have I done, or not done, Jupella wondered, a little anxiously, as she approached her boss. It was not her usual time of duty, and it did not occur to her to associate her visit with the newcomers.

"Now, Jupella, this is not a punishment. I just want you to wait at table … no, you're not a spy. I just want you to be your charming self, and tell me your impressions. Can you do that? You'd better wear a mask, since you're in quarantine with the visitors … As a sensitive woman you are likely to notice all sorts of things my security team will miss."

Jupella went away excited. The visitors were already the talk of Kraab, and very few of the residents had even seen them. "Ma'am, I'll do my very best," she said.

The Energy ministry was housed in a building at the edge of the park, just a few minutes away. Qu's chauffeur ran up as she left the City Hall, but she shook her head vigorously.

"I must set an example, Senton. I will walk."

Which she did, accompanied by two security guards.

"Ground floor? This is not your usual meeting room, Suidon."

"No ma'am, but we're not using the lift at the moment—only for the handicapped."

"Good. And you think I'm handicapped?"

"No, ma'am."

"Come on, everyone. We take the stairs to the meeting room. I can do with the exercise."

CHAPTER 12

While Qu was reorganising the meeting with the Ministry of Energy, the crew were taking stock of their situation in lockdown. They had been joined by seven others. There were the three from Dream Hunter, two from Rangolia's armed forces, and two from Qu's own staff. In spite of Qu's assurances of a comfortable week, the sixteen were rather cramped. There were just three private rooms, each with a heap of rugs and a low sleeping platform, a shared bathroom, and a large common room with two long tables and benches for sitting. As Guidon had told Qu, Euse had taken control of language learning. He was moving about the common room, pointing at objects, while Hamul gave them a name, and the crew repeated in chorus. Ess, as always, had a recorder in his pocket, and was tracking Euse's movements.

"I feel devastated," said Jelani quietly to Aleb. "How dare she!"

"I expect it will be all right," Aleb whispered back. "These travellers look healthy enough to me."

"But the disruption to the company!"

Portable phones were rare on Rangolia, and very expensive, since the technology had only recently been developed, in the usual way, from newly discovered records and artefacts. However, Hamul had been provided one for the whole group, and had maintained contact with the office.

"I expect we'll manage, as long as it's no more than a week," said Aleb. Jelani turned her attention to Euse, who was pointing upwards.

"Ceiling," said Hamul.

"Light!" cried Jelani.

"Ceiling, light!" chorused the crew of the spaceship.

It took most of the week, but by the end of it the crew were beginning to learn a great deal about the situation on Rangolia. How the 'old people' had a very advanced technology, now fallen into ruin, had exhausted most of their fossil fuels and turned much of the arable land into desert.

"And nobody knows what happened to them," said Aleb.

"Usually, when this sort of thing happens there are folk memories handed down through the generations," said Euse, with some difficulty and a great many hand gestures.

"No plausible ones. There is a story about a cloud that travelled around the world eating everything up. It was supposed to have simply appeared in the sky, sent by some evil people living above the clouds called Gravelings. Maybe the cloud ate up most of the oil and coal. There's certainly not much left!"

"But surely you have plenty of thermal energy?" said Euse. "We've seen steam rising off the sea."

"Yes," said Hamul. "The big problem is how to store it. When we're out of here I can show you one of our current projects, a solar power station to generate electricity for the city. Once again, we haven't found any really good methods for storage."

The Croans nodded sympathetically, but did not hide their greatest interest, which was in the Dream Hunter appliances. Hamul had pulled out Dream Hunter mark one, or D1 (in production), and D2 (plans only). When he had enough language, Euse praised their work. He and Ess put the D1 to work, first by some rather unsatisfactory 'tuning' and then by exchanging images. Euse's image was of a large pink globe bobbing in a purple sea, while Ess envisioned a small white hexagonal cell, one within a vast hive, with a curious moon-faced creature staring out of it, and moaning. Neither of these made any sense to Hamul, who had asked them to think about actual scenes they had experienced. Euse refrained from mentioning that the D1 was not actually designed for creatures who lived in exoskeletons, and had their own unique style of brain. Ess had intervened, making slight modifications to the devices so that at least some images could be produced. Now, after some hesitation, Euse passed the D1 to the rest of the crew, but they had no more satisfactory results. Of the nine, only Andrew produced an image that seemed remotely plausible, and Hamul finally concluded that one of the headsets must be faulty. He said as much later, when talking to Qu. "Either there is a fault or these guys have found a way of fooling the device—and me, for that matter."

"Very well, Hamul, you can follow that up, but I'd appreciate a preliminary assessment. You have been locked in with them for a week. What are your thoughts?"

"I wouldn't have said they were spies, ma'am, and I don't think they are telling lies, but just the same ..."

"Yes?"

"Just the same, I think they are hiding something. "

"So you believe it is they who are at fault, and not your gadgets?"

"Well in every other test we've done, after we get people to talk about themselves, and recall memories from their past, the images they conjure up, if they are being truthful, are solidly real. Otherwise, the images may be plausible, but they are flimsy or indistinct. Probably because of the way they have been using their brain. Now in the present cases, the images are solidly real, but completely implausible. So perhaps they are all a little bit crazy? I don't understand it."

"Hamul, they wouldn't all be crazy, so what do you think is going on here?"

Hamul paused, looked at the floor, and back again at Qu. She was giving him what he had come to regard as her 'penetrating look'.

"I think they are being evasive. The stories they tell us about their origins are always vague, and sometimes ridiculous. In addition, I have the feeling I am being studied. We are being studied. They want to know a lot about our technology, and our progress in deciphering the old peoples records. I think they are very possibly direct descendants of the old people and they've inherited some of that ancient knowledge. They've come here to check us out, although with what purpose I couldn't say. Of course, they've only just learnt our language, so I may have them all wrong."

"No, you've done well, Hamul. I've been thinking along the same lines. They're clever, but it's all too neat. That absurd stranding of their ship on top of an island, for example. They found a very good way to get right into the heart of Rangolia—and to me." Qu hesitated. "If you can, stay friends with them—perhaps even assign them work in your company? Don't worry if you do that, because we'll keep them under very close observation. Sooner or later one of them will slip up."

Hamul frowned. The company was at a delicate stage, with the initial publicity driven mainly by the novelty of what they had to offer. Bad publicity was what he did not need. On the other hand, the nine travellers were all clearly smart, had learned the language with great speed, and always made sensible comments and suggestions.

"Yes," he said at last. "Yes, I can give them work, if they'll take it."

"And one more thing. I've been told there is no easy way into their ship without causing damage. Security wanted to search it in their absence, in case there were incriminating records of some sort. They particularly wanted to have a look at their log book. I'm thinking it may be better to have them along in any case. Any suggestions?"

"Oh, I agree with you there, ma'am. I have a suspicion they will be only too willing to oblige."

"Very good, Hamul. I have a feeling our new year is going to be very interesting indeed."

Qu watched him go, and then called her personal assistant.

"Sorry, Rain, I know you've been working really hard, but I do need you this evening. It's a formal occasion and we both have to be looking absolutely fresh and alert. Fresh and alert, Rain! No excuses."

Qu sighed. She wondered if being in charge was going to get any easier. "Rain," she said, "get me Jupella, if she's still in the building."

Jupella came in looking flustered. "Ma'am, I hadn't …"

"You're looking fine, dear. I just want to know what your impressions are so far."

"Oh, ma'am, they're amazing. They make a big fuss of me, they say I look very pretty …" Jupella blushed.

"Yes, yes, but what do you think of them?"

"Well, they're very kind and polite. And they are amazingly quick at picking up our language. They seem to know so much about us already, and they ask me all sorts of things, especially Euse. Mister Euse asked me if I knew anything about portals."

"Portals! Are you sure he said portals?"

"Oh yes, ma'am. And I said I was sorry, I didn't know anything. And than he said he was sure I was a great help to you. And oh ma'am, I'm sure I could be a very great help."

"You are a great help, Jupella. I want you to carry on just as you are. And right now I want you to tell me what you think they are like in themselves. Never mind what they say about you."

"That's a bit harder to explain, Ma'am. They're not like our folk, and not just in size. There's almost a stiffness about them when they move—not exactly like stiff joints, but something sort of measured … I'm not sure if I'm explaining myself."

"You're doing very well. Would you say they are open, meaning not guarded when they speak?"

"I wouldn't say they are guarded, but they are definitely not open. No, definitely not open."

"Thank you Jupella, that will be all for now. Just carry on as you are."

Rain and Qu watched the servant go, Rain smiling, Qu frowning.

"You mean a lot to her, ma'am. And that Mr Euse. He must be quite a charmer."

"Yes. And Euse is a she, not a he. I'm sure of it. Ah, here she is, right on time."

"Ma'am, I'm at your service." Euse smiled. "I'll be very happy to help you any way I can."

"You can tell me where you come from, perhaps when your language skills are a little better? Right now, I'd like you to arrange a guided tour of your boat. It will be just for some knowledgable seafarers who are part of my security team. So will that be possible?"

"Ma'am, I'll be honoured."

CHAPTER 13

"There was a legend about this planet," said Andrew to Aleb, gesturing as he went, and suspecting he was getting many of the words wrong.

"Entrance, exit, doorway," he continued, since he did not know the Groobian word for portal. He pointed to the door of the hall, from which his fellow captives were still emerging.

"Ah, door," said Aleb.

"No, no, not door!" Andrew continued to mime. He, and they, were free at last, and the crew of the Duvra had endured seven straight days of language instruction.

"Ah," said Aleb at last. He went and talked to one of Qu's own servants, who was still in attendance. The woman smiled, and beckoned.

"Come on," said Aleb to Andrew, "this way."

"Come on, I think we're getting somewhere," said Andrew to Euse.

A trip by car, right to the outskirts of Kraab. Here there was no special lane for cars, and the woman in front was urging on the driver, and the driver, honking his horn, was veering side to side to go around assorted carts, people, animals and bicycles. It was not a very restful ride.

"Why are we going so fast?" Andrew tried to ask Aleb, very much wanting a more pedestrian pace, but the message was entirely misunderstood. Aleb leaned forward and urged on the driver: "Hurry! Hurry!"

But finally they pulled up at a single story stone building that looked a little like a fortified redoubt. The woman ran on ahead, up a short flight of steps, and rang the bell.

"They want to get you two back for a special banquet," Aleb explained to Euse.

After a long pause an old man opened the door, and was introduced to the visitors as an expert on the history of the 'old people'.

"Kefu, meet Euse and Andrew."

Andrew looked with interest at the first person he had seen whose hair was pure white rather than red, black or grey.

Kefu's eyes lit up after Euse explained the purpose of their visit. "Yes, yes, grand entrance way," he chuckled, and led the group down a passage to a room lined with paper-laden shelves. There was another longer pause while he began turning over volume after volume, until finally one was opened and laid out on a table in front of Andrew and Euse.

"This is old paper, very delicate," said Aleb. "Better not touch."

"Grand entranceway," the old man kept on saying.

"He means a gateway," Aleb whispered.

"Here, here," said the man.

It was a plan of some sort, that was certain. It took a while to understand, since most of the lines were faint, and the paper stained.

"I know what this is," said Aleb at last. "There was a great palace in the middle of Kraab. It burnt down before I was born, but for years people would talk about the amazing entranceway into the grounds. Rich, colourful carvings on either side of a covered passage, and all very old. These must be the original plans."

The old man turned a few more pages, and there was an etching of the portal, hinting at its former glory and the even greater glory of the palace in the background.

"This," said Euse to Andrew, "is going to be harder than I thought. Sir, do you have any more grand entrance ways?"

The old man looked puzzled. "More places? No, all here, all here."

The woman was now speaking impatiently to Aleb.

"Sorry," said Aleb to Euse, "but we have to leave now. You two are wanted for that banquet."

"I will certainly want to come back here," said Euse.

Andrew braced himself for another alarming ride, but the streets were quieter, the sun was setting, and the white painted woodwork on the tops of the buildings had a golden glint. "It's beautiful," he said, looking out, and fully expecting to be happy. Instead he felt desperately, achingly homesick for planet earth.

CHAPTER 14

On the Duvra

"Welcome, everyone. Welcome to our little ship, the Duvra. Here on your left you will see the chamber which houses the compressors." Grice had to stand on the tips of his exoskeleton's toes to see over the heads of the burly service agents.

"We're just wondering where you put the mast," said the foremost agent, who was ignoring the compressors. He had come to the foot of Grice's platform, and was looking him up and down doubtfully.

"And the sails of course," said another, who was thoughtfully tapping the metallic side of the chamber.

"And where do you stow the anchor?" a young man at the back, who had just managed to make it aboard, cried out. He was called Cavron, newly appointed to be one of Qu's private staff, and as this was his first assignment he was very keen to make a good impression.

Grice, alone among the crew, was guiding the special agents through the ship. 'Just tell them something, it doesn't matter what,' Euse had said, and so Grice decided to enjoy himself. The remainder of the crew were on their way to the Dream Hunter offices, in the company of Jelani and Aleb.

"Our good ship doesn't normally need an anchor," said Grice. "It's now ten Cronalink years old, but still full of some quite advanced features."

"Yes? What did you say it is called?"

The name and registration details are above the door, but of course, you can't read them." Grice gave the assembly an encouraging smile. "On board we just call it 'ship' but if anyone wants to call us they have to use the call number, which is also the registration number."

"You don't have a name?"

"Yes, it is registered in the name of the captain, which of course is Captain Schyl. If you wanted to talk formally to the ship instead of the captain you would say 'Captain Schyl Ho'. There is a more permanent name, Duvra, which appears in catalogues. It just means Sky Rider, which is the name of a mythical animal. But we don't use it much when we talk to the ship."

"You talk to the ship?"

"Frequently, but we have a lot to get through. Now, as I said, this is the compressor that runs the fore and aft ballast tanks." Grice pointed it out once more and the agents crowded around the tiny window. What they saw were a number of boxes mounted on slender pipes, a number of larger, egg-shaped tanks, and a row of winking red and green lights.

"What does it do?" asked the first, and burliest agent who had inquired about the mast. He towered rather intimidatingly over Grice, even Grice on his platform, and did not look as if he would tolerate any nonsense on the part of his host.

"It enables us to move rapidly when we come into the denser atmosphere of a planet. It takes in the air, compresses it, and therefore increases the weight of the ship. Down you go. When you wish to rise you reverse the action, create a vacuum, and up you go. We can also use it for heating or cooling the cabins, of course." Grice looked around the blank faces, perhaps waiting for a question. None came. " It's mostly just a back-up for the graviton, though in some circumstances it can save energy. And speaking of energy, I should tell you that all the materials, including the outer skin and internal walls, use molecular lattice arrangements, making them extremely thin, strong and light."

The burly agent, who had been frowning throughout this speech, waved his hands dismissively. "That's all very well, but we want to see the mast."

"And the sails, of course," said Cavron, who by this time had managed to edge his way through to the front.

None of the group could make the slightest sense out of what Grice was saying, but they were not going to admit it.

"On the ship we do use solar panels during interstellar travel, and of course radio masts," Grice admitted.

"So you travel by the stars?" Cavron was starting to feel he had a glimmer of understanding.

"Yes indeed, we take regular bearings."

"Using a sextant?"

"Radio bearings, usually," said Grice. "I think it's time to move on, as there's a lot to see."

Thereupon the agents crowded round the window, taking shots with their cameras at the little boxes with the winking lights, and hurried after Grice. They had no idea what those lights were all about, but assumed that mystery would be solved once they consulted the appropriate experts.

"All these outlanders must be very small people," hissed the burliest agent, who had already bumped his head several times on the ceilings.

Stooping low, the agents filed through a tunnel, down a ladder, and then, standing up straight in the wide, lofty space they had entered, stared in amazement. Confronting them was a dragon-like creature, lovingly assembled by Grice with the assistance of Cherg, the young communications officer. The monster towered above the visitors, looking down on them with half-open jaws. However, in spite of the big fangs it displayed, it did not appear at all threatening. Its expression, evinced mainly from its eyes, was kindly, although perhaps confused, as if it felt very lost, out of place or even embarrassed to be where it was.

The agents all stared at it a long moment, and then turned to Grice and began clapping. "Taapino!" they cried, and "Bravo!" they cried, and all intensified their clapping.

This time it was Grice who was confused. The 'space monster' which Cherg had lovingly constructed in the first place to entertain a child on Planet Earth, appeared to be a close match to the mythical Taapino, beloved of children and adults alike. And now quite suddenly all became clear to the agents.

"We had heard that you outlanders were often tricksters, but this is wonderful," said the burliest agent. Cameras were out once more, and soon the agents were enthusiastically following in Grice's footsteps.

"So they came to us with a message of goodwill?" Qu later asked Cavron. "I understand they have a very large container of gifts?"

"That is right, ma'am, and the container itself will be very useful. They must have had it towed onto that island for us to find."

"And all along they've pretended it's their ship. Well, we must make every effort to give them a good time while they are here. Find out as much as you can about their tastes. Oh, and start thinking about what gifts we can send back with them when they leave. Do we by any chance know when their real ship is likely to arrive?"

"No ma'am." Cavron looked thoughtful. "As for their tastes, I believe the Dream company will be the best place to gain information."

"And do we know anything more about their homeland?"

"Only that it took them months to get here. It sounds like somewhere in the Five Kingdoms area, or even beyond, outside the range of our maps." Cavron frowned. "I think they are playing a game with us. However, if we give them a good time and have them using those mind reading gadgets we should learn something."

"Very good, then, Cavron, See to it."

CHAPTER 15

Aleb's house

"Attention, ship! You are not permitted to land."

A crowd on the jetty gave various calls, mostly sympathetic.

"Poor outlanders, let them stay. … Shame!"

However, the boat began to turn, thrust away as it was by stout poles. The gap to the jetty was growing by the moment when a bundle in a white baby blanket flew out of a porthole and was deftly caught by someone in the crowd.

And as it landed the shock went through Aleb's body. He jerked himself awake. He lay still for a long moment, his heart beating fast. Breathe, he told himself. Breathe slowly and gently.

He was already late as he rose from his bed, as he washed, and dressed, shaking his head all the while as if trying to shake away that dream. He reached the door just as the paper was delivered.

"All right for some," said Ormond as he handed over the Kraab Monitor to his still yawning customer.

Aleb gave a sheepish smile. "I just dreamed I was thrown out a porthole."

Euse, Ess, Grice & Cherg to join Dream Hunter Company, ran the main headline. *The Croans have opened relations with a wonderful gesture of goodwill. It is now up to our government to reciprocate.*

Ω

Dreamland Centre, Kraab

"Ah, Belzic, you can help me with this. It's my second report to the big chief."

Belzic and the Croans were on the third floor of the Dreamland fortress, where Belzic had been busy directing traffic: a stream of beds, tables, chairs and other furnishings for their temporary accommodation. Now he came to look over Euse's shoulder.

Report from Senior Science Officer Euse to Area Commander Queyn

(Date: 50988/532)

Dear Commander

You will be pleased to know that we are managing well on Groob, and all the crew are safe and healthy. Our energy usage at this stage has been somewhat greater than we had anticipated, so we are conserving fuel. However, the sun is adequate (warmer than expected) and we will certainly be making use of it. Evidence of intelligent life has come in the form of both autonomous machines and hominoids. We are currently guests of these hominoids, and living in a modest little city, which sits on the edge of the desert where we first landed. These creatures are most likely the remnants of a more technologically advanced race which appears to have destroyed itself. They are making some progress by excavating the desert for artefacts they can make sense of and perhaps replicate. They are kind enough to let us 'help' them, which will enable us to probe their present understanding of their science and their origins. I think it unlikely that they will have any knowledge of portals, but you can be sure we will investigate this aspect of our mission thoroughly.

All our crew, along with our two passengers, are fit and well.

As usual, a technical report, including details of the air and sand, is appended.

"What do you think, Belzic? I need to keep the crusty old beggar happy, which means assuring him that everything is going well. Not a word about the crash landing, or Ess getting stung."

"What about mentioning the gravity, and something about the atmosphere?"

"Thank you, Belzic. Yes, all that is in the technical report, but a passing reference or two here would be good." Euse looked thoughtfully at his companion. "Of course, you and Andrew are the ones most challenged by the gravity here. The rest of us simply adjust our exoskeletons. Though we might be able to fix something up for you two. Which reminds me, we need two large tubs."

"Yes, Andrew's dealing with that. They told him, first of all, that we should send our clothes to the laundry, and then, when we explained they were for sitting in, that we should use the showers. The tubs are coming though."

"I should hope so, Belzic. Now, does anything else come to mind?"

"Portals," said Belzic thoughtfully. "Do you think there is anything in that story?"

"I haven't the faintest idea, but I mean to find out."

CHAPTER 16

For Qu, the visitors had created a problem. As spies, they would have been easy to deal with, and indeed, as idiots who had gotten themselves lost they would have been no problem. But as ambassadors? Rangolia had begun trading with four countries, all within twenty days' sail, but it was almost thirty years since any meaningful contact had been maintained with those more distant, when Rangolia had sent its ships off to the east laden with coal and fine linen, and received in return all kinds of clever artefacts, including, yes, miniatures of Taapino and some of his friends. And the traders had all been big strapping men, rivalling the strongest in Rangolia. But why these tiny fellows? And what was the meaning of that large ovoid container of curious artefacts? Suggesting the birth of a new friendly relationship? Qu decided she would need to send a delegation ahead of the return of Euse and his companions. They would bear modest gifts, and radio all details of their contacts. In favourable winds, it should take about three months to reach the nearest of their lands. Radio of course had been a recent innovation, following the recovery of more ancient records. Qu doubted if any of the outlander countries would know about it, so that would be an advantage to Rangolia. She turned to an ancient wall map, one that had, like most things, been rescued from the desert.. Twelve islands in addition to the mainland and a number of rocky islets represented her domain. Beyond Rangolia the ink had not coped well with the passage of time. Twenty 'outlands' had been drawn in with varying degrees of confidence by her own team, and a few other land masses were represented merely by tentative squiggly lines. Qu however knew there were hundreds of other habitable (and probably inhabited) land masses. She rang a bell. A young woman (barely recognisable after the encouragement the Croans had given her) marched smartly into the private study and gave a little bow.

"Jupella, could you get the office to contact the old man—what's his name, Kefu I think?—and get him to come here with all the information he has on the outlands? I particularly want to know what islands have natives who are tiny, and have brown skin and blond hair.

Kefu, the old man in charge of the archives, was chauffeured into Kraab and arrived in Qu's office with a bag of papers and a big smile on his face.

"The people you want are the Duramas, ma'am. I can find no record of their hair colour but they are small, and their skin is dark. They are also natives of a country that is about two months away from where that boat was found. There is just one thing though."

"Yes?"

"They are thought to be pirates."

"Perhaps they are, perhaps not," said Qu. "It hardly matters. Oil, Kefu, oil. We are desperately short of the stuff. We need to look everywhere."

Qu watched as Kefu departed, stooped as he always was, long shaggy white locks drooped each side of his neck. She had a moment of envy for one who could devote his entire life to old manuscripts, old records that would never complain, or answer back, however you treated them.

She called her PA. "Rain, get Guidon for me, please. Then find out if Blue Patrol is in port. If so get them to cancel their schedule and plan for a trip to Durama."

Debate about the ship's ultimate fate continued, with some (notably a company in competition with Qu's own support base) wanting it converted into an entertainment centre for the exclusive use of the Rangolian elite. Others, including most of Qu's own staff, wanted it set up on a pedestal as a monument to the new enlightened age they believed was coming. Nobody took it seriously as a ship that had actually gone any distance, without so much as a mast and sails. Obviously, it had been towed into Rangolian territory, and left for the Rangolians to discover for themselves. In the meantime the chief naval engineer was struggling to uncover its secrets. He had managed to open several compartments, and was astounded to see a table and chairs rise out of the floor. Efforts to discover how the trick worked merely succeeded in breaking the mechanism. The assistant to the chief engineer suggested, a little hesitantly, that Grice might be brought in to assist, but this the chief engineer curtly refused. He was not going to have an outlander call his skills into question. He consoled himself by breaking open a few more compartments and removing the items therein, to be taken away for further study.

"Welcome to Dream Hunters," said Hamul, as Euse, Schyl and Groose were escorted through the rooms on the top floor, Euse giving little exclamations of appreciation, and Groose asking the occasional question. The greeting was somewhat redundant, since the trio had looked in several times already, and were accommodated just two floors down in the building. However, Hamul was the company's CEO and this was his moment for a formal introduction.

"You are familiar with our first product, Dream Hunter mark one," said Hamul. "You have seen the plans for mark two. Now I want to introduce you to the prototype."

Euse took the headpiece, bigger and heavier than the mark one they had used in lockdown. He noticed that there were terminal points that would press against his head when he put it on.

"This may not work."

"Try it anyway," said Hamul.

Euse fitted the cumbersome apparatus over his scalp, surreptitiously adjusting the electrodes as he did so. When he signalled that it felt comfortable Hamul reached over and pressed a switch. This time, after five minutes of tuning, a visual field opened up in front of his eyes. He was about to say,

"It's just the same as with the other device," when he saw that it was not. A creamy golden light suffused itself not merely ahead of him, into the remote distance, but on either side.

"What you are seeing this time is boundless, and you can move into it just by using your eyes. Try it!"

The strange world in the headpiece came to life as Euse let his eyes focus into the distance. Groves of tall trees were interspersed with grassy plains, and little dells with running streams, and large white flowers growing out of ponds. Euse's eyes roved on. There were canals now with floating barges and tall cranes, and vehicles moving swiftly on broad highways.

"Do you recognise anything?"

"No!"

"Keep looking."

He was looking down on a beach: crowds of people were spread out under bright sun umbrellas. The mood was lazy, lethargic, peaceful. Euse felt at peace, blissfully happy, and he was just thinking how much he'd like to live in such a place when a jolt of fear passed through him. He gave a shocked cry and wrenched off the headset.

"You felt that, didn't you? We are now recording feelings, not merely visions. Can you guess who was the subject of this recording?"

"Nobody I know."

"It was Andrew, and then Aleb. That is, the images came mostly from Andrew, and Aleb contributed a good deal of the emotion. What we have here is a nostalgic, child's view of places that transformed over time. I'm not surprised you recognised nothing, since children see the world in a very different way. These were sanitised memories, if you like."

"But the fear?"

"You'll have to ask Aleb about that. Aleb watched the recording we took from Andrew, and added stuff of his own, including that fear. It would be a childhood fear, of course, and we forget just how intensely children experience their emotions. Incidentally, you were receiving Andrew's and

Aleb's emotions all the way through, but until the end they were obscured, overlaid with yours."

Euse passed the headpiece over to Groose. "See if these Outlander scenes evoke any memories," he said, giving Groose a slight smile. Groose, however, kept his face expressionless as he put on the device.

"Can you see the future?" said Hamul. "The D2, when it is spread widely, will revolutionise the way we relate to one another. Groups will connect up, maybe six to ten at a time, and share experiences without any kind of censorship. Now, how can you judge another person when you experience their feelings, and they can experience yours?"

He was at that moment disconcerted to see Groose pulling the device off his head and plonking it down on the table.

"It's dangerous," said Groose. "Take it from me, you have to preserve your fictions about other people, as well as about yourselves. Without them, your civilisation will collapse."

Hamul frowned at this unexpected outburst, and then turned away as he heard the lift door opening. Into the room came Grice and Cherg, followed by Aleb and Jelani.

"Hamul, I've been with Qu and she's very interested in having a demonstration of the D2."

"Well done Jelani," said Hamul.

"Ah, Euse, you are joining our staff, are you not?"

"Yes indeed, along with Cherg and Grice here, and Ess."

"Now that's another thing. Cherg has become so good with our language he has been able to tell me all about his home town in the outlands. I *so* look forward to visiting!"

"I'm sure," said Euse, "that Cherg's home is a wonderful place." He glanced up in time to see Cherg and Grice, who had paused at a window, coming across towards him. "And what might be the name of the island where your wonderful home is located, Cherg?" he asked.

CHAPTER 17

Hamul sat alone in his office, shirtsleeves rolled up, pondering sales figures. It was hot. The steamy heat from the sea blended with the heat from the desert, enticing those who moved to remain still, and those who were still to sleep. Now that the season of water was nearing its end, it was a time when mists and heat often intensified. Rangolia was holding its traditional market day holiday. A steady stream of traffic moved along the main highway, which ran close beside the Dreamland Company's stone fortress. The sound of moving vehicles, the hooves of horses, and the cries of people mingled, and in reaching Hamul's ears, had him thinking about the waves surging up the beach; waves, and the cries of gulls. He struggled to remain alert and turned his attention to a report from the sales manager. D1 sales were increasing steadily, but D2 (the more elaborate, networking version of D1) had hardly moved. Evidently people were wary of revealing their feelings—or was it simply that they needed time to get used to the idea? Or was it more to do with price? Hamul turned to the note left by Umus, head of production: 'Almost out of lithium. Do you want us to keep producing D2? If so, better do something—Umus.' Lithium seemed to be costing more by the day. Hamul had agonised over the price of the mark two product, since he wanted it to reach as many people as possible, and yet cover the increasing costs of labour, raw materials, overheads, and all those hidden and unexpected expenses. And then there was the problem of the mark three model, now being tested, for which no price had been decided. In the end he decided to play for time. Let the public get used to D1 first. Worry about the other two later. Not to mention the projected D4, which was to be a diagnostic tool for physical ailments. He wrote: 'Umus, cease D2 production for now. More lithium available soon—Hamul. (Take a break for a week, you've earned it!)'

There was still Groose to consider. Groose had made an ominous warning, even a threat, about the devices, and Hamul very much wanted to know what was behind his outburst. Groose had promised to call by for a few minutes—and here indeed he was.

Groose marched in, looking uncharacteristically Groose-like. "I'm sorry for what I said, Hamul. I just want you to disregard it," he said gruffly.

"Groose, you can't do that to me! You said the D2 was dangerous. I need to know how, why."

"I'll just say, the world you know, I know, is a construct of the mind. It can be easily disturbed, so take care with your devices. When disturbances happen the chances are you will experience them as things happening in the world rather than in your head. I think that you in particular should take care."

"I'd appreciate it if you could be more specific. For example, we already have a warning on the D2 that it is not to be used by the mentally disturbed. Is there anything we should add?"

Groose hesitated. "I think you should monitor the use of all your devices very carefully; perhaps restrict sales to a small group, and get them to make regular reports. Just remember, you don't know what these things were originally for, or what unintended consequences you might produce by fiddling around with the settings. There. I've said more than I meant to."

Groose took his leave, and Hamul, after giving the matter some thought, jotted down an extra two sentences 'to be added to the D2 instructions': *While this device has been very thoroughly tested a bad reaction is always possible. Please contact the Dream Hunter Company immediately if you have any concerns.* Hamul next packed up the remainder of the messages on his desk and headed for the lift. He would go home, take some refreshments, and take a trip by bicycle to a little bay where the water was cool, where a great many birds roosted each evening, and few people came. Birdsong was always a help. Birdsong, yes, the sounds of nature, yes, he could do with these. He would sit and think about the mark three, with the mental clarity that his retreat always brought him. However, he would never make use of any dream hunter device on himself.

Hamul had a problem: a deeply irrational terror could come upon him without warning in the most tranquil, most Arcadian of settings. He was deeply embarrassed by this fear, and did not seek help. Instead, he took refuge in the feelings of other people.

Yes, he thought as he headed home, he would bicycle in the cooling air, settle in his favourite bay, and perhaps, to begin, turn his attention to lithium, and the D3.

Ω

Jelani's House, Ridge Road

"We need to test it as well," said Jelani.

Aleb nodded solemnly. "We could just use the transmitter piece for a start. Only perhaps not today. It's getting late."

"No, that's just wasting time."

It was dusk, and Aleb was in Jelani's living room, the first time he had visited her house since his interview. He noted that the jumble of stuff that had almost covered her floor that time was largely cleared. Just a few corners and crannies housed little piles of books, papers, boxes, recording devices and clothing. He picked up the heavy transmitter headset of the D3 prototype from the little table, weighing it in his hands. Jelani giggled.

"It's no good just holding it."

"I know. I tell you what, you transmit and I'll receive."

"That's not what we agreed. Come on, you've already tuned it."

Aleb felt suddenly very reluctant to lay bare his thoughts and feelings to the woman in front of him. Jelani had the receiver set in her hands and was already preparing to put it on. She was calm, and very relaxed. He hoped she wouldn't see that he was trembling.

"I want you to think well of me," he whispered. Raising his head from the device, he caught her eyes.

"I do think well of you." She was smiling, but then her look became serious. In another moment she had put down her headset and stood up. Aleb had not consciously moved from his chair, but now he found himself standing up very close to her. She leaned up against him. "This feels like a dream, dream hunter lady," he whispered.

They were standing so close that walking was slow, but quite suddenly Aleb found he was tumbling backwards onto a bed. He raised himself on his elbows and looked at her. Both were solemn once more.

"I think," he said slowly, "I think we should be together."

"I think that too."

"Oh Jelani, I love you so much!"

He reached out, suddenly wildly joyful, and ran his fingertips down the side of her face, across her neck, down the line of her arm, down the line of her torso. She sat very still, watching him, and then she moved in very close, so the two were fully touching the length of their bodies. "Oh Jelani," he said in a soft whisper.

"I want to feel you, dear reporter man. I want to feel every part of you."

For a long time after that there were no more words.

CHAPTER 18

Down by the docks the crew of Blue Patrol were preparing to embark. Their cargo included rations for six months, photographs of the ship and all the crew members, a package of fine linen and another of ceramic objects by Rangolia's best potters, letters of introduction from Qu, and several others among the Rangolian elite, and a dozen radio sets. There was also a small canon and two shotguns, although the crew fervently hoped that these would not be needed. Their trip to Durama would take six to eight weeks for the ketch, and their mission was to establish trade agreements, and if possible secure a supply of oil. For these purposes two diplomats would accompany the crew, along with two members of Qu's inner circle who had at least a vague knowledge of Durama, and of the languages and customs of the outlanders in general.

Qu came in person to see them off, and stood watching as the yacht with its crew and passengers sped away in a freshening wind.

Ω

The westerly wind from the desert was clearing the air and dispersing the steam which had clung along the shoreline all day. It was warm still, but not excessively so, and the city of Kraab, which had gone to sleep for the afternoon, was waking up once more. The evening markets were beginning, with stalls and awnings being set up, items set out for display.

Andrew, Belzic and Cherg had taken a trip to the central market, where they were to meet Euse and Ess.

Andrew had been busy rearranging furniture in their new apartment. The unexpected weight of objects on this large planet still sometimes caught him by surprise. His wrist was still a little sore from such a surprise, and now his whole arm ached once more. However, he felt very ready for action, if a little annoyed with himself for his carelessness. Everything he saw at present struck him with that vividness and vitality novelty can bring.

Alighting from the car with their escort, the three of them were noticed at once. Shoppers came running across, calling out to one another excitedly: 'There's another of them! There's another of them!' They were referring to Cherg, not Andrew or Belzic, since the Croans, with there nut-brown skin and creamy white hair were celebrities throughout Rangolia. Andrew noticed another crowd not far off, and guessed, rightly, that its kernel would contain Euse and Ess. He turned to his escort: 'Can you get us over there?'

"Leave it to me," said the escort, and combining a stern voice with a few physical gestures he made a path for the three to follow. However, when they reached their goal they all stopped, amazed.

"Now this is our number three version," Euse was saying. "Mark number three. As you can see, it's a little more elaborate, but not much, and it's very light weight. Euse was using, not the Dream Hunter devices, but comic imitations. Some of the observers, obviously aware of the originals, were clapping. Euse was advertising the company in his own way, but mostly, he was having fun.

"Now, Ess, don't be shy, stand right here, in the circle of light. Ess will demonstrate what happens when you use the mark three. Watch, everybody!" Euse handed the device over, and Ess put it on his head. Immediately there was a loud bang, a brilliant flash and a great deal of smoke. When the crowd's eyes were back in focus, there was Euse holding the gadget once moret, and—nothing else. Ess had vanished utterly.

"Now where can Ess have gone?" said Euse. "Come on, Ess, you don't have to be quite so shy!"

After their astonished silence the crown burst out in wild applause. Rangolians love conjuring, and Euse was exceptionally good.

A man with the official city police livery came running up before Euse could continue. He spoke to Andrew's escort, who then called to Euse, Andrew, Belzic and Cherg together. Ess hastily threw off his disguise and joined the others. The policeman spoke urgently, quietly, as they clustered round. "Do you know where Groose is? Or Schyl?"

"Groose will be at the Dream Hunter building," said Andrew, puzzled.

The policeman shook his head. "We want those two as soon as possible. Listen. The guard on your ship has been attacked, and was found lying unconscious nearby. We have reason to believe Groose or Schyl may have been involved."

"Groose? Schyl? They couldn't have!"

"They were last seen at Docklands, and there is nobody else who would have attacked that guard. I must ask you to contact the police or Docklands security the moment you see them or have any news."

CHAPTER 19

Deception Dell

The tree under which Hamul was sitting bore clusters of little buds. The sun, still quite high, shone through a haze of vapour. Hamul had his head tilted upwards, his eyes closed, allowing the heat to bathe and soothe his face and neck. Just in front of him the water lapped sluggishly over the white sand, and in the tree above a pair of birds were coming and going with nest material. Hamul watched them for a while, feeling a kind of empathy. He too had been working hard, making calls, writing letters, calculating, planning, pondering, pondering. Sales were increasing, but so were costs. Costs, the hard reality.

Hamul wriggled round on his perch. He was sitting in a nook formed by two rock walls, one on either side, and behind a sloping line of bush that made its way up to the brow of a hill. It was a headland, complete with watchtower, that pushed itself boldly out into the steaming thermal sea. In the little dell there was a solitude, and air that was almost always still, and often, as now, languorous and heavy. After a little while he found a more comfortable position, and lay back on the soft turf, thinking it was time to move, but not wanting to be bothered. Not now, not yet, when he was so comfortable. He slept.

The light was dimming when he woke. There was a cool draught of air flowing down from the heights, and his cosy little niche had changed utterly. A red light shone out from the watchtower, mingling with the dusk. He shivered. The tide was in, almost up to his shoes, and he saw at once that the only way out would be the difficult climb up the cliff. Or he could wait out the night.

Hamul wrapped his coat around himself, and then the waterproof sheet he always took with him, and retreated a little further away from the water line. Ahead was the remote horizon, an orange expanse of sky reflected onto the sea, with Groob's second moon, Rubilis, moon of illusions, a pale blue oval sitting just above the water. The sky was darkening, and as it did so the sea appeared to shine with its own light: a vast, luminous mirror. A large fish breached the surface nearby, and gave him a look which he felt to be positively demonic. He retreated further back on his perch, suddenly, irrationally, afraid. *All I need to do now,* he told himself, *is get comfortable and have a proper sleep. I won't be missed, not until the morning.* He dozed. An image flashed into his mind, a woman who lived in the village where he grew up. She was, he supposed, not so very old, but at the time she appeared ancient, a wizened old crone dressed in black. The children were cruel, and would sometimes follow behind her when she walked abroad, taunting: *an outlander, a witch, ooh, an outlander!* He would be among them, often at the lead, and when she turned and glared he would see the anger in her eyes. *A witch! She'll cast a spell on you!* The children turned to teasing one another, or one would play the witch, prancing ahead with a black cloth draped over her head, and then turning and chasing all who dared to follow.

Hamul fell fully asleep, and when he woke an hour or two later his little world had changed utterly. At first he was confused, disoriented. He imagined himself to be back in his own little house, in a peaceful cul-de-sac at the top of Kraab. But the light was all wrong. He had trouble focusing his eyes. All around was a red glow, and dark looming columns that shouldn't be there. He jumped up in alarm, but then saw, to his relief, that those black objects were merely trees; and that at a short distance to his right was the reassuring shadowy precipice that was part of the enfolding barrier of his retreat. The cooling air from the heights was flowing more briskly now, driving back the steamy sea mists and sculpting them in fantastic shapes. And then he saw it.

Only the head was visible at first. Hamul could not, even in the darkest recesses of his mind, have imagined that head. It was high on the cliff, appearing to emerge from the rock: a grim mouth partially concealed by a huge protruding nose, and surmounted by a tall, tapering forehead. The eyes were black shadows, but the red light from the tower passing across in periodic flashes made them glance out knowingly. Hamul found his own eyes locked onto that face, and then, as it slowly emerged, the dark outline of the whole body, colossal, ponderous, reaching right to the ground. It wore a padded tunic, and its massive arms terminated in long, clawlike fingers. A veritable giant emerging out of the rock. Hamul gave a little whimpering cry, at last turning his face away, stumbling and falling as he retreated from the horrible sight. He crawled into a patch of scrubby bush, curled up, and tried to calm his breathing. You're not there, you're not real, you're a trick of the light he now said, over and over. A trick of the light. But he was shaking; his fear was defeating him.

Breathe, breathe, slowly, slowly, gently—and then at last he dared himself to take another look. The spectre had gone. Where it had stood, a small shrub swayed idly in the breeze. There were cracks in the wall, and the tendrils of tenacious plants, now thrown into relief by the oblique light, produced a pattern of shadows that may have suggested a great ogre. Hamul slept once more.

Pain brought him back to consciousness. One bruised leg was aching, and a rock was pressing into his side. The breeze was stronger, and he had lost his thermal blanket. He shivered, aware suddenly of the cold. The tree that arched over him creaked and shook. He was, somehow, entangled in the undergrowth, and took some time to get free. Something, meanwhile, was happening to that tree. There was a face in there, a witch's face; the face, surely, of the woman from the village. And pressing against him, clutching, was a withered arm. For a long moment Hamul froze, and then with a strangled yelp tore free. He turned briefly to the sea, saw Rubilis, now riding high and casting its pale glow on the waves. A tentacled monster, cruising just below the surface, passed like a shadow a mere few feet away. He found his legs. He didn't notice his pain, or his scratches. He pushed himself forcibly up the ever steepening slope towards the tower, scrabbling forward, grasping anything and everything ahead of him, groaning, gasping, and never looking back.

CHAPTER 20

Docklands

At the eastern edge of Kraab there was a bay, and a little cove that had once been a popular swimming spot: the water tepid only, never boiling, and the air sheltered from the north by a peninsula that jutted out a good mile, and formed the edge of a rising tectonic plate. In this area first one jetty and then a dozen had extended themselves, and by degrees the spaces between had been connected, using some of the precious timber ferried over from neighbouring islands, with assorted offices, huts, sheds, and even a small tower erected. It was in this area that Cavron, Qu's private eye, was escorting Schyl and Groose. They had arrived just in time to see Blue Patrol heading off on its three month journey to Durama, and Cavron, sounding as casual as possible, was wondering what Croans did during their long voyages, and were they missing Durama?

"What do you do, Groose?" Schyl asked with a little twinkle in his eye.

"I follow your commands," Groose responded, rather coldly.

"Commendable of you. Now as for me, I keep an eye on Erg. 'Are we navigating the right way?' I ask him."

"You mean, following the right star?" Cavron asked eagerly.

"Absolutely. We can't afford to get our stars mixed, or heaven knows where we'd end up."

At this moment the three arrived at the Croans' ship, which had been hoisted out of the water onto a landing stage. It was the largest craft present, and the most unusual, a silvery, ovoid machine rising to the height of the sheds around it. There was a wall with a gate, closing it off to public access from the jetty, and a signboard, on which someone had written 'DUVRA' in large letters.

"We'd better have a look and make sure she's seaworthy, don't you think, Groose?" said the captain. "There is a nasty gash on the side I want to look at."

Cavron at once leant over the gate, and gesticulated. A guard hurried up, and let the three in.

"We're keeping folk away, but of course that doesn't mean you," Cavron said anxiously.

"Of course not," said Schyl. He walked up to the craft and ran his hand along the damaged area. "We could fix this very easily, couldn't we, Groose? We have just what we need inside."

"Sorry, sir, you'd have to speak to the commodore," said the guard. "My orders are that no—one is to enter unless the commodore gives his permission."

Schyl, still looking thoughtful, turned his attention to Cavron.

"It's a pity, you know, since the damage was done by creatures from Rangolia while we were in Rangolian territory." Schyl exchanged glances with Groose, and looked again at Cavron. "You see, I'd hate anything like this to cause harm to our diplomatic mission."

"Yes, I see," said Cavron uncertainly.

"I wonder if you do." Schyl kicked at the plank in front of him. "It's not just the mission. You see, Euse particularly asked us to pick up a recording device from the ship. You recall him saying that, Groose?"

"Oh, yes, I certainly do, captain."

"And Euse is in charge of the mission. I'm just the captain of the ship; so where might this commodore be?"

Cavron looked at the guard, who looked sadly back at Cavron and the Croans. "I'm sorry, sir, he didn't say. You see, it's a three day holiday starting today, and I guess he's got a lot of things to attend to."

"If you don't mind waiting, I'll have a look," said Cavron. He gave an apologetic little wave and sped off. The others watched him go, and there was silence for a little while. Groose then looked meaningfully at Schyl, who turned to the guard.

"It would only take us a moment to get what we want, you know. You could follow us in."

"Well, I suppose …" The guard's voice trailed away. He ran his hand around under a tight collar.

"Oh, thank you sir," said Schyl. "I'll recommend you to Qu next time we see her."

The guard watched as Schyl drew a little cylindrical device from a pocket, and pointed it at the closed door, which shuddered a little, and then burst open with a grating sound.

"Heavens! Someone's tampered with the door. You'd better stay outside while we do some checks."

"Certainly sir." The guard sounded relieved. The other two scrambled through the opening.

"Number one, better check the door. See if it shuts again."

This time the grating was louder. Something flew off the door, and below them there came a short, sharp cry. Groose looked out and saw the guard lying on his back, his cap off and a red welt running from one eyebrow to his hairline. Groose called out to him, but the fellow did not move. Schyl came over and looked down.

"You'd better check him out, Groose. I want to see what else they've messed with."

Schyl worked his way through the rooms, noting broken hatches and empty cupboards. All the more important gadgetry appeared to be secure, the coverings undamaged. He came back to the entrance looking more reassured.

"Groose? It looks like they've taken away a lot of our entertainment equipment. It looks like we'll have a boring trip home, and it won't be any use to them! Groose?"

Schyl looked out the doorway, and saw Groose still working with the guard. He had taken one of the survival blankets from the ship and wrapped it around the fellow. He looked up at Schyl and grinned.

"This chap will wake up in an hour or two with nothing worse than a headache, I should think. It serves them right for damaging our door!"

Schyl came down and stood beside his first mate. Then he bent down and picked up the guard's wrist. "The guy has a strong heart, at any rate." He thought for a bit. "I don't think you should wrap him up like a present, Groose. And I don't think you should make it look as though he's sleeping on duty. He won't thank you for that. He's the sort of chap who will obey orders to the letter, but would be horrified if expected to think for himself. There are plenty like that on our home planet."

"So what do you suggest, captain?"

"We need to make it look as though he was engaged in a desperate fight against multiple assailants, determined not to yield, and if necessary die at his post."

"And what, captain, are we supposed to have been doing while all this was going on?"

"A good point, Groose. A good point. One thing we can do while we're here is pick up the spare recording pack. Now I think of it, I owe Euse a favour. A private matter, Groose, nothing you need to concern your-self with. I suggest we conceal ourselves on the ship, our equipment at the ready. We'll study the brain processes of these Rangolians when they find one of their own damaged."

Some time later, while the captain and his mate rested in their ship, Cavron returned with the commodore. Cavron gave a horrified cry, and ran to the guard, who was lying on his side, his clothes torn, his helmet and one shoe missing. While the Croans watched the events unfold on an internal screen, Cavron knelt beside the victim, and the commodore ran backwards and forwards, circling the nearby buildings, shouting oaths and flourishing a dagger. After a time he left the surrounding buildings alone and focussed on the ship itself, hammering on the closed door.

"He is a brave commodore, prepared to take on multiple assailants with just a single knife," said Schyl.

The guard had meanwhile regained consciousness and risen to his knees. He looked at first bewildered, and then terrified to see the dagger-waving commodore. He sought refuge in Cavron, clinging to him as the two gradually stood up.

"Fascinating," said Schyl. "Euse will love this. What do you make of the commodore, number one. Is he angry?"

"Not at all, captain, that's just bluster. He is afraid."

"Strange that he has to conceal it—his culture, I suppose."

"Ah, at last! He's off to communicate with someone, presumably by phone, since there is surely one on the wharf."

But almost immediately, before the commodore had gone more than a few steps, people were arriving on the scene from many directions. They formed a tight knot around Cavron and the guard, and many were bent on giving advice, much of it contradictory. The Croans kept on recording.

"A lot of excitement here, Groose. Can you single out someone?"

"Not easy, captain. It's a real tangle, with everyone affecting the behaviour of everyone else. Ah, I think I have a good subject."

"It's the commodore again, Groose! I see that he is at ease, now he has lots of people he can control."

People were, indeed, being directed to and fro, and the unfortunate guard, still looking bewildered, was being thoroughly examined.

"I can see it now, Groose. That guard will be proclaimed a hero. Ah, here's a man with a camera, doubtless a newsman, and here at last are the police. Everyone is happy now, Groose!"

"No, there is an undercurrent of fear, or should I say anxiety. You see it in the sideways glances. Where are those assailants, the eyes say."

"You're right about the fear; in fact I sense it everywhere, Groose, ever since we came here. And the interesting thing is it's always concealed. Why do you suppose that is?"

"I cannot say, captain, but I suspect it has something to do with what they call 'the old people'. I've tried to elicit some information, or even some theory about why that civilisation vanished, but they refuse to discuss the matter. It's just 'Oh, they've gone. We don't waste time on that sort of talk. At least they've left us plenty of records.' And then they clam up."

"So let's think of specific cases. Who comes to mind as fearful?"

"The Dream Hunter folk for a start: certainly Hamul, and probably Jelani. Then there's our escort Cavron, and some others that I've noticed in the service of Qu."

"And Qu herself?"

"I'd say she's the most frightened of the lot."

"And what about you, Groose? Are you afraid?"

"I certainly am. I'm terrified Euse is going to get us trapped on this planet. He's taking far too many risks. And as for you …"

"Sorry, Groose. I can do nothing unless the ship is in clear and immediate danger. In that case, as you know, I get to override his orders. I can't do anything about a few scratches."

"A few scratches!"

"Quiet, Groose, listen. Do you hear what I hear? That sound will be the local constabulary knocking on our door. I expect we'd better go down and talk to them."

CHAPTER 21

The third day of the festival goes with a ritual to mark the founding of Rangolia, (now three hundred and thirty-one years ago), and welcome the time of new growth and new birth. For some this day marks the 'true' beginning of the year. Tokens are cast into the Pool of Stories which sits at what many claim is the exact centre of Kraab, and an official seer from the temple studies how they land and gives his pronouncements for the days ahead. Qu will of course be there, and make herself visible at as many events as possible through the day.

Right now Qu is dreaming. There is a statue in a high place, shining with a beautiful glow, and it comes to her that she is that statue, unapproachable, safe at last. But then to her horror she set that she is bleeding; blood dripping down her legs, visible to all. And she can hear the shouts, the laughter: Come and see! Come and see! She's bleeding! the crowd are crying. Now she is trapped, discovered, most horribly visible, and with that a sense of fear, and shame. She wakes with her heart racing as Jupella comes in with her morning drink, the dream still vivid in her mind. She gives her maid a rueful smile. "The past chases me Jupella", she says, a statement that leaves the maid puzzled for a good part of the day. But now there are genuine fears to be dealt with. Today, perhaps, there will be life-changing decisions to be made. To begin, and perhaps to assuage those night-time fears, she takes a look through the popular press, searching for comments about her policies and her performance. Here, gratifyingly, is a sign that her ratings are lifting, thanks mainly to the visitors from Durama and the way she has handled them. But amidst all the political commentary the old criticisms continue on her dress sense, her hair style, even her make-up. Her occasional appearances in peasant dress, which she is particularly fond of, are generally slated as 'brash' and 'hypocritical'.

'Once again Qu has failed to gratify her office with the dignity it deserves', was how one article began, although the piece dealt mainly with the cost of food.

Her head of security arrives soon after she has had her routine massage, and broken her fast with milk, eggs and vegetable juices. She receives him in her small private interview room.

"Sorry, ma'am, I'm almost sure they are spies after all. The gifts were simply a ruse. I have to say they have been very clever. Shall I have them arrested?"

"No, Guidon, no. That would make us all look like fools, which I certainly don't want. And if we really are fools, that's all the more reason not to look like fools—and certainly not today, of all days! Now first of all, I want you to go over everything you know, or suspect. Never mind your report—I'll look at that later."

"Well, ma'am, to begin with, their stories don't make a lot of sense, especially comments from the one called Cherg. I know we don't have a lot of knowledge of Durama, but what he's told us doesn't match up with anything we do know. And what's more, he always looks as if he's daring us to challenge him. But it's not so much that—they seem to be recording us all the time, and that with devices that I'm pretty sure are beyond our technology. That's what really worries me."

"So what is your conclusion from all that, Guidon? Considering that spies usually try very hard not to be provocative, or conspicuous in their behaviour."

"I think, ma'am, they are deliberately aiming to keep us confused, and in the meantime their country is preparing to invade us—or I should say, that is a real possibility. They are certainly sending information somewhere."

"Thank you, Guidon. We must certainly prepare for that possibility. I will also have a message radioed out to Blue Patrol. As for what action to take on these Croans, I'll let you know later. In the meantime, behave exactly as before. Remember, they are honoured guests, and must be treated as such."

Qu stops abruptly as an urgent call comes through. "Yes? What! Keep me informed." She turns once more to Guidon.

"It seems that two of our Croans have attacked the guard who was on duty at their ship, and have since vanished. Apparently there was a witness, although at a considerable distance. She does admit it may not have been them, and simply a trick of the light that made her think otherwise. You'd better have a talk with Cavron, find the Croans if you can, and then chase up Hamul."

Ω

There were six steps leading from the ground to the entrance door of the spaceship, and when the door swung open the constable, on the fourth step and in the act of climbing up, teetered and almost fell. The empty space where the door had been was now filled by Schyl, smiling broadly, and looking benignly at the swaying constable.

"Oh, do be careful sir! On this planet, even a little fall could break a bone, you know."

The policeman smiled ruefully, and descended cautiously to the ground. He had not met the Croans, but had been warned to expect eccentricities.

"I must ask you to come down, sir."

"Certainly sir, we are on our way," said Schyl, who was not to be outdone when it came to trading 'sirs'. Schyl had been working hard on improving his skills with the Rangolian language, and relished the present opportunity. Behind him, Groose descended, planted himself slightly apart from the group, and prepared to take a surreptitious record of whatever was to happen next. The three joined a growing number of people around the guard, who had been the centre of attention for some time. He continued to look dazed, even bewildered, and was sitting once more, but he was at least sitting upright.

"I must ask you if you know this guard, and have any knowledge of the attack on his person?"

"Attack! Oh my goodness! Is the poor man hurt?"

"He certainly is, sir." Rather superfluously, the policeman pointed to the vivid red gash on the guard's face.

"Well, sir, first of all that needs treatment. Groose, do you happen to have … ?"

Groose at once plucked a little tin of ointment from his tunic, and gave it to Schyl, who rubbed it across the bruise. The guard had been starting to resist all the attention, finding it now embarrassing rather than flattering, but Schyl had taken him by surprise.

"Well, that is very gratifying, I must say." (The policeman decided to dispense with the 'sir'.) "However, I have to ask you about your movements over the last …" (the policeman here checked his watch) "three hours."

"We've been right here, sir, in this boat, and this lovely guard has been protecting us. That he should have been attacked in his line of duty, why, that's absolutely terrible."

The guard was here making hand gestures which could have meant, 'Don't mention it', or even 'Leave me out of it'. It was too late for either suggestion, however, for both Groose and Schyl were now close beside him, patting him on the back, commiserating.

"You were in the boat all that time? We have a report …"(the policeman consulted his notebook) "a woman in one of those high buildings saw a couple of individuals bending over a person on the ground. Are you sure you know nothing about this? Did you, for example, happen to hear anything?" The policeman gave Schyl what he considered was his 'steely look'. He was gaining in confidence, after what he felt was an unfortunate beginning, and looking forward to what a little bit of pressure might unearth.

Schyl turned to Groose. "Now that I think of it, didn't we hear something? A sort of cry, wasn't it?"

"The woman thought the two individuals were short of stature." The guard looked Schyl and Groose up and down.

Schyl glanced towards the tall residential towers, and back at the constable. "I must say I'm impressed by that woman's eyesight, to be able to tell a person's stature from such a height, not to mention the distance involved. Did she happen to see what the individuals were wearing?"

"No, unfortunately."

"Sir, you look sad," said Schyl compassionately. "We must help you find these miscreants."

"Thank you, but no." The constable hesitated. "Leave it to the force. We are sure to find them."

"Oh, but we must help! Groose, we must work our way all around the docks and speak to as many people as possible."

"Very good, captain, it will be a pleasure."

CHAPTER 22

Jelani's house

The following morning Aleb awoke to find he was lying in the sunniest, most cheerful bedroom he had ever seen. It occurred to him that the whole house was lavish, and particularly this room. There were a great many crystals hanging in the window, and sending rainbows racing around the walls as they slowly rotated. The window itself looked out on a sloping lawn which ran down a series of terraces to an expanse of pebbled beach, and beyond that wisps of steam from the ocean drifted lazily to and fro as they made their way into the upper atmosphere. Jelani diverted him from his musings by suddenly appearing at his side, and snuggling against him.

"I have coffee brewing. You'll smell it in a minute."

"Coffee! Wherever did you get coffee?"

"I have a store of it—just for special occasions. I admit it's not cheap."

"I thought it was unobtainable." Aleb looked around the room. "You have the nicest bedroom I've ever seen. In fact the whole house … I hardly noticed it the first time I visited."

"You hardly noticed anything. Not good for a reporter man. I waited forever for you to get in touch with me again—I mean properly in touch after that last outing."

"I thought you and Hamul … You seemed very close."

"Hamul? Hamul! Hamul has one passion, and that's his mission—to invent gadgets that he imagines will save the world. You don't need to worry about him. He barely notices me except as a colleague."

"But this beautiful house …"

"I inherited it as a tumbledown wreck desperately needing attention, so I sold the house I'd shared with Gijor and used the money to restore it. I love the place."

"Clever you."

Aleb raised himself a little, and bent over Jelani. She kissed him, and rubbed her face over his. "I don't think we have much to learn from the mark three," she said, " running a finger down his nose. "Just the same, Aleb the unobservant reporter, up you get. We'll give it a good test."

Presently Jelani and Aleb were sitting at either end of a table in Jelani's lounge. Aleb had the mark three transmitter and Jelani the receiver. Both had a pencil and notepad lying alongside. Jelani had attached her D3 headpiece, with its built-in screen, but Aleb was still hesitating.

"Come on, reporter man, what are you waiting for?"

And at last Aleb fitted the transmitter. He had in mind to think about his first visit to interview Jelani, and take matters from there, but the moment he had the transmitter switched on and tuned he had the most alarming sensation that his head was being probed, completely against his will. "Whoa! Whoa!" he exclaimed, reflexively.

"Better start with early memories," said Jelani.

Aleb relaxed a little. He looked into his screen, which at the moment was blank, and at the band of colour that sat beneath it. At present the colour was changing from red to a cool green, with little pink ripples flowing through it.

"Don't look at the colours! We want this to be very natural, for a good test."

"Right you are." Aleb focussed on the empty screen, and quite suddenly a movie began to play, quite outside his own volition.

"Are you receiving, Lani? I'm not doing anything!"

"All good here. Don't talk, just relax!"

He was just nine years old, and he had ventured out onto the waste-land between the highway and the sea. It was early morning, and the grasses that brushed his legs as he ran were alive with activity. Little hop-ping things, and bigger creatures with eyes on stalks that would bite if you came too close. Some boys came by, ones he recognised from school, and others mostly bigger than himself. There was one with a mean face and a scar on his cheek. He was holding a creature with a body almost as long as his arm, a snake-like thing with many legs, its body twisting this way and that, while its legs flailed impotently. Scarface confronted the young Aleb, pushing the animal almost in his face.

"Hey, you, Snowpatch. Bite its head off. Come on, bite its head off!"

"No! Let it go." He looked with distaste at the writhing creature with its sharp little eyes and gaping mouth.

"What a softie! What a little baby! Come on Trigger, show him how."

A little black and white dog with a long snout and wicked protruding teeth took a high jump, caught the thing, hung for a moment and then fell with the head in its mouth. The body continued to convulse helplessly.

"I'll get another one for you, Snowpatch."

"Leave me alone!" He started to move away but Scarface grabbed his arm and stood up intimidatingly close.

"The police will find you and send you away."

"Will not!"

Just the same he felt a jolt of fear.

"You don't have a registration."

"Do so."

"You're an outlander. The cops will find you."

"All right, that's enough, Aleb!" Jelani disconnected. "Oh my God, you poor little kid!"

"It was a long time ago." Aleb gave a rueful smile.

"Who told you?"

"No-one exactly. It was just a remark my mother made, and then my father said he had to get me a birth certificate, so I could go on an outing; and then I must have said something at school, because the older boys said I shouldn't be at school, because I came from the outlands. When a policeman came to see my mother I got a real fright, because I thought he was coming for me."

"Well, you sure gave me a shock. You must have been terrified. That's what your colours told me. Lots of red flashes." Jelani turned to her notepad and wrote, 'fear transmits very well'. "What else have you got hiding away in that head, mister reporter man?"

"Just that I'm sorry if I gave you the wrong impression of that waste-land. For a small child, it was like opening a door and discovering a wonderful new world. There were all kinds of funny insects, and rock pools with the most amazing little animals inside them. It was when I was exploring that place that I decided I would write about the world when I grew up." Aleb smiled, thinking back, and then pushed his headset across the table.

"It's your turn with the transmitter, Lani!"

They swapped, and Jelani gasped at times with amazement at the clarity and vividness of the recall that the machine provided. Her childhood had been less happy and more fretful than she had remembered, although there were unexpected, and forgotten, moments of sheer bliss. She noticed, as Aleb had, how even the worst experiences were lightened when shared. "It's as if they had happened to someone else," as she told Hamul later.

"You haven't talked about your children, " Aleb said presently. "What are their names?"

"Rihan and Holanna." Jelani looked into the distance, and was silent for a time.

"I need to take a rest from all that," she said.

Ω

Mukihano Island

"I wish we were back on the mainland. There's nothing to do here." Rihan kicked disconsolately at a stone. He looked at his sister. "We're exactly the same age, except I'm older because I was born first."

"I'm just as old as you!" Holanna had followed him out of the house. She now stamped her foot, frowned and hardened her eyes.

But Rihan had lost interest in the matter. He picked up the heaviest stone he could find and carried it the few paces necessary to drop it over the fence, where it rolled down into a shallow muddy stream.

"Daddy's going to take us for a row," said Rihan. He frowned. "Daddy's all right. I don't like Aunty."

The two children were in a designated play area set aside for them and fenced off by Gijor, who had promised his children an exciting life on Mukihaano Island 'with your lovely Auntie Yooriko'. 'Auntie' had not lived up to expectations, becoming bored quickly and being inclined to take her frustrations out on the children, as well as her lover.

"Yoorie, it's only for a little while," Gijor had pleaded. "This is a perfect trading base."

"There's nothing here. If I'd known you were going to take me to such a place..."

"It's the location, darling, it's the location! In another year it'll be a trading post, away from all the restrictions we have on Rangolia. We'll be rich in no time."

The children filed in from their play area and looked expectantly at their father.

"When are we going out in the boat?"

"Gijor, you can't take them out here! It's too near the river mouth."

"It's all right Yoo. I'll keep them away from the river."

"There's no time now anyway. Your daddy has lots of things to do."

"When are we going home to mummy?"

"Listen, Holanna dear, your mummy is much too busy to look after you. That's why you're here with your Auntie Yooriko!"

"Children, go outside and play now. Later you can come and have a wonderful story, and something to eat." The children remained standing, astonished at this betrayal.

"Look, sorry, I'll take you out another day. Promise."

Gijor watched his children file out, Rihan with his head bent forward, walking slowly, Holanna following closely behind.

"I don't know what possessed you to bring those children here."

"Yoorie, they're lovely children, and they're my kiddies, not just her ladyship Jelani's. She's too busy with her precious brain stuff. That's another thing. I don't want their heads contaminated with all that nonsense."

This was the beginning of an argument they had had many times. Yooriko opened her mouth to speak, almost a reflex action, but stopped herself just in time. Instead she poured a glass of wine from a flask, raised her glass, and looked into it critically.

"Why in heaven's name you can't get us something better than this rubbish I can't imagine. It wouldn't be hard to get a cask of something decent from Kraab."

"In another month, I promise. It's just that we're a bit short of cash right now, and there's a lot here that needs doing."

"Yes, you're always promising. And right now there's a festival on the mainland and we're stuck here."

Gijor sighed and went to the doorway. It was true there was a lot to do, such as scythe the backyard, and prepare it for planting. He had the seeds, newly purchased at a ridiculous cost, and there were more legal fees to pay. His latest challenge was for Jelani to sell the house and pay him a half share of the proceeds. Her lawyers were arguing that since she had purchased the house after they had separated he had no right to any of it. 'It's not that simple,' he said under his breath as he watched his children. Holanna was digging in the earth with a stick, and Rihan was throwing stones at the fence. As he watched, Rihan came and looked at Holanna's activity.

"Let's make roads, and build a town right here," said Rihan, in a burst of inspiration.

"We'll use stones for houses," said Holanna happily.

Gijor was in the act of turning away when the messenger came up the drive, hitching his horse to the gatepost and waving across the fence.

"Telegrams for you, sir."

Gijor tore them open, his heart beating fast.

The first told him that he was entitled to half the value of Jelani's present house. The second said that Jelani had equal rights as himself to the children. 'Since you live at a distance to your ex-wife, the court's decision is that you share them month and month about. Of course, you have the right to appeal.'

Gijor frowned. It was a Pyrrhic victory.

About the same time, Jelani received the same information. She called out to Aleb, who was just leaving. He came over, read the telegrams, and began to commiserate.

"Listen, reporter man, I'd give up everything I own in order to get those children back!"

"Listen, darling Jelani, you can come and share my place. We'll be a bit squashed with the children there as well, but it needn't be for long."

"I'll drink to that. Come inside mister reporter while I break open the wine."

Aleb took the bottle, and they both watched as the golden liquid flowed into the cups.

"Here's to victory," he said.

"Yes. Victory at any price!"

CHAPTER 23

Report from Senior Science Officer Euse to Area Commander Queyn
(Date: 50988/546)

Dear Commander

We are now domiciled in a very pleasant building provided by the inhabitants here. They regard us as emissaries from another country on their planet (they know their own country as Rangolia) and we are very happy to play that role. We live in their largest city, in the largest land mass in Groob, which they refer to simply as the 'mainland'. They are interesting as the first case of a people we have come across who are developing their technology by using what they can glean from a vanished civilisation. The scientists here are archaeologists first, engineers second: they excavate the deserts and find artefacts of various kinds. Most machinery is repaired, if possible, (and if it is understood) and attempts are often made to replicate it. Thus they have motor cars on their roads alongside horse-drawn traffic. The name Groob, by the way, is a close approximation to their own word, which they associate with the old people, and use in the names of various corporations. It can mean either Rangolia or the Rangolian mainland. A curious coincidence!

More interesting are what they call feral robots ('frots'), autonomous machines that move about, form quasi-military units, and attack others of their kind, or anything that will yield them the metals they need to replicate themselves. This is not something that has been reported elsewhere. These creatures are a menace, but are nonetheless protected by the inhabitants in the hope that future study will allow their scientists insights into the technology they exemplify. They run on powerful batteries, and we are currently searching for the source of that power.

The scientists have a limited understanding of the energy sources they could use: there are a few windmills and waterwheels, and they are experimenting with solar energy, but the main focus is finding petroleum, or other fossil fuels, which apparently were mainly exhausted by the 'old people'. Almost no use is made of their geothermal energy, apart from a little cooking, and nuclear power, which they know about from old records, is well beyond their technological abilities. I must admit I feel a touch of nostalgia for those remote, simpler times, and the easy pace of life!

Their government is also unusual, and is a sort of hybrid democracy/autocracy. There are six big companies that control almost everything, including (via a voting process) who gets to be president.

Crew:

Our crew are all well, and presently have various roles assisting the natives with their technology. Our passengers Andrew and Belzic have been particularly helpful. Incidentally Andrew has proved of value in providing a very non-croan perspective on our doings.

Ess continues to contrive useful situations in which to study the native population. I have to add that so too do Schyl and Groose, both of whom have been extremely helpful. Groose keeps a close eye on the risk element that inevitably accompanies our exploration of this remarkable planet, and we are all grateful for his prompting to show due care.

Portals:

So far we have made no headway with this target, though we suspect the concept derives from an old folktale. We are continuing to investigate.

Our present situation:

As I mentioned, we are in a very comfortable apartment, paid for by the government of this place, and are able to operate with very few constraints. *Neither of the other planets allowed us such freedom. Four of the crew (myself, Schyl, Cherg and Ess) have joined a company that works with equipment sensitive to the brain's electrical activity, and this gives us an amazing amount of freedom to explore the mentality of these people. The natives believe we are 'outlanders', that is, inhabitants outside the jurisdiction of Rangolia's territory. This too gives us an advantage, since the natives are all very keen to show their hospitality. If there are portals on this planet, or ever were, we will surely find them.*

Commander, I will transmit this short description along with the technical report from the house we inhabit, since that is where we have moved our more important technical equipment. Expect more detailed reports from us in days to come.

Sent by PB Euse, Senior Science Officer.

"Check that over for me please, Cherg, and then see if you can get us anywhere more comfortable than this place, since you've got the best grasp of their language."

"I think something is coming up very soon, chief. I'll work on it."

Ω

Confidential to Qu from Guidon

Ma'am,

Concerning the Croans, presently domiciled in the building owned by Dreamland Enterprises:

Following research from the old records, and reports from my agents, I respectfully suggest the following conclusions, and course of action:

1. There have been no reports of people similar in appearance to the Croans living in Durama, or any of the surrounding islands, over the past 100 years. While we have been in isolation for part of that time, I believe we can assume these visitors are not from Durama.

2. The Croans have a technology that is superior to our own, at least in respect to communications. We followed up reports of radio interference that were coming from the embassy, and when we enquired they apologised and said they were 'calling their base', and would adjust the frequency. There was no sign of a radio mast, and their transmission must extend well beyond the range of anything we can achieve (perhaps being bounced off our nearest moon?)

3. Their ship the Duvra (if it is their ship?) has no visible means of propulsion.

4. We have had reports of a large orange balloon (airship?) lifting off from the embassy.

5. Therefore, we continue to monitor their movements, and compile a record of, as nearly as possible, everything they say that has any factual content. I have approached Jelani, who has taken over the running of Dream Hunter in the absence of Hamul, and she has agreed to 'ask innocent questions', particularly with respect to their homeland. Jelani will also make available copies of recordings from the Dream Hunter devices.

6. I suggest that Blue Patrol is contacted and instructed to make a trade offer with Durama as if this is a purely Rangolian initiative, as it probably is.

Ma'am, I trust this finds you well, and you find this report of value.

I remain, your obedient servant, Guidon.

"Rain, we need to have another conversation with our visitors."

"Yes ma'am. Would you like me to bring Euse in?"

"No, not Euse. Not yet, anyway. I think perhaps I'll quiz Jelani and Hamul to begin with. Which means we must find Hamul."

CHAPTER 24

"Aleb darling, please make sure a message about Hamul goes in all the papers. It's so unlike him." It was the third call Jelani had made concerning Hamul that day.

"You don't need to worry about that, Lani. The police put those messages in, and one is already prepared for the Monitor. They'll run it for a week if there is no news."

"I'm so worried about him. I'm terrified he might have drowned, or been taken by a monster fish."

Giant fish came periodically to feast on the underwater life that flourished around the thermal vents, sometimes coming in close to shore and casting a speculative eye on the inhabitants of Kraab. There were 'safe' designated swimming places where one would not expect to be either eaten or scalded, but Hamul's little bay was not among them.

Jelani's house went on the market, and she moved in with Aleb. The following day Rihan and Holanna arrived, accompanied by 'Auntie' Yooriko. Gijor was not there.

"There now, here's your mother, darlings. Be sure to give her your school books. Auntie will say goodbye."

"Goodbye Auntie," said Rihan mechanically. Holanna said nothing. Both children looked with trepidation at their mother, who stood for a moment with mouth agape, stunned by the sudden appearance, and immediate disappearance, of Gijor's 'fancy woman'.

"Oh, Rihan, Holanna, I've missed you so much!" Jelani squatted down, arms outstretched, but with a look of fearful uncertainty on her face. The children hesitated for a long minute, and then walked slowly forward.

Ω

The headland to the north guarded Kraab from the worst storms, and served as a lookout towards the outlands, from where in the past raiders had come, burning, looting, raping and killing in the bad early days of the current epoch. Two generations previously a substantial tower had been built out of the local black stone. It contained a hand operated lift to supplement the external ladder, a viewing platform, a lamp fed by some of Rangolia's precious oil, and a number of red glass panels. Its companion, a little further along the coast, shone a white light, alerting ships that they were approaching the port of Kraab. The red light signified the proximity of a dangerous reef.

A man from the coast guard came every evening to feed the northern light, set it going for the nightly vigil, and exchange a few words with the departing day attendant. However it wasn't until the third morning after Hamul's disappearance that either of them heard a sound that was other than that of the wind, or the seabirds.

"That, Buraat, sounds like a bird in pain," said the departing keeper. "I'd better check it out."

Thus was Hamul discovered, two yards short of the clifftop, on a little platform of rock. He was confused, frightened and exhausted. He had no clear idea how he came to be in such an odd place. The day keeper called Kraab's civil defence unit, who called Kraab security, who called Jelani. Jelani arrived at the lighthouse, sitting in the back of an official car, in company with her two children. She was closely followed by another official vehicle that was part of Kraab's health and hospital service. Then when Hamul was guided out of the tower, and to the ambulance, Jelani was the first close associate to meet him, and be shocked to see his blank and puzzled face.

"Something very traumatic must have happened, and of course his memory loss will have caused further dismay," she was told. "But don't worry, he appears strong and fit. He will recover in time if he has absolute rest, and plenty of reassurance." Jelani felt unequal to the task, but Aleb came to the rescue. "Thank you, thank you!" Jelani responded. "Don't worry, don't worry," rejoined Aleb. "That's the mantra for you!"

"Idiot," she said, but nonetheless gave him a hug and a kiss. "You'd better get on with the reassuring bit. Off you go!" To be fair, Jelani had both the office and two children to manage, not to mention the problem of adapting Aleb's house to fit the needs of four.

In the Dream Hunter offices, the Croans took on more and more roles, arranging orders, delivering, even assisting with the design of future devices in the Dream Hunter range. Umus was amazed at the speed in which they absorbed both the science and business needs of the company. Then when Erg offered to join Euse, Ess, Grice and Cherg on the staff he was welcomed by all the senior staff. Meanwhile the government purchased Jelani's house: officially as an embassy for all 'outlanders' but in reality as a base for the Croans' operations. Guidon, chief of Rangolia security, continued to receive reports on their activities, but found nothing he could act on.

CHAPTER 25

Jelani came home each evening exhausted, but not too exhausted to spend time with her children. Usually, there was a cuddle, and a story to be read after she had had a talk with the day nurse.

"They're bright kiddies, and they get bored very easily," the nurse complained. "I keep running out of ways to keep them occupied, and I've never had that problem before. Today I took them to visit that outlander exhibition, where they have a giant model of Taapino as the key exhibit. They've been asking me about Taapino ever since, and I can't say I know much. Do you think you could … ?"

"A book? Of course, I have one with Taapino stories, which I think Rihan will just about be able to cope with, and Holanna is almost as quick." Jelani pulled the little book with its brightly coloured illustrations from her bag. It was a new publication, lovingly reconstructed from an old, damaged volume discovered recently at an archaeological site. The language had been modernised, but otherwise the stories remained the same.

"It's the children's things that get to me," said Jelani as she flipped through the pages. "When we see a broken toy, or a torn book pulled out of the ground, I do wonder what had happened to the owners."

"They'd have been long gone by now anyway, ma'am," said the nurse, packing up her things. "It's the future we need to be thinking of, not the past. I'll be here at the usual time, bright and early." The nurse looked around the room. "You should see if you can get some more money out of that husband of yours. It's a scandal the way he's taken half, and him never giving you any support. Well, I'll be off now."

Jelani heated some milk at the stove, while Holanna came and pulled at her skirt. "Mummy, Rihan's taken all the blocks, and I want some. Mummy, make him give me half the blocks."

"Rihan!" Jelani called out, without looking round. "Rihan, give her half, don't be greedy."

Aleb came in, came up close behind Jelani (who, again without turning round, said 'Back off!' in her firmest voice) and then engaged himself with the children, who were building rival castles on the floor.

"Mine's best," said Rihan complacently.

"It's certainly the biggest, but look at the imagination that's gone into your sister's."

"Mine's the best," said Holanna.

"I say they're both excellent. It's a tie," said Aleb.

"Lebby, can you get them to bed? I'll bring them in warm milk, and you can read them a story."

Soon the children were sitting, one either side of Aleb, in the biggest padded chair. Rihan had given conditional approval for him to be the 'new daddy' on alternate months. Aleb said he would try his best. Now he took the new book Jelani had brought home, opened it, and began to read.

Long, long ago a terrible monster came to live in the world of animals. It was a huge terrorsaur. It flew in and sat on the highest mountain in the land, and it called out in a big loud voice, "I'm hungry! Feed me!"

A giraffe stuck its head up out of the trees and looked at the big creature. "Why should we feed you?" the giraffe asked.

The monster at once swooped down and ate the giraffe. Then it said, "Because I'm a terrorsaur, and I say so!"

The terrorsaur made its home in the jungle, and all the animals had to bring it food, and if they didn't have any the terrorsaur ate them. Now, there was a family of gruffalumps living nearby, and they only ate grass. There was a big daddy gruffalump, a medium sized mummy gruffalump, and a little pink baby gruffalump, and his name was Taapino. On the day when it was the turn of the gruffalumps to feed the big terrorsaur, daddy gruffalump made his way through the jungle carrying a huge pile of hay on his back, with mummy helping, and at the very top of the hay sat little pink Taapino. Right in the middle of the jungle was a big empty space, because the terrorsaur had burnt down all the trees. So when the gruffalumps came to that big empty space they stopped and looked at the terrorsaur.

"Please, mister terrorsaur, we have food for you," said the daddy gruffalump.

But the terrorsaur gave a scornful snort when it saw the hay. It said, in a big thundering voice, "take it away, but leave that little creature you have with you, because I'll eat it." At once mummy gruffalump cried out, "That's our baby! You can't eat our baby!" Then the terrible terrorsaur gave an enormous roar and chased the mummy and daddy all the way through the jungle. After that it came back and looked at the pink baby gruffalump, and the baby gruffalump looked at the terrorsaur. "Hum," said the terrorsaur, "there's not much meat on you, but you look nice and tender. Come closer, and I'll eat you up."

"I bet you can't," said the baby gruffalump. "I can eat more than you!"

The terrorsaur stared at Taapino in great astonishment. It walked around Taapino and looked at the young animal from every angle. Then it let out another big roar. "I can eat more than any other creature in the world!"

"I bet you can't," said Taapino.

That made the terrorsaur so angry that it ate two elephants and five crocodiles in a row.

"That's nothing," said Taapino.

Then the terrorsaur became so, so angry that it ate twenty-one monkeys, seventeen tigers and a thousand eggs all at once.

"And now," said the terrorsaur, "I'm going to eat you!"

"I bet you can't," said Taapino.

And indeed, the terrorsaur couldn't. It couldn't move because of the huge weight inside it. But presently it began to groan, and then out of its side there poked a long snout, and the snout was followed by the rest of the crocodile, because it had been swallowed whole.

- Then out from the same place came the other four crocodiles.

- Then out came the two elephants.

- Then out came the twenty-one monkeys.

- Then out came the seventeen tigers, and they began chasing the monkeys, who all jumped up on top of the elephants.

- Then out came a thousand little fledgling birds, because the terrorsaur's warm stomach had hatched them out.

After that nothing came out, and Taapino, who was hiding behind a tree, called out, "Hey, terrorsaur!"

But there was no answer, because the terrorsaur's insides had all been eaten up, and it was dead.

Then the crocodiles began eating what was left of it.

Then Taapino went riding home on the first elephant, with the twenty-one monkeys all sitting in a row behind.

And all the little hatchling birds followed, riding on the second elephant.

And all the animals except the crocodiles followed, bringing presents for Taapino and his family, because they were so pleased that the terrorsaur was dead.

Aleb finished reading. He turned to look at Rihan, but he was fast asleep, and then he turned to look at Holanna, but she too was fast asleep. So he put the book away, carried the children to their waiting beds, and tiptoed out of the room. He had had a very busy day, dividing his time between Hamul, the Dream Hunter office, and a reporting assignment, and now he was looking forward to sharing experiences, the highs and lows, with Jelani. He went into the other bedroom in search of her, and then stopped. She too had put herself to bed, and was also asleep. However as he came across she roused, and smiled at Aleb.

"The kiddies?"

"Very much asleep. I read them the first of the Taapino stories."

"That's what I like most about the old people, the folk tales that have survived. I'm not so sure about the rest." She reached out her arms and Aleb sat beside her.

"You look so lovely I could eat you," he said.

She giggled. "I bet you couldn't." She nestled in against him and went back to sleep.

Aleb stayed sitting, listening to her breathing, to the faint wind gusts against the house, and the slow, gentle surge of surf on the pebbly beach. He was thinking how lucky he was to have Jelani and her delightful children right there in his house. He looked around the master bedroom. In every nook and corner there were signs of Jelani's presence. He had few possessions of his own, and the house, which had previously seemed almost too spacious for him, now had a cosy, closed-in feeling.

He did wonder at times where everything was going to go.

EARTH

The second season, Earth,
develops all those things that were started in Water.
Earth time is about processes, about growth,
about setting in motion both the good
and the bad trends that began at the start of the year.
Great things can be achieved,
while things long buried and forgotten
may begin to emerge once more.

CHAPTER 26

Hamul's house

Jelani made her way down a long path to the cottage that sat on the edge of the desert. An immaculate garden of flowers and fruit greeted her, and then the little house in black stone and white painted wood, with its tall chimney stack. Behind it ran the high wooden fence that marked the edge of the desert. She reached the door, and found it opening at the same moment, with Hamul in front of her, smiling, holding out his hand. She hugged him, noting with relief that the confusion had gone from his eyes. "Thank God," she said involuntarily, "you're back with us."

"Thank you for coming, Jelani. I'll get you a drink. A hot herbal tea?" Hamul chuckled. "I'm not allowed anything alcoholic, but for you …"

"Oh, no, herbal tea will be fine. Can I help?"

Hamul laughed, made her sit in what he called the 'cosy corner' looking out on the garden.

They sat drinking tea, discussing the garden, discussing the sand, uttering pleasantries.

"I suppose the frots could be a nuisance here? I mean, you're a bit isolated."

"Frots? No. The sand is more of a nuisance. It's so fine it gets into everything. See that strip of white along the grass? The wind produces it. It's the sand coming through a little hole in the wall."

"Yes., I see." She paused, and looked out not so much at the white strip as at the white, dust-like sprinkling over the remainder of the lawn and the garden. "So how are you feeling now, Hamul? Keen to be back, I expect?"

"Not allowed to for another two weeks, but to tell you the truth I'm rather enjoying doing nothing. And before you ask, I have no clue about what happened to me. The last thing I remember is setting out for my little cove, and I think I'd prefer to leave it that way." He met Jelani's eyes and she nodded, commiserating. "I'd like to hear what's going on at the office, just the same. Aleb doesn't tell me much."

"Oh, very good, Hamul. Sales are up, including for the D2. The D2 is still a bit experimental, so we're getting new tests."

"Is Umus managing all this, with his team?"

"We've had a bit of luck there, with the outlander visitors offering volunteer work. They're very smart—Umus says they pick things up very quickly. Oh, and we've warned them they may not copy anything when they return to their own country. They're strange, but I believe they are trustworthy."

Hamul chuckled. "They wouldn't be able to get working models if they tried. If I wasn't sure of that I wouldn't have let them near the place. What I'm hoping is that we can export some. Now, is there anything else you should tell me?"

"There is one thing. I'm not sure how significant it is."

"Yes?"

"Two families have contacted us. The parents have both used the D2, and in both cases their children seem to be hallucinating. The little girl in one family insists there is a big black spider on a wall in her room. The mother says there isn't even a shadow, and even when she shines a light on the wall the girl can still see the spider."

"And the other case?"

"There are twins in this family, a girl and a boy. They both insist that a 'little elf man' as they call it, comes to visit each night. At first only the girl saw it, but now the boy insists it is real. So what do you think, Hamul?"

"How many of the D2's have we sold? A couple of hundred?"

"Almost a thousand now, Hamul."

"And only two cases. I wouldn't worry about them—lots of children see things, or have imaginary friends."

"I was just wondering if we could produce a device that shows imaginary things as imaginary?"

"Not with our present technology. In fact, one of the reasons why we don't let children use these things is that they make everything seem real, and it won't matter how fantastic it is. No, tell the parents to stop using the D2 for a while to see if it makes a difference—otherwise, business as usual."

Jelani left soon after. The warm sun slanting onto the lawn, the flowers and the faint soughing of the wind, quite as much as the presence of Hamul, made her want to linger, but there was much to do, and the horse-drawn carriage that would call by at the bottom of the lane was due in a few minutes. She gave Hamul a quick hug, gathered up her things, and was gone.

"Take care, Hamul, we'll see you soon in the office."

"Not running the show you won't," he called after her. "I'll talk to the board, and I suspect they'll put you in charge. Would you like that?"

Jelani gave an ambiguous wave of her hand, and was gone. She did not, however, stop wondering about childhood fantasies and the use of the company devices. Could there be a connection? And might it not be as well to talk to other families who had been customers—without, of course, giving any cause for concern. She frowned. It would be a delicate business.

One thing was certain though: there would need to be a lot more testing.

CHAPTER 27

That was how it started—with the children. Hamul had thought nothing of it, and after all, why would he? With only two cases from a thousand sales? However, the worst pandemics all have a starting point, usually something very insignificant, and even if this was the strangest illness ever known, was it all really so very different?

Two months have passed. Jelani is running Dream Hunters, and Hamul is chairman of the board of directors. Jelani has settled in with Aleb, with the two of them, plus the two children on alternate months, being a little bit squashed together, but on the whole happy. Aleb works on assignments for various news services, while the children are with their father Gijor and 'Auntie' Yooriko. In between times Aleb either works at the Dream Hunter office or takes care of the children, assisting with schoolwork provided courtesy of the Kraab education centre.

"Daddy, a lady came to see us today while you were out," said Holanna one evening as Aleb returned from work.

"Yes? What did she want?"

"She was looking for a man called Andrew. I ran to tell mummy, but when we came back she wasn't there any more."

"Andrew? That's the name of one of the outlanders—I'm sure I could find him. Did she say who she was?"

"Yes, she said she was Maria."

Aleb found Jelani in the kitchen, stirring a pot. He resisted, with difficulty, the temptation to creep up behind her. Instead, he sat at the dining room table and gave a little sigh of satisfaction. A warm room, and a moment to sit still.

"Damn! There goes the power. Oh Lebby, this was so nearly cooked."

Aleb walked over and inspected. "Look, we'll put the lid on the pot and wrap it in Rihan's old blanket. What do you say?"

Jelani's expression hardly changed. "That's another thing I wanted to talk to you about. There was a strange kid with squinty eyes round earlier. He said you'd sent him, and he was there to play with Rihan. I didn't like the look of him—for one thing, he was quite a bit bigger than Rihan …"

"I sent him? I've never heard of him! Where is he now?"

"I sent him away. Rihan didn't like him, in fact was quite rude to him. I want you to talk to Rihan—it's useless asking Gijor, and someone's got to teach him manners."

"But Lani, he's usually very polite—quiet perhaps, but definitely polite."

"Not this time!"

"I'll go and see him. I'll get the blanket while I'm about it."

Rihan was quiet, but firm. "No, I'm not sorry, 'cause he's scary. He keeps coming, he's a nuisance."

"He keeps coming? When does he come?"

"Just about every day."

"What's his name? Where does he come from?"

"He doesn't say, he just turns up. He says, 'I've come to play.'"

"He doesn't tell you his name?"

"He only says one thing, and he looks funny."

"All right, son, I'll get to the bottom of this, but in future, if he's a nuisance, just call your mother. Don't be rude, don't say anything."

"All right, daddy."

The following day, Umus was in charge of the office while Jelani and Aleb ran tests on the D4. The D1 and D2 models were now both selling well, while D3 (which showed emotions as blocks of colour below the main screen) had at last been launched on the marketplace. The D4 was more of a diagnostic tool for health professionals, which Jelani and Aleb were not, but at least they were familiar with its intentions. They had put out a call for medical folk to come visit.

"A bad cough," said Aleb unnecessarily to the latest visitor. Instinctively he pulled the surgical mask closer against his face, and gave the D4 headpiece a final disinfecting wipe. "Let's see what the machine tells us."

"It's not that," said the earnest young man. "It's the children. I'm wondering if we could check them over. I know we're not supposed to use these devices on children, but in this case ... you see, our lad is usually very truthful, very matter-of-fact ..."

"I'm so sorry, sir. I'd need something official in writing, preferably from the medical council."

Thus began the imaginative mania, as it was deemed, among the youngsters of Rangolia. Increasingly, children were being taken by parents and caregivers to doctors, psychologists, counsellors and other helpful figures. The link between imagination and the products of Dream Hunter was not made for several weeks, and even then was strenuously denied by men and women of influence who had a stake in the company.

The mark four, like the mark two, was a 'networking' model, a concept dreamed up by Hamul and endorsed by the board. It included an external viewer, or the patient could look into his own brain functions, and transmit the images to others. Thus the patients could be examined by health professionals, or students, or in fact with anyone who had the equipment and the access code, and, presumably, the permission of the patient.

'Be as private or as public as you like' was the legend on the mark four, as on the mark two.

"I'll look at something, and you tell me what it is," said Jelani, turning on the external viewer.

"You could start by just sending a message."

"All right, I love you."

"You too. I meant, through the transmitter."

"Transmitting now. Now I'm looking out at the sea. I'm sending you wave pictures. My God, there's a boy, just appeared out of nowhere."

"No boy, Lani. I can see your waves though. Beautiful colours."

"You must be able to see him!"

"No Lani."

"He's still there, coming up slowly from the beach. You must be able to see him."

"I can't!"

The boy stood motionless, gazing vaguely around. Aleb tore off his headset. The boy appeared. He was mooching along, looking at the ground.

"We'll switch, and see what happens."

It was a problem. The boy appeared not to 'transmit' although everything around him did.

"I'll talk to him, Lani, find out what his secret is."

Except that he was now not to be found.

"I bet he's the boy who visits Rihan," said Jelani at last.

"Wretched boy! Where does he go Lani?"

"The children! He always says he's 'come to play.'"

Rihan and Holanna were busy hopping around the house, and counting how many hops it took for a complete circuit. And no, 'that boy' had not appeared.

"He only ever comes when I'm in my room," said Rihan. "I only have to go in for a minute and he turns up and says he wants to play."

"How very odd," said Jelani.

"Must be a coincidence, or Rihan exaggerating. "Holanna, does he visit you?"

"No daddy, only the lady visits me."

"The lady?"

"She says, 'I'm Maria and I'm looking for Andrew. Have you seen him?' "

"To you!"

"Yes, daddy."

"What do you think, Lani?"

"I think we need a lot more testing. It's got to transmit everything we see, or we have to understand why."

Aleb shook his head. "We're getting near the mid season, Lani, and that's the time when things go wrong, so people say."

The next day Maria appeared to Holanna as usual, and by good fortune Jelani was on hand with the D4 transmitter. She sent the image to the hub she and Aleb had created, but when they checked, the image of Maria had failed to register. However a second test, using the D3, had the image coming through clearly. Aleb then contacted Andrew at the embassy, and said 'there was a lady called Maria trying to contact you'. Andrew said he would come at once.

CHAPTER 28

The Embassy

The house at the lower end of Ridge Road that Jelani had owned had four bedrooms and a small common room—for a time Jelani's office. Andrew and Belzic shared one room, with Ess, Euse and Cherg in a second, and Schyl, Groose, Erg and Grice in the third. The fourth was devoted to recording, processing and communication equipment of various kinds. It was also supplied with a telephone which could communicate directly to the Dream Hunter office or to the Town Hall. The Croans all had their own personal phones, of course, but always made use of Rangolian technology when dealing with the natives. The sign above the front door, newly mounted, read 'Outlander Embassy'.

When the call came through to the embassy Andrew and Belzic were working with Cherg in compiling a record of the Rangolian language and customs. Most of the others were at the Dream Hunter offices. Andrew froze when he heard Aleb saying that 'a lady called Maria is looking for you'. He then found himself, as it were, watching his own actions.

"Maria is alive and has found her way to this world," he said, wondering. His mind rejoiced, but, strangely enough, his body felt cold. "How could that be, Cherg, Belzic, how could that be?"

Belzic caught his wrist. "Do not think about that, Andrew. This may not be what it seems, so don't think ahead. I'll come with you, so keep calm, let me do the thinking."

Andrew nodded. He found his body was shaking, and realised he was actually afraid.

$$\Omega$$

Up in her penthouse suite Qu sat looking out over Kraab. Her old childhood fears that had been buried beneath her public life, along with the laws, the protocols and the ceremonies of state, were, she suspected, beginning to break free. A memory came to her now: an airship hovering over the little island of her childhood, and a voice booming out from it: 'Is there anybody here? Is there anybody here?' While she, bedraggled, dirty and shivering, stood inside a hollow tree.

Another memory: her mother looking very serious. "Do not let anyone find you while we are away. Be sure to hide yourself! We'll be back when we can, and in the meantime, go to Nevala if you need anything."

There were many tiny islands in the world; probably more than a few held their own secrets.

Qu looked over the message that had been delivered that morning:

Urgent dispatch from Blue Patrol:

To: The President of Rangolia.

We hope this finds you well. We will transmit this dispatch to the station at Julvar. We ask for urgent advice.

We came within sight of Durama: a place of sheer rocky cliffs, and overshadowing it, smoke from an active volcano. Since we have no good charts of the place we were hoping for a pilot and signalled thus with our flags as we cruised the coastline. A boat did arrive, so we came alongside and assisted them to board. Two did so, but once aboard they were hostile. They pointed to our ensign and made it clear we were not welcome! Mooch took one of our radio sets from the hold and gave it to one of the natives, who looked at it as if it were something disgusting, and threw it overboard!

Clearly, the trade initiative did not come from Durama. I have to say also that the people on the ship did not look in the least like the Croans, or like Andrew or Belzic. They are very tall and thickset, and have red hair which they tie back with coloured bands.

We have few provisions for a longer eastward venture, but having come all this way we are reluctant to return. Please let us know your wishes as soon as possible.

Signed: Filly Ampwooler, Captain, Blue Patrol.

Qu hesitated. Nothing was as it seemed, and in particular, her visitors were not what they seemed. She called through to security. "Get a radio message out to Blue Patrol: 'Return immediately'.

She turned to another message, which was also labelled urgent and which dealt mainly with the Dream Hunter products. "*There is no doubt that the rise in violence, in suicides and madness can be linked directly to these products*" that note concluded.

There was a third message from her security chief: *These outlanders have never declared who they really are. They have charmed their way around Kraab with all sorts of stories, and have gone along with any assumptions we made. Their real purpose remains obscure, and is more than likely to be to our detriment. It may be that Umus is in league with them. Here are some recent episodes involving Umus ...*"

Qu folded up the three messages once more and headed for the meeting room, where twenty-three heads of departments and eleven secret service agents were already gathered and waiting.

CHAPTER 29

Out in the desert

"Move the screen a little further out, Aleb. Yes, that's better."

Hamul was at last out of hibernation, and working with the team, who were in the desert, well clear of Kraab, and indeed of any habitation. A long wall that marked the barrier at the edge of the desert appeared as a thin dark line a half mile distant. Aleb was standing inside an arrangement of screens, in wood and metal, and on a table in front of him were the D1 and D2 transmitters and receivers. On another table, about a hundred yards away, were the D1 and D2 counterparts, in the company of the sturdy dark-eyed Depoon, a gap scientist who had transitioned to Dream Hunters.

"Better sit while we do this next one," said Hamul. "Otherwise your head will be above the screen." Depoon squatted awkwardly in front of the table.

"Okay, you know the drill. Aleb transmits, you receive. Then we put the screens up on your side and repeat. Then the rest of you (nodding to twelve assistants who were standing by) mill about in the area between the stations. We need to find out if your actions can create any kind of interference. ... What should you be doing? Why not start an argument, or a bit of horseplay? ... Jukaan, you're an actor, can you get them to try out different scenes, or something? ... Think about it for now—we'll need to do a lot of tests, but we'll start with the simple stuff."

The current tests were in part a response to criticisms from customers, and in part an effort to allay the suspicions of some of the Board members. Criticisms, because the D2 range seemed to vary widely from the 'recommended thirty yards or less', and suspicions, since it was becoming believed that the mental activity of anyone beyond that range could interfere with the result. Hamul had rejected such comments, but Jelani was not so sure. She now worried that in some mysterious way she or Aleb had somehow 'infected' her children; that the mystery visitors the children were encountering were somehow mental creations to do with them. It had not helped allay her fears that Rihan's 'visitor' was very likely the deceased son of a customer she knew, who was the proud owner of a D2.

A small dune buggy, a new vehicle in Dream Hunter's growing fleet, now drew up with Jelani at the wheel.

"Depoon, you've received?" Hamul continued. "Good. Now send it back, and we'll see if it changes."

Jelani came across and looked over Aleb's shoulder. The image was from a photo of her old house, now the embassy for the Croans. Jelani saw at once that while the original transmission was fairly close to the original, in the image back from Depoon the foreground trees had all changed. "Take the screens away!" she called out.

"Jelani, no, we'll try someone else first."

So it went on: transmission with and without screens, with different images, (some abstract, some loaded with emotional tone), with different subjects transmitting and receiving. At the end of three hours the desert heat had intensified, and fatigue was having a perceptible effect on the results.

"Call it a day, Jelani?"

"Yes, Hamul. Another session next week, weather permitting. Are you—?"

"I wouldn't miss it. Okay everyone, that's it! Time to pack up!"

Jelani had her field glasses out, and she beckoned to Aleb. On the horizon was a tell-tale sign

"Better move quickly!" Aleb called out . "Frots coming this way!"

Ω

"Why don't you do something about the frots?" Andrew asked on his trip around the bays.

"If we don't interfere with them they don't hurt us," said the guide.

"Unless you're wearing something metal," said the driver.

"Now why would anyone be so silly?"

Andrew was sitting in a six-seat passenger car, lovingly reconstructed from diagrams and broken parts that had been recently excavated. The internal combustion engine was well understood, and with it the need for suitable combustible material. The Rangolians had yet to find a replacement for oil, and thus Andrew's present tour signified more than anything else his special status in the community. At the time he was inclined to feel critical, even belligerent. Maria had been elusive, asking for him but not appearing when he called. And Belzic had said, most tiresomely, 'You see, she is most likely just a fantasy you are creating for yourself. She won't withstand an actual meeting.'

With Andrew and his guide were two reporters, a diplomat, and a member of Qu's staff. It was the last who had questioned the notion of wearing metal. Qu, in fact, was very defensive about the frots. "They will ultimately be a tourist attraction," she predicted. And in truth they had been found nowhere else in Rangolian territory, or indeed heard about anywhere else on the planet, as far as the Rangolians knew.

"Now here," said the guide, "we are coming to the timber mills. We get the raw timber from Huvaan Island, which is two day's sail away. "There is an independent community of about five thousand, mainly farmers and lumberjacks. They mostly holiday here, so you will have seen some already. We buy their grain and timber and we send them many things in return, most recently radio sets, so we are in continuous contact."

"Have you anything like that?" Andrew was asked. "I suppose you've never heard of radio?"

"I've never seen a radio quite like yours," Andrew responded cautiously. He had been finding questions about his life as an 'outlander' a trifle embarrassing, but mostly he'd been able to talk almost exclusively about his experiences living in the wilderness, in which the most complex technology owned by the community was an old bus and a bicycle. He often felt waves of nostalgia for that bus, that bicycle, and that community. His great surprise now was the amount of attention he was receiving. He was not, after all, a Croan, and he did not have Euse's flair for handling all sorts of people, or indeed Cherg's ability to make up all sorts of stories on the spot, whenever asked anything. He was dimly aware that popular opinion had already identified the island he came from, since early speculations, transmitted mouth to mouth in confidence, had soon grown to certainty in the transmission. What was less certain was the matter of what he did there. His air of being quieter and more reserved than the Croans convinced many that he had some far superior rank. He was a special envoy. He was in secret deals with Qu. He was a great traveller, scientist, or even magician. He had secret knowledge of the stars.

CHAPTER 30

Rather more surprising than the attention given to Andrew was the almost total lack of interest in Belzic. Belzic was as short as the Croans, and readily merged with them in any group situation. He was plump, but somehow had a talent for becoming virtually invisible. At least, it never occurred to people to ask questions about him. Belzic was simply Belzic.

Right now he was visiting Aleb's house. Rihan had just returned from school, walking down a leafy glade in company with Holanna and the day nurse. Holanna was feeling tired and irritable when the group reached the house at the same time as Belzic. "I don't go to school. I don't go anywhere," said Holanna (referring to the fact that Rihan had been squeezed into a junior boys' class at the local school, to supplement his correspondence lessons, but there was nowhere for her).

Belzic loomed up in front of the trio, a grumpy Holanna in the lead.

"I need you to help me. Will you help me?" said Belzic.

Holanna stopped and stared, speechless.

"Ah, Belzic, isn't it?" said the day nurse. Belzic gave a little bow. "What do you want with Holanna?"

Belzic frowned. "A woman comes to see Holanna. She says she is Maria, and she is looking for Andrew. You will know this of course?"

"I certainly do. She's like a conjuring trick. I hear her voice, and I go running to the bedroom, but she's never there when I arrive."

"Exactly so. I'm hoping Holanna will direct her to me. I want her to say, 'Talk to Belzic, who is Andrew's friend.'"

"Do you think you can say that, Holanna?"

"Yes."

Belzic bent forward. "What do you say now, Holanna?"

Holanna began to cry. "I don't say anything."

"That is very wise of you, and you are very brave, but just this once tell her to talk to me. Can you do that?"

"Yes."

"Good. I'll wait for a while today and see if she comes."

Rihan had not listened to this exchange, but had gone straight to his room.

"He's quite a little artist," said the day nurse. "He'll be painting or drawing, if he isn't building something. I must say I'm grateful both kiddies know how to entertain themselves—well, some of the time. Will you join me for a cuppa?"

Belzic accepted. He sat down in the little kitchen while the nurse set fire to the stove and filled the kettle.

"It's a tiny house, a tiny kitchen, but they seem to be managing. You must excuse me while I prepare food. I usually leave some cooking for the family."

The sound of raised voices made her pause. Mostly, it was Rihan's voice. Belzic jumped up in an instant and raced to his room. He saw Rihan standing, looking frightened, and a taller boy with tousled, flaxen hair confronting him. He took the boy by the shoulder and spun him round.

"Who sent you!"

"I've come to play, I've only come to play. I mean no harm." The boy was in tears.

"I said, who sent you!"

"Please, please, I don't know, I've only come to play," said the boy, sobbing more loudly.

"Enough of that. Look at me, look at me!"

Belzic caught the boy's face in his hands, and twisted it up. The eyelashes flickered, and the eyes behind them appeared to be entirely white.

"Now listen! You don't belong here. I want you to go away and never come back."

There was a long pause. The nurse was watching, Holanna was staring wide eyed, as was Rihan. The boy suddenly turned on his heel and walked out of the room. The others ran to the passage, and then out to the front door. There was no sign of him anywhere.

"We are so grateful," said Aleb later when he returned. "I'm just sorry the woman never turned up."

"With a bit of luck she's given up, but if not Holanna will send her on to me. Ah, here's Andrew now."

Andrew alighted from the car, having completed the 'grand tour' of all the major features in and around Kraab. He hurried across to see Belzic, and, wordless, cast him a hopeful look. Belzic shook his head.

"It's as I feared, and the probability is that Maria is dead. If she wasn't she would have come to you, not to a child, if she came at all. As I was just saying, there is a good chance she has given up, or if not Holanna will refer her to me."

"Thank you Belzic. I know my hope is absurd, and yet I can't help hoping."

"Of course not. But now to our conveyance. Sorry, it's not nearly as grand as the one you've been in."

Euse stepped out of the embassy door to meet them, just as the coachman brought his horse to a stop. "Hear the news, boys? Six of our Dream Hunter customers have just complained that their children are receiving unwanted visitors. It looks like you're going to have a busy time, Belzic."

Belzic and Andrew now joined the Croans for a trip to City Hall. Roads radiated from the Hall like spokes in a wheel, and traversed extensive green spaces. As they crossed, the group looked out on a park vibrant with music and dancing.

"Stop!" called Euse. "We must watch this."

Teams in matching tunics formed circles that intertwined, merged, expanded and contracted.

"These are earth dances," said the driver. "In this country, this is the way we drive away ghosts and demons.

Euse grinned. "Wonderful! Wonderful!"

CHAPTER 31

In fact it was Andrew rather than Belzic who was becoming the busiest of all the outlanders, and for this he was grateful. The news about Maria had disturbed him a good deal. It had rubbed open an old wound, and he did not feel at all sure that Belzic had driven away this phantasm for good. He needed distractions. He was now acting as the go-between cum mediator cum booking agent for the rest of the crew, quite apart from being in a good deal of demand himself. The government had imposed almost complete isolation on Rangolia and her territories for over ten years, and had thus escaped the worst of the wars and plagues that had afflicted much of the planet. Right now Andrew was answering another request for Schyl and Erg, the captain and the navigator of that 'adventurous ship that had made it to the shores of Rangolia'. Both Croans were enjoying themselves, not least because of the interest they aroused in their audiences.

Andrew made the booking. Yes, a car would arrive at the embassy, and they were so looking forward to the privilege … etc. Andrew hung up the phone. (Phones were becoming more plentiful, and were in huge demand.) He had barely time to consider his next move before another call came through. This time it was from Qu's security chief. He was wanted … when, now? … yes, and yes, a car would be arriving in a matter of minutes. … Yes, Qu wanted an urgent word with him.

Qu dismissed the last of her advisers. She was in her penthouse at the top of the Town Hall and she needed to be alone for a time. Her meeting had been noisy, almost hysterical, and even though the press had been barred it was certain that many of the details would be leaked, would be being leaked right at the moment, as she contemplated the situation.

Details had to be teased apart, she had cautioned, not all lumped together, and she felt she had at least been partially successful in guiding the attendees through what she described as a 'minefield of provocative events'.

Right now she went over some of the chief ones as she had noted them down:

- the visitors were a surviving remnant from the elder days—a little pocket of technological knowledge hidden in the outlands, that now planned to expand its reach and take control of their country—the devices that Dream Hunter were making were instruments of mind control—they would ensure a compliant population when the invasion took place

- various 'ghost people' were appearing, particularly to children, and clearly there was some dark purpose intended here. ('If only it wasn't my little Beth' one of the security staff had moaned.)

- other children were having hallucinations, pleasant and unpleasant

- suicides and violent acts of all kinds were increasing—were up by a quarter since the arrival of these outlanders.

- the outlanders were known to be spending time in the desert—for what purpose other than to train the frots? Rangolia had a small standing army, and half a million fishermen, farmers and artisans who could be called up on three day's notice, but few had any training that would help in dealing with those dangerous robots.

Qu sat back in her chair, closed her eyes, and thought hard. Half an hour went by and then the call came through. "Andrew has arrived, ma'am."

"Good. Send him up. ... Yes, right to the penthouse. We need a quiet discussion. ... What's that? ... Danger? Nonsense! Send him up."

Andrew had felt a mixture of surprise and awe at the summons. On all other occasions he had been in the company of the Croans, and they had met in a downstairs room. On this occasion he was going alone, and to Qu's own private penthouse. He looked in despair over his wardrobe. Unlike the Croans, and even Belzic, he had not taken advantage of offers the Rangolians had made to outfit him. In the end he wore a fashionable Rangolian jacket over his own shirt and trousers that the embassy servant had cleaned and pressed for him.

The lift, the best working lift in the whole of Kraab, whisked him quickly to the penthouse, and he stepped out to be greeted at once by what he presumed was Qu's personal servant. "This way, please sir. Madam will be with you in a few minutes."

It occurred to Andrew that servants on Rangolia, on Earth, and probably throughout the entire galaxy were almost exactly the same; and maybe could be exchanged one with another without causing more than the most minimal interest. He gave a half smile at this reflection, before Qu entered the room to greet him.

"It was very kind of you to come, and at such short notice. Can I offer you a drink?"

Presently he was settled back in the most comfortable chair he had ever experienced, and sipping a rather sweet liquor. Qu's presence was however compelling, almost hypnotic, and he soon became oblivious to the chair, the drink, and every other detail of his surroundings. Even his difficulty with the language somehow ceased to matter. Qu conveyed everything slowly and succinctly. She began by simply laying out all the suspicions that had been brought to her attention: the mind control, the frots, the spectral beings, the suicides.

"What shall we do, Andrew? I don't believe for a moment that your party has come to prepare the way for an invasion, but I think you will agree that there are certain points that need clearing up. Are you prepared to work with me? My security staff, I'm afraid, tend to become very suspicious over very little. Well, that is there job, and I mustn't complain." Qu got up and stood before one of the big scenic windows that looked out over Kraab. "What shall we do, Andrew?"

Andrew felt a strong impulse to tell her everything, to have done with pretence, even though such an act would be in violation of all the principles the Croans had instilled in him. He was also aware that, of all the crew, Qu had singled him out as the one most likely to reveal the true purpose of their visit. And after all, why not? What difference did it make for them to be regarded as interstellar travellers, rather than simply outlanders. Andrew wrestled with the problem. Qu seemed to be still glancing out the window, speaking almost more to herself, than to him.

"Actually," he said at last, "we have come a great distance to get here."

"Yes? What distance would that be?"

Andrew joined Qu at the window. He looked out over Kraab, out over the sea beyond to the remote, misty horizon, and then into the cloud-flecked sky.

"A star," he said at last. "A distant star."

"Yes, I thought as much."

"I do hope I can speak in confidence?"

"Of course, Andrew. My thoughts are my own. You may tell me anything you wish." She hesitated. "I think we'd better create a plausible place for you all to have come from, to keep my staff and the rest of your crew happy."

"Ma'am, I am very much obliged."

"I'll have some maps sent up, but first I'm going to need you to tell me absolutely everything to do with your mission, beginning with why you are here in the first place."

Andrew told her all about the mission, and felt a great relief in doing so. The Croans seemed to thrive on pretence and deception, but for him it was wonderful having someone he could be totally frank with. "So you see," he concluded, "we came here firstly to see if there was anyone here at all, and secondly to find out if there was any truth behind the legend of the portals."

"Thank you Andrew. There is just one piece of the puzzle that doesn't fit, and that is the large model of our popular fantasy figure, Taapino. Why was he on your ship?"

"Oh, that! We knew nothing about Taapino. You must understand that in space travel there are long periods when the crew have little or nothing to do, and it was in one of these that I helped reassemble a model that had been made for an entirely different purpose."

"Good. That explains everything. You are here to find out about us, and to look for portals, which are apparently ways of travelling quickly between stars. You knew nothing of Jelani and Hamul's thought transfer machines until you arrived?"

"Absolutely not. ma'am."

"I believe you, Andrew. Now, come back to the table and we'll work something out. The problem is how to present you, or re-present you to the public. Are you aware that you visitors have become very divisive figures, adored by some and suspected by others, including some of my own staff, of all sorts of things?"

"I'm sorry, ma'am. Maybe we just have to explain …"

"No Andrew, no. The last thing we want is to have you coming from the sky. That would really stir things up. They're bad enough as it is. Now let me think … What I'll have to do is give you identities, and give you a mission. Do you think the Croans would go along with that?"

Andrew had a feeling that the crew would be more than happy with the idea. "I believe they would love you for it," he said fervently. He was back in that comfortable chair, relaxing, and feeling positively complicit with Qu. A cough behind him made him glance around: a servant had arrived with a scroll of maps.

"Good. Tomorrow is a festival day." Qu dropped the maps on the table between them. She smiled brightly. "We'll find a place for you all to have come from, somewhere remote, but with some definite facts you all can quote. I want you to have the Croans along here tomorrow, at the downstairs meeting room. A car will pick you up at noon. Now, as for the portals,

I have never heard of them, but it will do no harm for you to continue you search. And as for the Dream Hunter Company, you should carry on as before. We'll deal with that problem separately. Now, let's look at the maps. There is one place I have in mind which might suit: Dufalia. Ah, here. Take this map away and get your Croan friends to think about Dufalia. It's suitably distant and is supposed to contain a number of different racial groups. You will find some notes on the back." Qu flipped through the rest of the scroll. "Yes, I think that's everything for now."

Andrew went away with a light heart, and a feeling of confidence he had not had for a long time.

And I won't stay shackled to the Croans, trying to make my stories fit in with whatever they say. I'll be my own person, the 'great traveller' that a lady I met today called me.

Andrew took out the card she had given him: Deb Trooms. *Do come and visit*, she had written under her address.

Would he?

CHAPTER 32

The Troom residence

Mrs Troom scanned the table. Was anything missing? Each place had a glass (for water or soda water), a napkin, plate, and of course a D2 receiver. Tea and coffee would come later. The cookies! Mrs Troom ran back to the kitchen. Ah, good. Almost done, but not, not quite perfect. She adjusted the oven temperature. "No, Ramen, no! They're for the guests!" Her husband had come up unnoticed.

"The family meal is for later, nine o'clock in the other room. "Although," she added, "you could always join us."

"What? Me step into that den of tigers? No thanks, dear."

"Really, Ramen. Ah, there's the doorbell now. Please answer it for me."

Mr Troom, skirting round his wife, grabbed a few crumbs from the baking tray and went to the front door.

"Mrs Tring, Miss Vermont, Mrs Toomali, Mrs Herbert, welcome. My wife threatened to put me in with you lot. I wouldn't have the courage."

"What a lot of nonsense you talk, Mr Troom." Mrs Herbert went to her rightful place at the table, and bristled a little when she saw that the transmitter was not sitting there, where it should be.

Mrs Troom came in, all smiles She looked brightly around the table. "You've all found your places? Wonderful. Mrs Toomali, I thought I'd have you on the left of Mrs Herbert, if you don't mind, dear. And Mrs Herbert, I know we usually start with you, but just this once I'd prefer Miss Vermont to start us off. She sometimes gets left out altogether, and we can't have that."

Mr Troom walked into his daughter's room upstairs. She was tossing about fitfully in her bed.

"Daddy, the spider's still there. Mummy said she'd shooed it away, but she hasn't."

"Where is it, darling?"

"There, there, there!"

"It's just a shadow, darling. I'll put a candle on the dresser. See, it's gone away."

Except that, for Tessa, it hadn't. She began to cry.

"There, there." Mr Troom sat beside his daughter. "You've had a nasty bug, and you've been hallucinating. That means seeing things that aren't there. In the morning you'll be fit and well, and … and no more spiders!"

Tessa continued to cry.

"Look, I'm putting a lovely bunch of flowers up against the wall."

Tessa quietened. She looked at the red roses, and saw immediately that the spider was still there. Two of its muscular black legs were sticking out from behind the flowers. Not moving.

Mr Troom went back down into the kitchen, which was now inhabited by a long-haired youth.

"Better not, son. We have to wait for our dinner."

Mrs Troom had left the tray out for the cookies to cool.

Upstairs, Tessa had pulled the sheet up over her head, leaving just a little space for breathing. She had looked several times at those black legs. Not moving.

In the front room, Miss Vermont was in full flight.

"So when the storm was over, me and Hebby pulled out of the cove and followed the coast all the way down to where the old lighthouse used to be. That ketch moves well in the lightest of winds, and we made good speed. Mainly, we were looking for folks fishing in protected waters, although we came across a group that were frot catching. See what I mean?"

The group gazed into their receivers. They saw a group of men standing near the top of a cliff.

"See what they're doing? They coax the frots to the cliff top using bits of metal and then … you can see for yourself."

"Miss Vermont, was it just the two of you? Against all those people?"

"Oh no, we had two guards on the boat, with guns. There you are. They move pretty quickly when they hear the shots.

"After that, nothing doing for a while, and then we saw them. The poachers! They were trawling. See what happens now. They're trying to haul in their net as fast as they can, and we're after them. I'm steering. Watch!"

"Oh Miss Vermont!"

It was clear that the ketch was easily overtaking the trawler, and the men on board were in a desperate struggle with the net.

"Now see! Hebby and I are up at the prow, ready to grapple the boats together. The guards are shouting at the men and our boat is right up against theirs."

The group gasped as the net opened.

"Now see. Hebby goes overboard, but I don't see that. I get an octopus in my face, with one sucker across my eye. Our boat is swamped with fish while theirs, minus its catch, gets clean away."

The screams from upstairs interrupted all else. Mr Troom reached the room first, with his son close behind.

Tessa was sobbing. "It was the spider, all over my face, and its leg was in my eye. It was as big as my face."

"Sis, there aren't any spiders as big as your face."

"That poor girl, that poor, poor girl, to get a spider dumped on her, and her being sick into the bargain," said Mrs Toomali later to her husband.

"But there wasn't a spider, was there?"

"There was for her! I don't think I'll go to any more of those meetings. They're downright dangerous."

Mrs Toomali did not care for spiders.

"Oh, I forgot. I've had a talk with Mrs Therim. She has two little twins, just like ours and about the same age."

"Therim? Is that Jelani Therim, the one who split up with her husband?"

"Yes, she's with that reporter chap now. Anyway, we agreed that her two and our two should get together—a picnic perhaps?" Mrs Toomali looked anxiously at her husband. "I know you like to rest up when you're not at sea, but it would do you good, you know. And I want our two to get out of themselves more. Imaginary friends are all very well, but they need to … well … open up a bit, if you see what I mean."

Mrs Toomali paused for breath.

"Go ahead and arrange it, Mrs T," said her husband. "If it stops them thinking about elves I'm all for it."

"They're away half the time—that's the thing."

"As am I, my dear. You'll just have to catch us when you can."

Mr. Toomali was a sea captain concerned with the security of the Rangolian mainland.

CHAPTER 33

The Toomali residence

"Come here, young Toomali, don't let me chase you!"

Mrs Toomali had her neighbour round, hoping to relax and have a little respite from her overactive twins. Except that the nurse hadn't arrived and the children had been let out early from school. They had run in shouting and singing. "We've come to help you mummy!"

"That was all I needed, May," Mrs Toomali said to her neighbour. However, Pookah, on prompting from his twin sister, had come back, allowing his hair to be brushed and the medication administered.

"It's supposed to slow him down," Mrs Toomali said to her neighbour, "but I can't imagine anything doing that."

Pookah, released from maternal care, raced off after his sister. "Remember," said Sesha as he reached her, "remember what the elf man said."

"Maybe—not exactly."

"You do so!"

"It was about being good," Pookah admitted.

"He said, if we were really good all of today he'd give us a present."

"We've been good."

"Not really, really good. We've got to help mummy."

"Doing what?"

"We'll do the cooking, and the dishes, and—and everything. Come on, Poo-poo, it will be a surprise!"

"All right," said Pookah, suddenly interested. "We'll go round the back way and get into the kitchen. Keep your head down, Sesh."

The two children, bending low, half running, half crawling, made their way behind the hedge and half circled the house. Pookah could not resist a quick peek as they left the cover of the hedge. He saw his mother leaning a little forward, making some point with her hand, while her neighbour, with a cup half raised to her lips, was affably responding. "Once those two get talking they'll go on for hours," he said with satisfaction. "We've got loads of time. What shall we cook, Sesh?"

The twins slipped through the front door, taking care to close it gently, and a minute later were in the kitchen. Now that they were actually there both felt a little nervous, but were anxious to conceal it. Pookah looked at the cupboards, which stretched way out of reach, almost to the ceiling. More easily accessed were the rack of knives, the row of shiny cooking pots, the big iron oven. "We'll have to light the stove, won't we?"

"I'll make a pie," said Sesha.

"Let's make some sweets—decent ones, like they have at the fairs. Come on, we'll have to go through the cupboards and find everything."

There were little round drums containing various grains. When it came to it, Sasha wasn't sure how to make a pie, or even what ingredients were necessary, so she decided to put a little bit of everything into a big mixing bowl. Then after a few blissful minutes she took a critical look at her brother, who had loaded a great many sticks into the oven firebox and was attacking them with a flint.

"You need to put in straw first." She stopped making her pie and watched Pookah with interest as he fiddled with straw, sticks and flint. A puff of smoke burst out of the firebox and made its way to the ceiling.

It came as no surprise to either of them when the elf man appeared. He was sitting on the edge of a shelf, up near the ceiling, and he was wreathed in smoke.

"Work the damper, you idiots, work the damper!" he called out in his shrill, elvish voice.

Pookah guessed there was something in or on the stove that had to be 'worked'. There were a number of knobs to turn and levers to move about, but when next he looked up the elf man had even more smoke about him. He had taken off his hat, and was waving it in front of his face, and coughing. However, Pookah then moved a lever that made such a decisive clang that he wasn't surprised to see that the smoke was at last clearing, and the oven was roaring with such a noise that all three of them had to raise their voices.

"Is the pie ready? We could put it in now!" Pookah shouted.

But Sesha looked worriedly at the dry mixture she had in the bowl. It didn't look as though it would turn into a pie, or in fact anything other than what it was. Pookah looked. "It needs eggs, or something."

Eggs! She knew about eggs, and had a good idea where to find them. In fact she found six, and broke them very professionally into the mixture. "It's ready!" she shouted.

In the meantime Pookah continued his experiment with the oven, and at last shut off the vent, which reduced the sound dramatically. He opened the oven door, and gave a cry of astonishment as a blast of intense heat flowed out, enveloping both him and his sister as she came forward with the grain and egg mixture.

Down on the deck, Mrs Toomali's neighbour turned her head. "You have someone working in the kitchen?"

"Oh no, not today. In fact I'm giving myself and the kitchen a rest. I'm taking the kiddies out to dinner."

"Strange, I thought I heard shouting."

"Quick, shove it in," said Pookah, as he backed away from the heat.

Sesha half thrust, half threw the pie into the opening, and slammed the door shut. Then she looked around for the elf, who was still up near the ceiling, and at present dusting himself down.

"When did you chaps learn to cook?"

"We haven't," said Sesha sadly. "Mummy never wants us in the kitchen."

"Not surprising, not surprising," said the elf.

"Do we get a present?"

The elf man looked around the kitchen, suddenly furtive.

"There's nobody here but us," said Pookah.

"I'll give you a present, but you'll have to keep it secret. Hand me up a cup." Pookah did so. "Now, take the cup, but be very careful."

"There's nothing in it!"

"Yes there is. Put your hand in."

"I can feel something but I can't see it," said Pookah, wondering.

"Keep it safe, keep it secret. Don't let any grown ups get hold of it!"

Sesha next put her hand in the cup, and felt something rough, and hard, like a piece of stone. "What is it, mister elf man, what is it?"

The elf gave them a cunning, calculating look. "It's a piece of the old foundation stone that was here before the world began. Don't lose it!"

"Why are you giving it to us? What can we do with it?" asked Pookah.

However Sesha became distracted by a strong smell coming from the oven. She opened the door and a cloud of very dense smoke poured out, followed by a long tongue of flame.

"Quick, get some water!" cried the elf man.

Down on the deck Mrs Toomali set down her cup and stood up. "I heard that!" she cried. "Who's there?" There was no further noise, so Mrs Toomali turned to her neighbour. "Hand me that stick, May, and stay close behind me."

"Oh, do you think you should?"

"I'm not going to be frightened out of my own house. Come on!" Nonetheless, she paused a moment before the kitchen door, before flinging it open.

The kitchen was full of smoke, steam, and soot, and the floor was swimming with water. Also on the floor was a bent tin encrusted with something black.

"My mixing bowl!" said Mrs Toomali.

"Anyway, he gave us that present," said Sasha, much later. Her mother had been too stunned to say very much. She did finally ask who had put them up to such a thing, but the twins were careful not to mention the elf. It had become a forbidden topic. "We just wanted to make you happy, and do all the cooking, and everything," said Sesha. In spite of her anger, Mrs Toomali was touched. She cancelled the dinner engagement, and put the children to work scrubbing and mopping, after which she put out cold food for them, and their babysitter, and went off to the local Dream Hunter Club, where, in spite of her previous resolution, she used a D2 transmitter to report on their latest escapade.

Pookah wrapped the invisible stone up in a handkerchief, and then carried out a number of experiments. He found, to his disgust, that apart from its invisibility it appeared to be totally boring. He put it away in the bottom of his socks drawer and stopped thinking about it. Until, that is, his mother confronted him a few days later.

"Pookah, what on earth possessed you to put a dirty handkerchief in the bottom of your socks drawer? You put your dirty clothes in the wash. If you keep them with your clean things you make everything dirty."

"Mum, was there something in the hanky? I had something wrapped in it."

"No, Pookah, there was nothing there."

Pookah went upstairs and passed his hand all around the bottom of his socks drawer, and then all over the floor in his room. Then he shrugged his shoulders. The following day the elf man whistled to the twins as they were coming home from school.

"Is it safe?" he asked.

Pookah did not trust himself to speak.

"Be careful. Beware of the shapeshifter."

"The what?"

"Sometimes he's a man, and then he's a bear, or a wolf, or anything at all. He mustn't get the stone."

"I don't understand. Please explain!"

But the elf man had already vanished. Pookah turned and saw a schoolboy friend coming towards them.

"Hello, who were you talking to? Is there someone in the tree?" He looked suspiciously up into the branches.

"I was talking to Sesh and I was looking to see if an old bird nest was still there," said Pookah.

"Well, I don't care what you were doing." The boy looked into the tree. "I want you to come to my party next week. It's going to be the biggest party ever."

"All right, thanks," said Pookah.

"He's always got the biggest everything," said Sesha.

Back home, while Sesha went into the kitchen and was given a cooking lesson by her mother, Pookah crawled about on the floor of his room, trying to discover something he could touch, but not see. Anyway, he thought at last, if I can't find it probably this shapeshifter creature can't either. Just the same, he woke in the night, trembling. He had dreamt of something ghoulish floating around the house, and looking in all the windows.

Sesha slept peacefully. She wasn't sure about the shapeshifter, but she didn't like the elf. She remembered the calculating look in its eyes whenever it was talking to them.

CHAPTER 34

Aleb's house

Aleb's doorbell rang. Qu had arrived with her PA, Rain.

"Thank you so much for letting me come at such short notice," she said.

"It's an honour, ma'am," said Jelani. "We could go to the office—there'd be a bit more room," she added, rather conscious of the crowded state of the house.

"No, no, this will be more discreet." She gave a laugh. "No, don't tidy up or anything. I can squeeze in anywhere."

"This way," said Aleb, leading the way into the main room. He had cleared the dining room table, replaced the cloth, and spread out a number of D2 and D3 headsets.

"Would you like tea, or a tisane?" Jelani asked.

"Perhaps later." Qu smiled brightly. "What a lovely room." She looked around. "And what a lovely little girl!"

Holanna had come in, holding a soft toy. "Mummy, I can't sleep."

"Aleb, could you … ?"

"Come on darling, Mummy's busy," said Aleb.

"Can I have another Taapino story?" Aleb took her hand and ushered her out.

Jelani handed a D2 over to Qu. "Aleb and I have worked mainly with the D2—I think it's best to start with them, and then perhaps move on to the D3."

Upstairs, Rihan was sleeping soundly. Holanna looked into the darkened bedroom. "Can I stay with you and mummy tonight? I feel scared."

"You should be asleep, my sweet," said Aleb. "There's nothing to be scared about." He thought for a bit. "All right, you can sleep in the big bed tonight."

Holanna settled down quickly, and seemed to go into a deep sleep. Aleb too felt unaccountably drowsy. It must be the weather, he thought. So warm, wet, and misty. He sat in a chair alongside the little girl, watching her breathing and feeling a protective glow of satisfaction. He began drafting out in his mind a report he was to make for the Dream Hunter management: *transmission works most efficiently where there is an emotional bond between sender and receiver, although transmission can also 'leak' to a third party, such as a son or daughter* …

Downstairs in the front room, Jelani had used the D2 to send a few simple images to Qu and Rain, her PA. She now passed the transmitter across. "One of you could just think of some image, or look at one, and send it to me."

Qu took the transmitter, which very quickly tuned itself to her mind. Her worries of the day then poured out into the machine, rather overwhelming Jelani. Early memories had been stirred up, and they came out as well. Jelani and Rain could not repress little gasps of astonishment as the images flowed. Jelani was congratulating herself that it was not the D3 equipment they were using. Emotions transmitted with similar intensity would probably have reduced them all to tears. She waited anxiously for the end of the session, expecting a devastated Qu, but when eventually Qu took off the headset she merely smiled. "It is a relief to unburden myself a little," she said. "And I must say I'm very impressed with this equipment.

You must tell me, what training is given? Ah, you have it all written down on this pamphlet?"

In the main bedroom Holanna tossed about and whimpered. Aleb, startled out of his drowsing, leaned forward.

"It's all right dear, you're quite safe," he whispered.

Meanwhile Rain followed Jelani into the kitchen. "Just show me where things are, she said. "I'll make the drinks. You stay with madam and talk about the devices."

Jelani dutifully returned. Qu was looking curiously at the D3. "The D2 is the networking model, and the most popular," Jelani explained. "The D3 is more for therapy—it picks up on the intensity of emotions, which users don't always wish to display. You can, though, hook up two or three receivers, but it's a little more complicated."

"Do you think it would be good for lie detecting?"

"Well, I suppose so, though a trained actor could avoid detection from any kind of technology, I suspect."

Qu smiled. "I'm not thinking of trained actors."

The conversation was interrupted by the sound of footsteps running down the stairs. Aleb came into the room. "Is she here? Did Holanna come in?"

"No, Aleb. What's happened?" Jelani ran across to him.

"God, I thought she went downstairs. She must have slipped out the front door."

"Aleb, calm down, she'll be in the kitchen."

"Rain!" Qu called, as Rain came in with a tray of tall glasses. "Rain, did you see the little girl?"

The house was searched, and then the area around it.

"She was asleep, and Rihan had come out of his room, looking very unhappy, so I took him back and spent time with him, and when I came back Holanna had disappeared." Aleb looked deeply worried. "I went back to see if she'd slipped into her own bed. Someone must have gotten in and taken her!"

"Aleb, they couldn't have," said Jelani. "They would have had to get past us, or go through the kitchen."

"Where is she then?" Aleb sounded almost belligerent.

"Calm down, everyone, stop talking!" It was more of an order than a suggestion, and it came from Qu. "Just be quiet, be still and listen." Qu's voice now dropped almost to a whisper. "I believe that your little girl is still in the house, and I believe that someone, or something, has indeed entered this house. So just be still, listen out for any strange sounds, or smells, or even feelings that you might have." There was immediate silence. Jelani started to feel really afraid. She began to shiver uncontrollably.

Presently everyone heard a curious mewling sound. It was almost, but not quite, the sound a cat might make if it was in some way trapped. Qu put her finger to her lips, cautioning the group to keep listening. The sound gradually changed in tone: from being animal-like, it became more distinctly like that of a child. Until, that is, everyone knew with certainty it was a child, was in fact Holanna crying upstairs.

It was curious, Jelani thought later, how completely Qu had taken control of the entire situation. Now, she motioned to Jelani to go ahead of her, and the two crept very quietly upstairs, and Jelani called, in a soft voice, "It's all right, darling, mummy's here."

Holanna was sitting at the foot of her parents' bed, distraught. It was clear that she had been badly frightened.

"Do not question her," Qu whispered. However, after a period of hugs and tears shared between mother and daughter, Holanna became very talkative.

"It was this horrible thing," she said, "sort of like a big cat, but it put words in my head. It said, 'Have you got it?' but I didn't say anything. And then it kind of hurt me, so I said, 'Got what?' And then it kind of looked at me, and it said, 'I'm the shapeshifter. I want it' so I said, 'What?' And I felt I was being looked at some more, and it said, 'You're not the one,' and it pushed me away into some really dark place, and I was so frightened!"

"Oh, my poor darling."

"Mummy, when was I hiding in a tree?"

"Darling, you were never hiding in a tree."

"Oh yes I was. I was inside a tree, and there was a man walking about, and he was shouting, 'Is there anybody there?'"

Jelani looked helplessly at Qu.

Aleb beckoned. Rihan had settled back down in his own bed, but was giving little twitches, and cries. He appeared to be in a kind of trance. The others crowded round. Aleb sat beside the child, at first stroking his face, and then holding him. Rihan was giving periodic shudders that went through his entire body. "Come back, Rihan, come back," Aleb said, calling gently.

Presently Rihan opened his eyes. "Mummy? I want mummy."

"I'm here darling."

"Mummy, an awful thing came and it pushed me."

"It won't hurt you again, sweetheart. You're safe, I won't let anything bad happen."

Later, when the children were settled and sleeping normally, the adults gathered to discuss the situation.

"No more sales, please, Jelani, not till we know more," said Qu.

"No, I wasn't going to."

"And no more use of the D2 if there are children in the same building. Can you estimate how much use it's getting?"

"It's mostly used in gatherings of up to about ten people, mostly women only, though I gather there's a mixed sex group and a couple of men's groups. They usually meet in the evenings, and of course if there are little children that's when they would be sleeping."

"And I think it's about time the rest of us were," said Qu. "I want you to send me a report on your progress at least once every second day. Good luck. Come, Rain."

"God, Aleb, I had no idea things were this bad. Please hold me," said Jelani as she watched the pair ushered by the chauffeur into the state car.

"It's okay, Lani, just a technical hitch. We'll get it sorted."

"But this shapeshifter business … can horrible things just get through the walls? Or do you think it's the house?"

"I don't know. I've never felt anything here myself. It's more likely to be something to do with the transmitter."

"I suppose there is no doubt? These things infect the children?"

"No other explanation. Holanna, at any rate, has acquired a memory that had nothing to do with her."

"And that frightens me too. What if I end up with half my memories inherited from other people?"

"Don't be silly, Lani. I'll check your memories over, my sweet. If I find any really great ones I'll let you keep them, no matter how fantastic they are, and no matter how jealous they make me feel."

Jelani broke into an hysterical laugh, which eventually quietened. Aleb held her, rocking her gently. "Do you know," she said, "I think I'll keep you on."

Ω

"Well, Rain, what did you make of that?"

"Those devices, ma'am? Very interesting, but I can't say I cared for them much."

"In what way, Rain?"

"Too intrusive, too personal—and it seems to me they are dangerous, if they give the children such frights."

"I'm inclined to agree with you, but they may also be extremely useful."

Qu sat back in the big official car, and closed her eyes in thought as the pair were returned to City Hall.

"We need more information, Rain. We need a lot more information. And we need to take a controlling interest. If these things turn out able to control minds we don't want any private company owning them. Get the Board onto it Rain, and find out if they have shares on the open market."

Back in her office, a message was waiting.

"Rain, wait a moment. The old man has some information he thinks is important—and it's all about this Dream Hunter business."

"Kefu, ma'am?"

"That's the one. The archivist. I want you to get me an appointment with him as soon as you can—find a space for me within the next couple of days. Move the bookings around, postpone them, cancel them even, whatever it takes. Get me an hour with Kefu."

"I'll get onto it first thing in the morning, ma'am."

"And make sure we have a car available to pick up the Croans."

CHAPTER 35

The Toomali residence

Pookah had not forgotten the warnings of the elf man, and had made several more unsuccessful attempts to find the invisible stone. It was time now, he told himself, to put the matter out of his mind, especially since his father was due back after six weeks of patrolling Groob's territorial waters. Later, he could ask questions, casually of course, in the spirit of gaining information, and not implying that he actually believed in elves, or shapeshifters, or magic stones. Pookah had learnt to be circumspect when dealing with his parents.

The chance came that very evening. Mr Toomali had heard all about the twins' kitchen exploits and had nodded sagely. "Yes, they're mischievous little urchins, but they're big-hearted. They take after me, I'm afraid."

"And Sesha here has been helping me this evening," said Mrs Toomali.

"Well done, Sesha, it was a lovely meal. But what about young Pookah here? What have you been up to, young Toomali?"

"I've been learning things, dad. I'm just wondering what a shapeshifter is."

"A shapeshifter! Good heavens, what do they teach you in school? A shapeshifter is a person who can turn into an animal, or a bird, except there's no such person. They come into old stories."

"Yes? How old, dad? Did any of the old stories say anything about the world's foundation?"

"Well you're in luck there, young Sesha. One of the old stories said that when the world was planned it was to have a magical foundation of white marble, which would stop any evil spirits from entering. However the demons who lived in the abyss got to hear of the plan, and as the foundation was being laid they attacked it, and it was smashed into a great many pieces. According to the story, it is still being put together, and there are still lots of missing pieces where evil spirits can enter. Now where did you hear about this, Sesha. At school?"

"Yes, daddy."

"Good. Just remember that there are still a lot of evil spirits about, so take care to always be good."

"Yes, daddy."

"Father, you'll have them believing it's real! Don't listen to your father, children."

"Come now, mother, there are worse things they could believe."

In bed that night Pookah pondered the problem. Was the shapeshifter good or evil? Was the elf man good or evil? He decided that the best thing would be not to find it at all, and having decided that he felt better. "Confab, Seshi," he called out softly.

"Confab, Poo Poo."

"Sesh, I've lost it."

"A good thing, too," she whispered back. "Don't find it!"

"I won't!"

But as is so often the case, that resolution amounted to very little. Pookah returned to his bed, and the very first thing his hand touched when he put it under the sheet was the familiar shape and texture of the missing stone.

Ω

President Qu's office, City Hall

Rain, I want you to take copious notes, if necessary. Anything and everything he has to say could be of use to us."

"Yes, ma'am. I think that's him now."

Qu smiled a little more than usual when the old man came into her office. How exactly like a piece of old parchment he is, she thought. Aloud, she said "Kefu, I'm so pleased you could come. Do take a seat, and perhaps I could get an assistant to help with that bag of yours?"

"I can manage perfectly well, thanks ma'am." He took a seat and chuckled. "Yes, it looks heavier than it is, but it's mostly protective wrapping for the things I carry. Now, if you'd like to move your chair just a little closer, I'll take you through what I've found over the past week. Yes, your assistant could be closer too. That's right." He gave a little smile. "Sorry, nothing about oil at this stage."

In what followed Qu found herself being treated like a young junior, being instructed in the ways of ancient manuscripts. There was certainly no bowing and scraping from Kefu.

"I don't quite see …" she began tentatively at one stage.

"Oh, but you will," said Kefu. "This is a palimpsest, and you can see the original writing if you hold the parchment under a strong light, which I have here. Now, the practice of washing parchment and reusing it only happened when the old civilisation was already in serious decline. Previously, they had used some sort of electrical writing, along with a great deal of paper, most of which has perished, and right near the end they turned to ancient parchment. Why they did so, we can only conjecture. Now usually, the original text is more interesting, when we can read it, but in this case both the old and new are worth taking note of. I will translate sections of both, but I must apologise in advance for the original writing, for parts of it are lost."

Kefu then went ahead, beginning with the erased words which he could, in the main, discern, but which Qu could barely even see.

"So," she said at last, "let me summarise: This man whose name begins with K was a tyrant, but was extremely popular, with several million disciples. He was seized by the authorities, and his brain was treated so he would change his ways. They used something similar to the Dream Hunter devices to detect the problem, and then they gave him an operation. The personality change worked, but it caused an outrage."

"Yes ma'am, and not just from the original followers."

"So the argument was, once a thing like this starts, who knows where it will end?"

"Exactly so, ma'am. Now, the later writing appears to have occurred about a hundred years after, judging by the style. By a strange coincidence, it is on the very same topic, but this time it has a name: personality engineering. Here is how it goes:

To those mothers and fathers who are still taking their children to clinics for personality assessment and engineering, our message is, do not take this risk. The infection rate is nearing ten percent, and the resultant illness is incurable. Furthermore, brain infection transmits rapidly, particularly among those who have subjected their brains to reading and transmission mechanisms. There is not even need for close contact, since the infection can simply jump mind to mind over almost any distance.

"That's the relevant bit I wanted to show you, ma'am."

"Infection, Kefu? What do we know about this infection?"

"I'm sorry, ma'am, nothing. I'm not even sure if 'infection' is the right word. What is clear though, is that once you start using devices to examine people's thoughts and feelings, it may not be too long before you find ways to control their minds. Or, you might damage their minds in irreparable ways. Not to mention the possibility of some kind of epidemic resulting from your actions. So be warned: the mind is both a very delicate and very dangerous instrument.

"Now read this. It's only a fragment, but it's significant."

The flame came again: a little fireball which floated just in front of my eyes. With practice I found I could move it about: push it further away or move it closer. When it was close, I could feel the heat. Clearly, I had found a new kind of reality, neither objective nor subjective, but some kind of meld. As a further experiment, I tried passing my hand through the flames. Done quickly, I felt nothing, but more slowly and I became most unpleasantly burnt.

"Now what do you make of that? I think if you persevere with these gadgets you will be taking this country into very dangerous places. Do not do it ma'am!"

Ω

"Well, Rain, what did you make of all that?"

"He didn't have much to say after all, did he, ma'am."

"No, the reference to an infection was interesting, if it even was an infection. I'd love to know more about that. Otherwise, I suspect this brain engineering could be a very useful tool, if we ever get that far."

"What about that little fireball? Do you think that was real?"

"Real? Rain, reality is whatever people like to think it is. There's no other kind—or if there is, it doesn't concern politicians."

"Just the same, ma'am, it could be a little dangerous." The PA hesitated a moment. "You know, a threat to our democracy, if people's thoughts are manipulated, or if they start conjuring up fireballs."

"Oh Rain, Rain, we don't have a democracy in the first place. We have an oligarchy, which is why I wouldn't be here without the backing of some of the richest companies in Groob. And as for people's thoughts, they are mostly ephemeral trash, easily manipulated by a good speaker. What I have to do every year is cadge, cajole and manipulate the thinking of the few who support me, and vote for me. Sooner or later, I'm going to lose, but in the meantime, if anyone starts conjuring up fireballs, I'll make sure they're declared insane, and locked away."

"Or perhaps, put them on the stage."

"Yes, that would be safe. As for me, I won't be safe forever. Sooner or later the companies are going to want a fresh new image. Right now, I'm still the protector of the people, and I'm associated with these Croans, which are still a little bit of a novelty. It won't last, Rain, it's all about branding. It won't last—not unless I can find some oil."

Qu walked over to the big picture window.

"There's a bad storm coming in," she said. "I'm glad Kefu left when he did. You'd better postpone the Croans. I'll catch Euse on his own later."

"Ma'am, I've already put them off." Rain looked for a moment out the big picture window to where the air hovered, sullen and still over the city.

"I can feel the change beginning even now," she said.

CHAPTER 36

At the embassy

Euse was outdoors, sniffing the air, and contemplating the towering clouds. He beckoned to Ess, who stepped down from the embassy and joined him on the beach.

"If you want to have your swim I'd suggest you take it now, Ess."

"You could join me, master."

"I never swim on an unfamiliar planet, as you know," said Euse crossly. "Your only defence is your exoskeleton, if you keep it on, and that makes swimming impossibly strenuous."

"I would never keep mine on, master," said Ess sweetly, "and if anything happened I would rely on you to rescue me."

"Well, go then Ess, go! You've already been bitten once on this planet, so maybe you'll learn some sense if it happens again."

"Yes, master. This swim is in celebration of our new identities as Dufalians, and of course our new homeland, Dufalia!"

Ess disconnected the wires from his head and the restraining straps from his limbs, and in a matter of seconds the enclosing humanoid form had been cast aside and he had slithered into the sea. As a Croan, it was his second home, and now he moved about like the lithe, amphibious creature he was. Schyl came down and joined Euse, watching. "How fast can you go, Ess?" he called. Ess promptly waved a tentacle, and sped through the water, sending out a creamy wake that glowed under the light of the two rising moons.

"Things are about to change," said Grice, looking up at the rolling, roiling blackness that was now racing across the sky.

"Come out, Ess, you fool. Come out now!"

An intense light enveloped the group for a full second, and then a vast, deep sound, felt as much as heard, rumbled across the heavens. Ess, now far out on the Pond, waved a tentacle once more, flipped in a racing turn and headed to the shore. Euse stepped into surf which was now racing up the beach and caught the struggling form in his arms. The wind began. It whipped up the rising sea, drenching the pair, while Ess, now partly in his exoskeleton, clung to the science officer. Grice and Cherg, waiting behind the embassy windows, applauded as the two made their way up the steps and into the shelter of the porch.

It was a storm worth watching, as Ess said later. The embassy was pelted as much by sea as by rain and hail, and part of the garden was swept away. Grice had the primitive radio tuned, and for those who could receive, messages were going out constantly: keep off the beaches, and keep under cover! Certainly, in addition to the huge tide produced by the two moons, and the ever more aggressive incursions of the waves, a succession of fireballs floated over the embassy roof, exploding somewhere in the desert behind.

Groob Trade and Warehouse Company

Durhain felt the change coming as he packed up for the day. Just one day had gone by since his last change, and he'd begun to wonder if the 'process', as he thought of it, was speeding up, would perhaps in time leave him permanently as some nonhuman creature. Here it was, at any rate, coming upon him once more: a subtle change in his breathing, a faint prickly feeling at the back of his neck, and most of all the heat that began to spread up his spine, around his shoulders and down his arms, even reaching his hands as he shut the drawers of his desk. He nodded to his assistant Marty. "I'll leave you to do the security checks tonight."

From respectable office manager to what? There was no telling in advance. 'You can get help if you want it,' his father had said. Durhain did not want it. The changes were at once terrifying and intoxicating, something he needed now every bit as much as the urbane respectability of his other life. He drove away, humming quietly to himself, and sniffing the air. A storm was coming. Good.

Outside he moved quickly to his car. It was approaching that time when the second moon, rubilis, moon of illusions, makes its closest journey to the planet. Indeed both moons were showing in the darkening sky as he drove swiftly along the main thoroughfare of Kraab. With his heightened senses he could smell the storm coming, ahead of the messages that were soon to go out on the airwaves: secure your boat, check the waterways near your house, flooding is possible.

He did not return to his house. A little way out of Kraab, he turned off the main road and gunned the car up a rough track to a grove of trees. There was just room to squeeze his vehicle between the trees and the stone wall that held back the desert. Securely hidden, he killed the engine and sat still, listening. Dim sounds came from the highway, and fainter still, the sea. A wind blew, rustling the nearby leaves. Sound and movement emphasised rather than diminished the waiting silence and the stillness that so often heralded a storm. Durhain could now feel it racing towards Kraab.

Satisfied with his hideout, he let out very human groans and gasps, sounding very much like a person in pain. Then over the course of a few minutes the sounds became more strange, less human, something, one might have said, between a squealing pig and a howling cat. Then there was silence, until the car door opened, and a shadowy figure in a hooded black robe emerged. Durhain sniffed the air appreciatively, and began to move catlike down to the highway.

There were few pedestrians now, but those few took one glance at those eyes looking out from under the hood, and stepped well aside.

Durhain was never confronted, let alone molested. He made steady, unhurried steps down to a certain shack, once a boathouse but now being claimed by the sea. The water was lapping round his feet when he stopped, and looked all around the tilted walls and the broken roof. "You are late," he said, when the elf man appeared. And then, "Where is it?"

The elf smirked. "It has passed on. A child has it now."

Durhain stared angrily at the elf. "I anticipated that, and I've checked already."

"You checked the wrong child. It is owned by a boy, and he won't give it up."

Durhain continued to stare at the elf, and he saw that this was true. "I will get it," he said. "It does not belong to him, or to you."

The green skin of the elf turned a shade paler. He had deeper magic than the shapeshifter, but the shifter was stronger, having a foundation in the world of men as well as the world of spirit. "Find the boy, if you can! There are a lot of boys in Groob," he called out as a parting shot.

Durhain was already moving away, but he glanced back a moment. "I will! And afterwards, look to your own safety."

It was true, there were many boys in Kraab alone, but not many would have been visited by the elf. Durhain in his animal guise could smell out the ones that were. It was time for him to go hunting.

Moving now into the heart of Kraab, Durhain glanced briefly up as a lightning bolt split the sky and the deluge began. The streets were nearly empty, and those few people he met were running for shelter. But Durhain moved at the same pace, swift but unhurried, indifferent to the storm, and to everything but his quarry.

Aleb's house was a little south of Kraab, up on a ridge that overlooked both desert and sea. It was the smallest in the row: a tall narrow box that had admirably suited Aleb as a roving reporter, but became a challenge when Jelani and her children moved in. It had a picket fence, a neglected garden, and a tall green front door emblazoned with the word 'Welcome'.

The children had taken over Aleb's upstairs office, while he and Jelani shared the main bedroom. The children certainly loved the office, with its view over the garden, the scraggly trees and bushes (with plenty of places for hiding), the wall and the desert dunes.

As the storm moved into Kraab the children set themselves up by the large picture window. They watched the ball lightning floating away into the desert. "Stay away from the windows!" their mother called. "Lebby, go and make sure they're safe."

Holanna had draped rugs over a collection of chairs. "Come down Rihan, I've made a house," she said.

Rihan had built an airship out of cushions, rugs and an old mattress, which he had piled up on the play table, and he was sitting at the very top. "Here's the good ship Stormcloud sailing above the seas of Rangolia," he chanted. He was, in fact, becoming frightened, what with the lightning flashes being so intense, and the thunder so severe, and the house shaking in the wind. Of course he wasn't going to admit as much to his twin sister. He gave a little squeal, but was pleased rather than otherwise, when Aleb scooped him up and popped him on the floor. He had had a bad experience not so long ago, while asleep. Something threatening. He could not remember it now, but that, somehow, made it worse.

"We'll do houses," he said. "We'll make a really good hideout."

CHAPTER 37

All the while Durhain maintained his unvaried pace through Kraab. He passed a succession of shops, all in darkness and with their frontages boarded up. He was passed, once in a while, by a hurrying vehicle, its lamps illuminating little more than the sweeping, horizontal rain. Other lights were few, except at street corners where hanging oil lamps swept their feeble glow over the puddled pavements. He began climbing, moving more into the outskirts of the city. He went up a back street that took him along a ridge, and here he found his first target. A candle was showing in an upstairs window of the tall, narrow building. Durhain had been here before, had looked in on the children, had interrogated the girl, but the boy had woken too soon. At a pinch, he could handle a woken child, but the transition from sleep to waking was a dangerous one, and to be avoided. He sprang over the little gate that Aleb had recently repainted, and ignoring the welcome sign at the front door followed the walls around to a garden shed, and then to the gaunt, rattling trees in the untidy garden. And there he waited.

The wind quietened, and the thunder faded as the storm moved north. Rihan had been busy with Holanna's house, adding the last chair and taking rugs from his airship, but now that the storm was easing he decided to climb up one more time and look out over the dunes.

At first he took it to be an illusion: perhaps it was the street lamp shining in a puddle that suggested two beady eyes and a long snout. But then the face floated upwards into a tree, growing larger all the time, and quite suddenly rushing towards him. *Where is it?* The words, coming directly from that thing, formed in his head, and simultaneously a blinding light burst in front of his eyes. Rihan screamed, and fell.

The window burst open and a gust of cold, salt-laden air rushed in. Rihan lay on the floor, sobbing. "I can't move my arm, I can't move my arm," he said, while Holanna ran howling to fetch her mother.

But Durhain moved on. Another failure, but he was getting closer.

He could positively smell the stone now. Never mind what boy had it, he would go straight to it. Moving away from Aleb's house, he trekked south. His black, hooded robe almost completely concealed his face, and his gait was not the pad-pad of a dog or wolf, but rather the soft stealthy movements of a panther. He glided through the night, seemingly oblivious to the cold, the fitful wind, or his dripping cloak, a figure so fearful that one man he encountered backed away shouting, and flourishing a stick.

Now and again he stopped and sniffed the air, and then, as if reassured, moved on at a greater pace.

Pookah Toomali's house was in the most wooded area of Kraab, at its very edge. Here, the encroaching desert had relented, and drawn back a little. The trees were for the most part stunted, because the drainage was swift and the soil struggled to hold water. Still, trees there were, along with plans to plant more.

"Stay indoors tonight, you two," Mr Toomali had said. "There's a big storm coming, straight off the sea. We should miss the worst of it, but I don't want my young scallywags struck by lightning."

"We're being good," said Sesha defensively. "I'm cooking, and Pookie is helping with the oven."

"Are you indeed? And when can we expect the house to burn down?"

"I'm keeping an eye on them," said Mrs Toomali. "But as for you, Mr Toomali, I was hoping you would be here to protect us."

"Sorry, Mrs T, I'm on duty, and I've got to keep an eye on the beach. Some idiot is bound to get swept out to sea."

"Just you be careful then. No point in getting drowned as well! Here!" She thrust a parcel into his arms, simultaneously leaning forward to kiss him.

"What's all this?"

"I knew you had to go, so I've packed some decent food. You'll need it if you're going to last the night!"

A cold gust whipped around the door as Mr Toomali made off into the gathering dark.

Upstairs, Pookah was taking pride in managing the oven. He had fed in just the right amount of straw and kindling and was working the damper, while his twin sister, with an assortment of bowls in front of her, was strictly following her mother's instructions.

Pookah had felt a growing anxiety right through the day. He had checked the stone, and double checked it. Twice he had ventured outdoors, intending to bury it in the garden, but had changed his mind at the last moment. It was at present underneath a corner of his mattress, wrapped in paper and sealed down with wax. Even now, as he focussed on working the oven, his thoughts kept returning to his bedroom, and in particular to the corner of the bed, and the secret it held. It's almost, he thought in despair, as if someone, or something, is messing with my mind. Every so often he would look out at the storm, but there was nothing to see but the rain, the wind and the fierce flashes of the sheet lightning.

"Pookie, come and help me!"

Pookah rallied. With her mother's help, Sesha had made a splendid pie. The storm and the stone faded into the background of his mind.

The Toomali house had been built for the view. At a lower altitude than Aleb's, it was nonetheless on a little rise. The front rooms looked out over treetops and across the southern section of Kraab to the distant sea, and from Pookah's room one saw first the spacious garden, then the boundary wall, and then the desert dunes rolling away to the remote horizon. Durhain vaulted lightly over the gate, untroubled by the almost total darkness. The rain had eased, but the rumbling continued. The storm was moving north. A flicker from a candle picked out the window of the front room, where Mrs Toomali was settling a tired and slightly fractious Sesha, and another flicker from the corner street lamp played over the stone frontage. Durhain glided along close to the walls, gently checking windows and listening for animals.

Pookah had said good night to his mother and sister, had climbed into bed and was in that state between dreaming and waking where images flow random and unbidden through the mind, when a strange animal sound reached his ears. He opened his eyes, sat up, and immediately fancied he saw something moving in the garden. A black outline like an arched back flashed across his vision, black merging into black. No, the movement was all too quick and elusive. He went to the window and stared out for a long time, but there were no further movements. A street lamp, nearing the end of its life, picked out odd anonymous shapes, while a late flowering shrub flashed its petals on and off as the flame guttered. In the far west the sky was clearing, revealing a dusting of stars and light from Rubilis, moon of illusions, now riding high and casting its strange light across the desert.

A wind was stirring in the trees. They were still barely more than outlines, but the expiring lamp captured some gaunt branches that projected towards the house. And wasn't that a face nestled in there? Eyes that appeared to be looking directly at Pookah? He looked more carefully, and there indeed was a cat. He watched it arch its back and spring onto the roof of the garden shed below. Just a cat. Satisfied, he returned to his bed, stretched out, yawned, and closed his eyes. The stone was safely nestled an inch from his hand. Tomorrow he would bury it in the garden. He had spent much of the day fretting about what nameless horrors might happen to him if he gave it away to the shapeshifter, refused to give it away, hid it, or lost it. He wanted most of all to give it back to the elf, but the elf had not returned. But nor had the shapeshifter come. So tomorrow he would bury the stone in the garden, make it not his problem, and all would surely be well.

CHAPTER 38

When Pookah woke from his troubled sleep and knew with certainty that something was wrong. He was most forcibly struck by the silence and the absolute stillness of the night, but it wasn't that. No, it was something else— it had to be something else. He looked carefully all around the room, and then out the window. There was very little light, the street lamp having used its quota of oil being finally extinguished. Rubilis was riding high, and the still clouded Numilis was following in its path. The hunter and its prey, the old men used to say. A dark rectangle showed the location of the door, and he could see at once that it had been opened. As he watched two green eyes, low down, looked back at him. He gave a half cry, and was on his feet in a moment. His hand groped down through the bedclothes, grabbing the stone. The stone! It was all about the stone. He took it and walked trembling towards the passage. Take it, take it, he thought, whatever thing you are, please take it! But the eyes had gone, and there was no other sign of animal or man. He crept along the passage, listening at Sesha's door, and then at his parents' door. Nothing. He returned to his room and went to the window. The garden remained a patchwork of dim, grey shapes. The tree where the cat had sat for a time was almost indiscernible. Now, there was no movement at all that he could see, but the stillness brought with it a tension of its own. It was a heavy, sullen stillness and there was a sense of waiting, of purpose.

Pookah found in himself not so much fear as a cold anger. Something was getting at his mind. And it was all about the stone … He stayed at the window and watched.

Surely now there was movement, a gathering in the darkness that assembled itself into a face—a face neither human nor animal, with a long snout and red eyes that sought to capture his own, and which radiated human intelligence. Now it was rising into the branches, floating, a thing surely of air, that was coming towards him, and tugging at his mind. And now words were hammering into his mind: *Have you got it? Where is it? Give it to me!*

The pressure in his head became intolerable. He opened his mouth to shout, scream, anything, but no sound would come. He wrenched open the window, took the stone, and threw it with all his strength towards the face. There was a flash of light and a loud crack, as if something in or near that face, that thing of air, had broken. Then silence, darkness. He closed the window, and leaned with his head against it, sobbing quietly. At length he groped for matches, and lit a candle. The cheerful glow enhanced the darkness beyond the glass, but he knew with some strange inner certainty that the thing had gone. The illusions had all gone, and with them had gone the elf and the shapeshifter. He returned to bed, lay down and listened to the night. The brooding stillness had gone. He could hear the innocent rustling of the wind in the trees, and far, far further away, the surf made a lullaby as it rolled up and down on the shingle beach.

"Sleeping well today, son?"

It was his father in the room, back from his storm watch.

"I have to leave early tomorrow to catch the boat, but today we have a car. It's a perfect day for a long drive and a picnic, so give yourself a big stretch and a yawn, eh, son? Hey, I haven't had much sleep myself, but it's too good a day to waste. Have a stretch, a wash and go help your mother."

"It sounds great, dad. A picnic! I can't wait."

Pookah ran to the window and stared out at the garden, and the gaunt tree with its branches groping towards the house. His father joined him.

"You loved that tree, but I'm afraid it's dead now. You can help me take it down—just not today."

Pookah looked carefully over the entire garden, but could see no trace of the drama that had unfolded during the night. It was true that some of the bushes looked wind battered, and there were broken twigs everywhere, but nothing looked actually squashed, or trampled.

"I hope you weren't disturbed in the night. Your mother tells me one of those big wild cats got into the house. I hunted it down this morning—it was trapped, and terrified. Got it out in the end, but I fear I may have woken you."

"No dad, I slept well."

"No bad dreams, no shapeshifters?"

"I'm through all that." And Pookah felt, very strongly, that this was true.

"Great, son. That means you're growing up. If you're going to be a sailor you'll find there are enough real threats in the world without having to invent any."

The Toomali family had recently acquired a radio, to which they eagerly listened over breakfast. There were the usual personal messages from outlying islands, and from ships at sea, followed by various items of news. The most curious was the announcement of the death of Mr Durhain, Chief Executive Officer of the Groob Trade and Warehouse Company, who was known for his eccentricities. He was discovered in Harlan Street, and had choked on a piece of quartz stone, which he had apparently been carrying in his mouth. His face looked so strange it was only when the contents of his pockets were examined that identification was possible.

"Why, Harlan Street is not two minutes walk away," exclaimed Mrs Toomali. "The poor chap. Any of us might have come across him."

CHAPTER 39

Aleb, waking, became aware of the silence. He looked out the window and saw a clear sky adorned with a glittering arc of stars. Next, he went to the children's room. Both were sleeping soundly, his son propped up with a plaster across his head and his arm in a sling. He glanced around the room, noting that the window, now with a large crack across the glass, remained firmly shut, the play table beneath it now devoid of mattress and cushions. All was quiet, and he felt, for the first time after a somewhat traumatic evening, positively cheerful. First Holanna, now Rihan, he thought. But they had not been visited by anyone, not on a night like this, and Belzic had dealt with the 'kid who wanted to play'. And nor had he or Jelani been using any of the Dream Hunter devices. Surely, then, Dream Hunter was exonerated—in this case at least. Returning to his bedroom, he found Jelani already awake.

"Come here, you big baby," she said. "You mustn't worry about my kiddies—I've already checked, and besides, they're tough. They'd survive a hurricane."

Aleb bent over and kissed her. "Duty calls," he said. "There'll be a lot of stories after a storm like this, and I want to get ahead of the rush."

"Wrap up warmly then!"

Aleb had recently acquired a new bicycle, managing to get ahead of a long waiting list. He wheeled it out now, and looked up and down the

185

street. It was, for the moment, quiet. A couple of street lamps continued to flicker, but there were extensive pockets of darkness. A black cat emerged from the shadows and leaped up onto a high wall. Aleb kept scanning, but found no more movement. He decided to head first for the docks, but after coasting downhill and turning a corner, he almost ran into a group of frots. They were busy tearing apart a car that had been parked at the side of the road, and at first they ignored Aleb when he pulled up and was beginning to take photographs. Then without warning two turned on him, and he came within an inch of losing the bike. Frots move far more quickly than humans, but Aleb had the advantage of a large burst of adrenaline and a downhill run. A block further along there was a call box where he was able to alert Kraab security.

Deciding now to search along the barrier walls to find how the frots had escaped the desert, Aleb took a turn and a loop through the central business district before beginning another climb. Here and there he saw damage from the storm: tree branches blocking roads, a street lamp down, a broken window, washing draped over the edge of a roof. The wall, when he reached it, looked secure. In places earth and rubble was piled up against it, but the stones had held. Aleb took his bike along the 'wall road', a narrow track used for excursions and inspections. The stone section gave way to wooden posts, boards and rammed earth. And here at last he found it: a section blasted away by lightning strike, judging from the blackened timber. The boards were scattered a long way, with many already disappearing into the sand. Aleb took photographs, and decided to head back at once to his home. Here he could ring the news through, alert security and develop the pictures. On his return he passed a group of men with poles and nets, rounding up the frots. He stopped again for more photos. The frots, for all their menace, did not seem to understand nets. Two, with swords, were making dangerous swipes, while some men parried with their poles and others threw nets or lassos.

Aleb moved on, heading for home. Holanna, watching out the window, called out, "Here comes dad!"

"Dad number two, coming in with the dawn," said Rihan.

"We were all awake and worrying about you," said Jelani as he entered. "The news came out that there were frots all over Kraab, and people should stay indoors."

"The news was exaggerated, as usual," said Aleb. "Actually, I got some good photos of the creatures."

"Aleb! You should have stayed well clear and left all that to the experts."

Ω

All night long the wind had roared about the embassy building. The sea was close by, and the windows facing it, in the room inhabited by Andrew and Belzic, were pelted with salt spray and rain in equal measure. Belzic settled down, yawned and slept, as he always did, and thus was little comfort to Andrew, who sat up and with each wind gust watched nervously to see if the glass would hold. He fell asleep at last and was alone when he woke to an intensely bright day. Everything sparkled. He sat up and listened. Belzic had gone, leaving his part of the room with its usual tidiness, but the other rooms appeared equally silent. Andrew tiptoed out into the hall. There was a very faint and rather odd noise coming from the third bedroom. Andrew hesitated. It was the room shared by Schyl, Groose, Erg and Grice, and he did not like to intrude. However, he was bursting with curiosity. He gave a quiet knock and opened the door. And stood still in shock. The centre of the room contained a great knot of entangled, wriggling flesh, and scattered around that were odd, and for the moment unrecognisable items. The rest of the room was empty. Andrew stood transfixed in the doorway for a long half minute, thinking, insofar as he did think, that something terrible had happened. Then he felt two hands on his shoulders, pulling him backwards.

"Leave them alone," Belzic whispered in his ear, and shut the door. "Haven't you noticed what's been going on? Grice has been after Schyl for a long time, and mostly been ignored. Something must have happened during the storm."

"Are you saying that that—that thing in there—is Grice and Schyl?"

"Andrew, you are shocked. And I agree, they are breaking one of their nine rules for planetary visitations."

"So they strip off their exoskeletons to ... to ..."

"That, among other things. But don't refer to Grice as 'she', since on a mission everyone is unisex. And if you want to know where the rest are, they are out in the desert, inspecting some interesting old ruins which the storm uncovered. I believe your lady friend Qu is going there as well, and one of the official cars will pick us up in a couple of hours, if you want to come. I am most interested."

The car took Andrew, Belzic and Qu's PA on a steady climb along the wall road to the nearest gate, from where they had to walk laboriously over soft sand for some distance. The storm had transformed the dunes, sweeping them away in some places and raising them high in others. The usual tracks had disappeared, and scattered everywhere were a great variety of items which the wind must have picked up and tossed across the wall. Among a multitude of small things they found an old bed, and a considerable collection of roofing iron. The site, when they came within half a mile, advertised its presence with a cluster of dazzling lights. The wind had scooped out a wide hollow, from which rose an assortment of metallic spires and domes. It looked to the visitors like a magical place, a city dressed out in greens and golds and purples that had arisen all fresh and pristine out of the ground. As Andrew said later, everything looked as if it had been newly created.

A score of people were working around the buildings, while another group were busy setting up barricades against the frots. The trio made their way past the barriers and found Qu talking to one of the scientists. He had a magnifying glass out and was studying a structure which Andrew took to be made of steel.

"See," said the archaeologist, "the surface is very slightly roughened at the vertices, but most of it is pristine. If it was ever pitted, it has been polished smooth since." He picked up a handful of sand. "This is very old, and no longer coarse. It's been ground down over the centuries, so any action of sand on metal will polish rather than roughen."

"And what is this structure made of," asked Qu.

"That we can't yet say. It's not steel—it's some kind of alloy, but we're not sure which."

There was a shout from nearby.

"It appears that someone has found a way into one of these buildings," said the archaeologist. "I strongly recommend nobody goes in yet. Excuse me."

Andrew and Belzic continued looking around the buildings, until they were politely moved on by the scientists. They found Cherg and Erg amid a cluster of reporters, who were busy taking photographs. "Come on Andrew, Belzic," said Cherg. "We've organised a car and we're going exploring. I want to see what else the storm has uncovered."

On the way to the car they encountered an extremely cheerful looking Grice. "Cherg, is your car big enough for one more? I have a mind to go travelling."

Cherg at once agreed. "If it isn't, we'll get a bigger one."

Grice then turned to Andrew. "I understand you looked in on me this morning?"

Andrew felt his face go crimson.

"Andrew, you don't know how much I envy you. You're a natural hominoid, and the galaxy belongs to your kind. We came out of the sea, and you've no idea of the hassle involved in managing an exoskeleton."

Andrew had nothing to say to that, but Cherg spoke at once: "So what have you done with our captain, Grice?"

"I expect he's still sleeping, the poor man. The men always get worn out."

"Poor chap," Cherg agreed, looking critically at Grice. "But here's the car. Let's move! I want to see what else the storm has brought to light."

CHAPTER 40

The excursion

"Faster, dad, faster!" Pookah was in the front seat, sitting between his father's legs and clinging to the steering wheel. The car was in the slow lane, easing its way along behind a donkey cart.

"Dad, we've got room to pass!"

"Pookie, I want you to get used to steering—watch it, you nearly had us in the ditch!"

In fact the man on the cart, all dark skin, leather jacket, shaggy hair and straw hat, at that moment turned and beckoned the car to pass. Then he saw Pookah, smiled hugely, before taking off his hat and waving them on with it.

"That's one fan you've got today," said Mr Toomali, who however relented, gave the motor a burst of speed and guided the car to the inner lane.

"He must think you look cute," said Mrs Toomali. "He doesn't know you."

Suddenly anxious, she turned her head and checked the back seat.

"Sesha, what are you sitting on? Not the picnic basket I hope!"

The Toomali's were on the south coastal road which meandered for miles about the little bays and inlets, now and again skimming along close to an ancient sea wall before abruptly curving inland to round a headland; and finally expiring altogether in a maze of horse tracks and wild flowers. Pookah had at last relinquished the wheel and joined his sister in the back seat. The two were engaged in some activity which involved a lot of giggling. Mrs Toomali looked behind more than once.

"Are you sure you two are feeling all right? It's a very bendy road."

It was a wild, wayward road, a little doubtful at times where the sea had made a secret incursion before breaking triumphantly to the surface and sending out plumes of spray. Mr Toomali slowed the car to a crawl.

"Are you sure this is all right, Jaan?"

"It was checked over at dawn, mother. They just said people would have to be careful."

"Hey look mum, dad, look at that!"

'That' being a precarious stairway up a near vertical rocky face the car was at the moment passing.

"It leads to a beacon and a lookout, son," said Mr Toomali. "It tells mariners they're on the way to Kraab. I'll take you there one day, and you'll see how messages get sent by flashing lights."

"Pookah, you must never go up there, it looks horribly dangerous!" Mrs Toomali sounded outraged.

"Mother, there's an easier way, although I have to say that was how the signalmen used to go."

Everywhere along the road there were signs of the storm: heaps of rubble that had been hastily pushed aside, stranded, dying fish in pools, a number of damaged or dead seabirds, including one with a broken wing that was running ahead of the car.

"Stop, stop!" Sesha cried out. She had seen a lost hatchling struggling in one of the shingly heaps at the road's edge.

"Oh, Sesha, dear, it will never survive," said Mrs Toomali. She knew what was coming.

"It will, it will!" Sesha was out of the car in a flash, and came back cradling the little creature.

"You'll have to feed it," said Pookah. "You'll have to find icky slugs and worms and all sorts of horrible things."

"Now, now Pookie, don't tease your sister."

"Sorry, dad."

"I can give it some milk," said Sesha. "I'm going to keep it."

"Here is where I had in mind," said Mr Toomali. He pulled off the road almost at its terminus. The car was slightly above the road on a level patch of scrubby grass and sand that, like some big marine animal, had shaken itself dry and stretched itself out to toast in the sun.

Close by was a shallow lagoon into which a good many fish had been swept. The air rang with the cries of birds that were sweeping in, diving, and grabbing their prey.

"There's not much shade," said Mrs Toomali doubtfully.

"Look, we can sit under the bushes and spread a tarp over the top," said Mr Toomali the practical.

They were in a little patch of calm. The wind was rising, and echoing against the cliff faces. Mr Toomali had just enough room to lie back while the picnic things were spread around him.

"Dad, why don't we gather up some of the fish?'

"Eh? No, son, we'll get some bigger ones from the market."

The outside world was fading fast for Mr Toomali.

"Jaan! Jaan T! You haven't eaten or drunk a thing. Come on, sit up before it all goes!"

"Right—ho mother, pour me something from that thermos if you will."

The food and drink went quickly.

"Mum, dad, can we go and explore?"

"Right—ho son, take care of your sister. Keep away from the water."

"And you mustn't go far. Stay within sight of us!" Mrs Toomali anxiously scanned the surroundings.

Mr Toomali yawned, and lay down once more. "There's nothing dangerous here, as long as they're sensible. Don't worry Mrs T."

The wind dropped a little, but the heat from the sun intensified. Mrs Toomali gathered up the empty bowls and glasses, and stacked them in the basket. Then she too yawned. I must learn to trust my children, she thought. Otherwise they won't grow up. "Move over a bit Jaan dear, I want to lie down with you."

Mr Toomali gave a little snore, but he obligingly yielded, sliding sideways on his back without really waking.

But Mrs Toomali lay a long time awake, looking through the leaves above her head to the bright sky. There were no clouds, and the wind was now still, as if the air itself slumbered in the heat. Nearby a thin trickle of steam flowed up in an almost vertical line. She followed it with her eyes, watching it fan out and ultimately merge into the sky. She wondered what was up there. She had heard said that all the little lights in the sky were other worlds, perhaps just like this one. She liked to think that there would be some that were kinder, without wars, or plagues, or vast empty wastelands, or all that wasted life of men and birds and animals.

Of course there were the gap scientists, bringing all that knowledge out of the sand, knowledge that provided them with a car, and a radio, and so much else. There were also those who said the scientists would sooner or later unearth terrible secrets; secrets that would doom them all, as surely as it had done with the elders. And already the stories she heard frightened her, and she sometimes sensed an undercurrent of fear all through Kraab. We can be happy with what we've got, she thought. Why delve any more? Let the dead civilisation rest in peace. Let it not harm the living.

She had had very limited schooling, unlike the children today. There had been some elementary reading, some geography, and lots of practical work, such as how to cook, manage a house, make clothes. Almost all the stories, such as the beginning of the world, the divine beings that guide us through life, or where we go when we die, had come from her mother, that fount of reassuring wisdom. It was all being torn away from her now, and even by her own son, who was always coming back with a new story from school. Mrs Toomali thought now of her mother, that amazing woman that the plague had taken from her too soon. Then she sat up very cautiously, careful not to disturb her still sleeping husband, and looked around. The children were out of sight, certainly among the horse tracks and the wild flowers that were the road's return to its original condition. She now got down on her knees, closed her eyes, and said a prayer to her namesake Maaven, the goddess of hearth and home.

Dear Maaven, I pray that you may keep my children safe, and my dear husband, and the whole city of Kraab. May it thrive and be happy. May I stay strong and well and brave to look after my family, and accept their views, no matter how much they may challenge my own. And oh, please Maaven, may my family stay good and strong, and not be swept away by the madness of the world. Give them guidance, dear Maaven, especially if I am not around. I once heard that even in the most waterless wasteland there will be some-where a fount of knowledge, and wisdom, like a pure crystal fountain flowing up from the deep heart of the earth. Dear Maaven, if it be your will, if it be in your power, show me a sign that the world is not all meaningless, a blind accident, as some say, and that you yourself are real, and that you care?

Mrs Toomali rose from her knees. The wind had returned, and a gust blew through the bushes.

Mr Toomali woke up with a start. "Goodness, have I been asleep long? Where's the sun? Already behind the hills! We'll have to leave soon. Where's the kiddies, Mrs T?"

A moment later they heard them.

"Mummy, dad! Come and see!" Pookah was racing ahead, Sesha not far behind.

"Come and see! We've got something to show you!"

"We'd better check this out, mother," said Mr Toomali.

Mrs Toomali noted that the shallow lagoon, now nearly dried up, was empty of birds and presumably fish. She followed the others along little humpy trails, wading at times through shrubs and ubiquitous red poppies. Then, over a spur of rock into a little bay, she saw what the children had discovered. A fountain of clear water spurted up as high as her knees, and then sank with a gentle hissing into the sandy slope that led down to the sea.

"Aha," said Mr Toomali. "This comes from the aquifer under the desert. The water filters down through the sand and becomes very clean, which is why springs like this supply half of Kraab."

Mrs Toomali merely smiled. She had quite a different explanation.

"Will it stay here?" asked Sesha.

"It may. If it does it will form a proper little stream, and over time the vegetation around it will change—and even the little beasties you see hopping around. It might even make a lovely little pool, with things that love fresh water swimming in it."

"I want to come here again and see if it stays."

Back at their picnic site Sesha made another discovery, and was heartbroken. "Mummy, dad, you didn't look after it!" It was the little bird, and it was very clearly dead.

"Darling, it couldn't have survived," said Mrs Toomali as she held her daughter.

"Look, sweetie, we'll take a trip through town and see if we can get you a pet bird. Will that help?"

He doesn't understand, thought his wife. Nothing can replace the one that died.

"Well, son, now you've helped drive a car you don't need elves or shapeshifters any more?"

"No, Dad, I want you to teach me properly."

It was dusk. The car was heading home, and although the shadowy shapes along the side of the road might once have been monsters of various kinds, they were now merely rocks, or piles of rubble. Pookah in fact felt he had walked, or driven, into another world, and one even more extraordinary than that which had been controlled by his childhood fears. All his terrors seemed indeed to have gone old, and stale, and have transformed themselves into little scraps of idle childhood fantasy.

"And you, Sesha, what do you think?"

"Yes, daddy, I want you to drive through town and get me a bird."

"It will be busy in Kraab," said Mrs Toomali anxiously. "It's the turn of the seasons."

But Mr Toomali was not to be discouraged. "An excellent time to buy a bird," he said. "The car is due back tomorrow."

AIR

Now, the season of Earth gives way to that of Air.

Air is about consequences,

about things coming to fruition,

and especially about mirages,

dreams and illusions

that may tempt the good people of Groob into folly.

Many of the processes begun in the earth continue,

for the Air season is also the time of gathering in,

of harvest, as well as of secrets revealed,

and matters achieved,

for good or ill.

CHAPTER 41

Maria

"Hello? Yes, this is Andrew … Umus? You said Maria? Where are you? Where is she?"

Andrew was out with Aleb when the call came through. He felt a prickly sensation down his spine when he heard the name Maria. Not really excitement—more a sense of foreboding.

"She came to the office. I don't know why. No, I don't understand why she came here, or even how she got into our building. I couldn't contact you, so I told her to wait at the Embassy."

"Thank you, Umus." Andrew hung up. His mouth was dry and he was frightened. Oh dear, the place is probably locked up, he thought. But she won't turn up anyway.

There were no taxis available, and Andrew decided to walk back to the Embassy. He felt very strange, and he wanted to prepare himself. Maria wanted to see him—or was she, as Belzic thought, merely an aspect of his mind that had, somehow, cruelly activated itself? The sky was heavily clouded, and a sea mist was blowing over the city, so the evening light was dimming faster than usual as he approached the Embassy. The lamp over the entrance, that would normally be burning at this time, was also extinguished. Andrew tried the door, which was locked. He had a sense of mingled relief and disappointment. It was another false alarm, or perhaps the phantom Maria had melted into thin air. However when he found his key, turned the lock and stepped inside he had the immediate sense that he was not alone.

It was very dim in the passage. He shut the door and leaned against it, his heart beating fast. There were no discernible sounds, yet he had the very strong feeling that someone was there. Resisting the temptation to be silent, he checked the front rooms, and marched down the passage, knocking loudly on each bedroom door before opening it. The house seemed utterly deserted.

The third bedroom was his own, shared by Belzic. Nobody had any reason to go there. Just the same Andrew paused and listened outside the door before swinging it quickly open. There, sitting on the chair beside his bed, was Maria. She was outlined in light, reflected in through the window, and she was wearing a familiar, pretty dress. She jumped up at once as the door opened, and came to Andrew with her arms outstretched.

"My darling, I've missed you so much!" Both said it, almost at the same time, and Andrew gazed at the shadowy figure that was holding him, feeling her back, her arms, the pressure of her body on his.

"Let me look at you properly. I'll light a candle." He pushed her back gently, and fumbled around in the dim light looking for matches. He was shaking all over.

"You must come back, come home, we're all lost without you."

"Lost?"

"Oh yes, Jack and Elizabeth especially. Bill as well."

"Bill came back?"

"Darling, I'm sorry I drove you away. I need you. We need you to lead us."

"Are you real?" The question slipped out because it had to. Andrew held the candle up between them.

"Even if not for me, think of the group."

Andrew tried to look into her eyes, but they were turned away from him.

"Darling, take the candle away. It blinds me."

Andrew took the candle to a little side table. "How are you all lost, my dear?" he asked while his back was turned. "Like frots in the desert?"

"Yes, exactly like that."

Andrew slammed the candle down and came back. "There are no frots on planet earth!"

"It's just that I can read your mind, Andrew."

Andrew grabbed her by the shoulders and shook her. "You are a sort of trick! A mirage!"

Maria burst into tears. "I'm real! I'm real!"

Andrew felt a wetness on his hands. He released them and found they were covered in blood. He cursed, ran to the bathroom and came back with a wet cloth. He began to sponge her shoulders.

"You've hurt me!" There was blood dripping down her dress.

"How did you get here? Was it a portal?"

"Yes, yes, a portal. It's right near here. Come quickly before it goes!"

Maria pulled persuasively at his arm, and he followed her, straight to the bedroom's big picture window. For a brief moment they stood together, looking out at Numilis, which, devoid of its companion, was rising alone above the horizon. Then Maria melted into the glass, and he was alone. And he felt certain at that moment that Maria was truly dead, not on earth or any other planet, inaccessible forever. On an impulse he knelt down in front of the window, looked out at the rising moon, and said a prayer.

Shortly after he heard the sound of the front door opening. Belzic came in. He put his arm about Andrew's shoulders.

"She's really gone now, and I've said goodbye." He looked at his hands. They were damp from the cloth he had held, but there was no sign of any blood.

"I thought my hands were bloody, but they are in fact spotless," he said. He began to laugh, and then weep.

CHAPTER 42

The Toomali residence

"Pookie, Sesha, your father is coming home a day early," said Mrs Toomali. "That means tomorrow, and if the weather holds we can hire another car. Would you like that?"

"Mummy, can we go the other way?" Sesha asked. "We've never been right through the town, and I want to see all the shops."

"Nah, she just wants a swing for that silly bird of hers," said Pookah.

"We can decide when your father comes home," said Mrs Toomali diplomatically.

"It's not a silly bird, it's very pretty,"

The bird in question was a kind of small parrot, for which Mr Toomali had provided an enormous cage, mainly at the instigation of his daughter. ("It's so we can get another bird and they can have a family," Sesha explained.) The cage hung from a rafter in the spare room, once a retreat for Mr Toomali, and a place where he was supposed to be writing his memoirs, but now largely taken over by the children.

"Mummy, you can let Mr Chips out of his cage," said Pookah. "He can't fly away because he's got his wings clipped. Here, let me get him out."

"But he mightn't know he can't fly," said Sesha, almost in tears. "He'll go out the window and fall and get killed."

Pookah wanted a bird that hopped around the house.

"Leave him in the cage for now, dear," said Mrs Toomali.

Pookah put his face up against the cage, wrinkled his nose, stuck out his tongue, and made sick noises. The bird watched calmly, seemingly indifferent, before spreading one green, yellow and black wing and beginning to preen.

"Leave the bird alone, Pookie dear. You can tidy your room, and Sesha, do come and help with the lunch. I want to show you another recipe."

After lunch Mrs Toomali received a telephone call from Jelani Therim. It was quite a long chat, and once it had finished she brought the good news to her children. "You haven't met the Therim children, but they're about your age, and we're all meeting up in a couple of weeks."

"What for?"

"You'll like Rihan and Holanna, Pookie dear. Anyway, we're all going on a picnic if the weather holds."

Ω

"There," said the doctor, "how does that feel? I want you to wiggle your fingers."

The doctor had removed the sling that had supported his arm, and was carefully feeling round his shoulder. Rihan wiggled his fingers.

"I think we can do without the sling now. Just be careful for the next few days, little fellow. No rough play."

"Thank you so much," said Jelani. Rihan ran out of the surgery to join his sister. Presently, Jelani emerged and the two children crowded around her.

"Mummy, can we go with you to your work?" Holanna asked.

"Sorry dear, the building is off limits to anyone under sixteen. I have to take you home. Your father's there, but he's working, so you'll have to be very quiet."

Aleb was at the kitchen table, writing up a report. He looked up and smiled when the trio came in. "Get yourselves some water, and then go play. Quietly now!" Jelani warned, and hurried away.

Back at the office she checked over the reports of the past week. Her main concern was the various kinds of visitations, as they were now officially called. They mostly concerned children under twelve (thirty-six) as opposed to eight for older children and adults. She now had five categories: fantasy visits (goblins, elves, gnomes, trolls, and a small dragon); 'real' people (three identified as recently deceased, and one uncertain); activated memory (remembered events experienced as 'real' repetitions, often with a different outcome); threats (something hidden and about to attack, or something standing or walking close behind the subject); and finally composites (such as an actual person or animal endowed with supernatural powers, or multiple visits of different types). Jelani had, with some regret, included her own children in the list of those experiencing this last category. Then there was Andrew. She wasn't sure if Andrew had experienced anything at this stage. However, she wrote his name down, and against it put a large question mark.

Umus put his head round the door, questioning. Jelani sighed.

"Yes, we put a stop on the D2. Had to. Forty-four cases in the past week. I've given up counting the cases where children pick up on their parents."

"Mind you, we've had nearly five thousand sales." Umus suddenly grinned. "Nobody can say you were wrong."

Jelani scowled. "Wrong about what?"

"Experiences really do transfer mind to mind."

CHAPTER 43

Office of the President

"Ma'am, it's Euse."

"Good. Let him in, Rain, and get Jupella to bring in some drinks, and take a break—and off you go."

Euse walked in, beaming.

"Ah, Euse, I trust you Croans are happy with your new identities?"

"Ma'am, we're delighted."

"Excellent. In that case it is time you and I had a serious talk."

Jupella followed Qu to a side table, holding a jug and glasses.

"Your favourite tipple?"

"Anything warm and sweet, ma'am."

Qu leaned back a little, fingering her glass.

"I think you appreciate my position. So far, our talks have been more about my needs, and what I expect from you. I have gained a lot of popular support from your visit. You have come in the guise of ambassadors from a distant country, and you have brought gifts. You are popular, and we have given you the freedom of the city. None of this will of course last—not if it gets out that you are not ambassadors, and your purpose has nothing to do with trade, or alliances." Qu stopped abruptly, and watched Euse's face.

"Now, I want to know a good deal more about where you are really from, and what you want from us."

"Well, yes, it is true that we are not ambassadors, and we are not interested in trade." Euse paused, weighing his words. "Nor are we the remnants of what you call the elder people. Rather, we are explorers from a distant place. I have to say we are grateful for your support, and we have tried to reciprocate in a way consistent with our rules."

"Yes? Tell me about your rules."

"Certainly. I must say that our policy is not so much to deceive our guests as not to disclose more information than we have to," said Euse. "You people made some assumptions that weren't so different from the truth. Yes, we are from a far country, and yes, you are welcome to our gifts."

"Very good, Euse, but let's get more to the point. You are, I believe, from a country that is so distant it is from another planet?"

Euse had been looking out on Kraab, but now he shot a startled glance at his interviewer. "Perfectly correct, ma'am. It is normally against our policy to declare this, and if we do, and are believed, it can be highly dangerous to us, and to our ship."

"You have nothing to fear from me or my government, Euse. I have prepared some papers that give you a plausible home on this planet."

"Ma'am, that is appreciated. We already have some knowledge of Dufalia, as provided by Andrew."

"Good. I want you and your crew to memorise all the details I have for you now, so you will have a consistent story when you come to talk to our people. No more wild and conflicting tales!" Qu paused in thought.

"We can explain past confusions as problems with the language. But now you will be Dufalians and have a consistent story, which should help your credibility. In return I expect you to reveal a good deal more about yourselves, and your purpose in coming here."

"Certainly, ma'am. We are Croans, that is, we are creatures that came out of the sea a very long time ago, and we wear a support that enables us to move about on dry land. We are clever, curious creatures with highly developed technology, and one outcome of this is we make a habit of visiting other planets. There are four other species that we know of that also pay visits, so we have formed an agreement which takes the form of nine rules, or articles, about how to behave when we pay visits. These rules were the outcome of a number of unfortunate events, and one of them is not to be conspicuous, if at all possible, when dealing with other intelligent beings. From our point of view it's a very sensible rule, because we want to study the way they behave in their natural habitat. Though I must confess we have rather stretched that rule, at times."

"From what I've learnt I would say you have, and you have been anything but inconspicuous. This leads me to suspect there are other reasons for your visit."

"There certainly are. The main one is to investigate what may turn out to be merely a legend."

"Indeed? A story about this planet? Do please explain."

"A folk tale tells that an ancient civilization developed a set of portals to enable their folk to travel easily from one planet to another. This planet was supposed to be the hub of their network. I don't particularly believe in the story, but there certainly was a technically evolved civilization here, and you people are conceivably the survivors from it."

"Thank you. I want you to compile a document which lists everything you know about this legend, along with all the reasons why you have come to our planet. I also want a copy of your nine rules, and a little more about yourselves, and the planet you come from. In return I will give you your cover—that is, details of Dufalia, the country you will say you have come from. Can you have your information sent to me by this time tomorrow?"

"Why yes ma'am, that should not be difficult."

"Excellent. I will help you with the portals if I can. I think we can do things for our mutual benefit. Thank you for your visit." Qu now flashed out her charming smile.

"Our mutual benefit," Euse repeated. "That is what I was hoping for." He stood up, gave a little bow, and began to turn away when Qu stopped him one more time.

"One more thing, Euse. I want fewer of your crew working with this Dream Hunter outfit. Don't move them all out, and certainly not all at once, but get them onto other things. I suggest helping the scientists out in the desert. I will have a word with them."

This time Euse flashed out one of his own smiles. "That too ma'am is what I want."

Euse met Ess and Schyl back at the embassy. "Things are getting better and better, crew. We're going to be off digging in the desert."

"What, with their primitive equipment, master?"

"Yes, my trusty assistant. Or on second thoughts, one or two things from the ship could be useful. Why not get Grice onto it, Schyl? I gather you two have become quite chummy lately."

"Very well, Euse, what shall I get him to provide. Automated? Semi-automated? Hand tools?"

I will leave it to his judgement. Now, Ess, I want a printed copy of our visiting rules, along with everything about why we came here. And all about the portals. If you don't know anything, nor do I. Make something up. We've got to keep Qu happy."

"Yes, master."

On the last point Euse was perhaps unduly cynical, since a good deal had been written about the portals, although most of it was speculative, and concerned not so much the legend as its origin. Ess at any rate had plenty of material to play with, and was soon happily at work.

In the meantime, Jelani was settled in the chair that a short time previously had been occupied by Euse. Umus was there as well, and both were looking a little worried about what the interview might portend. However, when Qu came into the room she was looking as fresh and untroubled as ever.

"Thank you so much for coming, both of you. Oh, do be seated, Umus … yes, I certainly know who you are, and it's nice to meet you at last. Now, I know you have been very busy testing your gadgets, which are unfortunately still meeting with quite a lot of controversy. Crowd hysteria, perhaps? People seem to love them or fear them. I assume you have warned all your customers not to have children in the house when your gadgets are in use? And your tests are continuing?"

Jelani and Umus exchanged glances. "We give all our devices a great many tests before we launch them, but we found nothing at the time," said Umus.

"However, we've stopped the sales of the D2 for the moment, and if our further tests find anything really troubling we'll recall them all," Jelani added. "They are continuing as we speak."

"Are there any leads at this stage?"

"I think the maIn one is that family connections are very power-ful, especially where mothers are involved, but children generally are very receptive."

Qu frowned. "I hope you can pin that down a little more precisely. I gather you two are the brains behind the company?"

Umus smiled. "That would be far too big a claim for any of us. It was Hamul who got things started, but he only built on data and speculations that Jelani had already provided. As for me, I have been fortunate to dis-cover some material taken from the desert. The D1 was developed out of it, and to some extent also the D2."

"Umus has been essential all the way through," said Jelani.

"So what do you imagine could be the problem? I assume you don't believe that things of the mind can acquire actual substance? I recall that on the wall of your office is the sign, 'The Dream Hunters of Groob: turn-ing your dreams into reality.'"

"That's just advertising," said Umus.

"I can explain the point of it," said Jelani. "If you have good dreams, such as things you wish to aspire to, the devices will make them seem more powerfully real. They will seem more achievable, and so make you more confident, more likely to succeed. But if you have bad dreams, such as phobias, you have a chance to confront them in a safe way, and so overcome them."

"Preferably with a qualified therapist sitting at your side," said Qu drily.

"There's a men's group where they all work together, sharing secrets in confidence," said Umus. "They tell me they've had some great results."

"I wonder if you can explain a problem one of my security guards has," said Qu. "He's a very down-to-earth chap, but he's used one of your devices, and now he's started seeing things that aren't there." "Such as, ma'am?" Umus said, for Qu had paused.

"He was reticent about that, but he said they look like demons, or giants, goblins, dragons—all fantasy things."

"I would advise him to stop using the devices," said Umus. "He has a very active imagination, and they are not for him."

"That certainly sounds sensible."

"Does he have children?" said Jelani.

"I believe there is a little boy, and a much older daughter."

"That is very suggestive. He has very likely been reading stories to the boy—the sort of stories with lavish illustrations—and they come into his mind while he uses the devices. Once he knows where the images come from he should have no more troubles."

"Thank you Jelani, I will tell him."

Jelani dipped her head very slightly, and the two exchanged smiles.

"There is one other thing. I understand your children have had actual visitations? Creatures that appear to be physically present, standing in front of you?"

"That is so, ma'am, though fortunately the visits have not been at all threatening. The main one was a boy who kept pestering Rihan, saying he wanted to play. "

"And have you found out anything about him?"

"Yes. There is a woman living a few houses away who lost her son. According to Belzic, she was using our devices to try and bring him back."

"Oh dear. Have there been other visitations where you know the source?"

"Yes, quite a few. I'll send you a report ma'am. There is one other case I've been involved with, in which the source was obviously Andrew. He lost his wife, or left her behind when he came here. At any rate, he believes she is no longer alive."

"I'm sorry to hear it." Qu made some slight movements, as if preparing to rise. "It does seem as if you have everything well in hand."

"I hope so, ma'am," said Jelani. "We are a down-to-earth company, and our devices are not to be used if children are in the house."

"Or, indeed, in the house next door, if we can avoid it," Umus added.

Jelani and Umus both stood up, and made little bows.

"And do discourage talking with the dear departed," said Qu with a laugh. "Thank you both very much for coming."

CHAPTER 44

"Rain, I want you to stay a little later this evening, if you will. I have the information from the Croans. I must say they are very prompt."

"Yes, ma'am, I have no commitments."

"Good. Now firstly, they've sent me some general information about their history and their lives, which are incidentally about three times as long as ours. Now let's see. They came out of the sea in ancient times, and on dry land they wear a supporting framework, giving them a human shape."

"I had wondered, ma'am. That is certainly a deception!"

"To be fair, it enables them to move about. Now, as to their gender, they profess to be 'gender neutral' while on missions."

"I don't believe that!"

"While on missions ... and we are to refer to them all as 'he' and 'him' since we have no gender neutral pronouns. As to what sex they actually are, it is apparently a private matter."

"They keep their sex hidden?"

"It's difficult to believe, Rain, I know."

"Easier, ma'am, to believe it's another deception."

"To continue, they report they have always been fascinated by the humanoid form, and they keep genuine humanoids in reservations on their home planet!"

"Heavens! Do they keep them in cages and feed them?"

"They say they have always wanted to visit us, and have some ancient legend connected to this planet. They feel highly privileged to be our guests."

"I bet they do. No doubt they are chiefly interested in digging up the technology in our deserts."

"While their interests are chiefly scientific, they are more than happy to be our friends."

"I bet they are."

"They say they love art, mathematics, and exploring the galaxy. They do not play sports but they have many strategy games."

"No doubt we feature as the pieces in one of their games."

"Now Rain, I want to sound you on what follows. Here we are: *Rules for visitors.* As Euse said, it's all about science—or so they pretend. Let's see: *Article one: Visitors must as far as possible blend with the inhabitants in their daily activities, and not exhibit themselves as in any way special.* Hum! They've hardly followed that rule. *Normally* (it goes on) *secrecy about the visitors' place of origin is essential.* I don't think they tried very hard with that one. Let's look at another: *Article three: Visitors must not make use of technology that is not already extant on their host's planet.* What do you make of that one, Rain?"

"Why, ma'am, I like that 'extant'. If you have them digging in the desert ..."

"Exactly. Our old technology is probably equal to anything they might have with them."

"I could send a message ... "

"Don't bother. I'm sure Euse will have worked it out, and from what I've seen, these fellows have a very oblique way of following their own rules."

"Do tell me some more of their rules, ma'm."

"Here's a good one: *Article six: Visitors must in all cases obey the laws of their hosts during their stay.* And this one: *Sample material such as metals, fossils, artefacts or living specimens may be removed from the host planet only for the purpose of scientific investigation.* That's article seven."

"I see a conflict there, ma'am. I'm sure we don't want them carting off any pretty gadget they might happen to find in the desert. That would be against article six."

"Indeed, Rain."

"Were there any others that looked interesting?"

"The last one of all is good: Article nine: *Members must at all times conduct themselves with dignity and decorum, both in their behaviour with one another and in their dealings with intelligent beings in the planets they visit.* Most of the rest seem to be about getting permission from SCOG before they do certain things."

"I see. What is SCOG?"

"It says, the Supreme Council of the Galaxy."

"It sounds like a grandiose title, even for the Croans, don't you think?"

"Yes, Rain, considering that by Euse's own admission they have knowledge of not one thousandth part of the galaxy. More to the point, our own permission is the one that should generally be sought. But now I want you to listen to the third pretty missive they sent us. It begins, 'My dear Madam Prime Minister ...'"

"Heavens! They are appropriating you now!"

"Also, see the pretty way the message has been folded and decorated, Rain. What do you make of that?"

"Why, either they are in love with you or they want something very badly."

"It goes on, 'We are honoured to be able to offer you the story of the portals, as told on our home planet. It is a legend that goes back many generations:

There was once, in ages long past, a powerful wizard. He had a wife, who was very beautiful, a daughter who looked just like her, and two sons. It would have been a very happy family except for one thing: the younger son. While the older son was gentle, loving, and obedient to his father's wishes, the younger was wayward and rebellious, in fact attempting to undo all the good things his brother did. The wizard was deeply grieved because he in fact loved the younger son more than his older brother, and had taught him many secrets. Now the day came when the wizard and his family were invited to be guests to attend the coronation of a new king. The younger son was not to be found, so the family had to go without him. "I will say he is indisposed," said the wizard.

As the king was being crowned, and the family were kneeling with all the other guests, and affirming their allegiance, the son was breaking into his father's private study. He grabbed bottles and flasks and vials, and, while consulting various secret scrolls and grimoires, began tipping their contents into a large cauldron. The contents soon began to swirl and bubble, and pungent vapours rose. The son breathed them in deeply, and presently he took a small vial, filled it with the liquid, and began to sip. Soon he dropped the vial and fell down groaning. His body began to swell, and he became deathly white. The whiteness extended to the walls and ceiling. The son stood up, huge now and immensely strong, but his strength was hardly needed, as the entire house was crumbling into dust. The son marched out like an enormous white ghost, and wherever he went all the colour drained from the things around him. The trees turned white and crumbled into dust, and so did the houses, and so did every creature he met. And all the colour rose into the sky, which eventually turned completely black.

In the big city people looked up at the sky and were astounded. Somebody went and told the new king, and the courtiers, who promptly told the wizard.

The younger son, now monstrously large, met his family on the road. He ran towards them, crying, "Father, father, help me!"

The wizard cried out "Stop!" but his family rushed forward, and the younger son embraced them, with tears in his eyes, and, for the first time, love in his heart. Then his mother and brother fell with him to the ground, and the two brothers crumbled into fine white dust, but the daughter ran to her father to comfort him. The two knelt beside the mother, and the wizard put all his knowledge, strength, and passion into keeping her alive, and his daughter helped him.

Meanwhile in the high heavens a messenger to the gods watched the sky turning black, and he heard the chanting of the wizard. He flew at once to the great Lord of All to inform him of the problem.

"Your Majesty, the sky is black, there is absolute darkness, so should any of this family be allowed to live," he asked, "or should I call on the High Chancellor of the Underworld?"

The Lord of All pondered a little while, and finally gave his pronouncement. "Normally," he said, "I would allow nature to take its course, but since this is a special case … yes … a special case, and the young son finally had love in his heart, here is my judgement: let the sons be moons to circle this world, and give a little light to what would otherwise be a terribly dark place for the next thousand thousand years. Now the beautiful mother who did so much for this family, for her I had in mind a beautiful star …"

"But Sire, it will surely not be seen for a thousand thousand years," said the messenger.

"Yes, that is rather a long time," said the Lord of All. Not to me of course, but it would be to mortals. "Very well, in that case, while she cannot remain in human form, I will preserve her loving heart, and put it right in the centre of the world, so the land and sea will stay warm, and not freeze, and all living things will take heart, in spite of the darkness, and life will go on."

"That is very wonderful," said the messenger, "but there are just two problems.

"Name them," said the Lord of All. "I am in a tolerant mood."

"The first is, what should become of the wizard and his daughter?"

"It has already happened. They have turned into ice statues, and they will last as long as there is darkness in the sky. Name the second."

"It is no longer possible for me to report on what is going on in the world, with the sky so dark. It will make life very difficult if I have to stay here forever."

"I have already considered that," said the Lord of All, "and I shall make the world a hub, with passages everywhere, even to the most distant stars. You will be able to travel in a twinkling to wherever you wish to go."

And so it was. Life continued all through the darkness, and the seas and the lands remained warm, as indeed they do to this very day. For the mother's heart continued to beat, and it always will.

"Well, Rain, that was what the Croans delivered. What do you think?"

"A very pretty story, ma'am, and interesting, if true."

"If true?"

"I mean, they could have made it up once they saw our enormous white desert. And as a story, of course, the mother and daughter had to be beautiful, not just loving, or the whole thing wouldn't have worked."

"Yes, I see that, but what I really want is your overall impression of these visitors. You have seen them, and you have an idea of their rules. For example, would you trust them?"

"Not for a moment, ma'am. Not for a moment. I think they will cooperate with us as long as it suits them, and no longer. Apart from that, I see them as thoroughly condescending."

"Thank you, Rain, that's all I wanted, and I have to say I agree with you. So far, we have been mutually of use to one another, but this will almost certainly not last. Especially if they find something in the desert that they want for themselves. We must be ready for them. But now, if you wish to stay a little longer you could dine with me."

"Why, thank you, ma'am." Rain gave her boss a brief little bob of her head, before attending to her papers. "I'll just put these away and get ready."

Qu watched her leave the room. She had employed Rain three years before becoming president, and it had taken her all that time to discover she was in love with her assistant. More frightening to her was her discovery, by the most subtle of signs, that her feelings were reciprocated. Even so their relationship remained strictly formal, perhaps the more so as their feelings grew. The possibility of anything more overt than the briefest meeting of eyes frightened Qu. But maybe it is better this way, she mused.

CHAPTER 45

Aleb's house

"This is Pookah and Sesha; say hello Rihan, Holanna," said Jelani, as the visitors arrived, the aforesaid children running in ahead of Mr and Mrs Toomali.

"How are you both? Great that you could finally come," said Aleb, shaking hands.

"Jaan's tour finished a day early," said Mrs Toomali, with a touch of pride, as if her husband had had something to do with the favourable winds. "My goodness, what a lovely little house," she added, startled to find the passage ending rather abruptly at the bathroom.

"No, this way, Mrs Toomali," said Aleb, advancing ahead, opening doors.

"Oh, do call me Maaveni, stress on the second syllable, please." She gave a little laugh. "Do you find the place just a little tight for four, Mrs Therim?"

"We manage, don't we, Aleb." She gave Mrs Toomali the benefit of a big smile. "My name is Jelani, of course."

Aleb was inclined to go into details of the management, such as how the kitchen had been moved, with the benefit of a hand pump and an extra drainpipe.

"Do let me see your kitchen," said Maaveni. "We can leave the men to talk about engineering, or carpentry, or whatever it is."

The children were running up and down the stairs. "I can go down in six jumps," said Rihan.

"I'll beat it," said Pookah.

"Can't." He looked dispassionately at his rival. "What sort of name is Pookie? Pookie, Pookie!"

"Come on, leave the stupid boys. Come and show me your dolls," said Sesha.

Holanna lined them up for inspection. "Now this one has been sick so it's mostly in bed."

Sesha examined the dislocated arm. "It needs surgery. Come on, we'll take it to the hospital."

They were interrupted by a very loud crash, and a few seconds later by a babble of anxious voices.

"Pookie, Pookie, what have you done?"

"Rihan, Rihan, what were you doing?"

"My leg, my leg!"

"Oh dear, oh dear!"

"Help me move him, Jaan. Don't move the leg!"

"Pookie, can you wiggle your toes?"

"We'll have him attended to in no time," called Jelani, who had gone straight to the recently installed telephone.

Pookah was placed gingerly on Aleb's old sofa, now sited to afford the best views in the newly arranged lounge. Maaveni Toomali arranged the cushions behind his head while Jaan Toomali attended to the injured leg. Pookah groaned. Sesha and Holanna stood alongside, impressed by the gravity of the event, and with their own doll's casualty forgotten.

Pookah was duly whisked away in the recently mechanised ambulance.

"It's just a slight break. We'll put a cast on it and he'll be good to go," said the doctor cheerfully.

Ω

"Whatever did you think you were up to, son?" said Mr Toomali later.

Rihan was impressed by the cast. "Sorry I called you Pookie."

"It's all right, it's my name." He was sitting up in his bed, which had been moved into the front room.

"Your house is much bigger than ours."

"Yours is okay," said Pookah generously. Then, feeling that response was a bit inadequate, he looked thoughtfully at Rihan. "How's your arm?"

"It's okay. It was my shoulder, actually, but it wasn't a real break, more a sort of crack." Rihan nonetheless felt a strong bondage between the two of them; bonded, he thought, in the best possible way, by their own battle wounds. "I say, will you be able to go on the picnic tomorrow?"

"I guess so."

Holanna meanwhile was looking over Sesha's dolls. They were all lined up for inspection, and in fact, smartly dressed, as if they were indeed on display. "You have eight," said Holanna, amazed. She gazed at the immaculate dresses. Holanna's dolls were somewhat improvised, as were their clothes.

"Oh, come on," said Sesha, already bored. "Come and see my bird."

Mr Toomali had strung the cage high in the middle of the room, and Holanna stared at it expectantly as the now confident Sesha climbed up on a chair to release the bird. "Out you get Mr Chips," she said, pulling open the door. The little bird was out in an instant, flapping its wings as it fell straight to the floor.

"They did something to it so it can't fly," said Sesha. "It means it can't get away. Watch."

She dropped a line of seeds across the floor and into Pookah's room, and the bird hopped obediently along behind. "How's that for something?"

said Sesha, indicating the view. Holanna gazed out over the sand dunes. The horizon was concealed in a grey haze.

"See that branch sticking out of the sand? That was a tree that got blown over the wall in the storm. It sat on the dunes for a couple of days but now it's getting buried."

Holanna looked at the tree, and then at the pattern of shadows from the clouds that intermingled with the shadows on the dunes. She noticed something else. "Look, there are different colours in the sand."

Indeed, there was no pure white, but grey merging into green, or blue, the colours constantly interchanging with the wind in what seemed an intricate dance.

"The desert looks alive," said Holanna."It's so pretty."

"Dad says it's stuff in the atmosphere that makes the colours change."

But Holanna noticed something else. "Sesha, look, a long way off. Those are people aren't they?"

Sesha took a pair of binoculars and studied the landscape. Presently she gave a scream. "Oh God, that's terrible. I'll get dad."

Holanna continued to study the figures, screwing up her eyes for greater clarity. The binoculars had gone with Sesha.

Certainly something was going on, but it was all very distant. Sesha would say nothing, and neither, later, would her father. He went out, merely saying he had an urgent matter to attend to, and returning as dusk was falling and the Therim family had gone home.

In the night the wind increased: a hot moist wind that had been warmed by the steam from many volcanic vents. As dawn broke, Aleb called Jaan Toomali to discuss the plans for the day. "It's a strong south-easterly, isn't it? I thought we'd go north along the coast, and then take the desert road. It's only a short trip across to a beautiful beach, which will be sheltered. Does that interest you?"

"Give us half an hour," said Mr Toomali.

"Fantastic!" said Rihan when he heard the other family was coming.

Holanna, who wasn't sure about having hers mix with Sesha's 'posh' dolls, decided, on due consideration, she would take only her favourite, Naala, a swarthy, defiant looking creature that Aleb had (not without some consternation from her mother) recently presented to her.

Ω

The news was still under wraps when it reached Qu's office.

"We don't want people to panic," said Qu to her PA. "We need more detail, much more detail." And to her security chief, "Warn people to stay off the desert roads, especially the northern ones, apart from essential travel. Yes, an immediate alert by radio, but stress that it is just precautionary. And find out all you can from the road patrol services. We have to know if this was just a freak event or the beginning of a trend."

CHAPTER 46

In the desert

"What do you think, Groose? What does number one make of all this?"

For some days the Croans had been working with the gap scientists out in the desert. They had been lifting sand out of old, newly discovered buildings, carefully sifting it as it was bailed away. Cherg and Groose were working at an improvised machine near the surface.

Groose inspected the little, spherical piece of glass. "If I was to take a wild guess, I'd say it was part of a robot's brain. There's a lot of circuitry in there." He held it up for the light to catch.

There was a cry overhead from two of the gap scientists. "Defences needed! Defences needed!"

Cherg cursed. "That's the second time this week. We'll never get anywhere at this rate." He was up the ladder in a flash, however, in time to see Erg, already on the job. The frots had broken through the archaeological barrier, and Erg was swinging a large wooden stake, battle-axe style, at the ones closest to the digging.

"Get away, you stupid things, get away!"

"Aim at their legs, you can topple them!" Cherg called out.

But the foremost creature, a good deal taller than the Croans, was fighting back, and getting in some telling blows. Erg retreated, Cherg grabbing the pole and jabbing it into the frot. And shortly after the Desert Service Unit of the military arrived, and in a very practised style moved in with ropes, nets and a variety of slashing blades.

The Croans can move fast, but were no match for the frots, and as the last frot was trussed and taken away they lay back on the sand, bruised through their exoskeletons, but intact.

"That's enough for today," said Groose. "It's time to investigate Belzic's cooking."

"Provided we're in time," said Cherg. "Provided it hasn't all gone down the throats of Grice and Schyl."

They were in time to hear the news that was being broadcast throughout Rangolia. It was described as a 'freak attack'. A man with four children had his car break down in the desert not far from Kraab. At first he decided to stay in the vehicle, hoping to attract attention, since they were close to frequented areas. However, as the heat of the day increased he decided to risk leaving the car and leading the children to the city. In what was described as the only known unprovoked attack on humans, a band of frots tracked them down, killing two of the children and leaving the rest of the party prostrate on the sand.

In Kraab at least one person in ten now had a telephone, and the lines were soon humming, many from outraged parents calling for Qu to resign.

"She doesn't have a family, or even a husband. She can't possibly understand!" was the refrain most commonly voiced.

Ω

"Yes, this is the turnoff I had in mind," said Aleb. "Just watch out for frots while I open the gate. It's just a shortcut to the bay."

The newly acquired Therim family car having pulled in behind the rental, Aleb and Jaan Toomali were conferring over the route. Mr T scanned the desert.

"I expect they would have closed the road if there was any real danger?"

"Surely, they have patrols on these roads all the time," said Mr T. "We should be safe, but to make sure I'll give you a big stick, since I have a spare one."

"A stick? Not a gun from the patrol boat?"

"Guns? Guns are useless against frots. Here, take this. I'll close the gate."

Both vehicles were based on a design found in a book retrieved intact from the sand: The Nature of the Internal Combustion Engine. The Toomali's hire car had a few improvements, and was on the whole a safer option for the desert. However neither car would be able to outpace a band of frots in full racing mode.

The road was no more than a narrow track scooped out of the sand, and marked at intervals by little stone cairns. The cars made good progress. The boys, in the back seat of the leading car driven by Jaan, kept their faces glued to the windows. "I bet this could go faster than anything else in the world," said Pookah.

"Not as fast as a big hawk," said the knowledgeable Rihan.

"Yes, could."

"No, could not."

A ground mist was closing around the car, and with no reference points but level sand, both boys had the curious feeling that the car was barely moving at all. Rihan, looking all around, felt that the entire world had been swallowed up. Occasionally, one of the little cairns would float by.

"We're halfway through already," said Mr T cheerfully. "Sorry, boys, there's not much to see until we get to the bay."

But Mr T was wrong, because a moment later the world opened up once more. The desert ahead, running level to the remote horizon, sparkled in the gentle heat. However, dim shapes in the far distance moved like ghosts. Both cars came to a stop.

"That's a storm," said Jaan.

"It could miss us," said Aleb the optimist. The sky above remained defiantly blue. The sun beamed down. Jelani came across to talk to the men.

"Are you sure this is the quickest way? Couldn't we go cross-country?"

"No, Lani, there's a big hole somewhere. You don't see it until you're in it, I'm told."

"We could always go back," said Mr T. We're about halfway now, but we wouldn't want to get stuck at the bay."

"Go back? No way, dad!" Said Pookah.

"Full speed ahead then."

"Full speed it is, chief," said Jelani. She gave a mock salute and returned to her driver seat.

CHAPTER 47

"It really sounds as if we should close the roads, ma'am."

"Yes Rain, but for how long? Lots of people rely on those desert crossings, and they'll be outraged if we just lock the gates. And with some justification, in my opinion. Let me think, and in the meantime see if you can contact Desert Patrol one more time."

Qu called up security, and this time managed to contact the head immediately. "Still just the one event? ... What? The Kraab excavation? They'd be after the metal, wouldn't they? ... I see."

Qu disconnected and was immediately put through to the Desert Patrol Unit. Then after a short interview she rang off frowning, and turned to Rain. "There have been several incidents, but all of them are ambiguous."

"Ambiguous, ma'am?"

"Humans were attacked, but only because they were blocking access to metal. The worst incident was apparently at the excavation works just out of Kraab, where our guests the Croans helped fight them off. No-one was seriously injured, so we are left with the one incident: that poor man and his children. So, Rain, we're giving the country three hours' notice, after which the roads will be closed for forty-eight, and our scientists will have time to carry out tests."

"I only ever met one frot, and it terrified me, ma'am. It was its eyes. It looked at me, you see, and I could see nothing behind those eyes—no intelligence, just a sort of emptiness."

"And yet the things are smart, Rain, and possibly getting smarter. They may have decided that the best way to get to metal is to destroy any intervening humans. Anyway, I've requested the Desert Patrol round up all frots within twenty miles of Kraab. I want them destroyed, or decommissioned, or whatever can be done."

"They are legally protected, aren't they, ma'am?"

"Not if they turn homicidal, Rain. There is a clause in that law about destruction in the case of a clear and serious danger—or words to that effect."

Another call came through. Qu answered, and hung up smiling. "It looks as though we're going to have a storm over the desert. An excellent time to close the roads."

Ω

The procession continued. Jelani drove the second car, while Maaveni admired the scenery and the girls discussed dolls in the back seat.

"I haven't been out in the desert, or at least not nearly so far out," said Mrs Toomali. "It's all so … so …"

"Big?"

"Vast, utterly vast." Mrs Toomali eschewed the trivial word 'big'. She gazed up at the rapidly changing sky, noting its varied colours, with all the graduations from white to black. "It all feels so open, without all that steam."

"You can see different weather systems forming and changing," said Jelani, dropping a gear as she felt the sand softening under the vehicle's wheels. "It looks as though the storm will miss us."

"It must be wonderful to know how to drive," said Mrs Toomali admiringly.

"Oh yes, it has its uses." Jelani squinted ahead. "There's a definite change in the weather coming this way."

Mrs Toomali lapsed into silence. She sat back in her seat and stared into the distance. The sheer emptiness of the desert was now making her feel slightly uneasy.

"They say the stars up there are all different worlds, just like ours," she ventured presently.

"I think that's almost certainly true," said Jelani. "Probably not exactly like ours, mind."

The wind was picking up, and little white spurts of sand lifted up from the car ahead.

"Oh dear, we'll need to put the bonnet up," said Jelani. She gave the car a little toot, and Mr Toomali obediently stopped. The two men wrestled with the levers that raised the protective top. "There's a trick to it," said Aleb, "but it's not always easy."

With the car moving once more, and the canvas top making gentle flapping noises, Mrs Toomali felt lulled into a pleasant dreamy lassitude. She removed her hat, slid a little in the seat, and rested her head, aiming for comfort. There was a trick to it, she thought, but it was not always easy in a bouncing car, to get her head in exactly the right place at the top of the seat, so it was relaxed, and not strained. She achieved it at last and turned her attention back to Jelani. Scientific like, she thought, clever.

"Mrs Therim, do you believe in the old stories?" she asked tentatively.

"Jelani, please. And which stories do you mean?"

"Well, Maaven. I'm named after the goddess."

"Oh yes, I recall. Was she in charge of childbirth?"

"Hearth and home," said Mrs T firmly. "Everything to do with the family, really."

"Oh, a sort of general overseer. I haven't really thought about the old divinities. I think if we believe in them they do have a kind of guiding effect—they're reassuring, at any rate."

Mrs Toomali tried one more time. "Could they be real, along with those worlds in the sky, and all the rest?"

"I somehow doubt it, Mrs T. You see, we have to go by the evidence."

"Even if the evidence is dug out of the dry sand?"

"Especially then. We must respect the achievements of the past."

But Mrs Toomali scarcely heard the last remark. Go by the evidence, she thought. We have to go by the evidence! And wasn't the evidence a crystal clear fountain of water, spurting from the dry sand, and that after she had prayed to Maaven to give her a sign? She thought of that fountain. Forever flowing it would be, with a pool below it, and a pleasant stream making its way to the sea. And creatures of all kinds would come to drink that life-giving water, an oasis in the dryness. Perhaps shady ferns would grow around it, and the water would sparkle through the shadows, and her own family would return in time, and exclaim, How beautiful! How wonderful! Her pool. She would go there often, and sit beside it, and say a prayer of gratitude to Maaven.

Mrs Toomali's reverie was disturbed as the car jerked to a stop, and she pitched forward, only saving herself by putting both hands on the dashboard.

From the back seat came giggling, and then an indignant cry from Sesha, "You're sitting on my doll!" But Jelani's exclamation eclipsed even that outburst:

"Oh my God, it's a sand dragon!"

Both cars had pulled up, and Mr Toomali ran across to consult with Jelani.

"We'll be safer off the road. Do you think you can manage? Just follow me, and watch out for holes!"

The passengers looked ahead at the towering column of grey, moving sand that at the moment sat astride the road, and was moving steadily towards them. It glinted wickedly as it swayed like an unsteady top, and coils of black dust spun upwards, mingling with the whiter sand and dispersing into a densely clouded sky. Mr Toomali revved his car engine and turned away from the road, bouncing and bucking over the ridged surface of the desert, with Jelani's car in his wake. The way ahead was treacherous, with unexpected holes and protruding rocks demanding full concentration. The tornado was making a high pitched wailing sound as it approached. "Aleb, what's it doing? How close is it?" Mr Toomali was shouting. "Keep this direction and it should miss us!" Aleb shouted back. But the sand was already blasting against the cars, stripping off the paint, blinding the drivers to whatever lay ahead. The cars bucked one last time and began to roll down the slope of a steep dune. "Keep steering downwards!" Aleb shouted to the following car. "Don't let yourself slide!" It was his last instruction. The cars hit the upper lip of a rock face and fell, tumbling, rolling and sliding faster and faster. Jelani gripped the steering wheel as she spun, and shouted to her passengers. "Hang on to something, don't get thrown!" It was not clear if they heard above the crashing, rolling of the cars and the roar of the approaching tornado. No-one was really capable of thought as the cars spun and rolled. When at last thy came shuddering to a stop there was no movement, there were no voices. There was almost no sound. Jelani became aware, in a confused way, that she was largely inverted. Her legs a long way above her. There was empty space up there which she would have liked to reach, except that her neck was tilted on a very unpleasant angle. She very much wanted to move it, or at least rub the sore spot, but her arms were also trapped. So she stared upwards, searching that empty space above, and calling out, and presently she saw a very strange face looking down at her. "Help me," she begged. Then as her head cleared, and her eyes became more focussed, the face began to make sense. It belonged to a frot: a face on the end of a long flexible neck that manoeuvred over the twisted metal above her, and then remained quite still. "Help me, please," she said again. Other sounds came to her: Sesha crying in the back seat, and then shouting, 'Go away, go away!' Further off, now dull and remote, came the moaning of the sand dragon.

CHAPTER 48

"Where are we at, Rain?" Qu laughed as she pulled off her dripping coat. "First we have steamy heat, then dry heat and wind, and now horizontal rain, and nobody is satisfied with any of it. I could swear that downpour waited until I had to go out. Ah, drinks!" A servant had come in with a tray of refreshments. She gave a little bobbing curtsey and departed.

"So, Rain, what's happening?"

The personal assistant held up a sheaf of papers. "Six personal calls, none of them urgent, and a heap of correspondence that I'm still working through. Oh, and a couple of items require your signature."

"Thanks, Rain. I'll let you get on with the correspondence—I'm sure you'll sign on my behalf where you can. Just update me on the frot situation."

"Very good, ma'am. The three hour warning worked fine; all the cars were cleared from the desert and the gates locked. We've got the patrol people in there right now. They want to gather up a couple of hundred frots for various tests. They have some keen gap scientists, I gather, who want to experiment with trying verbal commands. Oh, there are some scientists still working among the ruins, but they can look after themselves. They have keys for the gates."

"I thought those experiments with verbal commands had been tried some time ago, Rain."

"Yes, quite a long time ago, and of course with very limited results, but now they think they have a better idea of the command language that was used. Something that's come out of the latest excavations."

"That sounds encouraging. How many are in the ruins?"

"Actually, ma'am, it's just two of our visitors: Andrew and Cherg."

"Well, I wish them luck. Now, I suggest we both have a ten minute break, shall we? Would you like to pour the tea?"

Ω

"If you'd like to take one end of this old door, Andrew, we can set it up as a table."

"Great. It's time for a break."

Andrew and Cherg had been working their way down, floor by floor, through a large circular building, and every floor had been disappointingly empty of everything other than sand. Now at last there were things to study, including fragments of furniture, or what the two presumed was furniture. There was the rectangular slab that Cherg was calling a door, and all around were other unidentifiable items, along with some ancient but miraculously preserved sheets of paper. Andrew obediently took one end of the 'door', and the two juggled it over projecting pieces of metal until it settled firmly.

"Now I need to spread these papers out and photograph them before they turn into dust. These scientists have nothing we can use—nothing to fix them," he grumbled. The papers were their first real find.

"Fine, but let's have those drinks first, Cherg, I'm famished."

"Yes, in a minute." Cherg continued to study the artefacts. "This is the so-called new script, not more than a thousand years old … I can recognise words! Listen to this: 'All of sector nine taking the leap'. Now what could that mean? Ah, here's another, 'The white death has reached the northern peninsula'. What does that mean?"

"I don't know, but I'm famished! Come on, put that stuff away and help me set out the food."

Cherg continued to photograph.

"Look! What do you think this means?" There was a diagram, faintly outlined, of a globe, a cylinder inside the globe and at the very centre what appeared to be a star. Cherg struggled with the text. "Trans ... trans something ... physic, or maybe physical ... vortex. Trans physical vortex. And underneath a list of numbers, possibly dates and times."

"I think," said Andrew slowly, "I think it's some sort of power generator."

"Power? Solar power? There's a sun image in the diagram."

"Portal power," Andrew continued, surprising himself. "I bet it's something to do with portals."

Cherg considered. "That is possible. The diagram is most likely just a sort of logo—a sign the company used. Look, it's all set out in a hexagram." Cherg examined the lines more closely. "There was once colour in this," he concluded. Very carefully, he packed away their find, and Andrew poured out the drinks.

"Aleb," said Andrew suddenly. "Aleb said something about coming through a portal. He said it as if it was a joke, but there was something about the way he said it ... We need to talk to him."

Ω

Aleb was trying to be calm, but his voice was breaking as he dictated his story over the phone.

Some of our readers will remember Jerome Foulkes a distinguished diplomat and trade negotiator, who went missing ten years ago, at the time of the outbreak of war. He is now on his way back to Groob. He has spoken to his son by radio, (that is, the Monitor's reporter Aleb Foulkes) and is presently ten days' sail away. The Monitor looks forward to presenting his story in a future edition.

"That must have been a shock for you," said Jelani. "How did you find out?"

"The Monitor called me this afternoon. They managed to get me a hookup."

"Well, that's wonderful. Damn, I haven't got a babysitter, or we could take a meal out." Jelani began to bustle around the house. "I can set up a bed for him. I'll use the sofa."

"Lani, he's ten days away."

Aleb's memory of his father was in fact limited, and, as he knew himself, somewhat idealised: a tall man with reddish black curly hair and a razor sharp mind. He had wanted his son to be a diplomat, an expert on the politics and history of Rangolia, a skilled debater. Aleb didn't like arguing the point of anything, but rather (in the course of his journalistic work) presenting the point of whoever he was interviewing. From his father's perspective, Aleb kept on taking 'wrong turns'.

"Was he the one who told you you came out of a porthole?"

"That was my mother. And of course she might really have said portal."

"Well, you'll be able to ask him anyway."

CHAPTER 49

Belzic tried one more time to contact Aleb or Jelani, and then put the problem from his mind. He went to the Dream Hunter offices, and joined Umus, who was sitting back in his chair with a pile of messages on the table in front of him. He wasn't looking at any of them, but rather, had his head tilted upwards, and his eyes closed.

"See what you can make of them, Belzic. I've added notes to the ones that make sense to me: the usual story of someone recreating some visual memory, often one they didn't know they had. There are also quite a few oddball ones."

"Children?"

"Not so many. Most people are following the rules, I would say, and not using the devices if there are children in the house."

Belzic pulled up a chair and began to flip through the messages. After a while he raised his eyebrows, and looked at Umus. "This chap says he went back in time and met himself!"

"You'll get some that are even stranger."

"Your company is not responsible if they are crazy, surely?"

"True, but these ones all had certificates of sanity."

"Meaning?"

"They got themselves checked over."

"Ah, another very strange one. A chap who got swallowed by a monster. Doesn't say exactly what kind of monster. Hmm. I see that a good many are critical, with some threatening to sue us. On the other hand there are others where much gratitude is expressed."

"Do you think you could go see some of the ones with grudges?"

Belzic hesitated, then flipped back through the pile. "It seems to me that most of these have a problem with the way their life is going. For example, this one: a chap who went back in time. He probably felt he had taken a wrong turning in his life, and being reminded of it has upset him a great deal. If I was to work with him I would want to take him back to that time and place."

"And the one who was swallowed?"

"Clearly, he feels that something has taken over his life entirely. Really, it would probably need a skilled therapist to sort out either case."

"But you could help?"

"I could sound them out. I promise nothing, of course."

Belzic left the Dream Hunter offices and headed towards the Embassy, walking quickly. The air was cool and still, but the sky retained a brooding quality, the dimming light emphasised by black low clouds. He took a shortcut across a section of the beach, and stopped for a moment to watch where, not far out, a turbulence in the sea represented the spot where some underwater drama was being played out. From the deserted Embassy rooms he put a call through to the City Hall, who switched it to the Desert Patrol Office. After a brief talk he got to work in the kitchen.

Presently a vehicle pulled up at the embassy. On the tray were four children, and four adults within. The children were staving off sleep by attempting to keep their eyelids open, but when they ran into the embassy they had a lot to say. Hard on their heels came the adults (one moving with the aid of crutches, and one with a bandaged head) and hard on *their* heels came Andrew and Cherg from the desert, and the rest of the Croans, who had been out visiting Kraab's museum and archives. Everyone had a tale to tell, and seemingly wanted to tell it, not least Pookah. "It was the biggest adventure anyone's ever had in the whole world!" Pookah was saying to anyone who would pause a moment to listen. "And I wasn't even frightened."

"You were too. You kept saying don't harm us, don't harm us," said Rihan.

"Well, they didn't," Pookah responded. "They might have if I hadn't spoken!"

"You were both very brave," said Mr Toomali.

"I told them to help me," said Jelani, wondering.

I asked for help, thought Mrs Toomali. Her prayers had actually been directed to the goddess of hearth and home, not without some fear. Would she even be heard, she had wondered, so far from hearth and home? But now a happy thought occurred to her: "I wouldn't let go of my purse! They didn't take my purse!"

Maaveni had escaped with nothing worse than a few bruises, and was able to assist Jelani, who had twisted her ankle. Aleb meanwhile had cut fabric from the car, and from his jacket, in order to bind up Jaan Toomali's bleeding head. The children had largely escaped unscathed, although Sesha had lost her doll.

"They took my doll! I want my doll! Daddy, make them bring back my doll!"

The frots had ignored the cars' inhabitants. They had torn away the doors and parts of the bodywork, gathering up what they wanted from the wreckage, while the released inhabitants scrambled away, grabbing what they could carry. When the frots left Mr Toomali had walked up and down over the trampled sand, feeling certain the doll would not have been taken.

"I'm sorry, Sesha," he said at last.

The little girl was distraught.

It was a long, difficult climb back to the road, with a still groggy Jaan helping Pookah, whose leg cast had in fact helped shield the two boys from any serious injury.

"We may have to burrow into the sand tonight," Mr Toomali said. "It is likely to be cold." He peered up and down the narrow track. The marker stones were fading into the dusk.

Mrs Toomali, who had indeed kept her purse (holding it tight against her body as the frots attended to the car) stood up beside her husband, while the rest lay or sat on the ground. She studied the way the road narrowed with distance, until, as it neared the horizon, it was no more than a pale hairline that blurred into the darkening nothingness.

"Someone is coming," she said at last.

"Daddy, I want another doll," said Sesha.

But the big patrol car, when it pulled up, drove every other thought from her head.

"How many are you? Eight? You're lucky we didn't miss you. We won't be coming back this way today!"

"We're lucky they found us," said Mrs Toomali at the Embassy. "It was their last tour for the day."

She had to speak loudly to be heard over everyone else. She yawned, and looked across at the desperately tired children. Belzic, standing close by, nodded solemnly. He was doling out soup, and listening to everything.

CHAPTER 50

A journey back in time

"No, I don't want compensation, I just want to warn other people!"

"Can we then go over what happened?"

"Yes, if you must. Come in, then."

Belzic was ushered across a soft carpet into a luxurious lounge. His host, who was lean to the point of emaciation, gestured to an enormous armchair, into which Belzic, after some hesitation, subsided. The host however continued to pace up and down. "You see, I hadn't fully taken in what had happened, not until my daughter ... you see, she's an adult really, but a bit innocent, so I wanted to try out one of these ... er ... devices, just to feel comfortable about what she was doing."

"Mr Haan," said Belzic presently, "the company will be most grateful for any information you can give. It will all be kept in the strictest confidence, of course."

"Well, yes, you might as well know—of course I had no idea, no idea at all."

"The devices were tested by six hundred people, but there is always more to learn. If you could just ..."

"Yes, yes, I know. So, ten days ago I joined this group—a colleague of mine from work and six others I did not know, all men. One was the leader. He said, 'think back to when you were a carefree youngster. Think of something really exciting you did. It may have been a birthday party, or an outing. Perhaps you went camping with a group of friends'. So we all put on these things that go right over the head, and cut you off from everything. You're just looking at a white screen. I could soon hear that the others were getting results; there were lots of 'oohs' and 'aahs' going on. I however just had this blank screen." Mr Haan sat for a moment facing Belzic, but then stood up again.

"I'll manage better if I have a drink. Would you—?"

"Why, thank you."

"It's a strong brew. We make it here."

Belzic sat back with his drink, while Haan took a few sips and continued.

"My family was running a farm in Perigaan, which is the most remote of our country's islands. I think things went well to start. We raised animals for wool and also produced garments out of flax—we had a small factory as well as the farm—and there were six men and a couple of women who worked for us. There was no radio at that time, but the boat came every week with mail, or things we'd ordered, and we often had things to send away. Then the war began. Our staff left first. A boat was coming to collect us, and I remember waiting at the wharf, each of us with a big bag of belongings. I had desperately wanted to take our cat, but that wasn't allowed. Anyway, the boat never arrived. When daylight came there were three ships of the enemy on the horizon, and a fourth heading straight towards us.

We took everything back to the house. "We carry on as normal," said my father. "Listen, everyone, be polite, but tell them nothing. Don't talk unless you have to—leave the talking to me." He hid his rifle, two swords and a couple of knives we used on the flax underneath the house.

We were all tired, I guess, but we made an effort to do all the usual chores—gathering fresh vegetables, cooking a meal, feeding the animals. The soldiers came. I think they were very surprised to see a family living on the island. They just stared at us, and I thought at first they were going to leave us alone—I think they did for a day or two, but I don't remember. I was eight years old—in fact I had my eighth birthday on that first day they confronted us..

Now this is what happened when the soldiers came into our house; and this is what I lived through again when I put on that terrible machine.

The family: my father, mother, older brother (fifteen), and young sister (six), and myself, sitting at our round dining room table. We all had drinks, and I had a little cake in front of me. The others were singing my birthday wishes. There was a banging on the door. My father opened it and four men, armed and in uniform, marched straight past him. They did not speak our language but when they gathered round they knew exactly what was happening. One of them slapped me on the back, the other three lining up to shake my hand. They seemed to think the whole event was a huge joke. They spoke to me, and of course I didn't understand a word, but I smiled and nodded.

My mother offered them drink, food. Only then, just like the ending of a film clip, my screen went blank. There I was, looking at myself, my siblings, my parents, and those soldiers, all so close I felt I could reach out and touch them; and there was this feeling of intense familiarity about a scene I had long forgotten. And then another image came: me hiding in the wood behind our little house, watching the soldiers.

One soldier in particular seemed to take a shine to me. He came to visit me every day. He showed me photographs of his family, and a drawing which I guessed represented his son, a young chap like me. He even helped wash the dishes on occasion, since the soldiers would sometimes share our meals. They began to seem like part of our family, going away for a day or two but always coming back. They had a camp set up just past our garden, and I would sometimes walk a little way towards it, just to watch them.

Once we watched a sea battle. It was hard to make out the details, since the soldiers had confiscated our telescope. Nonetheless, there were, far off, clusters of ships, puffs of smoke, and distant reverberations. The whole war seemed like that really, all around us, and yet remote, dreamlike.

Our enemy soldiers, when on the island, seemed to spend a lot of their time lying about, or entertaining themselves with songs.

We seemed to know when they were finally leaving. The whole atmosphere changed, and for the first time I began to feel anxious. I was sitting outdoors in the late afternoon sun, a book in my hand, but not reading. I kept looking towards the beach, and our little landing jetty. My favourite soldier came and sat beside me. He had the drawing of his son with him, which he pointed to, and then he shook my hand, and laughed. Quite suddenly I wanted to impress him in some way. I ran to the back of our house, crawled under it, and came back with my father's rifle. As soon as I showed it to the soldier I knew it was a mistake. He stared at it, his eyes growing big, then he took it away. He was no longer my friend; he was an enemy soldier. I had just wanted to show him that I knew about rifles, and my father was going to teach me how to use this one. It wasn't for war of course, just for shooting birds.

Anyway, my soldier friend went off with it, and then the other three came running, and orders were shouted. In the confusion I ran and hid behind a tree. I watched my mother coming out of the house, and being driven back in, along with the rest of the family. The soldiers searched everywhere. They found the rapiers, and the flax knives. Then I heard strange voices; more soldiers had arrived. I slunk away and hid under sacks in the room we used to store harvested flax. I lay there for a long, long time. I dimly remember that night, and the light from a lantern moving about in the store room, but I was not discovered. When I woke up again it was daylight. All the soldiers had gone, but my father had been shot.

A little later in the day our own soldiers arrived and took us away.

I never told my family what I had done.

Jay Haan paused, and then, since Belzic had made no sound, added: "Your infernal machine brought it all vividly back to me, scene by scene. In particular, I watched my childhood self crawl under the house, and run back, triumphantly, carrying my father's gun. I guess that was when I lost my innocence." He gave a dry laugh.

"So what happened to your life after that?"

"I worked very hard. I wasn't especially bright, but I did well at school. I slogged. I grew up. I started a business. It failed. I started another and was brilliantly successful. I got married. I have a daughter who still lives with me, but my wife and both my sons have nothing to do with me."

"Why is that?"

"I have periods of deep depression—if that's what it is. When I come out of it I go out of my way to annoy people, or I scream, I throw things around. Belzic, I have trouble living with myself—I feel … tormented. I watched your device through to the bitter end—I couldn't stop myself. And then I wrote to your company."

"In your letter you said you were going to kill yourself, and you hoped we all burned in hell."

"That's right."

Belzic looked thoughtfully at his client, who was now shaking, and huddled down in his armchair. It was very quiet in the house, but occasionally there were sounds. A woman went by the window. The daughter? More probably a servant. He caught sight of a man who was probably a gardener. He eased himself out of his own chair and sat on the arm of the one occupied by Haan. He put his hand on Haan's shoulder. "Let it all come out," he said. "Let it all come out."

For a long time Haan shook and sobbed. Then he said, "My poor father."

"Why did he have rapiers under the house?"

"I found them up in a tree. I think they were old fashioned duelling weapons. My father cleaned them up. He said he was going to sell them, or give them to the army. It's funny, you know. He hated war, wanted nothing to do with it; but the army declared him a hero, awarding him a medal which my mother received at a special ceremony. And the rest of the family went along with it. My mother got a state pension."

"And what finally did you get out of it?"

"I was eight years old, for God's sake!"

"That's not what I asked."

Haan said nothing, and presently Belzic continued, speaking very gently. "You are still fighting in that war, did you know? It's time to let go, forgive yourself, surrender."

"I'm not sure I know how."

"Yes you do. Reach out to that little boy. Tell him you love him. Tell him you forgive him. Tell him you understand."

Haan gave a long sigh. He closed his eyes and was still for so long Belzic wondered if he was asleep, but then he said, "Thank you, thank you. I think I want to be alone right now."

CHAPTER 51

Return of the diplomat

"My word, how things have changed! God, has it been ten years?" Jerome gave a quizzical look at his son. "I must say you're looking well."

"So are you, dad." In reality Aleb was shocked at how different his father was from the old photographs, not to mention the recollections of himself as a teenager.

"I'm better than I was. Ah, I take it this is how we travel?"

Having led his father off the wharf Aleb reached out a hand to help him into the donkey cart, but the older man forestalled him, moving nimbly. A wharf attendant hoisted up a large trunk.

"The place is a bit cramped, dad." Aleb looked anxiously at the luggage.

"No problems. They're putting me up at the hall."

"We had a car, dad, only it got wrecked. I'm on a waiting list for another." Aleb cracked a whip, and the donkey set off at a gentle amble.

"Ah, there he is! Aleb, you can't keep him all to yourself!" Two journalists were running up. "Whoa! Stop the cart!"

"You see, I'm a bit of a celebrity," said Mr Foulkes senior.

$$\Omega$$

"I do feel well. Better indeed than I've felt for a long time. As I told you, the buggers kept me locked up in a cell not much bigger than a box. I was one of the hostages, would you believe."

"We heard nothing of that."

Aleb watched his father stretch out on a bed. They were in a little outhouse, away from the bustle of City Hall itself. The journalists had been shooed away. Tea and food had been served, and Aleb, feeling comfortable and lethargic, mirrored his father's posture on the adjacent couch.

"And after I was freed and the buggers mostly shot I was treated as a hero, would you believe. I was no hero, son. Just doing my job, but being in the wrong place at the wrong time."

Aleb contemplated his father's deeply lined face: worry? More like sadness. Not the way a hero ought to look. And did he ever really know him?

"We never really talked. You were always away negotiating," said Aleb.

Foulkes senior said nothing.

"I expect you've come back for a rest," Aleb added hesitantly.

"Not for me, son. Not yet, anyway. I've had a word with your president. It's time to open the country up. Not just to trade, but to immigrants, tourists. Rangolia has been isolated for far too long, and you know what happens? Your minds narrow. You get into a groove, and become fearful of change. All this ridiculous fear of 'outlanders' as they call them. I don't like what is happening to my own country—it's time to let in some fresh air, some novelty, some newness. I must say Qu agrees with me."

"Dad, was I ever an outlander? I mean, was I adopted?"

"What in hell's name makes you think that?"

"It's just one of the things mum said that I still remember. She said I came out of a porthole."

Aleb looked anxiously at his father, who first stared at him, and then began to laugh.

"It's like this, son. Before I met your mother she had quite a career as a sailor. It's the reason we met, actually. At a sailors' dance. Anyway, your mother was much given to using nautical terms for everything, appropriate or not. I can assure you you were born in the usual way."

Aleb too laughed, and then groaned. "Oh my God, what a damn fool I've been, all these years. Anyway, dad, I can see you're exhausted." Aleb took a closer look at his father who appeared to be asleep. He was about to tiptoe out of the room when Foulkes senior spoke again.

"Even when you were a young fellow it was almost impossible to get into the country. To live I mean. There was quite a bit of trade, but there was fear of strangers. Reminds me, I must get to talk to these newcomers—clones are they?"

"Croans, dad."

"Croans. Adventurous travellers, from what I've heard. We need people like them. If this country is going to thrive it needs to share itself with the world."

"Yes, dad."

"Dufalians, did they say? I haven't been there, but I know a bit about that country."

"Would you like an interview? I'm sure I could arrange one. It would make great copy for the Monitor."

Ω

The rumours had been building up for some time: private talks whispered over drinks, or in cars and carriages. The suspicions were build-ing, and at last beginning to coalesce. The main focus was of course the Croans, and all those confidential talks they were having with Qu, with the Dream Hunter folk, and more lately with the gap scientists. There were two main schools of thought: they were an advance party preparing the way for a takeover of Rangolia, or they were (with the help of Qu's govern-ment) planning to turn the entire population into slaves with their minds controlled by the government. The Dream Hunter devices were, of course, an essential part of the conditioning. All who had used them would, at a certain time, be put into a permanent trance, ready to take orders. The frots, meanwhile, would be brought out of the desert, ready to round up and destroy all resistance. There were a number of variants on these ideas: the most intriguing being, perhaps, that the frots were a remnant of the elder people, who, aspiring to live forever, had converted themselves into machines. Neither Qu nor Jelani nor the Croans heard any hint of these thoughts, but one of the main corporations, with aspirations for political influence, knew about them, and decided they might provide useful material. Especially since the said corporation was planning to put forward a candidate for the coming elections.

Maradi Guriang was a young employee of the Groob Trade and Warehouse Company that Durhain the shapeshifter had once managed. He was wildly ambitious and he was in a hurry. The company board decided to groom him for the top job.

CHAPTER 52

The pamphlets

"Jelani, have you seen these?"

Jelani was once more ensconced in Qu's private office. She turned her gaze from the view over Kraab, and examined the flyers.

"They are turning up everywhere, and at this stage nobody seems to know who is responsible."

One of the papers showed a photograph of herself and Qu, both smiling and obviously posing for the cameras. "Why the smiles? What are they really planning?" was the caption beneath the photo. Another missive showed the offices of the Dream Hunter Company, with a transmitter device in the foreground. "Who is keeping a record of your thoughts? Would you wear one of these?" was the caption.

A third showed the Croans in a group, and below that image were pictures of Groose in the desert warding off a couple of frots who were trying to invade the archaeological site. "What are our visitors really up to? Where are they really from? Why are they training the frots?" were the captions. There were others, particularly more aimed at the Dream Hunter Company and their devices. "Do you know what these things do? Has your brain been modified lately?" was a typical caption.

"Well, do we really know what they do? Do you know?" asked Qu.

Jelani took some time to reply.

"Not in detail, but we are finding more out all the time, both from desert records and our own experiments. For example, what we do know is that the brain contains a great many complex maps, and it is chiefly from these that we build a model of the world around us."

"Maps, you say?"

"Yes, the world we experience is really a construct built out of our senses, and very dependent on these maps, along with our memory and our expectations. For example, we take in visual information, and then construct a complete picture. Sometimes the construct is a mistake—we think we see an animal in the woods, but it is just a pattern of shadows. Now, when we look into a headset and visualise something we use the same maps as for actual seeing, so we see what we are visualising, and the effect can be very powerful. The problem of course is, if our impression of a wild animal in the woods is picked up in the headset it will become more and more vivid. We will not necessarily come to realise it was just a pattern of shadows."

"It sounds very strange. I take it that most of this information comes from excavated writings? What harm could your devices do?"

"I would say none at all. You imagine your house, say. The device reads impulses off the visual map you carry inside you, and projects the result on the screen in front of your eyes. You are now in an interactive mode. You see what is already in your visual cortex, thus imprinting the same image over the map you already have. Then with your eyes and your memory working together you build a very clear and precise picture. It may not be identical to the original, but it will be a close copy. Now, all the tests we've done show that memory becomes sharper, thoughts clearer. And there are cases where people were virtually incapable of forming mental images, who were now able to have them."

"And could anyone read those images, I mean, people other than yourself?"

"Of course, you can transmit what you are seeing, and others with receivers, or who are very sensitive, or have an emotional bond to you, can pick up your image. Consider all the children who have been affected. However the transmitters have only a very limited range. Just don't have children in the house when they are being used."

"Thank you, Jelani. So these missives that keep turning up appear to be just mischievous, and not based on any evidence?"

"I certainly think that is the case, ma'am."

"Yes, that fits with my own experiences, but just the same, I'm worried. My agents tell me that opposition to my government is growing, and in particular, opposition to me is growing. I fear that when people look in our direction they construct out of the shadows some threatening monster. Could those machines be affecting our thoughts, our opinions, would you say?"

Jelani gave Qu an incredulous glance. "Ma'am, I don't think you need a machine to get people indulging in malicious gossip. They do it just to get attention. And as for our company, it aims for nothing but good, and I believe that is true for the Croans as well. They have been extremely useful for us, and I believe also for the gap scientists."

After Jelani left her, Qu pondered the situation. She called on security and handed over the leaflets, with a simple message: Find out who is behind these, and when you do find out as much as you can about them, and what they might be planning. Then she lay back in her most comfortable chair, and shut her eyes. Nothing to be done yet, she thought. Just the same, those Croans have been useful, but their days in this country are now definitely numbered.

Ω

Mrs Toomali gazed in astonishment at the glossy paper pinned outside her front door. It must be an important message, she thought, since glossy paper was a rare and expensive item in Groob. She brought it indoors and called her husband, who however laughed when he saw it.

"They're at it again! Don't read it. Throw it away."

But Mrs Toomali was not going to do that. She opened the missive and began to read:

Are you being fooled? Do you really believe our strange visitors, the Croans, have come for our benefit? Come and listen to Maradi Guriang. He will tell you the truth about this government, and the people it supports.

CHAPTER 53

The Founders' Temple

On the seaward side of City Hall there was a temple. It had been built in the early days of the city, when two tribes had come together, after struggling through great hardships, and decided that in unity there would be strength, and a chance of survival. The tribes were known, to themselves and others, as the suubs and the eldrons. They were officially equal in rights and status, but in practice the suub accent was not an advantage for the ambitious in any field. Nevertheless, in the temple they could come together as equals. And the two tribes together constituted the vast majority of the inhabitants of Groob.

The temple itself had become more elaborate over time. There were now wall plaques which told the past history (and mythology) of the tribes, mainly in bold, brightly coloured illustrations. There was also a statue of the tutelary deity of the suubs and eldrons; actually a mysterious merging of two gods which previously had entirely separate appearances and attributes. They were simply two aspects of the one being according to the temple priests, and this was accepted by the majority of visitors. The statue stood on a little stage, and to its right was the ancient 'Book of the Gods', taken from the desert sands in perfect condition many years previously. The book was behind glass, and was propped open at the first pages: on the left hand page was shown a man and a woman weeping, and on the right the same two rejoicing. The images were very faded but unmistakable, and beneath, also faded, were captions in an ancient writing which no-one had as yet deciphered.

The Book of the Gods as a whole was, in fact, indecipherable, and its present elevated status was simply because a Priest of the Temple, in a fit of divine inspiration, had declared that it would one day be read, the people would rejoice, and all the mysteries of the world would be revealed.

A more recent book, on the opposite side of the temple, was the Book of Answers. To use it one meditated or prayed, keeping a question in one's mind, and then went to this book (actually a copy, frequently replaced), opened it at random, and read what was hopefully a suitable response .

It was to consult the Book of Answers that Mrs Toomali had come. She was sitting in the back row of seats, her eyes screwed shut, asking her Goddess of Hearth and Home if she should go listen to Mr Guriang. A voice sounded close to her ear. "Can we help you?"

Mrs Toomali turned, astonished. Perhaps her Goddess had come to her, and in an even more dramatic fashion than before, when she had witnessed that fountain of pure water springing from the dry desert sands.

Euse was standing close by, and with him was Ess, and they were both smiling. Mrs Toomali stared at them, startled, frowning. They were rather small and harmless looking. There was certainly nothing angelic about them. She decided to be candid.

"I was just praying to my goddess, and you rather startled me," she said.

"Could we be the answer to your prayers?"

Mrs Toomali took a longer, more considered look at Euse. He did not, she thought, look very much like the answer to anyone's prayers. However, she handed Euse the missive she had received concerning Maradi Guriang.

Euse perused it slowly, frowning, but finally gave a delighted smile.

"Look at this, Ess. This chap knows all about Croans and he's going to give a talk. Do you know all about Croans?"

"No, master. I didn't think anyone did." Ess looked back and forward between Euse, the pamphlet, and Mrs Toomali. "I do have a working knowledge of the creatures," he added.

"I should hope so, Ess. Now ma'am, you are no doubt wondering about this chap Guriang. So are we. He must be a great sage to know all about Croans."

Mrs Toomali now felt a sense of connection between herself and Euse. "My husband thinks I shouldn't go," she confided.

"What! Not go to a talk by a great sage? You both must certainly go, and so must we. Now, the government gives the two of us a modest pension, so we could pick the two of you up and ensure you get good seats."

So, they were state employees, thought Mrs Toomali. That settled it: the matter was one of state security, and Mr Toomali would certainly be interested.

"I'll talk him round," she promised.

CHAPTER 54

Private views

"Hoots here? Good, that's the four of us."

Mingo put his head in the doorway. "You guys all got your cards?"

"What for?"

Mingo looked scornfully at Harper. "In case we get raided, dummy."

"We won't be raided, Ming. I gave our names when I hired the things," said Harper. "I had to sign saying we're all over eighteen."

Mingo and Harper were brothers, with Harper, a year and a half older, nearing twenty, and considering himself a good deal smarter than Ming. Along with Hoots and Jingo, the group privately regarded themselves as the 'gang of four', although there were some tensions among them.

"The government says they're getting tougher," contributed Jingo.

The four were in a garden shed on Jingo's family's property, a lavish place, complete with an artificial lake, as befitting the prosperity of the owners. "The lake was just a fluke," Jingo would say proudly to anyone who would listen. I was digging, and the water just sprang out of the ground. Jingo had taken pains to decorate the shed with Dream Hunter posters: ('Change your mind—change your world' and 'Your dreams are your passport to great achievements'), along with a few small tables and comfortable chairs purloined from the house. Jingo now turned from the lake and made an expansive gesture with his hands. "Take your seats, guys, I've got the gadgets right here." With the air of a conjuror he opened the box Harper had provided and brought out three D2 receiving devices.

"Hey, there's four of us!" said Ming.

Jingo brought out the transmitter. "Who wants to go first?"

"Me!" said Mingo.

"Okay, who do you want to think about?"

"Qu," said Mingo.

"Qu? You're crazy! She'd eat you alive!"

"No, she's cool."

"But the opinion of the other three was decidedly against Qu."

"How about Jelani?" said Hoots.

"Almost as bad," said Harper. "Hard as nails, I bet."

"What about one of the teachers?" said Mingo, but this was met by frowns and head shaking.

"There's a girl down the road," said Jingo. "She's kind of cute. I think about her a lot, but she's kind of private." The others nodded sympathetically. The girl down the road just wouldn't be suitable for group viewing.

"I know," said Harper, "we'll just invent somebody."

This was agreed with enthusiasm. "Don't spend too long, anyone," said Harper. "We'll all want a go with this." He looked impatiently at Mingo, who was tuning the transmitter to match his own brain patterns.

Finally, Mingo sat back, transmitting, and soon had a big smile on his face. The other faces were all so intensely concentrated on their receivers that nobody heard the knocking on the door. At length Jingo pulled off his device and went to open it. A cheerful face confronted him.

"Just the four of you, I see," said the cheerful face, looking over Jingo's shoulder at the easy chairs, the little tables, the oil lamp swinging gently, and three lads with their heads buried in the surreal Dream Hunter gadgetry. "That's good. ... No, no need to show me your cards. I'm sure you are all very upstanding citizens."

The time went quickly for the little group, and as they packed up Mingo couldn't resist a passing shot at his brother.

"See, we were raided."

"We were not," said Harper. Although, in fact, he had had a moment's alarm, since he had forgotten to bring the cards along with him.

Ω

Solaria had arranged her viewing in the front parlour, in a house a little less lavish than Jingo's, but in the same elite area of West Kraab. "Oh, do come in," she said as, one at a time, four young women from the same college class entered, and were handed their receiving sets along with iced sweets, specially prepared. "I'm going to start with a few memories of our last holiday. Watch out for the frots. The tour guide gave us little pieces of metal. We stood on a platform and threw them down."

Solaria's well planned evening went very smoothly and happily until the fourth young miss had the transmitter.

"What!" the others exclaimed. "Foli? He's over forty, he's ancient!"

"He's cool," said Kuran defiantly. "Anyway, I'm going to have him on my machine." She proceeded to do so, while the others ogled into their receivers.

"Kuran, how dare you?" Solaria finally exclaimed.

"Easy," said Kuran, "you just let yourself go."

Ω

Public speech

At a meeting not a mile away from Solaria's house, Maradi Guriang was letting himself go, was in fact in full oratorical flight. "What of our young people who have these dangerous machines? Don't you know that their brains are being sucked away? Their very capacity to think for themselves?

They are going to be easy prey for our new totalitarian regime, oh, such easy prey! And it's not as though any of us will gain any privileges from this new regime. Oh no! We are simply going to be an addition to the Five Kingdoms."

Mrs Toomali sat in the back row of the hall, along with her husband, Euse, Ess, Cherg and Groose. The Croans were now known by sight to many in Kraab, and for this reason had stayed in the shadows while waiting for the hall to open, and then moved quickly to the rear seats. Mr Toomali, at least, was looking suspiciously at Euse as the talk continued.

"Those mysterious visitors of ours, do you really believe them? Don't you know they are preparing the way? The Dream Hunter Company is just one of their tools, planned years in advance. The frots are another: at this very time they are being trained for their mission, to suppress any resistance. And digging in the desert! Nothing they find will be to the peoples' advantage. But not even that is the real threat. Not even that!" Guriang paused a moment for effect, and continued: "The greatest threat of all is this present government, now increasingly brainwashed by these creatures, these Croans and the Dream Hunter tools they are using on us."

"Hear! Hear!" shouted Euse. Groose glared at him, but Mr Toomali, who had been giving him puzzled looks for some time, now turned away. Ess continued recording the performance.

"Brothers and sisters, are we going to let these things happen?"

"No!!" roared the crowd. "Turn them out!" someone shouted. Ess continued to record, now standing on a chair and panning his equipment around the room.

"See, we have reporters here," Guriang continued. "You are welcome. Let the people know what is happening!" Euse stood up beside Ess and bowed. Groose tugged at him so that he almost fell.

"You're welcome to get yourself into trouble, but I'm not joining you," Groose growled. The four Croans made an unobtrusive exit.

Also leaving at this time was Qu's own security agent, Cavron. He made a hasty trip to City Hall. He followed up his report to Qu with a suggestion: "Ma'am, would it not be wise to send the Croans away immediately?"

"Send them away? No, Cavron, that wouldn't save us, and besides, I don't think we should exaggerate the importance of this gathering. I believe the Croans are still very popular, apart from being useful to us in other ways. So, what I want from you are the names of the key players in this little absurd drama, and, most importantly, who is behind it."

"Behind it, ma'am?"

"Yes, Cavron. In other words, who is financing it. It will be one of the big companies. Off you go. Find out everything you can, and then we shall have a better idea how to deal with it."

"Yes, ma'am, certainly, leave it to me."

CHAPTER 55

The opposition

"Well, Mr T, aren't you glad I dragged you along?"

"I admit it, Mrs T. I didn't like it, but it's important to know what is going on."

Jaan opened the front door of the Toomali residence as he spoke, and was confronted by the babysitter putting a finger to her lips. "They've all had a busy time and they're falling off to sleep," she said.

In fact Jaan had felt exasperated for the entire length of Guriang's rant, wanting either to run out or jump up and challenge the man on most of the assertions he was making. "There is no doubt," he continued to his wife, now in a whisper, "if you think yourself the next thing to God, and make all your pronouncements as if you are revealing sacred truths, you'll get plenty of followers."

"Next to God?" Mrs T queried, for she had not quite caught up with her husband, "which god are you talking about?"

"It doesn't matter, Mrs T. All of them, if you like. I'm just saying that nobody should be allowed to make claims like that unless they can back them up."

Mrs Toomali was silent. What if he was truly inspired, she was wondering. That would surely be like being next to God. Instead of making such a suggestion (which she knew would be met with outrage, and probably wake the children) she merely said, "What time would you like your supper, dear? Or should we go somewhere? It's a late night downtown, and you're not on call until tomorrow morning."

"You are right, my sweet, I'm not on call until the morning, and we have the sitter booked for another hour. Ah, here they are now. They might like to come with us." 'They' referred to Aleb and Jelani. Jelani had been working late, but Aleb had attended Guriang's meeting, coming into the hall with his scarf wrapped around his face (it was a cold evening) and intending to provide a report for the Croans. He had observed Euse and the others arrive, and was greatly astonished at their audacity. Now he was with Jelani, in the newly purchased car, and about to enter the Toomali residence, where they had left their children. "I'm just amazed at them. Euse was even standing up on a chair and yelling out encouragement to the guy."

"Probably the safest approach," said Jelani. "If they'd tried to hide, someone might have spotted them."

The two made their way into the house. "I hope my two behaved themselves?" said Jelani.

"Just fine," said the sitter. "The girls were making houses all afternoon. The boys? I don't know much about boys' play. I think it was some fantasy game."

"Our meeting was all about pure fantasy," said Mr T drily. "Wouldn't you agree, Aleb?"

Ω

"You sure told it like it is, Mr Guriang," said the last of the admirers. The hall was now closed for the night, and Maradi Guriang had been escorted to a car.

"Give me a drink, Buzz, I'm dry as dry," said Maradi Guriang.

"That was all right as a start, I suppose, but you need somewhere much bigger," said the driver as they moved off.

"Then it's got to be outside," said Guriang. "Outside, and daytime, and I'll need a good speaking trumpet. It's high time they dug up something decent out of the desert."

Elsewhere, little groups were gathering in bars, cafes and restaurants. The desert was a frequent topic, as in the following:

"I reckon he's right, you know. They should leave well enough alone."

"Mind you, they were a clever lot, those elders."

"Too clever! And look where it got them!"

The speakers were a young soldier and an old carpenter.

"Well, we could learn something," said the soldier.

"Oh yes, that's what I think, and that's just what we don't want. Who knows what's buried under all that sand? Just think, all those lovely cities and gardens and everything they were supposed to have had, all gone! That's what comes from being too clever."

"The gods don't want you to pry, that's what I think," said the publican, joining in.

"Exactly. They disturbed something down there, and if we go on digging ..."

"That's just superstition," said the soldier.

"Superstition is it?" said the publican. "And the desert—is that superstition?"

"All right, what should we do about these Croans?" said the soldier, calling them back to the main topic of the meeting."

"Get rid of them of course, and get rid of Qu as well," said the publican. "If we don't get rid of her she'll only bring in someone else."

"All right, how do we do that?" said the soldier. "Have either of you two got a vote?"

"No, but we can talk to those who have," said the publican. "And if they don't listen to us we boycott their shops and their businesses. That's how democracy works. You find out who owns what and you get them where it hurts—in the pocket."

The carpenter nodded. "I already know where I'll be buying my next lot of timber and tools," he said. "We'll have those Croans out of here in next to no time."

CHAPTER 56

The break-in

"Well, Euse, I hope you're pleased with yourself."

"Actually, Groose, I am, and I'm sure Ess had taken some excellent recordings. It was a wonderful meeting, and it shows us how quick people are to latch on to any kind of nonsense when they're feeling anxious."

The Croans were back at the Embassy, and enjoying a soup delivered by Belzic, who, after some trial and error, had discovered some culinary creations that were acceptable to all, including Andrew.

Belzic looked now at Andrew. "You're putting on weight at last. Why, you're almost back to the way you were during your earth days."

"I hope that is a compliment, Belzic."

"Absolutely. You were almost fading away on the ship."

"Well, thank you. The soup is excellent. I hope you have some more." He nodded to the door, where Schyl and Cherg were arriving from the desert, Erg still with traces of sand on his clothes.

"Schyl," said Groose, "do you think you could get Euse to listen to reason?"

"Nobody ever has yet. Why do you expect that miracle from me?"

"Euse," said Cherg, ignoring Groose, "just about everyone I meet now looks anxious. Why do you suppose people are feeling anxious?"

"It's because of what you are doing, taking dangerous secrets out of the desert," said Euse. "And there's no need to take half the desert indoors with you."

"Schyl," said Groose, persevering, "we need an escape plan and you need to get ready to overrule Euse. If the signs are what I think they are, it could even be quite soon."

"Aleb told me that feeling anxious is a seasonal thing," said Andrew, anxious himself to contribute to the conversation. "It's closely tied to the waxing of that second moon, Rubilis."

"Well, we're almost out of that season now," said Groose crossly, "and the anxiety, if that's what it is, is translating into action. I know we still have a following, especially among Qu's devotees, but there are plenty now who glare at us, and tell us to go home. I tell you they're going to do something, and it will be sooner rather than later, so don't think we're going to be safe in this building, Euse."

"That, Groose, is what makes it all so interesting. We have plenty of devotees ourselves, and we can relocate if we need to. Besides, I want to see a real crisis, and I still want to track down those portals. I'm now almost certain they exist."

$$\Omega$$

Maradi Guriang's headquarters were an easy half hour horse ride away from City Hall, and Guriang was there now, eating a sizeable meal, and in between mouthfuls talking to his committee.

"This is good ... yes, more of that goulash, whatever it is, and the seaweed salad if you please ... no, Buzz, no violence, not at this stage of the game, although breaking into the Embassy could be a good move ... more of the root vegetables, please ... yes, not by us, of course ... by professional burglars while we are miles away, talking to our followers ... yes, more of that green stuff ... Buzz, that's not so important, because what matters more now is more dirt ... dig it up or manufacture it ... doesn't matter which."

"Chief, there are some who say the Croans came out of the stars."

"Yeah? We want to win over the majority, not the totally dumb credulous ones. Find something that will stick, Buzz"

"Chief, I think I can do exactly that."

"Good man. Go to it, Buzz, go to it."

Two days later the Croans returned from the desert to find the front door of their Embassy building had been forced open and the place ransacked. All cupboards and drawers had been emptied out onto the floor, and a number of items, which would have been valuable to the opposition, had been unintelligible to the burglars, and lay in a heap along with the more prosaic food, clothing, and all other household flotsam.

"Yes, Groose, before you say anything, there is nothing here that troubles me unduly."

"Maybe not, Mr Science Officer, but it scares hell out of me." Groose emptied a chair of the crockery that had tumbled onto it, and sat, morosely staring at the muddle around him. Ess and Cherg, meanwhile, were darting about, gathering and sorting.

"Not much broken, master," said Ess cheerfully.

"No, it wasn't a serious burglary, Ess—more of a warning."

"And are you going to take it seriously, Euse?" Groose had not moved from his chair.

"I am," said Schyl, who had just arrived. "I take anything seriously if the crew or the ship are in danger. Groose, I authorise you to make an escape plan. If Euse gives you any trouble let me know."

Groose brightened. "Thank you, captain. Grice, find out what's happening with the ship. Say you need to inspect it, and check it over for a voyage. Euse, contact Qu and say we plan to leave in another ten days."

"Ten days! That's outrageous, Groose. This is a perfect time for us to make a study of how a society can divide itself when its stresses come to a head."

"Point taken, Science Officer. And if they come to a head in a great hurry we leave in a great hurry. If you and Ess wish to stay and collect data the rest of us will leave you to it."

The following day the *Groob Newsflash* came out with a big story that a young sleuth had put together with the help of Maradi Guriang. The story was paired with a photograph of a very pleased Euse standing in the desert and holding up an object that looked rather like a decapitated head with a cluster of trailing wires and tubes. In the background stood a smiling Qu. Euse was quoted as saying the following: *These brain monitoring and control devices are an enormously significant advance for your country, and we look forward to performing extensive experiments.*

To be fair, Euse was speaking to scientists about the D2 (the photograph was unrelated) and no political message was intended. Nonetheless, the circulation of Groob Newsflash tripled overnight, and thousands flocked to listen to Maradi Guriang.

"I think you will soon have all the data you want, Euse," said Schyl.

There was certainly not long to wait. The following day two protest groups clashed: one group carried banners with legends such as, 'Dream Hunters forever' and the other, who were more militantly and threateningly armed, (although somewhat diverse and muddled in their objectives) proclaimed on their placards: Throw out Qu, Cast out the Croans, Down with Dream Hunters.

CHAPTER 57

The mob attacks

The first calamity, as the good citizens of Groob were in time to call it, came at the midpoint of the season. Six young women were discovered in a garden shed. All were dead in what appeared to be a suicide pact. All were just eighteen years old, and none were considered to have been depressed or emotionally troubled. According to the early news reports they were sitting at a table on which was laid out a collection of Dream Hunter equipment.

Two days later a mob surrounded the Dreamland offices. They smashed the vehicles in the yard, broke down the door and rampaged up the stairs (the lift was held against them). Jelani and Umus were in the building, along with two technicians. Jelani had called the police as soon as the mob began to gather, and shortly after making that call she saw a delivery vehicle drive up and be overturned, with the injured driver being hauled out and beaten. Jelani made a further urgent call as the downstairs doors were being smashed open.

However the value of having one's offices in an ancient fort was soon apparent to the besieged staff, since the stairs made a tight, steep curve as the top was neared, and Dreamland Security had lowered several very large stones into place. These were removable from below only at the cost of grievous bodily harm to the besiegers.

The police contingent, with the support of the army, arrested a couple of dozen rioters that they found within the building, while the injured driver was rushed to hospital. The staff were unharmed and unmolested, with the remaining rioters retreating from the scene. The other offices, all empty at the time of the invasion, were untouched.

Aleb arrived while the invasion was happening. He was terrified for Jelani even as he took note of as much detail as possible, along with a number of photographs. He was driving his newly purchased car, and having pulled in with rash closeness to the mob had it attacked even as he was taking photographs. He drove Jelani quickly away as soon as she could be released. She sat beside him crying quietly into a handkerchief.

Aleb drove the car out of Kraab and up into the hills, stopping near the ancient watchtower. They were in sunshine, but dark clouds threw their shadows over Kraab, and much of the sea. Aleb remained silent, and the two of them gazed out over the empty ocean. A sharp dark line defined the horizon.

"I know what you're going to say," said Jelani presently. "But I'm not giving up, not now, not after all I've done, after all we've done. I won't let them win. I won't! I won't!"

Aleb said nothing. He watched the darkness deepen around them. Presently he saw flashes of lightning flickering all around the hills. The storm was rushing towards them. A sudden wind gust shook the car, and the deluge began. He turned the car and drove quickly downhill, half skidding on the dirt roads, and reaching home to find two unperturbed children but a frightened babysitter.

"There was a crowd of them and they were holding two big signs," she said. "It was horrible! I told them you weren't here, but they looked as though they didn't believe me, but then the heavy rain started and they went away."

"Thank God for the heavy rain," said Aleb.

"Come on, Rihan, Holanna, we're going away."

"Now?" said Holanna.

"Yes, now. Get your pyjamas and warm coats. Aleb, can you help me gather up some essentials?"

The crowd who had threatened Jelani had in fact been diverted by a more significant event, brought to them post haste by a messenger on a horse: the release from prison of Maradi Guriang. He had been involved in a fight with a policeman and was incarcerated for a few days in order, as the judge put it, to "cool off". The issue was really quite unrelated to any of the current areas of resentment, but nonetheless Maradi Guriang was being treated as a hero. Word spread quickly and the frustrated mob, retreating from Aleb's house and the Dream Hunter offices, rallied around the released prisoner. Later photographs showed him being carried aloft on shoulders through the rain.

Ω

"Interesting," said Euse the following day. "The focus now is all on the Dream Hunter folk. Jelani has gone into hiding, and nobody knows where she is; and if you go looking for a D2 or a D3 you'll have a job to find a single one."

"Don't count on your safety," said Groose. "In another month these folk have their elections, and your friend Maradi Guriang is going to challenge Qu for the office of president. Belzic here has found out all about it."

The days began late at the embassy, since away from the ship the Croans needed to periodically relieve themselves of their exoskeletons and bathe for an hour in salt water; and bathing facilities in the embassy were rather limited.

Right now Belzic and Andrew were bringing in plates of the overdue breakfast.

"At last," said Euse, eyeing the food. "We would have been ready a lot earlier if Schyl and Grice hadn't taken over the bathroom, with Grice barricading the door."

"We would have been ready a lot earlier if you hadn't taken over the bathroom and spent an hour fiddling with your exoskeleton," Grice retorted.

"Belzic," said Groose, getting back to the point, "tell us about the election."

"It's quite basic, really," said Belzic, taking up his bowl and sitting down to eat, "there are five hundred allowed to vote. To get a seat you have to pass an exam, and either pay or be sponsored by some company. The seats are auctioned in lots of five, with no more than four lots allowed per company. Or you can invest in one lot and on-sell the seats individually."

"So it's a rich person's game," said Ess.

"Or rich company. The people seem to be happy with it."

"We may not be," said Groose. "If this new chap Maradi Guriang gets in he'll have us all arrested."

"Could that happen?"

"Yes, Euse. If Guriang brings in his own heads of police and security it would be easy for them to lock us up, at least for a week or two. Eventually they'd probably have to either let us go, change the law, or charge us with conspiracy against the state."

"Meaning?"

"If we were convicted of that they'd kill us. You'd better hurry up and find those portals, Euse."

CHAPTER 58

Qu takes council

"It's a shame we can't blame that chap," said Qu. She was still tired after a late, uneasy night, and was feeling both anxious and irritable.

"Maradi Guriang? No, ma'am, we can't, unfortunately. He is never directly involved."

"Just the same, it's his inflammatory speeches that do the damage."

Apart from the attack on the Dream Hunter office, there had been various other incidents, and Guriang was always careful to be somewhere else.

Qu had just finished an early morning consultation with her security staff, and was now talking over various issues with her PA. Rain in fact had a heap of her own work waiting: letters and petitions to the government, complaints, threats, offers of assistance, cranks expounding 'ultimate solutions' and much else. And there was Jelani. Qu urgently wanted her to contact Jelani, but Jelani was not available, unable to be reached.

"God, Rain, I just try and do what's best for the country, and now you have idiots like Guriang stirring things up, as if they weren't bad enough."

Qu had her head down, and to Rain's astonished gaze she appeared to be weeping. She passed over her handkerchief, and tentatively laid a hand on her chief's shoulder.

"Oh, thank you Rain. It was just a bit of grit in my eye. It's gone now."

Rain removed her hand and took back the hanky. It occurred to her she had not previously ever touched her boss.

"I think things will settle down more today," she said.

"I need to sound people out, Rain, gauge the mood of the crowd," said Qu. "It's horrible that this is happening now, right when I have a campaign to run."

"I think, ma'am, that the real problem is the desert. A lot of people are saying that the digging should stop, that we should just live the way we are."

"Yes, Rain, and those are usually the ones quickest to demand access to the things we do pull out," said Qu. "Get me security again. If they can't find Jelani we'll try Umus, or even Hamul." Qu sighed, shuffled some papers around on her desk. She was beginning to feel, for the first time in years, something other than absolute confidence.

"You tell me people are afraid of technology? Give me technology any day, Rain. People are the real problem."

"I think they're mostly afraid of what might come out of the desert in the future, ma'am, and I often hear them say that something or other is just not natural. And of course they're always afraid of the frots. There was the case where that man and his children were killed."

"Yes, Rain, and that's because the father responded to the frots by threatening them. Hell, if they'd simply remained calm, or even requested help, there would have been a very different outcome. Rain, they are simply machines. They are predictable. When I was a little girl I spent a year with robots, all alone. They were my make believe guardians, and I had some of the happiest times of my life with them. The only times I was really afraid was when humans came looking for me, and of course I was hunted down in the end—hunted down, Rain, like a wild animal! And then what happened? I was put with a group of kiddies I was told would be 'like me'. They were nothing of the kind. None had been in isolation for a year, and guess what? They all regarded me as a freak, children and staff alike. Oh, how I wanted to be back with my robots."

"You've come a long way, ma'am."

"Yes indeed. And Rain, there is nothing to fear from the desert, nothing to fear from the frots. The big challenge is people, and especially their fear. If I knew how to deal with that fear I'd be happy indeed."

Rain smiled, and then turned to the ringing phone.

"Good news, ma'am. The Dream Hunters' management are going to meet at Hamul's place, one hour from now."

"What, the board?"

"No, just Jelani, Aleb, Umus and Hamul."

$$\Omega$$

When the two pulled up at Hamul's residence, Umus had already arrived, with Jelani and Aleb pulling into the drive shortly after.

Qu entered Hamul's lounge calm and relaxed, without any hint of her earlier distress. She took immediate charge of the situation. Hamul, Jelani and Aleb were each to speak of their experiences over the last few days, and then make a suggestion or recommendation of the future direction of the company. Qu then followed with her own suggestions. "Of course you will be free to take a different path, provided it doesn't endanger life or property," said Qu.

"I had largely been left alone," began Hamul, "but that changed two days ago, when I had filth thrown on my lawn and over my front windows. It seemed a bit rich, considering I've had no say in the company for a good long while. I confess I was confused—was there some neighbour I had offended?"

Qu simply listened, hands together, fingers interlaced, eyes half closed, while Rain took notes. The time passed quickly, and finally, as evening drew in, Jelani finished speaking, and Qu made her assessment.

"The main factor behind all this is fear, and how it is being manipulated by certain unsavoury characters. Therefore, we take fear away, as much as possible with good information, and where that doesn't serve by physical removal. Now, good information: Umus, get the latest figures out as soon as you can: those who've been distressed or harmed by the devices compared with those who say they've been helped. As for that tragic suicide pact with those six teenage girls, I understand the devices were never even used by them?"

"No ma'am," said Jelani, "they met in a shed which was shared with another group. I understand one of the girls had a rather unhealthy, hypnotic effect on the other five. They did leave a notebook, I believe."

"Aleb, can you follow this up? Get hold of that book if you can. Find out if the forensic people have finished investigating, and see what you can wheedle out of them. I know they tend to clam up and talk about privacy issues, but this is important. If the opposition keeps telling lies we challenge them. If necessary we threaten them with legal action. Now, physical removal is our second strategy. Get the devices out of shops so people aren't reminded of them. Buy them back, and then sell through mail or telephone orders. That leaves the offices—a very visible reminder. Any suggestions?"

"I've been thinking of that," said Umus. "A lot of the work can simply be carried out in people's homes. We still need a factory of sorts, but does it need to be on the mainland?"

"Your factory is in Folcorn, isn't it? Has it been threatened?"

"Not until recently. A threatening notice was put on the door three days ago, and the staff are very upset of course. We're in the process of moving everything to Kraab."

"Where it is even more vulnerable. Where else would you suggest it goes, Umus?"

"Well, Skerron is only a half day's sail away, and it's not visited much. There's not a lot to do or see, and landing there can be difficult. I think there are only a couple of small buildings, but there is timber on Skerron, and stone. I think we could build a factory and have it working in a few months."

"Jelani, what do you think of that idea?"

"Ma'am, I think it could be just the answer. We do the design work here, and the production at Skerron. The finished products could be stored anywhere. They don't take up a lot of room, and they don't need special care."

"I think the four of you had better take a little trip, and the sooner the better," said Qu. "I do share your optimism about the devices, but we keep them discreet from now on."

The four exchanged glances.

"I'd better stay in the office," said Umus.

"I think just Aleb and myself to begin with," Jelani said firmly, and then turned to Qu.

"Ma'am, a lot of people have radios now. You could address all of Rangolia, or at least the mainland."

"And the outlying islands, indeed I could. Thank you, Jelani, I certainly could, and I have been considering doing so. How would you like to be my speech writer?"

"Well ma'am, I'll certainly try."

CHAPTER 59

The death pact

Aleb's first thought was, what a dreary place. The shed had been stripped of everything except a large wooden table that sat firmly in the middle. There was one dirty, cracked glass window, and sacking tacked over the other holes that would once have held glass.

"That was where they sat," said the man from forensics, indicating the table. "Three on this side, one on the far side, and one at each end. Absolutely symmetrical. The chairs were quite spaced out, you know. It was quite a formal arrangement."

"And the Dream Hunter devices, where were they?"

"The headsets were packed neatly on a little side table just over here. We checked them and we're certain they were never used by this group. All very tidy, though. They'd even swept the floor."

"So it was all very … formal." Aleb tried to get his head around the formal arrangement as he pictured it. "I thought they would have been, you know, closer together."

The forensics man said nothing.

"They all took poison, did they?"

"Chloroform soaked rags over the nose and mouth, and tight-fitting bags over the head. They tell me there are worse ways to go."

"But they were only eighteen!"

The forensics man turned abruptly away. He reached into a bag and turned to look at Aleb one more time. "Here's the book. Take it to her lady-ship, or wherever it needs to go. None of the families want it."

Aleb returned to his house. His footsteps echoed in the empty rooms. Holanna had left a picture for him, 'our house', a tall thin box with four stick figures in front. The children though were with their father, and with 'auntie', while Jelani was at the office, or possibly in the desert. He made himself some food, a drink, and sat, toying with the notebook but not opening it. It was the first time in a long while, he considered, that he had a quiet, solitary moment, without interruptions and with nothing urgent confronting him. Presently, he opened the book, turned to the last page, and scanned the final two sentences.

There is nothing more to be said. What we leave to the world now is our silence.

There followed six signatures, all, obviously, their cult names. Two signatures were rather childlike, and it was these that brought tears to his eyes.

He decided it would take a full two hours to read—not something that 'her ladyship' would be prepared to spend time on. He would need to work through it and provide some sort of report. At least, he would be able to assure Qu that the Dream Hunter Company was not in any way involved.

He began reading from the front.

I, Rader Mafeo, begin my private journal on day four of the water season.

The High Priestess has agreed to admit me, since I will be eighteen in two weeks! There will be an initiation to begin with. I am squeamish about blood, but I am told there is nothing to it. We each contribute six drops into a saucer, it is mixed, and the High Priestess will daub a cross on my forehead. I will join the four already initiated.

Day seven: HP says that there will be no more members, that any more would be dangerous. Information could be leaked.

There followed a list of numbers and letters which Aleb could make nothing of. He decided they were probably memory prompts for the information that was 'not to be leaked'.

He skipped over a couple of pages.

Day twelve: Two days to go!

HP came to me while I was sunbathing. She kissed me on the lips, lay down beside me and stroked my hair. She told me I was a free spirit, that I was a pure soul. I asked her if we could be together on an island somewhere, but she told me this couldn't be. Every island worth living on gets visited, she said, and we could get taken away, killed, or made into slaves. We would always be afraid, always watching the ocean. HP then pointed up into the sky. Did I see that blue patch? And doesn't it give a sense of freedom to see clear skies, even if just a tiny patch of them? I said it did. She told me then that we would be going to the Pure Land, where there would be no more clouds, or mist, or storms. No more guessing games.

Day fourteen: It was easy! I was wearing my little white dress and my gym shoes, my face carefully washed and free of any make-up. I was shaking, and frightened I would need to run out somewhere to pee. The four who were already members came in and surrounded me. The tall brunette put an arm round my shoulder and just said 'It will be all right'. And it was.

(I am not to write down names.)

Day 16: Mother was at it again. Less time in books, more fresh air, get some exercise, get some colour in your cheeks, girl! God, I could speak her lines for her. And then there is always the 'What's wrong with Grant?' plea. He's a nice boy, and you should be socialising more. I don't say, get serious with him, but there's no harm in going out once in a while … etc. etc. I had forgotten to remove my 'Pure Land' badge, and she asked me what it was. I said it was just a girls' club, and she seemed satisfied with that. I must be careful about keeping this book hidden.

Day 20: More trouble with Grant. He keeps trying to make conversation that he imagines will please me, and it really freaks me out.

Day 22: Finished my last school assignment. Subject: On truth and mediocrity in Groob. Really pleased with it. Got a note from the Head saying I could get advanced studies paid for. Even said, 'We could make a sociology professor out of you'. Yuk! We found a new meeting location: an old shed, also used by one of those mad dream hunter groups, but fortunately on different days. HP says the Great Day is getting closer.

Day 24: My last entry. HP says too dangerous to put things in writing, but she will keep it for all of us to write something on the last day.

Aleb frowned. There was a lot more writing in a different hand, but it appeared to all be in code. He flipped over the pages, and found roughly drawn maps, one labelled 'Pure Land'. There were directions 'for the traveller on approaching the Pure Land' and various statements 'to be made to the Gatekeeper'. Aleb's sense of sadness intensified. It appeared that these girls, or perhaps 'HP' alone, had constructed a whole mythology, an 'escape' mythology, for their own benefit. He came across what appeared to be an address to the acolytes:

If you stay you will be married off, and you will have a husband to serve, and later children will come. All of your free, pure soul will be extinguished. You will have no identity of your own. You will just be Jaan's husband, Baat's mother, and you will be those things all day, every day. You will love your husband and your children, because there is no way you could do otherwise. You will have no choice but to love. And if you choose not to marry? Do not expect that way to be easy.

Aleb passed over the rest of the address, not wishing to know more about the unmarried. He was looking for something, he wasn't sure what, that would give him more insights into the mysterious HP. None of the names had been released, apart from Rader's (an oversight, he guessed) and he was not inclined to delve. He did, however, come across the text of what he presumed was the final address of the mysterious High Priestess:

I have chosen the five of you for the purity of your souls, and your capacity to receive the truth, for which no adult is ever likely to be capable. And yet the truth is so simple: It is joy. Not wealth, not power, not property, not influence, not admiration from your neighbours. It is simply joy. It is the only thing you really need to know: to be blissfully happy. And that happiness depends on very little from the outside world: a little food, a little clothing, a little shelter, and the ability to see the world clearly, not swathed in the mists of ignorance. We are going now to that beautiful place, where all this is possible.

There was one more bit in Rader's hand:

Today is the day! The season of air reaches its climax and melds with the soon to begin season of fire, so they say. How fitting that we should be heading for the Pure Land above us! I am so happy!!

CHAPTER 60

Advice from Belzic

"Rain, stay with me please. I've got Belzic coming, away from the others, and I want to pick his brains."

"I must say you're looking bright this morning, ma'am."

"Yes Rain, I think we can win this one." Qu rubbed her hands. "Thirty-five more days to go—I can't wait."

Qu wandered to her favourite spot, the big picture window overlooking the city. "We're nearly at the end of the season, and I see that preparations for the fire festival are already under way. By tradition we're supposed to let go of something next season. Are you letting go of anything Rain?"

"No ma'am." Rain took her drink over to a side table. "I'll just sit in the background, ma'am, take a few notes?"

"I think that would be best. Ah, here the man comes. Come in, come in Belzic. It's good to see you. Take a seat."

Belzic came in, draped his jacket over a chair, turned to Qu, gave his short, stiff little bow, and sat facing her.

"Belzic, I have watched you watching everyone and everything, saying little but sizing everything up. I think you have a very shrewd mind." Qu paused, weighing her words. "I would appreciate an honest assessment from you. You have made contact with a wide range of people, I would think, whereas I mostly hear from devoted fans or virulent opposition. So, we have come now to the time when campaigning begins in earnest. What do you think my chances are at the coming election?"

Belzic frowned, and took a long pause. "You are asking a lot of me, ma'am, and all I have to go on is what the surveys say: that Rangolia is fairly equally divided in its allegiance between you and Guriang. Do the voters really see it that way? I couldn't tell you."

"Come now, Belzic. You have more insights than most. Do tell me your thoughts."

Belzic paused, and turned his gaze to the big window. "I think," he said at length, "if you stand on a confidence vote you will probably win narrowly. On the other hand, if you decide to resign and compete on an equal footing with the opposition you are likely to get a better win. The risk is, if you lose on the confidence vote you are more likely to lose on the second vote. It's a matter of psychology."

"Thank you, Belzic, you certainly have gone into the matter. I must admit I certainly hadn't considered resigning. What do you advise?"

"Ma'am, I don't want to advise you."

"Belzic, I trust you, I trust your advice, and I think it would be best for you visitors if I was to win. I know there is dissatisfaction in the streets now about my government, and I want to turn it around over the coming days, so I would welcome any advice."

"I'm sure you are right about the dissatisfaction, but as for advice, I don't give it lightly. I do think you have a good chance, whichever option you take." Belzic paused, and frowned in thought. "There are just five hundred votes to be cast, are there not?"

"Yes, but most of them are sponsored. They must do what they are told." Qu smiled. "The sponsors naturally support whoever they think will best support their interests."

"In which case you should definitely win, since your policies sound a lot more progressive."

"If only it was that simple." Qu smiled. "Thank you for your confidence anyway, Belzic." She looked at him thoughtfully. "Who are you? I mean, what were you doing before you came here?"

"I was a fashion designer." Belzic turned fully to the window and looked out over Kraab. "I've done many things, but nothing for long." He turned back to face Qu. "I guess I've picked up a lot of knowledge, and I can see the direction in which a country is heading."

"This country? Do tell me."

"I think you're on a knife edge, and could go either way."

"Belzic, please explain!"

"I'll just say that many countries that develop an advanced technology end up being driven by fear: fear of another country, or of failing, or of missing out on what the next person has. Life gets very complicated, resentment builds up, especially among the impoverished, and it may coalesce around some power-hungry fanatic, so you end up with a police state. In your case the pace of change is too great, and people are being taken out of their traditional ways of living too quickly. They are troubled, and look around for things to blame. You are one target, the frots are another, we are another, the Dream Hunter Company yet another."

"And yet they all enjoy the new things: the radio, telephones, cars."

"Those that can afford them."

"Belzic, I understand what you are saying. The problem is what to do. How do the Croans manage?"

"I believe they have a very complex caste system, and they have all sorts of controls on how money can be used. You'd have to ask them, ma'am."

"I may do that, Belzic. And thank you so much, you have given me a lot to think about."

Belzic retrieved his jacket and gave another stiff little bow.

"Just one more thing before you go. I understand that one of the objectives of your visit is to find portals, magical doorways of some sort that lead to other worlds?"

"Certainly, ma'am, that is one objective."

"If you found them, what would you do? Give us control, keep them hidden, or what?"

Belzic smiled for the first time. "We would need to talk about that, ma'am." Belzic took his leave.

"Well, Rain, what did you think?"

"He's a close one, ma'am, but I think he's right about you winning, especially if you stand with them on an equal footing."

"Rain, I'm hanged if I'm going to resign. All my instincts tell me to go for the confidence vote."

CHAPTER 61

Belzic left City Hall on foot. He made his way uphill, away from the sea and obliquely towards the river. He passed through a green space with a lookout platform and children's playground. Then came the stone wall with its stout wooden gate, and the desert beyond. He could just see over the gate to some excavation works not far beyond. Something large was being winched out of the ground. Belzic watched awhile, and then carried on to the narrow footbridge over the Kraab River. The river was flowing swiftly, splashing over black rock projections, and with little fountains erupting here and there from the riverbed itself. At the bridge he joined the queue who were waiting for the traffic from the other side to complete their crossing. Belzic watched them cross, young and old, men and women, some carrying the tools of their trade, most dressed against the searing, drying winds. He assumed they would in the main be factory workers coming for an afternoon shift, perhaps to assemble the cars or bicycles they might never be able to afford themselves.

Over the bridge, he climbed once more to the track along the wall, which continued up a steady rise. The hill below was covered with small trees, through which he had intermittent views of the whole of Kraab, and the south coast road winding into the distance. The way now became more rugged, with steep ascents and descents. A stream flowed under the wall, and then rushed on into a deep ravine. Although portly, Belzic moved with agility, making his way down a dizzying but well—trodden path, and at last finding the start of the road, and the little hidden place where the shapeshifter had parked on some of his night-time excursions. In a few more minutes he was back in the busyness of the city, negotiating bicycles, horses, foot traffic and the occasional motor car. The sound of the sea now mingled with the street noises, and very shortly, as the road took a turn round the last big building, there was the bay, and the embassy building directly ahead.

A collection of messages awaited him, some general ('to the Embassy visitors', which he now always dealt with), some specifically to Andrew, and several to Euse. He gave a wry smile, thinking of how the Croan rulebook required impartial observation and non-involvement in the affairs of wherever they went, and yet here they were being nothing if not fully involved. He quickly sorted out the mail, pausing in astonishment when he saw an item addressed directly to him. *Dear Belzic* (it read) *please can you help me. I am haunted. I am terrified and there is nobody who will listen. Please call me. Please come.* There was no name, but there was a telephone number. Belzic duly dialled it, but there was no answer. He turned to the others, working through the ones that didn't specify a name other than a generic one, and reflected on the fact that he was now an unofficial secretary, as well as cook. He then walked through the empty building to the room he shared with Andrew, and sat looking out over the misty shoreline. A little further south, where the coast road began, was a wide border of wilderness between the road and the sea, but here two grass-covered terraces lifted the Embassy a little, and provided a view over the Pond.

Belzic was not indifferent to the pleas of others, and the short cryptic message he had received rather unnerved him. No-one who'd had trouble with Dream Hunter equipment had written like this, leaving out every detail, including their name. If it was someone deranged, even dangerous, he had no training in such matters. In addition there were issues of his own he had trouble with. Periodically an image would come to him while he was falling asleep. A woman standing at a door with her two children— and he was taking the children away. It was her sad eyes that hurt him most forcibly, penetrating right to his heart. The images came to him now:

that desperate flight, the ground below him erupting into flame. Then the mountain, a sheet of fire while he screamed out, Run, children, run! Into the tunnel! He had returned later to inspect that dubious tunnel, the few pines remaining standing like black skeletons, sentinels perhaps to the dead. The tunnel was gone, leaving no more than a scar to mark its place. He wondered now about that woman, was she still waiting in hope to hear from her two little twins? Belzic shook his head, as if that would erase the image of those eyes, and that thought. Dwelling in this place could reduce him to madness. To distract himself he went once more to the telephone, and dialled the number given in the note. This time there was a reply.

"Please speak more slowly," said Belzic into the phone, "I can't make out what you're saying."

The voice at the other end responded in what seemed a mix of static and some extremely broad Rangolian dialect.

"Where are you? Just say where you are," said Belzic. More static. "Just say where you are," he repeated. The voice faded out altogether. Belzic made other calls. Could that last call be traced? Not, apparently, once the caller had disconnected. Belzic went to the kitchen, made himself a drink, and prepared food for the evening. He was expecting Cherg, possibly in company with one or other of the gap scientists. Cherg had opted to continue working on the desert excavations, rather than go to Skerron. With his better understanding of the language, Cherg would be the ideal person to have on hand when he tried that number again.

He switched on the radio, and was just in time to hear Qu address the nation.

CHAPTER 62

The broadcast

Belzic, Aleb and many others across Rangolia put aside their activities and turned on their radio sets as noon approached. Aleb had finished with the notebook and was wondering how he could report it. Jelani had drafted a speech for Qu and was now anxiously awaiting her broadcast.

It began with an introduction from the announcer, an admirer of Qu, along with some spirited music. Then Qu began to speak.

Greetings, citizens of Rangolia. Many of you now have radio receivers, so it is my privilege to speak to you today. We now have radio communication connecting all of our six cities on the mainland, as well as the Faalim Islands. I should add that we are working to provide telephone communication throughout the mainland, and it will soon be a joy for me to talk more directly with more of you, and to listen to your concerns. This is how our government, any government, can improve its services. I believe we have a wonderful country here in Rangolia, with enormous potential for growth as we green the desert and develop our technology.

Now, the role of a president, or king, or minister, is not to rule but to be ruled. To serve, in other words, the wishes of the people: not to control them, or give them misinformation. It is also our duty to call out those who do misinform, who spread mischief, and lies. Unfortunately there are plenty of those, even here in Rangolia. So I appeal to all of you, if you hear something

extraordinary, something wicked, or barely credible, do not give it any cre-
dence, do not pass it on; instead contact this government immediately, if you
have a phone, or if not talk to the mayor of your town or city. In this regard
I want to assure you that our Croan visitors are not spies, or servants of the
state, and they certainly intend no harm to any of you. The same goes for
the Dream Hunter Company. Many of you have already found their devices
useful for therapy, and for those of you who have had unpleasant experiences,
please contact your dealer, or go immediately to the Dream Hunter office.
You will be compensated and offered free counselling. In future, the Dream
Hunter staff and their agents have agreed to vet all customers carefully, and
make sure the appropriate device, if any, is provided for them.

So, remember, my government is here for you, to help you, not tell you
what to think, or how you should behave. We urge you all to be wary of those
who are, and contact this government with your concerns. In another four-
teen days there will be a vote of confidence, or not, in our record over the past
year. We stand by that record, but we aim, always, to do better. And in order
to do better we rely on you, on your voices, and on your willingness to critique
our performance. Please do so.

"Turn that rubbish off, will you, boss?"

"Guriang, it's good for you to know what the opposition is up to."

Guriang was inclined to be petulant with his campaign manager. "All that rubbish about serving. A president's job is to be the boss."

The manager waived the comment aside. "We've got to keep them on the hop, but we mustn't be associated with violence. It was fortunate you were locked up when you were."

"Boss, I'll stir them up plenty, just wait and see."

"Nothing incendiary, Guriang, nothing they can pin on you, on us, if things go bad. And please don't pick any more fights! Just use hints and insinuations. Keep it vague. In fact, I'll get you a speech writer."

"Boss, I've got a story worked out about those girls that topped themselves."

"No, Guriang, no! Leave the girls alone. They're much too dangerous to touch, and anything you say could backfire on us."

Maradi Guriang sighed. He had been preparing that story in his head for some hours, and was smiling in anticipation of the effect he expected to produce. "Boss, I wouldn't say anything they could prove wrong."

The manager relented just a little. "You could refer to suicides in a general way, but no specifics. Keep everything vague, mind. Hints and insinuations. If we get crude the big companies might abandon us. I tell you what, I'll give you some speeches to consider. The politics of fear, Guriang, works best when it's subtle. Hints, Guriang, hints and insinuations. Nothing specific. Nothing you could be pinned down on. I would focus particularly on the dream hunter lot. Qu has a controlling interest there, and is part of the management. Not nice, Guriang, not nice for them, but very nice for us. Yes, very nice for us. And something for you to work on."

CHAPTER 63

The bones of a message

Out in the desert the excavators had improved their technique. Buckets were lowered by crane, filled, lifted and emptied well to one side of the increasingly large hole. Supporting poles and beams held back the sand, which had now given way to small riverbed stones, bones, and various charred remains. Cherg was down there now, in the company of two experts on the elder days, picking over some of the near complete skeletons of small animals.

It had been a busy day. Sand was everywhere, and every portion of it had to be put through a sieve before being removed. In this way Cherg and his companions had worked their way though one floor of a largely intact building and moved on down to the lowest level so far excavated, where the sand ended.

Cherg patted the stones he was sitting on. He gave a huge yawn. Wanting to listen to Qu, he had tried, without success, to get reception inside the hole, and the radio was now safely wrapped up out of harm's way. Cherg was now hungry and a little frustrated. "Would you two like to join us for a meal?" he asked.

Dylvan stood up and dusted down his trousers. "Yes, we'd like to go to the Embassy, and we could certainly use some food."

They arrived on the surface to find that the entire site was being shut down for the night. The original primitive barriers had been replaced by stout wooden posts, and a gate which, to date, had baffled the frots.

Back at the Embassy, the food and drinks were waiting.

"Belzic, how did we ever manage without you," said Cherg, once the introductions were made.

"It is slow work, and there are perhaps a hundred more hours of it in the present building alone. Cherg, could you …"

"No, not for much longer," said Cherg. "Sorry Dylvan, Sital, I'd like to say we could, but we're nearing the end of our stay. We don't want to overstay our welcome. But now let's enjoy the food."

Although he tried to hide it, Cherg felt unaccountably sad. Perhaps it was to do with the scraps of diaries they had come across. Very few manuscripts survived intact but there were loose pages and even whole segments of partly decipherable books, including diaries written by a hand long dead and forgotten. It was mostly on these that he itched to begin work. Nonetheless the transience of life, when he discovered it in his earliest years, had always upset him. He dimly remembered being put into his very first exoskeleton, and his father talking to him: "Now you have had your operations you will no longer be able to live in the tank."

"But I want to, I want to!" In the tank you could fly, you could zoom, as your swimming muscles grew stronger and stronger. The tank in his hometown was huge, could accommodate a thousand Croan shrimps, and yet you always knew if your father or mother came by, you could feel their energy and you would skim across the water to bask in their closeness, as much as the food they provided. Language was not yet possible. But now, there was the pressure and pain of the exoskeleton. And being told that father would no longer come. Dead? What is that? But he knew instinctively it was something bad. Like having his swimming muscles taken away. Like being taken from the water, feeling the weight of his body for the first time, and being locked into a metal container for much of the rest of his life. "You'll get used to your exoskeleton," said his mother, and, "You'll still be able to swim". Not, of course, the way fishes can swim.

Once the meal was over Belzic brought out the phone. He dialled the number on the paper, listened for a moment, and handed the phone to Cherg. Cherg listened, frowning in concentration, and handed the phone to Dylvan. There was a long pause, Dylvan leaning back in his chair, his eyes closed, the phone cradled against his shoulder. Eventually he handed the phone back to Belzic.

"Yes?" said Belzic impatiently.

"There is something there, but it's unintelligible. It fades away, comes a little louder, and fades away again. I could make out one or two words, such as 'help' and 'haunted' but not with complete certainty. Now, if we could increase the volume?"

"Ess could, but Ess is away," said Cherg sadly.

"Let's try, anyhow. We have a lot of equipment here," said Belzic.

The phone was dismantled and examined by Cherg. "It's very basic, so it should be easy."

After some further work Belzic and Cherg between them were able to increase the sound and take a recording, which was played at various speeds. At a fast speed no words could be heard, but when the recording was slowed right down the few words that were recognisable resolved themselves into static.

As news time on Groob radio approached the pair gave up and listened to the broadcast. There was one item of particular significance. *Various users of telephones have reported a good deal of static over the last two days. We are pleased to advise that the problem has been identified, and is related to faulty wiring. We expect it to be fixed within the next two days.*

"So your message is a bit of a chimaera, Belzic," said Cherg with a smile.

Dylvan was eager to explain it: "It's only static, Belzic. Some of it sounds like actual words, so you hear what you expect to hear."

"Not the written message," said Belzic crossly. "As I told you it said, 'Help, I'm haunted', and it was addressed to me. I'll get it to show you." Belzic went to the mail tray, where the letters were still neatly stacked. The one addressed to him was not there, and nor was he able to find it when he searched his room, his belongings, or any other possible location.

CHAPTER 64

Dreams and frustrations

Belzic's uncharacteristic frustration unsettled Cherg. Help me, he muttered to himself as he settled down for the night. Bother Belzic! Snatches of half remembered comments, instructions, flowed through his mind. "Always remember your caste," said his father. "You are a land animal now. You are a trader. Be loyal to your caste." "Yes, father." Except that his father had not been, had married a guardian. "I am half guardian," he had once said, defiantly, when sent away. "Can't I do guardian training?" It made no difference. Traders learnt languages and navigation, along with a smattering of history, art, music and mathematics. Cherg was good, winning his place in the expedition from sixty-two others. The expedition under Euse. Cherg dozed, dreamt a little, became half awake once more.

He half felt, half saw himself moving into Trilfarne, scanning the air waves for broadcasts that did not exist, sending our scouts to skim the atmosphere at high altitude. A white world, but ice, not sand. The crew dropped off Euse and Ess to carry out the main mission, while the ship went on to examine the remaining eight planets. When they returned news of what Euse had done rather shocked Cherg. He attempted to understand the relationship Ess had with the leader: the sardonic technical expert who seldom varied his cynical 'Yes master, no master' repartee. He felt sure there was another Ess buried away, but Ess had only ever once hinted at this, when the two were together, doing something routine. Ess had looked solemn and thoughtful for a moment. "I'm treated as the junior on this ship," he said. "I could have had a better job."

But it was Euse that most worried Cherg. Even on planet Earth he had done increasingly risky things, and now more so. And Schyl, who as captain was supposed to rein in any reckless leader, had not done so; had, Cherg suspected, even been charmed by Euse. It was left to Groose to do what he could, and Groose was going on no more missions, while Cherg most certainly did not want his career to end after a single expedition. Cherg did not dare complain. Euse, you believe you are God, but you are not. You have been lucky so far—we have been lucky so far—but for how long?

Cherg fell asleep.

Belzic lay awake puzzling over the letter that had disappeared, and the voice that had come over the static on the phone. Was he, perhaps, the one being haunted. He was now well versed in dealing with the ghosts of others, but himself? Or was it simply a trick of his mind? The letter imagined, and the voice a gestalt derived from the static? He fell asleep, and after muddled dreams woke towards dawn. The purple light of Rubilis flooded the room. The embassy was almost empty, since Andrew and most of the Croans were already away, preparing for their trip to Skerron. However, there was someone in the room, and that person was sitting in a chair with his back to Belzic. He gazed at the profile, a black silhouette unmoving in the stillness of the early morning. There was something familiar about that back, that posture. Belzic felt unaccountably afraid, but he rose very quietly and walked over. The figure did not stir. Belzic prepared to speak but the words would not come. Instead, he reached out and laid a tentative hand on the shoulder in front of him.

"Mother?" said Belzic uncertainly, and the figure in front of him slowly turned round.

"Beebee? There you are. The nasty daddy has gone now, and we won't let him back, will we? You've got to be my daddy-man now, Beebee. You must help me, Beebee."

"But Mummy, I'm only a little boy!"

"Yes, Beebee, you're my baby and my daddy man all in one. Now isn't that nice?"

Belzic was in a place he could only remember in dreams. Dark wooden panelling, the tapping of leaves against the windows, sun catching late blossoms. His father came and went, jolly and cruel by turns. Nature was moving in, crawling up the walls in the form of vines which found their purchase in the slow decay of the blistered weatherboards.

"You'll have to be a big strong boy and help me pull back those nasty branches, Beebee."

They were three hour's walk from the nearest railway station, and their occupation was deemed 'illegal' by the authorities.

"Daddy, what is illegal?"

"It means you can't get a drink anywhere." The father roared with laughter and cuffed his son on the ear with a blow that sent him sprawling. "One day, son, I'll toughen you up properly."

"I'll help you, Mummy, I'll help you!"

But Mummy was no longer there. He was at a picnic, and the children scrambled around a big sack.

"Gently now, gently, children! There is no hurry. Every child has a present. Just look for your name tag."

Belzic, who had been added to the party informally, at the last minute, had no present. He felt ashamed. He ran and hid in the bushes, losing himself in the sunlight and shadows.

He came back to find trampled grass in an empty field, the stream murmuring quietly. He could see tire marks where the bus had been. Darkness closed around him, and he floated, ghost-like, towards a distant light.

His mother with her back to him, obstinately not looking, not attending.

"Mother, I have to go, I have a job to do!"

And then at last his mother turned, face hard.

"Get yourself a proper job!"

Belzic designed fashionable automata, little dogs mostly; not the smart-suited, high flying executive his mother had wanted.

"There is someone who needs me, mother!"

His other job, and his excuse to be elsewhere.

He was in a lecture hall, his anatomy teacher on stage. A class was in progress, and the body on the table was himself.

"Now this is the cadaver we all assumed to belong to Belzic. The face looked right, the basic shape looked right. So Belzic, right? Not at all! Everything inside this body is second hand, the lungs from somewhere, the liver from somewhere else, the gall bladder somewhere else again. Belzic, you see, had no time to acquire his own organs, or have his own personality. He was much too busy looking after other people, anyone and everyone he could find, whether they needed help or not. So really, he was just a jumble of a person—or was he? If there was a real person inside we would find it by opening the skull, wouldn't we? So let us open the skull. There, what do we see? Yes, the neurones are firing right enough, but look closer … It's all automatic! It's an endless sequence, you see. It never varies … I'm sorry to say, if there ever was a real Belzic he stopped existing a long time ago."

"No! No! No!" Belzic woke up shouting. He stared, confused. He found he had left the Embassy and was sitting on the beach, the water lapping nearly at his toes. The dawn was breaking, and the images of the night were fading quickly, but his face was wet with tears.

"Ah, there you are, Belzic. What are you doing on the beach? Are you coming with us to the island?" It was Andrew.

FIRE

Fire rounds off the year:
a time of consequences, revelations, endings.
A time also of clearing and cleansing,
death and cessation, loss and departure,
for always the old must perish
to make way for the new.

CHAPTER 65

To the island

The Season of Fire is typified by an intense drying easterly wind, which, blowing relentlessly for days at a time, sears the green fringe on the eastern side of Groob and frustrates the efforts of farmers to green the desert beyond. The wind was certainly pushing the little yacht along at high speed.

"Lean well out, you two!" shouted the captain. "We don't want to capsize!"

"This is great fun," Erg shouted back. "Euse, we need to do this more often."

"Watch out now, he's going to swing the boom. Heads well down. Ess and Erg, get back inside."

The captain was a phlegmatic man, who had barely batted an eyelid when asked to sail to Skerron, a lonely place containing two failed farms, some tumbledown houses and a storage shed maintained and stocked by the patrol boats of Rangolia.

"And how long would you want to stay there," asked Captain Haas. He had sailed boats for twenty years, the first ten with his father, and believed he had met 'all sorts'. He had not met the Croans before.

"Oh, come back for us in a couple of days," said Euse. He introduced Schyl, Groose, Grice, Ess, Erg, and Andrew. The captain cast a sour look at Andrew.

"I can pack you six little ones in quite easily, but I'm not so sure about the big fellow here."

"Oh, we must have Andrew. Can you tie him to the mast, or something?"

"No sir, but I'll see what I can do."

So Andrew lay near the bottom of the shallow keeled boat, along with the luggage, from where, with his head propped on Schyl's personal bag, he had a fine view of the white capped waves, and rather more than he needed of their briny flavour. Close to him was Schyl, seated, followed by Euse and Groose, and, furthest away, Grice. Grice was taking the opportunity to make occasional disparaging remarks about Schyl.

"This captain knows how to pilot a ship. Maybe our own captain could take a few lessons from him," said Grice. Captain Haas remained silent, as did all the others except Erg and Ess, who spent their time hanging onto ropes, swinging across the boat on each tack, narrowly missing heads, and shouting like excited schoolboys. At last the jetty came into view, and the captain proceeded once more to give orders. "Two days you say?" he said as the last items were offloaded. "I'll come about mid afternoon, day after tomorrow."

There was a narrow path from the jetty to a clearing where the modern shed stood. A notice proclaimed that the shed was not to be entered except as a matter of absolute necessity, and a wooden structure over the door handle, which would have to be broken to allow unauthorised access, emphasised the point.

Andrew, who felt he had carried rather more than his fair share of the baggage, dumped the last load against the side of the notice.

"What have you got in all these bags, Euse? Rocks?"

"Andrew, you are looking splendid, the epitome of rude good health," Euse responded.

Andrew scowled, but on reflection turned the scowl into a grin. "At least the trees shelter us from the wind."

"You were pale and weak while on the voyage to Groob, but with the advantage of good food, a good strong gravity and plenty of exercise, you really are an example of the ideal humanoid form," Euse continued. "Now, if you'd just like to get the camp set up—we'll all help, of course."

Ω

"I think it's better if we skirt round the island," said Mr Toomali. "There's a jetty on the lee side, but unless you have a very shallow draught it can be tricky."

Mrs Toomali sat at the stern of the little ketch, admiring her husband's adroit handling of the boat, and catching an occasional glimpse of her children, who were doing something mysterious in the cabin. Really, the children nowadays lived in another world to the one we inhabited, she thought. We were far too busy to bother with spooks and goblins. "It's such a pity your two couldn't be here," she said to Jelani. "It would be such an adventure for them."

"Oh, I expect we'll take them another time. This is really just to check the feasibility of building company factories and offices here." Jelani scanned the rugged shoreline as they drifted past. She saw the marker rock, exactly as she remembered it when she had experienced the death of her father.

"There's the marker rock," said Mr Toomali. "I line it up with that little islet we call the Pyramid, and that gives me the bearing I need."

Curious, thought Jelani, I expected to feel something, visiting this place again. Shock, tears, anything, but really I just feel flat, and rather old. My poor papa, how remote you seem to me now. Another world.

"We lived in another world," said Mrs Toomali abruptly, "not a bit like today's kiddies."

"Oh yes," said Jelani vaguely. The yacht had turned and the wind struck them more forcefully.

"There's the bay, right ahead. I'll anchor under that outcrop, and put us ashore in the inflatable."

"It's very savage," said Mrs Toomali. The waves were racing to a steeply shelving beach, and forming a curtain of spray that half obscured the timbered territory beyond. Mrs Toomali looked anxiously at the inflatable, in which Mr Toomali and the children were already ensconced. He half rose and reached out an arm. "Quick now, when I say, jump!" She did so, giving a little squeal as she fell, and the others followed, throwing over their luggage and following it as the waves permitted.

The island was the result of a network of fractures in the ocean floor. In ancient times it had been born as a mountain of fire, but the volcano had, after a modest rise above the surrounding sea, given up on its early promise. It was now significantly eroded after centuries of winds, rain and storms, although the crater remained, along with a number of underground caves. Several modest streams also flowed from its higher reaches.

"This of course is the rainy side," said Mr Toomali cheerfully. "Rain and wind both. Someone tried to run a farm near here. We'll see if we can find it."

There was, indeed, the remains of a track. "Damn, I should have brought a slasher. We'll need to clear this out."

"Here, let me," said Aleb. "At least I have good boots." He kicked his way to the front, and presently the tall shrubs became less dense, diminishing in time to mere waist high plants. "This must be the farm. It's all new growth." The others pushed through alongside.

"Look, there's the house!" said Mr Toomali.

Certainly there was a building ahead, since a partially collapsed roof was visible above the wilderness of an overgrown garden. The party moved into the garden and weaved their way over, under and around various creeper-draped structures. Aleb kicked at a wooden wall that may once have divided the garden from the house. The wall fell with a crash.

"Watch out, my darling!" Jelani shouted, and the next moment the air was loud with the noise of screaming birds. They were the most ugly things she had ever seen, with their bright red heads, green eyes and long saw-indented beaks, and at least a score of them came rushing out of a huge gap in the house wall. They made it clear that the visitors' presence was not welcome.

Aleb grabbed Pookah, while Jaan grabbed his daughter, and the whole party made an ignominious retreat, the birds sweeping down relentlessly to within inches of their heads.

"What now?" said Aleb, once they were back under the cover of the trees.

"Keep moving, keep moving," said Jelani, "the birds are still hovering."

"Let's get to the top," said Pookah, pointing upwards.

There was a rocky wall ahead, the eroded face of the old mountain, and the hint of a track that skirted it.

"It looks rather steep," said Mrs Toomali.

"Oh, come on," said Jelani. "You know we're bound to climb it sooner or later."

"Sesha, do you want to wait here with me?" said Mrs Toomali.

"If Pookah's going I'm going," said Sesha.

In fact the track to the top was little more than a grassy scramble, and everyone made it, half tumbling over the lip of the old crater. Sesha and Pookah lay on their backs in the shallow dip, while the wind whistled overhead.

"This would be a cool place for your new building!" said Pookah.

"All right, Pookie," said Mr Toomali. "You can carry up all the building materials."

"Look!" said Jelani, "there's a boat at that jetty."

From the summit the land dropped away in a series of terraces, with a good deal of flat land at the lower levels. Also visible on the west side was the shed used by the patrol boats, and, alongside, a couple of tents and a pile of baggage. There were also two buildings that looked in better repair than the farm house they had visited. There was no sign of the visitors.

"There are just too many trees," said Aleb, who had been scanning the land through binoculars.

Jaan returned to examining the crater. In one place there was a substantially bigger dip. "Pookie, Sesha, look here. This was once a fire mountain, and here's where the fire would have come out."

"There's a hole down there," said Pookah excitedly. "Do you think there is still fire down there?"

Maaveni came to inspect. "Stay well back, Pookie dear," she called out in alarm.

Jelani meanwhile found something else: a hexagonal hole cut downwards into the rock. It reminded her of something, but she couldn't think of what. She kept looking, and found other obviously artificial holes.

"Oh, oh!" said Mrs Toomali. "I feel so queer."

"Quick, lie down, Mrs T," said Mr Toomali.

"It's no good, I feel terrible. It's this place. I've got to get off it."

CHAPTER 66

The sanctuary

"Easy, easy, Mrs T. You just rest a bit, and we'll take you straight back to camp."

"Dear, I've got to get off at once. I feel absolutely dreadful, and it's coming from here."

"But there's nothing here!"

"There was once," said Jelani. "Look at these holes. They go in a circle: little round ones, and these bigger hexagonal ones."

"You're right," said Aleb. "There must have been a watchtower here at some time. Some of the holes could have held pegs for guy ropes."

"Can you two get the kiddies down, please," said Jaan. "I'll help Mrs T."

"I don't think I can manage the slope. It's awfully steep, and there's that big drop at the end."

"Of course you can. I'll stand just below you, and stop you if you slip."

But Mrs Toomali, on looking down, gave a triumphant cry which so astonished her husband that he almost slipped.

"My God, it's the Croans," said Jelani.

"They came to help me when I was in the temple, and now I'm in trouble they've come again," said Mrs Toomali.

As they reached their camp, Euse assisting all the way, she was the happiest of the entire party. Everyone was astounded, not least Mrs T herself.

"I feel as though I've been given a whole heap of energy," she said. "I can't imagine where it came from."

"Take care now," said Euse as the Croans left for their own camp.

"Oh, he is so charming," said Mrs Toomali.

But Jelani scarcely noticed the departure. "City Hall!," she said suddenly.

"Lani?" Aleb looked quizzically at his partner.

"That's where I've seen those hexagonal holes—in the rock gardens at City Hall."

"So?"

"So there's some connection between Skerron and the Hall. I'm sure of it."

Ω

"So what do you think," said Andrew later, "could that hilltop have anything to do with the portals? Would they have had them there?"

"Absolutely not," said Euse. "Why ever would they have portals there? Just the same, it could be significant. We'd better check it out while we're here."

"Would you like to elaborate, master?"

"No, Ess, not at this time."

"So what do we do now, Mr. Science Officer first class?"

"Senior Science Officer, Schyl, I'm senior now. And as for what we do, we make a study of this amazing jungle here, and wonder why it has all but gone from the mainland. Soil samples, please, Ess, and plenty of plant specimens. And take a look at the way the island is terraced, just like the mainland. That too must be investigated."

"And Mr senior officer, do you have any first impressions to get us started?"

"You mean other than the obvious? That we are on the side of an ancient volcano, since the entire island was born out of fire? We take samples, and they will tell us a good deal about what's inside this planet; especially since the island has probably not been messed with for thousands of years."

Ω

"Lebby, it is so peaceful here," said Jelani with feeling, but she said it quietly, as if it would be sacrilege to make any more noise than the birds themselves. "I can't understand why this place is visited so seldom. It is so close, and so beautiful."

"That is obvious, my darling. There is no nice beach, and in any case a cold current flows around the island. It can also be dangerous getting in, or getting out. And unless you've been here the idea of walking about in a forest just doesn't appeal."

"There used to be visits, like the one I was on, but the landing was difficult."

"Yes, it can be hard to land here," added Jaan Toomali. "Don't move now, Mrs T. You have a beautiful bird sitting on your hat. A lovely little green fellow."

Maaveni stood stock still. She felt suddenly very happy, the grizzles of the children forgotten. A bird! Jelani turned and looked. The bird remained, quite unconcerned and unafraid. It pecked at something on the hat, glanced this way and that, and then suddenly, as if deciding that humans were of no particular interest after all, flew away.

"I'm glad people don't come here," said Maaveni suddenly, and with such emphasis the others turned to her in astonishment. "People coming here would ruin the peace, would ruin everything. So no, I don't think there should be a factory here."

"Now, now, Mrs T, we're not quite that bad."

"We could designate some areas as off limits, strictly for the birds," said Aleb placatingly.

The group moved on, Maaveni as if waking from a dream. They had made their way to the Croan's camp, and finding nobody at home had moved on past the storage shed, following a coastal track to a wide scrub-covered plain.

"This must have been a farm," said Jaan Toomali.

"It would be perfect," said Aleb. "What do you think, Lani?"

"Oh, I agree. The only problem will be getting the materials here. Not the timber, of course. We can use what's here. Once the office is running we will only need little boats for coming and going."

"It's a beautiful place, but won't you miss Kraab? And what about the children, and school, and all that?"

"Oh, Mrs T, they won't be staying here. You won't, will you, Jelani? Isn't it just for your production staff?"

Aleb and Jelani exchanged glances. "Actually, we'll have to be here quite often—or at least, I will," said Jelani. She looked at Jaan. "It's so hidden and so beautiful. I did think the children would benefit from one or two days a week here—and perhaps your two could join them? Ours are mostly home schooled, of course—entirely so when they're with their father."

CHAPTER 67

Andrew, climbing up behind Euse, rounded the lip of the ancient crater, dropped the bag he was carrying, and sat down.

"You managed that beautifully," said Euse. "Back on planet Earth you'll be a champion."

"Will somebody make him shut up?" said Andrew. He was still breathing heavily.

"Behave yourself, Euse," said Groose at once. "We've got enough problems already with certain other crew members breaking the rules."

He looked over the crater. "Ess, can you help Andrew with the bag? It needs to be in a clear space where we can unpack."

The other three (Grice, Schyl and Erg) were moving quickly around the crater. Erg had found a stick, and was prodding at the ground. "Aha," he said presently, "there's a big hole here, completely overgrown."

There were in fact a number of concealed traps that yesterday's group had, perhaps by good luck, managed to avoid. Euse opened the bag Andrew had been carrying, removed several pieces of heavy equipment, and with the help of Ess began to map out the area. They quickly discovered the hole that Pookah had found the day before, and presently crowded around it. Euse at once began to take measurements, and shook his head. "It goes a long, long way down," he said. "Out of range. Ess, I want to get a vacuum bottle lowered as deep as possible, for an air sample. Ess, do you mind taking it down a little way?"

Ess looked quizzically down into the hole, and then back at Euse.

"How are you going to get him back out?" said Groose. There was a short silence, and then Ess asked his own question.

'Where is my gas mask, master?" he said.

The hole was in fact barely big enough to fit a person. Euse leaned over it and sniffed the air. Then he took a bottle from the bag, attached a wire to it, and lowered it. After a minute they all heard the bottle bumping against a rock. Euse pointed a remote controller into the hole, and shortly after pulled the bottle up. The air inside was faintly discoloured.

"Put a camera down, Euse," said Groose, but Euse shook his head.

"No, I don't like what I'm seeing. There is something very wrong with this place."

The group were distracted by the sound of gasping and coughing. Andrew had walked a little distance from the others and was now rolling on the ground.

"Get him out!" Groose shouted. "Euse, Grice, help me."

But there was another victim. A sudden cry distracted them, and they turned just in time to see Erg fall to the ground, clutching his throat. Ess too was gasping. He ran to Erg, grabbed him under the shoulders and dragged him as fast as he could away from the hole before he too collapsed. Meanwhile Groose and Euse had Andrew over their shoulders. They reached the lip of the crater, stumbled across it, and then fell, all three together, tumbling down the steep outer slope.

Ω

"I do hope they're all right. I've had a sort of funny feeling about them."

"The Croans? Mrs T, they're the last people I'd be worrying about. Anyway, we can keep an eye out for them on our way back to the boat."

Jaan was feeling very pleased. He had it all planned out; a modest little jetty, and that rocky spur could probably be extended to form a breakwater. Not to mention the ease with which a track could be cleared through the scrub. "There are no big trees to cut down, but plenty of timber nearby," he said happily. He would have a crew working alongside the builders, and all of them on the bonus pay that went with Special Operations.

"We can make something of this island," he said.

"We'd better hurry now, Jaan, if you don't want to sail in the dark," said Aleb. He pointed to the descending sun, and just for a moment the party stood and watched, as a dark shadow began moving across it.

"That's Numilis. Not a good omen, so they say," said Jelani.

"It's just an eclipse, Lani, just an eclipse," said Aleb. Nonetheless, he turned on his heel, hoisted his pack higher, and began to move with greater speed.

Ω

"Easy, Andrew, easy, here, let me look."

"It's horribly sore, Grice, horribly sore."

"I can see that, I'm going to bind it, but first I need to know just where it hurts."

Grice began prodding around the knee, and every so often Andrew cried 'ouch!' in an agonised way, and Grice said 'ah!' in a pleased way, and while this was going on the other members of the party were picking themselves up and dusting themselves down. Andrew continued to lie where he was, and Grice continued to push and prod, and say occasionally, 'Great!' or 'Excellent'; and finally, perhaps feeling an explanation was due to Andrew for all those happy noises, he made a brief apology. "Learning about joints was part of my training, Andrew," he continued. "Most Croans don't even know how to fix their exoskeletons."

"That feels better, said Andrew. He was cautiously testing his newly bound knee. "I can't understand why the rest of you weren't hurt more."

"I'm sure we're all a bit bruised, I am anyway, but our exoskeletons usually protect us from really serious injuries," said Grice. "Mind you, if it hadn't been for all that young foliage to cushion us things would have been worse."

"Someone will have to go back and collect our equipment," said Euse, looking at Ess.

"Yes master, where is my gas mask?"

"It's not gas, it's an energy accumulator, Ess."

"And since our Senior Science Officer, First Class, is the one who knows all about it he is the obvious one to go get the equipment," said Groose.

CHAPTER 68

The big dry

In the drought that now afflicted the mainland, leaves hung lifeless on the trees and only the toughest, or luckiest, saplings would survive. In the headland towers the keepers added fire watch to their coast guard duties. And almost everyone in Kraab would at times stare through the seaward mists in the hope of seeing rain clouds. In the little bays south of Kraab the heat pooled and stagnated, smelling of rotting weeds. The tree that had so terrified Hamul, now totally dead, creaked as wind stirred, and looked indeed, in the evening shadows, very like a bent old crone. Hamul meanwhile had retired from all official duties and stayed mostly in or near his house and garden. Jelani, returning from Skerron, was shocked by his appearance and determined to get him out of his isolated little dwelling. She visited more frequently, and sometimes Aleb came with her. "What is it, Hamul?" he asked on one occasion, but Hamul shook his head. "Was it just a dream I had? Everything has gone flat." Later, Aleb talked to Belzic about Hamul.

"He really brought the company to life—he had such passion," said Aleb. "Now, he doesn't seem to do anything—or want to."

"We must get him out of that place," said Jelani. "He's too isolated. It's not good for anyone."

Aleb and Jelani, having combined their savings, went house hunting. They found a likely place, down near the embassy, and their concern for Hamul was mixed with excitement for themselves.

"It's exactly what we need," said Jelani after their first inspection. "My two kiddies will have their own rooms."

They were coming back from their inspection when the news broke. A popular entertainer who had used, and enthused over, the various devices was found dead, apparently by his own hand. The hostility towards the dream hunters had started to quieten, but it now erupted in protests in Kraab and the other main cities in Rangolia. The Kraab protesters assembled first outside the Dreamland fort, and on gaining no admittance moved to City Hall, where rocks and paint were thrown, and scuffles broke out. A guard was injured, and a brawl was imminent when Guriang and his supporters arrived and redirected the group to the Temple. Guriang had been well coaxed by his sponsors, and appeared like a natural leader. He was applauded after almost every phrase, as he abjured the crowd to avoid violence, to act smart, to work as a team. "Here, in this temple, this special place that some say is the heart of Rangolia, and its exact centre, we can change the direction of the entire country. And do you know what, we will change it!" said Guriang. "There will be no more digging, no more dangerous equipment! No more Croans! No more Qu!" The crowd applauded, after which most dispersed. Some thirty, however, moved off in a tight little group. Their target was the Embassy.

Euse and Ess had spent much of the morning in the Embassy, sending the scout off on missions, first in one direction and then another. The 'big orange balloon', as it was called, was becoming a familiar sight in Kraab, and was regarded by many with indifference, as just another 'thing from the desert' which might or might not benefit their lives. Not so by the followers of Guriang, who regarded it as just another part of the dark plot to enslave the citizens of Rangolia.

"Aha, it looks like we have company," said Euse. The scout had just returned, and Ess was calling out numbers and other data as it came in to land. It was followed by a crowd, equipped in some cases with poles or swords. Euse was out the door in a flash, first to secure the scout and then to greet Guriang's mob.

"Welcome, everybody! You are so welcome! Would you like me to tell you about our wonderful scout?"

The mob stopped. Their leader, Jufah, was not much taller than Euse, and keen to show his courage in front of his fellows. He had expected flight rather than confrontation, especially since there were only two Croans in evidence.

"We want you to leave our country. Go back to where you came from," he growled.

"Yes, yes, but just before we go we would like to give you all little gifts." Euse was still smiling, and Ess, now alongside him, was pointing something incomprehensible at the crowd. There were snapping sounds and lots of flashing lights.

Jufah wavered. He was deeply superstitious, and the scene in front of him was incomprehensible. Moreover, he felt that his mind was being probed. He waved his arm in a curious, swiping motion. He turned away to the group behind.

"Come on," he growled, "they've got the message."

Ω

"What did they say they wanted, Rain?" Qu asked.

"The usual, ma'am, but especially no more excavating in the desert. They say enough is enough. Some think there are demons buried under the sand, would you believe."

"Surely not many would be so superstitious!"

"They also want the Dream Hunter company declared illegal, and all their gadgets destroyed, all their money taken away, and they want the outlanders banished immediately, on pain of being locked up for life. But they blame the digging mostly, I think. They say it creates a widening gap between the suubs and the eldrons, since only the eldrons can own the fancy new things."

"And how widespread are these sentiments, Rain?"

"It's hard to say, ma'am, but I think the number is growing."

"Oh Rain, Rain, if I win this time it will be the last. Our world becomes more stupid by the day."

"Ten more days to go, ma'am."

"And seven campaign meetings. Do you think we could fit in another?"

"It would be difficult. You must have a day's rest before the actual speeches, and then there is all the travel time, if you are going to go right round the island."

"I should, you know, and even travel to the other islands."

"If you could have more of your speeches broadcast ..."

"I know, but we have to be seen to be fair, and give equal time to the opposition. At least I have the last word. Is it true, by the way?"

"Is what true, ma'am?"

"Only eldrons can own fancy things."

"No ma'am. It's more to do with your money, than dressing posh, or the way you talk."

"That makes sense. But I have to say that right now nothing much makes sense to me anymore. Time to turn in, Rain."

CHAPTER 69

The shareholders' meeting

"There is deep sadness in all of us," said Euse, "and I acknowledge that unless your devices are handled in a careful, informed way, with guidance, that sadness can be very harmful, can lead to a suicidal depression ... No, let me finish. Do not be on your own if you want to use the D3. Have a guide, someone with deep self-knowledge that you can relate to. This is what your company should require. Thank you."

Euse sat down. It was the day after the visit by the mob, and he was at a rather stormy meeting over the future of Dream Hunters; a crowded hall containing perhaps most of the shareholders along with various carefully vetted members of the public. Euse turned to Ess and smiled.

"This is heating up nicely, don't you think? How divided people have become!"

"Is there a deep sadness in all of us?" Ess responded. "I wouldn't have thought that would be the case for you."

"Oh, never mind all that. I want to keep everything moving."

Indeed, there was a strong push from those who argued the company should not be in the business of 'looking after' people. You want to buy or hire a device? Then you will be cautioned to read a paper explaining all the risks, which you accept. You sign the paper, pay your money, and take your chances. That, at any rate, was the argument put forward by many if not most of the shareholders. One of them stood up now. He was a compromiser, attempting to build a bridge between the two divisive groups.

"Sure, we'll provide back-up therapy, support, if people get into trouble," he said. "In fact I see a wonderful prospect for Dream Hunters: a therapeutic support wing, ready to race into action whenever someone gets into real distress."

Euse rubbed his hands together and smiled more broadly. "That's the stuff," he whispered to Ess.

"Master, aren't you getting just a teeny bit too involved in all this?" Ess gave an impish grin. "What about all those visitors' rules?"

"Come now, Ess. Those rules are for idiots; we would achieve nothing if we followed them. Consider: we are required to observe and record, but our observations lead to questions, and questions cannot be settled without tests, and tests require experiments."

"Which require our full involvement, master," Ess added.

"Exactly. The experiments you and I did on Trilfarne were a little crude, but I just needed to find out certain things about those beings."

"Not to mention finding a great source of wealth, master."

"That, Ess, is something we keep to ourselves."

Euse turned his attention back to the meeting. "It's not our business to look after people," someone was complaining more vehemently, bringing the argument full circle. "Consider: there have been accidents with guns, for example … "

"Yes! And motorcars!"

"And motorcars, and lots of other things. The manufacturers don't have to patch up the people who are harmed, and they wouldn't be able to in any case."

"Ladies, gentleman, fellow Rangolians, the point is, should the devices continue to be sold at the present time?"

"Isn't it enough just to keep them out of the shops?"

"Wouldn't it be enough just to have people sign an acceptance of risk?"

"Come on Ess, you've recorded enough, let's get back to the Embassy and have a meal. With a bit of luck Belzic will have something tolerable for us as well as for Andrew."

But Andrew met them as they left. He was somewhat out of breath.

"Thank God I've found you! Come quick."

"Whatever is it, Andrew?"

"Guriang's mob. They had a meeting with him, and then they all went to the Dream Hunter office. There was nobody there, but they set to work battering the door with rocks, leaving only when security arrived. I was worried they'd attack the Embassy next, but they went straight on. I'm not sure where to, but I don't trust them."

"Ah, we'd better find them," said Euse. "Have you talked to Jelani?"

"I can't find Jelani or Aleb."

"Did you speak to Guriang?"

"I didn't see him, but that's like him. He's always somewhere else, so he can't be blamed for anything."

"Come with me then. We'll contact Qu's security and get a car."

Ω

In his little house at the boundary of Kraab, Hamul beamed at his guests.

"Thank you so much for coming! That's it, come right in, take a seat in my sun lounge."

"We thought we'd come and see if you were still alive!"

"Pookie dear …"

"That's all right, Mrs Toomali. I fancy somebody needs to keep an eye on me nowadays. I used to see a lot of Jelani and Aleb, but now not so much. I suppose with all this political business over the company … Can I get you something?"

"Can I get you something, perhaps drinks for all of us? Just point me to your kitchen Mr Hamul."

Hamul subsided. "The fact is, I've been very short on energy lately, even for my garden. I'm thinking I should see a doctor."

Hamul did not mention a vision he had had a few days previously, the first since his terrible experiences in his little bay. He had gone to his bedroom, planning to have a rest after gardening. The sun was streaming in a most welcoming way onto his bed, but on the nearest bedpost sat a bird. He recognised it at once: a parrot that a neighbour had owned, with the most beautiful green and grey plumage. As a child he used to make frequent visits, just to admire the bird. Now, it looked at him nonchalantly, and turned its head as if to groom itself. Then he saw, to his horror, that it was systematically plucking out its feathers. He gave a little cry of distress and moved towards it—but the vision had already gone.

Jaan Toomali looked at him curiously. "Yes, I think you should. Perhaps I can take you?"

"Jaan, I must tell you something. It's crazy, I know. I don't understand it myself. You probably know I went missing for a few days, and the coast-guard found me on a ledge below the top of the cliff where they have their lookout. Well, I just couldn't have got there on my own. I couldn't! It was a sheer rock face, and I'm not that good at climbing anyway. I went back to check on it, and it scared me just to look at it."

"Yes? So what do you think happened?"

"One memory did come back to me. I was walking through a tunnel, actually inside the cliff. The tunnel was lit by a strange light, a sort of yellow gold. It was very beautiful, and I felt that I belonged there. I felt that I only had to walk a little way and I would come to my real home. Yes, it sounds crazy. Somewhere, I was going to find a door, and when I opened it …"

"Yes? Go on."

"A great fear took hold of me, and I began running … that's all I remember."

"So you think you were actually inside the cliff? A false memory, surely?"

A loud knocking at the front door startled them all. Jaan moved first, taking a peek out the window.

"Hamul, don't go to the door! There's a big crowd there and I don't like the look of them."

The knocking intensified.

"Can we get into the desert from here?"

"Oh dear, what have I got you into?"

"They'll be after you, Hamul. Look, I'll see if I can put them off—Maaveni, get the children into the desert. And you, Hamul, over the fence as fast as you can!"

"Open up! Open up!"

Jaan Toomali ran to the door, which was now being hammered on ever more violently.

"Open up! We know you're in there! Open the door!"

CHAPTER 70

"In a way, it might have been a blessing," said Rain.

"Yes, they did themselves no favours," said Qu.

"No indeed, ma'am. I notice that Guriang was careful to distance himself."

"And you think it might give us the edge we want? Let us hope so."

"Yes, especially since Jaan Toomali was also hurt, and he's highly regarded by everyone."

"So I heard. What happened there?"

"He tried to hold the mob back so Hamul could get away, so he got knocked down, and then of course Hamul was beaten and kicked. And Toomali started shouting out 'Enough! Enough!' And they all went away."

Ω

Opinion had been firming up against Qu in the past few weeks. The rich and privileged had telephones and radio sets, and many other items which were supposed to 'filter down' through the ranks, but were in no hurry to do so. The rich had cars which scared the horses, and the horses (sometimes by contrivance of their owners) got in the way of cars. The 'two tribes one people' mantra which featured in the temple, and on the walls of all public buildings,was being sorely put to the test. Qu's own sponsors, who had so enthusiastically supported her over the previous three years, had called an urgent meeting, and it was this that had shaken her even more than the decline of her popularity.

"Are you sure you can handle this?" she had been asked.

Qu's voice turned a little frosty as she responded. "I have handled more difficult situations. Why? Are you thinking of replacing me?"

Although indeed it was too late for that. Qu was hastily assured of 'our full support' and the meeting had moved on to a discussion of tactics. Now, sitting in her office with Rain and looking over the list of those who were to extol the virtues of her past year, she suddenly grinned.

"Rain, it is situations like these that bring out the best in me."

"Time we were making our way over ma'am," said Rain.

"It's lucky," said Qu thoughtfully, "that the fool Hamul went to meet the mob. Otherwise there would have been no incident, and no bad publicity for Guriang."

"Ma'am, my understanding is that he couldn't climb the fence."

"Whatever. In any event I've been given a gift, and I'm certainly going to use it."

Ω

"Hello, you look grumpier than ever, Groose."

Euse had just returned to the Embassy, having completed another round of talks, with the assistance of Ess, Cherg, and various devices from the Dream Hunter studios. The three found Groose busy with his phone. He now put it aside, and put all his attention on Euse.

"Base wants us out of here. Apparently you are too busy to answer their calls, so they're chasing me. We should leave right away, or at least say we're going to, except that no doubt the ship is by this time totally inoperable."

"A few more days, Groose. We definitely need to stay until after the election, both for our records and because we're as keen as the natives to see the final result. I am, anyway."

"Euse, have you given up on the portals?"

"On the contrary, Cherg, Ess and I have solved the whole mystery."

"What you've done, Euse, has stirred up the natives to the point we risk our lives being here."

"Come now, Groose—"

"And in addition we can't leave because our ship is locked up, and heaven knows how much it has been looted and vandalised."

"Groose, I admit some items have been removed, but that's the main reason why the ship is locked up. As you know, the door was damaged, and so I called on the port authorities to protect our property. I think we can trust them to do a good job. I've also called on Grice to arrange an inspection, and attend to any repairs. I'll lend him Ess, and anyone else who wants to be involved."

"Euse, have you really solved the problem of the portals?"

"Yes indeed, Cherg, and when we're on our way home I'll tell the crew all about it. Until then we say nothing."

"IF we get to be on our way home, Euse, *IF* we get that far. Right now, those who are still a little bit friendly to us are wondering why we are spying on them."

"Ah, you mean the scout."

"Yes, the scout. When a big orange mystery object floats about over the city people tend to be a little bit curious."

"Groose, I'm not being provocative—just doing my job."

"Which is just what frightens the good citizens—"

"Listen, Groose, the election is about to begin, and in a week after that we'll be gone. I've given Qu some useful information, but I can't please the world."

"It would have been smarter to have left yesterday. Heaven knows what will happen if Guriang gets in."

"Master, shouldn't we be talking to Qu about the portals?"

"Absolutely not, Ess!" Euse stared at his technical assistant in astonishment. "Absolutely and definitely not. This goes nowhere outside our own crew."

CHAPTER 71

Hamul in hospital

Hamul stirred. That dream again—or was it? Bright colours, applause, laughter; his sister, whom he barely remembered, and who appeared occasionally in dreams. On this occasion she was wearing a floral dress, and was on the stage—but doing that exactly? The dream had already faded, and he was left, as usual, wondering if this was a real memory—indeed, if any of his recollections were actual memories, or simply constructions built out of numerous retellings by his parents.

"Your sister—now she had real flair, real talent," said his mother, and his father echoed the sentiments.

Hamul felt diminished, always. How do you compete with a dead person? There was also the matter of her death—something his thoughts always veered away from, not least because the details had been kept deliberately vague. More than that—something that frightened him, although he wasn't sure what.

"Feeling better, are we?" The nurse was leaning slightly towards him, full of professional cheerfulness. Hamul welcomed the intrusion.

"They're going to broadcast the election, and I wondered if you'd like to listen, since we have a spare radio? Say, I do hope that Qu gets in again. She seems to know what she's doing. Not like that terrible mob who attacked you, you poor dear."

Hamul grinned, and brushed his fingertips over his bandaged head. "Yes please, I'd like that very much."

He leaned back and rested his back and head against the plump pillows, and looked with appreciation round the room. White curtains and walls, crisp white sheets, white pillows. A white, soothing, comfortable, reassuring world. This could be heaven. Hamul smiled and dozed.

Ω

The election

Aleb smiled ruefully at Jelani as the pair took their seats in the big hall.

The smile was intended to say 'Well, here we are again, another year gone by!'

Jelani squeezed his hand. "It wasn't your fault! Anyway, he's a tough old bird."

"Maybe it's not my fault, but I should've thought of Hamul sooner." They'd had this conversation a number of times in the past few days, in fact ever since Aleb had arrived to find Hamul prostrate, and Jaan Toomali, also bleeding, bending over him. Of the attackers there was no sign.

"Anyway, we've been so preoccupied," said Jelani. Aleb nodded. With their pooled savings they had been able to purchase the larger house Jelani had discovered and move in almost immediately.

"Your father will be able to stay with us."

"On the rare occasions when he's here."

"Hamul will have to come in with us," Jelani continued. "We can't have him going back to that isolated place of his."

She stopped, and the two turned their attention to the stage, on which the Speaker of the Hall had just appeared. The voices in the audience rose, and then died away.

"Thank you for your attention, honoured guests, ladies and gentlemen. As you know, on this day, the eightieth of the season of fire, we review the progress and the wellbeing of the inhabitants of Groob and its outlying islands. Welcome to you all. We especially welcome the visitors from our southern cities, and those who have made the long trips from Kaalon and Daarin.

"Now, as is usual when there are challenges to the office of president, the challengers are invited to speak first, either to find fault or to offer a vision of how Rangolia might be under their presidential care. Today, we have two challengers, and I shall shortly introduce them. The protocol in this case is, after they have spoken, Madam President will be invited to speak in her defence. Then, I shall ask the evaluators, which you see sitting to my left, to decide by vote on the standing motion: 'that this country has confidence in the future performance of the sitting president'. If the motion carries by majority vote that is the end of the matter. If it fails the president may resign, or may choose to stand against the other two contestants. The voting will continue until one contestant achieves an outright majority. Now, I call upon the first contestant, Maradi Guriang. Mr Guriang, please take the stage."

Aleb and Jelani exchanged glances as Guriang appeared. "Feel the tension," Jelani whispered. It felt, indeed, as though any who had previously been pleasantly relaxed were now on the edge of their seats.

"Fellow Rangolians, it is an honour to be standing here speaking to you all today. I wish to say, firstly, how saddened I was to hear of the recent attack by an irresponsible mob on two innocent, elderly citizens of this country. I hasten to add that these aggressors in no way represent my policy or attitudes."

"Very predictable," Aleb whispered.

"I like the way he presented Mr Toomali as elderly."

"Not even Hamul is elderly."

Guriang's speech continued with growing intensity, as he referred to the 'dangerous frots', the machines designed to 'control your mind', and the evil plotting of the present government with the 'sinister Croans'. The speech was applauded by many in the hall. Aleb gritted his teeth.

The second speaker came on with a very different message. "We must be bold, and we can be bold," said Laloo Maani. The man was a suub, and, surprisingly, his message was the precise opposite of Guriang's. "Don't you see what a wonderful opportunity we have in this desert, and from our visitors? We have marvels waiting to be discovered, things that will give us all the chance to live lives of leisure, lives of luxury, both in the things we can own, and the things we can trade." Maani went on to expound on his policies, including one to have the frots trained, and eventually turned into a branch of the military. "And probably other things," he enthused. "They could become your servants, and do all the heavy work." The Dream Hunter Company would continue to operate, with trained guides available, and indeed be used eventually as an educational tool.

Hamul had propped himself up on pillows, with his ear close to the erratic radio. He heard himself described as 'elderly' by Guriang, heard how under Guriang all the Dream Hunter devices were to be recalled, and placed under the control of an authority with powers independent of the government. After Maani's speech, a good deal more to his liking, Qu gave her own. She spent no time at all attacking the ideas of her opponents, choosing instead to talk about what her government had achieved, and had yet to achieve. "Our way is the way of moderation," she said. "There are uncertainties with any new technology. It has both dangers and rewards. It has the capacity to change our whole society—change the way it oper-ates, even—and this can be very threatening. Yes, threatening, and also very exciting. This is why I want our country to proceed, to be progressive, to look forward rather than backwards, but at the same time to proceed slowly, and with caution."

There was a brief recess after Qu's speech, and on the radio this was filled by a couple of boffins discussing the likely outcome of the vote. Hamul had been leaning over the radio, and now lay back, tired and shiv-ering slightly with a fever. The evaluators filled in their voting slips, which were checked and counted by scrutineers, who then followed the Speaker onto the stage.

"Thank you for your patience, ladies and gentlemen. We now have a result:

In favour of the motion, that this country has confidence in the future performance of the sitting president: 248 votes. Against: 251 votes, and one abstention. Therefore the motion is rejected. There will now be a second ballot, and since the sitting president has chosen to enter as a candidate, it will be a three-way contest."

"Oh my God, she might lose," said Jelani, her voice barely heard over the noise from the rest of the audience.

"Silence, please, silence! There will be no vote unless we have silence!"

The second ballot was counted amid simmering impatience.

"The results of the second ballot: candidate Qu: 248 votes; candidate Guriang: 200 votes; candidate Maani: 52 votes. Therefore no candidate has an absolute majority, and the evaluators have no mandate to appoint a new president. Candidate Qu retains her office as caretaker president, and a new ballot will be held one week from now. I declare this meeting closed, ladies and gentlemen. Thank you for your attendance."

Hamul, listening and shaking with fever, gave a cry and slumped back into his bed. A nurse came running.

CHAPTER 72

Convalescence

"Hamul was propped up on a daybed, and looking out at the sea. He had just been moved from the hospital to Aleb and Jelani's new house, since, as Aleb explained, his own house was dangerously isolated. "We need to keep an eye on you," said Jelani. "Those lunatics won't dare come here," said Aleb. Privately, he wasn't so sure.

"I can't intrude on you like this," said Hamul. "And besides, there's my garden."

"You will stay here until you're strong," said Jelani. "We can decide what to do later. Just call out if you want anything."

In truth, Hamul did not particularly want to do anything, think about anything, want anything just now. Just to lie here. He remembered running back into the house in time to hear Jaan Toomali remonstrating with the crowd outside. There was a lot of shouting, but that was all he could recall before waking up in hospital. Aleb, Jelani and Jaan were standing around his bed, Jaan with an impressive bandage around his head.

Now, of course, he was in the care of Aleb, and, particularly, Jelani, in the house the two of them shared. His fever had abated, and he felt pleasantly lethargic. In particular, he loved watching the sea, which he could do with no more effort than a slight turn of the head. Right now, it was forming itself in tiny dancing peaks that rose and subsided, over and over, always the same and yet ever changing as they rose into the midmorning sunlight, and subsided, each leaving a little circle of foam and a little trace of colour from the depths. The pond shimmered with life and vitality.

Jelani entered the room and sat in a chair beside him. Hamul gave a wan smile.

"Afraid I'm taking up quite a bit of your time, not to mention a whole room in your new house."

"You, Hamul, are welcome to stay just as long as you like. The children don't need a bedroom each at their age, and in this house we have three good sized bedrooms and a spacious lounge. In fact that's really why we bought the place. We were getting a bit cramped where we were!"

"Thanks. I'll be on my feet soon, mind, and I do have that garden to look after."

"No you don't. We could find you a place near us—unless—now this is just a thought, but we are going to need people on Skerron. We're going to set up radio communication from there to the mainland, so you wouldn't be completely isolated."

There was a pause. Hamul gave a little grunt, meaning (as Jelani suspected) that he wasn't at all keen to be away from his beloved garden, but didn't want to sound selfish or ungrateful.

Jelani gave him a little pat on the shoulder and left the room. Hamul suspected she was trying to keep the Dream Hunter Company together at a time of great uncertainty, as well as running the house and looking after him. He turned and looked towards the door, which she had pulled behind her, but not quite shut. Then he started. There was the bird again, perched on the back of the chair and quietly, systematically stripping away its beautiful feathers. "Don't, don't," he gasped. "Oh, please …" The bird looked at him calmly, and continued to pluck. "You don't exist, you don't exist," he repeated, over and over like a mantra. It made no difference to his distress.

Something was happening to his eyes. The door, and the wall beside it, had become hard and shiny, and had moved very far away. He wondered if he would be able to reach that door. The floor between bed and door was like a great brown sea, and like the sea it was rippling and sparkling in the afternoon sun. He looked more carefully, contemplating the problem. How to reach the door. The door itself was waving gently, like a limp rag shaking in the breeze. I must escape, he thought. But there were things in the way. Faces in the floor. Faces looking up. His sister. Hamul saw with a shock that his sister was crying. She was tearing off her pretty floral dress. "No, no! You mustn't!" But there was his mother, finger against her mouth, head shaking. "She was the clever one, Hamul. Not you!"

The faces were gone. The day had gone, and the room had come back. Hamul, waking, found Jelani beside him, and behind her someone he didn't know.

"Hamul, you haven't met Aleb's father Jerome."

"I've heard a lot about you, Mr Foulkes."

"And I've heard a lot about you."

"Are you staying long?"

"Just a few more days. Then I'll be away for several months."

Hamul smiled and held out his hand. "It's nice to meet you."

"Likewise." Jerome Foulkes took his leave.

"I'll pull the curtain, unless you'd like to look at the two moons? No, Rubilis has gone behind a cloud. How are you, anyway?" Jelani could not hide the touch of anxiety in her voice.

Hamul blinked, and smiled.

"I've been thinking about my sister."

"You have a sister?"

"Oh yes. She died when I was quite young. She was very pretty, but she got sick."

"I'm sorry."

"It's ok now. Somehow, I've carried her about in my mind, but now she's gone."

"Did you care about her very much?"

"Yes, I cared a lot. Would you open the curtain a bit more? There's still one moon visible and I'd like to look at it."

Ω

"What's he doing here?"

Hamul opened his eyes.

"Rihan! That's not very nice." Jelani knelt down beside her son. They both looked at Hamul, who was basking in the mid-morning sunshine.

Hamul looked back at the little boy and grinned. "I'm being rescued, that's what I'm doing, Rihan."

The children were impressed. "Were you being chased by a huge monster?" Holanna asked.

"Not exactly, but close."

"Come away children, Mr Hamul needs to rest." Jelani turned to Gijor, who had followed her into the room. He was looking all around. "Thank you for bringing them," said Jelani.

"You seem to have done all right for yourself. A nice house."

"Thanks. It's half Aleb's."

"Yooriko and I have a great little farm now. The kids like being with us."

"I'm glad to hear it," Jelani responded. She reflected that the two conversed, if at all, in short, staccato bursts.

"Well, I'm off. See you in a month." Then, noticing the recumbent Hamul, Gijor gave an awkward smile. "Sorry, I didn't see you sir. I do think I've met you."

"We did meet once. I'm Hamul."

The children meanwhile had lost interest in the rescued stranger. They were running through the remainder of the house. Rihan was disappointed that there were no stairs, but the beach close at hand made up for a lot. "If a bad storm comes the waves could reach as far as the house, and we might have to escape," Aleb had told them, and that made the house far more interesting. "We'll need an escape strategy," said Rihan, while Holanna excitedly grabbed pencil and paper and began planning for one. "Rihan, you'll need to help me make a list of our survival rations," she said. Rihan cast a slightly anxious look at the sea, which was lapping sleepily against the steeply sloping shingle below them. Holanna came up beside him and stared out in frowning concentration. A few tenuous threads of mist were drifting around the house. "There are terrible big monsters out there," said Holanna. "We'll have to arm ourselves and find places to hide."

"Come on then," said Rihan, who was thinking of the huddle of furniture in the next room, still awaiting suitable locations. "I'll make us a really neat hideout."

CHAPTER 73

Enter the army

"Four more days, Rain. Do you have any idea what they're thinking?"

"No ma'am. They're sequestered, as the law requires."

"It only needs three to switch and we're in."

"Yes, but the trouble is some may go the other way—I mean the ones that are sponsored. If a couple of big companies decide to make a deal, policies become a minor matter."

"Rain, I know, I know. It's just that I see this country on the verge of real prosperity, with everybody's lives made easier, and to have it all taken away by this superstitious nonsense I hear …"

"I know ma'am. You can't please everybody … Even if we win there could be trouble ahead. And I must say I'm worried. I walked by the temple, and even that had graffiti daubed on it—quite disgusting comments as well. And I see there are army units everywhere. I've never seen such a thing before."

"But surely that's good. The army will bring order; in fact my security staff recommended I call them in."

Ω

"General now, well, well." Aleb's father Jerome had been meeting old friends.

"Yes sir. We've both done well, haven't we? Are you in the country for long?"

"Just till after the election. But what's this I hear about Guriang, threatening to lock up the Croans if he wins? Can you reason with him?"

"Not my job sir. I stay clear of politics, though I have to say quite a few of the military feel the same as Guriang."

"Well, I've tried to talk to him. I interviewed one of the Croans, and I agree they're not to be trusted, but the real point is they have a technology that is way ahead of ours. And that makes locking them up the maddest thing I can imagine. But God, the military has special powers, and if ever there was a need …"

"The country could be in danger? That's different, Mr Foulkes. Leave it to me."

Ω

Therapy

In Jelani's house, two doors along from the embassy, Hamul was alone. He had left his bed several times in the morning. He felt positively cheerful for the first time since the attack, although still rather weak and light-headed. Now, he opened the box containing the food Jelani had left him. I can't stay here, and let them look after me, he was thinking. They have enough to do. However his thoughts were still a little half-hearted, and they melted away entirely when he smelt the food. For the first time in a long while he knew what hunger meant, and what food was all about. I've been a bit depressed lately. Maybe I shouldn't live alone, he thought. He looked across to the phone: the number of the embassy had been pinned up beside it. Hamul made a call.

"No, Hamul," said Belzic on the phone. "You want to confront your fear? I strongly suggest you don't use anything from Dream Hunters." Belzic hesitated. He had various calls for his attention, but Hamul's situation was special. His present location was hopefully still a secret, but that could not be guaranteed. The sooner he was mentally and physically fit the better. He hurried over. Hamul was in his dressing gown, sitting up on his bed. He appeared cheerful, or at least pleased to see Belzic, who took the bedside chair.

"Let's try something right now, shall we? You are game? All right, I think we should start with that bird you say was plucking out its feathers. Okay, imaginary bird. It doesn't matter." Hamul was making a series of nods and monosyllabic interjections while Belzic spoke. Belzic now paused, and Hamul said simply, "Yes, fine, the bird."

"What I am thinking, Hamul, is that the bird connects with your sister. Does that make sense? Now, if you think of your sister as that bird, metaphorically plucking out her feathers, what does that suggest to you?"

"To be less showy, conspicuous?"

"Keep going."

"To be more herself, maybe, less dressed up in fine feathers, maybe even less successful?"

"Keep going."

"Now that I think of it, Alaani was due to enter a singing competition. Our father, who was training her, kept telling her that she was going to win, and my mother was always saying she was the clever one in the family."

"And you were jealous?"

"And I was jealous."

"How did you get on with your father?"

"Mostly he ignored me. He was mainly interested in my sister."

"Who died. Do you think there was anything, say, not appropriate in that relationship?"

"Dad and Alaani? I doubt it. He just thought the world of her."

"Go back to this competition. What happened?"

"Mum and I went early so we could get good seats. Alaani had already been dolled up, but she wanted to wait. I sat with my mother in the audience, and she never showed up. Later I was told she was dead, and she'd had a bad accident."

"How did you feel?"

"Very bad, but then I was frightened."

"Yes?"

"I was just a little boy!"

"Go on."

"I was frightened I would die too."

"Were you afraid of your parents?"

"No."

"What then?"

"Lots of things. There was a picture in the hallway which terrified me. It was in a corner, away from the windows, and it was always dark there. I used to shut my eyes and hurry past if I had to go that way. And I was afraid of various other things around the house, especially at night."

"So you transferred your fear to things around the house?"

"When you put it that way, I suppose I did."

"Now what do you think really happened to your sister?"

"I think … she killed herself."

"Say it louder."

"I think she killed herself."

"Why would that be?"

"Because mum and dad were always putting expectations on her, especially dad, and she felt trapped. She felt she could never be good enough for them."

"Did you feel trapped?"

"No. My life was easy because nobody expected very much from me."

"Except you were afraid. Why?"

I suppose … if she was so good and she died, what hope did I have?"

"But you've managed your life very well, haven't you?"

"I found I was really quite smart. I've set up businesses and charities, and of course I got Dream Hunter started."

"What happened to your parents after your sister died?"

"Mum and dad separated. I went to live with an aunt for a while, but I kept in touch with mum. I never saw my father again. Do you know, I think my sister was the only reason they were together in the first place."

"And what about now?"

"They're both dead. I inherited some land, which I donated to the city."

"So how do you feel right now?"

"Strange. Lighter. Maybe happier. I've been carrying that fear around so long, so stupidly, so needlessly."

"Well done, Hamul. You are certainly sounding a lot happier. Let us celebrate with a drink—that is, if you are allowed, and are feeling strong enough?"

Belzic looked critically at his patient. Hamul in fact looked old, tired and gaunt.

"I'm feeling strong enough for anything now."

However, when Belzic returned with drinks Hamul was lying down asleep. Belzic took a closer look at his very pale face, and checked his pulse, which was fast and irregular. He put a drink by the bed and spread a blanket over the sleeping figure.

He stood at the window and looked out over the sea. It was mid afternoon, normally the hottest, sleepiest time of day, but the wind had changed and the sky had clouded. A cold wind flowing out of the desert made him shiver a little. He picked up the phone, intending to call Jelani, but a voice came out of that machine the moment he raised it: a voice that was remote and faint, but at the same time very distinct and clearly enunciated: *help me, Belzic ... please, please help me.*

"Who is that? Speaker louder!"

But the phone was dead. Belzic replaced it, and a moment later it rang.

"Who is that? Belzic? Listen, this is Rain. I want you to talk to the Croans urgently. They've got to get away. Listen, the army has taken over City Hall and Qu is confined to her rooms. They say they are here to take control, but everyone who worked for Qu is being arrested. I may be next. I want you to contact Jelani and Aleb, and Andrew, and Hamul. Tell them to leave the country, and get away yourself. Good luck."

The phone went dead. Belzic replaced it, and a moment later there was a thunderous hammering on the front door.

CHAPTER 74

Roundup

"Hullo? Rain? What's that? Leave the country? But there's nowhere ... it's too late anyway. The army has just driven in through the gates, and in any case ..."

The phone went dead, and a shaken Jelani hung up. She and Umus were conferring on the relocation plans for the Dream Hunter factory, while the rest of the staff were on leave. In fact most residents of Kraab were on holiday, this being the day in which Kraab was supposedly founded, some 332 years previously. Jelani now looked helplessly at Umus.

"It looks like the army is taking the place over."

"That is ridiculous! Let me talk to them. Come on."

But Jelani began to sob. She took up the phone once more and attempted to call Aleb. Aleb was not to be found.

Umus ushered her to the lift, and at the ground floor burst out into the foyer just at the time a squad of military men entered. Umus confronted them.

"Where is your commanding officer! I wish to speak to him."

"In due course, sir. I have orders to take you two into protective custody, sir. It appears your lives are at risk."

The sergeant was placating, embarrassed, while his corporal, who stood by, grinning, was clearly enjoying the encounter. Certainly Umus, aroused, was intimidating with his long hair, long red beard, and his sheer size. The sergeant stepped back a little way and motioned to the corporal.

"If you would just follow me, sir."

The corporal continued to grin, even as he spoke, which infuriated Umus all the more. However he was now hemmed in on all sides, and he followed, meekly enough, walking in step with the men, with Jelani close by.

Ω

Belzic took another quick look at Hamul and ran to the front door as the knocking intensified. He was confronted by three soldiers. They took a brief look at Belzic and pushed their way past.

"Excuse me!"

"Hamul? We have come to collect Hamul."

"Well you can't! He's sick."

They stood around the bedside, considering.

"We have orders to collect him."

"No, you can't possibly move him. Don't you see it might kill him?"

Hamul was sleeping heavily.

"He's wanted."

The corporal flashed a piece of paper in front of Belzic, as if that would settle the matter.

"So what good would he be if he's dead? It would certainly get you into trouble for failing to take care of him!"

The corporal looked doubtfully at the sleeper, and then, sternly, at Belzic. A worried frown crossed his face. Clearly, Belzic was an impediment. He glared at the man.

"We'll be back. Just don't move him!"

Belzic watched them leave, and then turned to Hamul once more. Except there was very little he could do. There was water beside the bed, and more blankets ready if the patient began to shiver. He suspected that Hamul would not wake again.

Hamul was back in the tunnel. The same golden light, and in the distance a yellow door, shadowy, but glinting, as if beckoning. Last time, he remembered, it was locked, but this time it opened smoothly as he turned the handle. In his sleep, he smiled, closed the door once more and returned to his body.

Belzic phoned the Embassy, and on receiving no reply went there just in time to see the Croans being escorted away by another squad of soldiers. Euse, as usual, was at the front, smiling and chatting with the leader, who answered in monosyllables, if at all.

"Ess, keep close to me, that's right, get a recording of all his responses. What a fine specimen he is, don't you think so, Ess?"

In spite of himself, the sergeant walked even more stiffly, more like a parade ground figure.

"My word, you must be proud to serve in such a country," said Euse.

Belzic watched them go, and shook his head. He tried again to contact Aleb, and was wondering what to do when Andrew arrived with two gap scientists. They had been in the desert, and were not aware of the events that had taken place over the last few hours.

Belzic made up his mind.

"You three have a car. Excellent. Take us all to City Hall, as fast as you can."

Ω

"Let me write my report. You want the people to know what's going on, don't you?"

"We just don't want you to write anything that will stir people up," said the colonel. "If you do that we'll have to close you down."

Aleb was trying, with difficulty, to keep his temper. He had been making phone calls for the past hour, and was still trying to contact Jelani. At least the children were back with their father.

"I tell the truth, when I can get it, and if you obstruct me that's what I will tell people. So tell me, where is Qu? Is she being charged with a crime? If so, what? The same goes for my partner Jelani. Where is Jelani? What crime has she committed?"

Aleb was competing for the colonel's attention. He was sitting in the office of the Speaker of the Hall, which the colonel had appropriated, and a steady stream of military personnel were coming and going with questions, messages, things to sign. But then at last the colonel turned to him.

"I have always enjoyed reading your reports, sir, and I certainly don't want to stop you now. You should rest assured that nobody is being charged with a crime—that is the job of the police, in any case. Our role is to protect the public in times like these, and that is just what we are doing. Your partner has been threatened, so she is in protective custody, as is the president, who gets, let's see ... about twenty threats every day. We are taking over the running of the country until peace is restored, at which time the vote for the new president can go ahead as planned."

"Yes, good. When will that be, please?"

"I can't rightly give you a time, sir ..."

Aleb, hoping to believe the colonel, wrote a reassuring article, and the paper had record sales. Later, the military broadcast to the nation a carefully crafted speech in which they promised to stamp out the 'lawless elements' that had infected the country. There was no mention of the election 'going ahead'.

Ω

"Rain! Oh dear, I thought you'd got away from this ungodly place."

"No ma'am, my job is to be here with you."

"Well, I appreciate that."

"How have you been treated, ma'am?"

"Oh, fine, it's just that nobody will tell me anything. I've just listened to a long, rambling speech by the military, which was mainly about stamping out 'lawless elements', and absolutely nothing about me, about the election—nothing really about anything other than 'keeping people safe' as they put it." Qu sighed, and looked glumly at her PA.

"So what can you tell me, Rain? What is actually going on?"

Qu pulled a chair up close to the big window which took in much of Kraab and the ocean beyond. She had been prevented from leaving her own suite of rooms, or using a phone. She very much wanted to contact her own security team, but this too was forbidden. Rain joined her and the two of them stared out over the city. Here there was curiously little to suggest anything out of the ordinary was taking place. Traffic continued to flow along the coastal road, as well as in and around the central streets. Most of the factory chimneys were smokeless, as befitted a public holiday in Kraab. A loudspeaker was booming out over the central park: *We will not interfere with your lawful daily activities.*

"What is actually going on? I wish I knew, ma'am. All I know is I don't trust them."

"No, Rain. They could protect us well enough without locking us up!"

CHAPTER 75

City Hall, where the future directions for Rangolia were invariably decided, was a number of connected structures: a residential block with the president's offices located at the very top, the theatre, where the voting was held, and where otherwise various entertainments took place, a smaller cabinet room in which political policies were ironed out, a great many offices, and a number of satellite buildings housing various government departments, along with accomodation for diplomats and honoured guests. A little to the east was the temple, which proclaimed itself to be the 'exact centre' of Kraab, and which also piously and rather optimistically proclaimed on its walls that all in Rangolia were 'equal'; with the eldrons and suubs declared 'two tribes, one language, one people'. Around the entire complex stretched a park, a green oasis containing a fountain and a lake, and coppices of the tall fern-like trees that were distinctive in coastal Groob. To the east of the park the terrain slanted down to factories, warehouses, the docklands, and the Pond, the extensive thermal sea that saved the planet from being a dead, frigid world. To the west, the ground sloped up in a series of terraces which accommodated the homes of the affluent, some nestled in the shelter of the wall that held back the desert. Snuggled very close to the wall, sat Hamul's old house with a 'for sale' sign attached to the front gate. ('A quiet, secluded little cottage with a beautiful garden' ran the advertisement in the Kraab Monitor) Hamul himself was at the moment, (and purely in his mind), on board a yacht piloted by Jaan Toomali, and containing the Toomali family.

Up at the masthead Hamul's sister was calling to him, 'Come and join me, come and join me', but Hamul felt heavy as lead, supine and immovable in the bottom most cabin. He tried to call out in reply, but even his jaw would not work. The yacht was bound for Skerron, where, in actual fact, four surveyors and a builder were impatiently leaning over a radio and waiting to hear further news of the army takeover on the mainland. (Nobody was at this stage calling it a 'coup'.) Hamul, all alone in the house that had been provided for him, twitched and shivered in his sleep.

Other radios in Groob, in the southern and western cities, and the outlying islands, were equally tuned in to the broadcast from City Hall. On Mukihaano Island Jelani's ex-husband Gijor also sat listening, with Rihan and Holanna playing nearby. 'Auntie' Yoorie, who was preparing lunch for the family, smiled to herself a sly, secret smile as the news trickled in. "I fear that woman of yours has got her comeuppance," she called out.

In the business centre of Kraab, as in every other business centre in Rangolia on this day, the markets were in full swing, with those places with radios receiving the greatest attention. 'What's the latest from City Hall' was the recurrent question on everyone's lips.

The main part of City Hall was in fact merely the latest in a series of structures on the site. Previously there had been a loftier and far more elaborate temple, with catacombs that ran six levels deep, and extended well beyond the bounds of the buildings. Even above ground some elements of this much older building survived in the form of elaborate stone facings. Euse stopped in front of one now, by the simple means of calling 'Halt!' in a most authoritative military way. The startled phalanx stopped.

"Observe, soldiers, the intricacy of these lovingly executed stone carvings. Observe, and ponder over the long ages that this magnificent face will have looked sternly out over Kraab."

"Inside, you," said the sergeant in charge, and the phalanx moved on."

Ω

"Please tell me where I may and may not go."

"Ma'am, you are free to move about anywhere within the building. If you leave it we cannot protect you."

"Thank you, officer." Qu turned to her PA. "Let us see who else has been confined."

The Croans were shepherded into the main hall to join Qu's security and support staff and several members of the Dream Hunter workforce. They arrived in time to see Qu and Rain walk in and begin moving around the gathering, talking here and there, shaking a few hands and, occasionally, putting arms around more upset members of the staff. A little bit later Andrew and Belzic arrived, Andrew going straight towards Euse while Belzic made a circuit of the hall.

Euse was escorted into an office, a small room with a large man behind the desk. General Greesh had not met Euse, and didn't particularly wish to meet him. He sat now reading reports, although he was very aware of the newcomer. The general liked to make people wait. Euse meanwhile studied him in silence for a few minutes, and then began to take photos, moving here and there over the floor to check out the best angles. The general, dimly aware of the movement, at last raised his head.

"Ah, thank you sir, look to your right if you don't mind. I think your left profile is going to be better than your right. Ah, that's good, I'll have these pictures made up for you. Would you like them framed? Or shall I just deliver them?"

A dawning awareness came to the general that he was actually dealing with Euse.

"Never mind the photographs," he growled. He gave Euse his special 'look' which usually worked, but not this time. "You are a visitor Mr ... er ... Euse, so you won't be aware of our customs. Now, we have been isolated until recently, so we don't have many visitors. So I think there have been faults on both sides. Both sides," he repeated. Euse nodded solemnly, and looked contrite.

"I know you have been useful to the president, but we have a very tense situation here." Euse brightened.

"Oh, Mr General, we can help you there."

"No! We have suffered enough from your help." The general pointed his finger.

"No sir, you will be leaving. We will show you all the courtesies that are your right as a visitor, including of course escorting you to your boat."

"Do your courtesies extend to provisioning our boat, and replacing all the items that were taken from it?"

"Yes!" The general suddenly looked very tired. "Yes, of course."

"When I said all the provisions I don't of course include Taapino. That was our gift to you when you arrived."

"No, no. Yes, of course, thank you."

"And thank you, Mr General. And of course I don't mean a number of items, some of which were consumed by us and our guests when we arrived, and some of which …"

"Take what the hell you want."

Euse beamed at the officer. "In that case, Mr General, we will take advantage of your courtesy. We are so much obliged."

Ω

Qu came out of her own interview looking pale.

"Rain? I'm being charged with conspiring against the interests of the state."

"No!"

"It means that because I have a case against me I can't be president until my name is cleared, so the army is in full control."

"When is this case against you coming to court, ma'am?"

"In two days from now, because they want to rush it through before the final vote. If I'm cleared I can still stand, but it means I have only tomorrow to prepare a defence."

"Ma'am, I'll start contacting people now. They can't stop us from doing that!"

"It's not only about me. It includes Jelani, and Hamul too, of course."

Ω

In Aleb's cottage, a few steps up from the sea, Hamul was half awake and hallucinating under the full moon. He was giving little cries, and flailing his arms. One swing hit the water glass, which fell and broke, sending little sparkles of glass across the floor. Nobody came for there was nobody to hear.

Three blocks away from City Hall, in the deepening twilight, most of the stalls stayed open for the fair, which was just getting started. A band started up, with various voices calling above it: come dancing, come try your luck with us, come for the lolly scramble, come learn how to drive a motor car. Out of all the year it was the most special evening.

CHAPTER 76

The evening wore on. Jaan Toomali, captaining Green Patrol, sailed into the harbour as the darkness intensified. A small group stood waiting as the boat was moored and the sails lowered, among them Mrs Maaveni Toomali, who burst into tears as she embraced her husband.

"Come now, Mrs T, anyone would think you were sorry to meet me."

"Oh Jaan, haven't you heard, they've taken Mrs Therim away—arrested her!"

"We did hear the army had taken control and were trying to calm things down, but what on earth has Jelani Therim been up to?"

Maaveni barely heard her husband's response. She was tugging at his arm.

"You've got to do something, Jaan!"

"I fear you overestimate my powers, dear heart."

When the Toomalis arrived at City Hall a large crowd was already assembled, and the air was electric with anticipation. A burst of cheering erupted as the Croans came out on the main steps, waving and bowing. They moved on, flanked by soldiers who were struggling to keep back the milling fans. Someone had produced a placard with 'We are sorry you are leaving' inscribed in giant letters, and now a voice called out, "Come again!" and the cry was taken up by others, and turned into a chant.

"I had no idea they were so popular," said Jaan Toomali, as the couple worked their way through the throng, eventually arriving at the front door of the Hall. They were stopped from going any further.

"I'm looking for Jelani Therim."

"And you are?" The soldier who confronted them was all angles, especially his sharp nose and jaw. That, and the tone of his voice, frightened Mrs Toomali a little, but she was feeling very determined.

"Maaveni Toomali, and this is my husband Jaan."

"Come in, you are wanted, Mrs Toomali."

"Whatever have you been up to, Mrs T?"

The pair followed the soldier with some trepidation into the crowded amphitheatre.

"My goodness," said Jaan, "this is where they hold the elections."

The big inscription above the stage read "Where destiny is determined". Jaan Toomali looked critically round, and soon spotted Jelani, with Aleb beside her.

"Thank God you're ok!" Aleb was saying.

"Lebby! At last, at last!" Just like Maaveni, Jelani burst into tears..

"It's all right, I'm here, I'm here." And by God, he thought, if they lock her up I'll write articles that will create a stink across the whole of Kraab.

"They're very polite, Lebby. They just won't tell me anything."

Jelani herself did not feel very 'polite', and the manner of the senior officer had made her want to scratch the man's eyes out.

"Madam, we are protecting you from certain threats, as is required of us in the armed forces."

Was she being charged with anything? Was Hamul? What was going to happen to Dream Hunters, all that equipment, property, hard work?

"Madam, it is too early to say. We are gathering evidence."

And also, she wryly noted, most of their manufacturing equipment, along with the entire store of devices.

"They say they're protecting you?"

"Oh God, Lebby, hold me, hold me. Is this really happening?"

"Listen, Lani."

A breakaway group had followed the Croans down to the docks where their ship was moored, but the greater crowd remained at City Hall. Someone had begun chanting, "Jelani, Jelani, we want Jelani!" and now more and more voices joined in as people from the fair were flocking to the Hall. Jelani however barely heard, since her attention was caught by new arrivals.

"Lebby, look who else is here!"

Maaveni came running forward, and behind her a bemused Jaan. Further back still came Belzic and Andrew.

"Oh Mrs Therim, whatever is going on? Tell us, because I'm sure Jaan will fix it," said Maaveni.

But whatever Jelani was going to say was cut short by a voice from the stage.

"You attention please! First of all, take note that this military operation is entirely for your own safety. If you are being charged with a crime, or summoned to appear as a witness, that is entirely the responsibility of the judiciary. I will add that if you have been charged with a crime you will be staying overnight in the Hall. You will shortly be taken to your rooms, so tell your escort if you have special needs or dependents … Silence please! … If you are being summoned as a witness you may leave once you have signed a statement, acknowledging that you have read and understood the summons. For this purpose, go to the front of the hall . If you wish to give evidence but have not been summoned go to the left side of the hall. Everybody else may leave immediately. The trials will begin promptly at noon two days from now."

Andrew and Belzic were among those being summoned as witnesses.

"Belzic, do you know anything about the criminal law on this planet?"

"Not much. I expect they'll tell us about it. Ah, this queue takes us to the front of the hall."

"Belzic! We have to go! The Croans were told they had to leave immediately."

Ω

"Ma'am, it's mostly about those Dream Hunter gadgets. If we can show them to do more good than harm they won't have a case."

"I'd like to share your optimism, Rain. Stay with me tonight, please."

Qu was back in her own set of rooms.

Ω

"Euse, we can't leave yet, we haven't got our passengers."

"Indeed we have not, Groose. Would you like to go and fetch them? Just remember, if we're still here after midnight we won't be able to go at all. They'll lock us up and take away our beautiful boat."

"Midnight is not far off, master."

The crew had been busy for some hours, gathering up equipment that the military had returned, running checks on the health of their ship, and generally organising for departure. Groose now stepped back on the wharf, had a talk with the soldiers and looked anxiously around.

A sergeant looked sourly at Groose. He was tall, and Groose appeared a midget in his eyes.

"Go, Croan, go, if you don't want us to lock you up." Groose retreated.

"There is no sign of them, Euse. We'd better go looking for them," he said.

"They'll be back at the Embassy, master, probably waiting on the beach."

"Yes indeed, Ess. Captain, we'd better move. We'll pick them up later."

"Take her out now, Erg. We'll lift off in twenty minutes."

360

Thus it was that the starship had left the wharf and was heading out to sea when Andrew and Belzic came panting into Docklands.

"They'll pick us up, won't they? We'd better wait at the Embassy," said Andrew, and the two turned onto the coast road for another half hour jog. However, instead of the ship the soldiers were waiting for them, and they were firmly and somewhat roughly escorted back to City Hall.

$$\Omega$$

"They're not here, master. What do we do now?"

"Try the beach. Everyone, keep looking."

"They're not down by the water, or anywhere near the house, master."

"Grice, how is our fuel?"

"If we wait we'll have nothing left over for contingencies. As you know, moving slowly in a gravity field is the worst thing we can do."

"Captain?"

"We leave now. Erg, plot a course to spin us around Rubilis. Everyone to their stations."

CHAPTER 77

Last report

Report from Senior Science Officer Euse to Area Commander Queyn

(Date: 50988/603)

From Space

Dear Commander,

This is my final report on Groob, since we are returning, as requested. I'm pleased to advise that our two passengers have elected to remain on this planet, so we will not have to detour to Earth, and will be arriving in a little under three months. We have now made a detailed study of all the main physical features, and can confirm that the planet remains habitable chiefly on account of the thermal vents which occur in many areas over the ocean floor. We can also confirm that a previous civilisation self-destructed some 1100 Groobian years previously, at least partly on account of nano-weapons designed to penetrate all forms of defence. Technical data, maps, graphs and evidence of widespread destruction (including the extinction of many life forms) are included as usual in the appendix.

All our crew are well, and have enjoyed a most interesting three-planet mission, during which our true origin and identities remained concealed, in accordance with the interplanetary visiting rules. We look forward to report-ing in person three months from now.

Sent from Space by P.B. Euse, Senior Science Officer, First Class.

"Ess, read this if you please and tell me if there is anything more to add."

"Yes master. Maybe write something about the mental states of these folk when they're in a crisis."

"A good point. We've got heaps about them under ordinary duress, and that's all been sent away. But a really good crisis … Ess, what a shame we've had to leave before that court action. I would have loved to be there and find out what's happening with Madam Qu. Still, we have a heap of evidence, quite enough to keep the old commander happy."

"Yes. I think I can guess what will happen."

"Can you indeed. What will happen, Ess?"

"I think they'll get rid of the Dream Hunter Company, or rather, the army will take it over. Maybe Jelani will work for the army, or maybe they'll lock her up. They'll certainly want experienced staff, so they won't lock up too many, maybe just Qu."

"Well, Ess, we'll see if you are right."

"You'll see if Ess is right? How do you propose to do that, mister Senior Science Officer?"

"I left a transmitter behind with Aleb. It only has enough power for a week or two, but that should suffice, mister Captain. Hmm, I think the trial should be starting about now."

Ω

The trial

"It's almost time, Ma'am."

"I'm ready. Where are they holding it?"

363

"In the big hall, as you suspected. I'm told the place is packed with spectators."

"Lead the way, Rain. I'm as ready as I'll ever be. Qu gave a little shudder, and on the way through to the main hall kept her eyes looking straight ahead."

Belzic and Andrew watched her, walking tall and unhurried amid a cluster of supporters towards the main entrance.

"She's a cool one," said Andrew. He watched, admiring. After her group came Jelani and Aleb, and a number of others from Dream Hunters.

"At least we can help Jelani, even if we can't help ourselves."

"Cheer up, Andrew, we're not being locked up. Besides, I wouldn't write off Earth just yet … Here we go, they're summoning us next."

The hall was indeed crowded, and Andrew wondered where everyone was going to sit. He managed to squeeze in after Belzic at the end of the row that was labelled 'witnesses'. He closed his eyes and felt, as much as heard, the noise of the crowd around him booming in his ears like a great sea.

"Attention! Attention! Attention, everybody. The court is in session. Silence, silence! … Have some respect! Those accused of a crime will now come on the stage." The court manager deferred to a clerk, who now read out the charges as the accused stepped onto the stage.

"Madam Qu, Acting President of Rangolia, you are charged with recklessly permitting the production of equipment likely to cause distress and harm to its users, and having no known useful purpose. Furthermore, you are charged with allowing the said equipment to be freely available, while knowing it to cause dissension and conflict within the domain of Rangolia. How do you plead?"

"Not guilty."

"Please be seated."

"Jelani Therim, Manager of Dream Hunter Company, you are charged with producing and selling dangerous equipment, having no known useful purpose …"

Apart from Jelani, Umus and two others, including the sales manager, were charged with crimes. Hamul was deemed unfit to stand trial. In fact he was delirious often, was under guard in Aleb's house, but at least receiving regular visits from a doctor.

The court manager was back again, eager to instruct.

"You will note that the accused have all been charged with the same offence, and that is because there was essentially just one crime, with each of the accused playing a different role. This means that if the Dream Hunter devices are found to be harmless all will be acquitted.

"Shortly I will introduce the examiners; but first, and especially for those of you unfamiliar with court proceedings, the jury panel is that row of seats directly above me. You will note that there are twenty in the jury, ten picked by lot and ten who are experts in court evidence. A conviction requires the agreement of at least fifteen of these capable men and women."

"Only three women among them, ma'am. I'm not sure I like that!"

"I wouldn't trust them any more than the men, Rain."

"To your right are seats reserved for our support staff. If you have a problem of any kind, that is where you should go."

"Perhaps we should ask them to help us get back to our home planet."

"Shush, Andrew."

"You must bear in mind that the examiners' job is to bring out the truth by skilful questioning. That is, they are not supposed to form any opinion concerning the guilt of the accused. That is the job of the jurors. Now, concerning the questions themselves, neither the accused nor the witnesses are obliged to answer every question, or indeed any question, but refusal to answer is usually unwise.

"Moving on, this area where I stand is the speakers' platform. Anyone called to give evidence, or answer questions, will stand here. Immediately below the platform is the recorders' box. Their job is to take note of all that transpires in this hall, such as questions and answers, names and occupations, dates and times, and a good deal else. There are always two recorders for a significant trial such as this one."

"God, I wish they'd get on with it. This court manager loves the sound of his own voice."

"At least we can sit together, Lani."

"You may have noticed that there are no specific places reserved for the accused. Unless or until they are convicted they are privileged, and can choose where they sit."

Andrew stopped listening. He was wondering in part what use he would be to the Dream Hunters, but mainly about how he was going to survive on this alien planet, without any hope of getting back home. It was all the more of a shock when a voice rang out: "Would Mr Conway please come to the speakers' platform". Andrew looked around, and seeing that all eyes were on him made his way to the front of the hall. "Will you please state your name, occupation and place of residence."

"Will you please state your name, occupation and place of residence."

"Um, yes, I'm …" For a moment Andrew was tongue tied, not having considered such matters as occupation and place of residence.

The examiner smiled indulgently. "You are a diplomat, are you not, a diplomat from Dangoogle?"

"Oh yes, a diplomat, um, from Ranfurly, ah 108 East Street, Dangoogle."

"I'm sure Ranfurly, Dangoogle will be sufficient to find you, Mr Andrew." This time the examiner smiled encouragingly. "Now, please tell us in your own words what experience you have had with these Dream Hunter gadgets."

"I have used them myself a couple of times and talked to others who have used them."

"Yes? And what have you found?"

"I've found they can greatly improve a person's recall of their own past life. Early memories, some very early, may come into sharp focus."

"Would you say that what you recall is always what actually happened?"

"No. I would say that what you recall is what you believed actually happened."

"Could you expound on that a little?"

"Certainly. Suppose you are a timid little child, and you get yourself lost in the woods. Someone, an adult, goes looking for you, but because you are so scared you believe a monster is after you. When you relive the experience the fear comes back and you might actually make a visual construct of a monster out of the trees around you."

"Does that mean you become traumatised?"

"Not if you are mature and healthy, because you are also aware that what you see is just a childhood fantasy."

"But what if you are not so mature or healthy?"

"You have to be over eighteen to use any of the devices, and you are not supposed to use them if you are suffering from depression or any mental illness—at least not without qualified medical support."

"You have heard that some people have had visitations of some sort from apparently other—worldly beings. Do you have any comments you would like to make on this matter?"

"Yes, two things. Firstly, children: they are susceptible and vulnerable, so obviously must be protected by an adult. You treat unwelcome visitors of any kind in exactly the same way: they are unwelcome and must leave at once. Secondly, I was approached by one of these beings. Thinking of that encounter, I would say, if you're not sure, make them look at you. Look into their eyes."

"Their eyes?"

"Yes. Their eyes will tell you all you need to know."

Andrew began to enjoy the exchange as the questions continued, and he realised that he loved talking Dream Hunter business. All too quickly the questions stopped.

"Finally, is there anything you would like to add about the Dream Hunter company or its equipment?"

"Yes. I think the company has much to teach us. It may not always make us happy, but it can make us wiser, and more compassionate towards others."

The second examiner took up the idea of 'compassion' with Belzic.

"If you are not already a compassionate person would using any of these gadgets actually make you compassionate?"

"It certainly need not, although there are circumstances where it might."

"Please explain."

"You receive a transmission from someone who has been through experiences similar to your own, or who has feelings that match your own."

After Andrew and Belzic, nobody had much more to add until a scientist Andrew had not met took the stage.

"State your name, occupation and place of residence."

"Jemma Grams, gap scientist. I live in Kraab."

"Gap scientist?"

"That means I study ancient artefacts, mostly found in the desert, in pursuit of my own interests. We try to bridge the gap between our own limited knowledge and that of our forebears."

"And what are your interests, Miss Grams?"

"Chiefly, what brought the previous civilisation to its end."

"And what have you found?"

"Briefly, that the prototypes of the equipment Dream Hunters produce had a very different purpose, namely, to control the minds of those who used them."

"Control their minds?"

"In three ways: to make them happy, docile, and obedient to the state."

"Do you have any evidence that they did these things?"

"They almost certainly failed, since this venture happened just before the terrible war that brought the old civilisation to its knees."

"Could the present Dream Hunter devices control the minds of those who use them?"

"Not, I think, in the way intended. However, I believe there is a risk of addiction, and a chance that excessive use could damage the brain."

"But you have no clear evidence of this?"

"Not as yet, but I see their widespread use as a violation of the precautionary principle."

"Please explain, Miss Grams."

"Certainly. It means that lack of evidence of harm does not ensure evidence of no harm. These devices should have been kept from the public for several years and undergone extensive testing. We need in particular to know more about brain functions and how the Dream Hunter equipment interacts with them."

"Thank you, Miss Grams. This trial will continue at noon tomorrow, Everyone may now leave City Hall, but if you are one of the accused or a witness you may not leave Kraab, and must return here by noon tomorrow. Thank you, ladies and gentlemen. The court is dismissed."

CHAPTER 78

On board the Duvra

"Well done, Erg, we're nicely positioned to leave this star system."

"Thank you, captain, but it was mainly our canny little ship's brain that did the work."

"Just the same, it needs a good working relationship, which you have achieved over the last four years. Now Euse, I understand you and Ess are to be congratulated."

"You could say we've made a little progress, although it's really a matter of one's point of view."

"Oh come on Euse, stop teasing."

Euse glanced at the young communications officer, and just for a moment looked annoyed at the interjection. Then he relaxed, and continued. "Cherg is right, because what Ess and I discovered affects us all. The decision now is technically mine, but I believe we all need a say. We'll put it to a vote."

"For God's sake, Euse, put what to a vote?"

"Cherg, he means, what to do about the portals," said Ess.

"It's easiest if I just show you," said Euse. "I'll put everything up on the screen. First, here is a map of the local area, Skerron on the right, Kraab in the centre, and now I add six little crosses, which represent places of high energy . Notice anything?"

"They form a perfect hexagon," said Cherg. "Kraab is in the centre."

"Yes, and the exact centre is where Kraab's City Hall stands."

"Tell us about these energy places," said Schyl.

"I picked them all up using the scout, and after I got the first three it was easy."

"The scout that caused so much trouble!"

"Yes, Schyl, it gave us a bad reputation."

"I can see that the first one was the volcano on Skerron. How did you get the rest?"

"That was easy too, captain. We looked for energy of the same type and range as that on Skerron. That is, a form of dark energy which up till now has been purely speculative for us."

"So what has Kraab to do with all this?"

"Kraab is the focal point."

"But Euse, there are no radiations coming out of Kraab."

"Of course not, captain. You'd soon have a lot of sick people. No, the radiation will be contained, probably deep under City Hall. What we can say is that the energy that came out of the Skerron volcano and the other five locations may have increased to the sixth power. Here is a graph showing the power potential in City Hall, compared with the power needed to drive this starship."

"But Euse, this was a long time ago. It surely wouldn't still be operating."

"Except that it is. Ess and I have run tests. It is operating, which means it is being maintained, which means various people, including probably Qu, know all about it."

"Euse, that is wonderful! It will be a simple matter to send in a team to find it."

"Do you really think so, Groose? Are we going to take over this planet?"

"Of course not! What do you think I am? It would be a partnership, at most, a co-governance. We could greatly enhance their living standards, to the mutual benefit of both countries. And just think what it would do for your career, Euse. You and Ess—in fact, all of us. Just think, rapid travel all over the galaxy. We'd better grab it for ourselves, before someone else finds out about it."

"I've seen what happens to planets that get taken into partnership. Oh yes, they get offered all sorts of goodies, with all sorts of strings attached. I wouldn't wish that on Groob, particularly since I've come to admire and respect Qu. To me it sounds like treachery. I also doubt if we are ready for such a leap forward in our technology. However, since what I decide affects you all I will put the matter to a vote. If you want me to tell the commander the portals really do exist, I will do so. I don't want you to decide right away, but rather think about it. We'll vote in a week, just before we go into hyperdrive. Remember, if anyone abstains, I have their vote as well as my own."

"Euse, are you sure you have detected a portal and not something else? Perhaps it was simply the way people ran their civilization a thousand years ago."

"Maybe, Groose, but unlikely. Why have it hidden? Why have so much of it? The amount of power needed to move this ship into hyperdrive is minuscule, compared with what they have there."

"And all the while Qu worries about finding oil."

"I'm sure Qu knows all about it."

"Why not vote now, Euse? I'm sure we all know how we'll vote."

"Very well, captain. Take your seats. Ess, hand out the ballot slips. I suggest you just indicate with a tick or a cross for yes or no."

CHAPTER 79

The verdicts

"That concludes the evidence, ladies and gentlemen. Shortly, the jurors will vote, and in the meantime I would like to introduce the judge of the court. He may confer with the jurors after they have voted, and he will mete out penalties for any person convicted."

"Thank you, Mr. Speaker. Yes, my job is to be as fair as possible, which means if someone is convicted I will attempt not merely to penalise the criminal appropriately, but also to compensate any victims of the crime. Mr Speaker, I suggest you adjourn the court for one hour."

"Court is adjourned."

"What do you think, Belzic?"

"I don't see much evidence of a crime, Andrew, unless it was in the early days, when young children were being affected. Just the same, I think these jurors will be out to get Qu for something. I'll go and talk to her, if I can get near enough."

Andrew, on his own, felt very much at a loss. The people he knew best were surrounded by sympathisers, and he was still trying to cope with the idea that he was stuck forever on this alien planet. He saw then that refreshments were being served and gratefully joined the queue.

The stage had changed. The judge was at the microphone, with three of the jurors alongside. People, some holding cups or plates, were hurrying to their seats.

"We now have verdicts on the people charged. Order! Order! Thank you. Firstly, on defendant Jelani Therim: ten votes in favour of conviction, ten against. Therefore Miss Therim has been found not guilty. The charges against Hamul and Umus were six for and thirteen against. I find that the employees generally did not break any laws. That is, they were conscientious in testing, and they took measures to protect the public when problems began to emerge. I conclude that the hostility towards them was based not on reckless behaviour but rather on unjustified fear.

"Now we come to Acting President Qu. Here the voting was sixteen for conviction and four against. Therefore Acting President Qu is convicted of a criminal offence and must relinquish her office. Her government's controlling interest in the company means that in her case there were measures that could have been taken early on, for example to restrict sales to within government, or perhaps to experimental groups. On the other hand I find no serious and reckless disregard for public safety, but rather concern to allow the kinds of freedoms the people in this country value very highly. Please now come to the stand, Acting President Qu. I find you guilty of failing to act with due care, and I sentence you to abstain from any public office for the next five years, effective immediately. In addition, I rule that the Dream Hunter Company be disbanded, since although no single employee was reckless, the company as a whole was. All the company's assets are to be surrendered to the state. As for those who own Dream Hunter devices, or who have invested in this company, that will be a matter for the next government to decide. Finally, I appoint General Greesh interim president, until elections are held.

"Mr Speaker, over to you."

"Thank you judge. The court is now out of session. Silence! I said silence! Please clear the hall."

Ω

"What will you do, ma'am? Whatever it is, we'll all support you."

Qu was pale, but dry eyed. She gave wan smiles to the group that clustered round her: Rain, Andrew, Belzic, Jelani and Umus.

"Thank you Rain. What will I do? First of all, invite all of my loyal supporters to my rooms. At least I think they are still my rooms, for tonight at least. Come."

There was no-one to meet them when the lift came to a stop. They filed out and followed Qu into the penthouse for the last time.

She walked to the big window. "This is a view I shall certainly miss."

The servants had already left, but there was food and drink available. There was even a note indicating what was where, and a little card with the signatures of those who had been her support staff. Belzic and Jelani got to work preparing a meal.

"I don't know when I'll see Aleb," said Jelani. "He's busy writing up a report for the papers."

"Your children are with their father?"

"Thank God, yes, ma'am."

A message came through that Hamul had died.

"Apparently it was a bad infection," said Qu.

"At least he didn't have to go through that ridiculous trial," said Jelani. "It was horrible, being stuck up on stage like some sort of trophy."

Soon after, Jelani and Umus left. Rain too had hurried off to meet someone. Andrew and Belzic were alone with Qu.

"I wonder what will become of us," said Andrew. "I don't fancy going back to that empty Embassy."

"Come, you two. I've got something to show you."

CHAPTER 80

"You're sure about these portals then, Euse?" Schyl toyed with his ballot paper. "Perhaps it's just your equipment? Perhaps there are faults in the ground that emit unexpected energy? Perhaps your calculations are just that, calculations, with no real basis."

"The energy is real enough, Captain, and I think that even if the portal conclusion is wrong, Space Headquarters is going to want to take another look."

Schyl thought about the consequences of actual portals becoming available on Cronalink. He would be famous. They all would be. A new source of energy that many had speculated about would become attainable, and the race would be on. A score of ships would land on Groob. The natives would resist. There would be a short, sharp civil war. The information would leak, and tensions would rise through the galaxy. Cronalink would be riddled with spies. And then there was Qu, whom he had come to admire very much …

"Very well, I support you, Euse. I'm not sure if anyone else will."

"Master, I abstain." Ess drew a line through his ballot paper and handed it in. Euse spread out the ballots for everyone to view.

"As you can see, there are three that say yes, and three that say no. There is also one abstention, and that gives me an extra vote; which means that the motion, that the likelihood of a portal system operating on Groob be concealed from space headquarters, is carried, four to three. Thank you, fellow crew members, for giving your attention to this matter."

Ω

"Stay close to me or you'll get lost." Qu shepherded the two Earthlings through several dimly lit basement passages.

"Most people don't know that there are far more than two levels of basement below City Hall. In fact I didn't know until I became president. Of course, you have to know where the lifts are, and apart from this one they're not easy to find. Here we are."

The lift door slid open. "Very efficient," Andrew murmured admiringly, as they were whisked down to a lower basement. The door opened onto absolute darkness.

Qu led the group by touch around several corners.

"Here's the next lift, and I'll give you some light."

Another lift, and another descent followed, along with more dark passages, so that the guests were soon hopelessly confused.

"I'd never find my way back unaided," Andrew conceded.

"It wouldn't be easy," Qu agreed. "We're there now."

Qu lit her lantern, and they found themselves in an almost circular cavern, high domed with walls of rough stone.

"Even if you had light all the way you'd probably never find this place. Now watch."

A shadow appeared on one of the rock faces, and while the two wondered where it was coming from it deepened, and quite suddenly became not a shadow but the mouth of a large circular tunnel.

"This is what your friends the Croans were looking for. It is also where, if you want to take the risk, you can return to your home planet."

A light formed in the tunnel, golden and enticing. It flooded the cavern, and lit the way ahead to a distance so remote it seemed infinite.

"This will take us to our home planet?"

"Planet Earth is one of the key destinations, and normally the first one, so I'm told. That's all I can tell you. The last person to use this portal did so ten years ago."

"Did he come back?"

"No, Belzic, there is no way back, at least, not that we know of. This represents the remnants of a complex system our forebears had a thousand and more years ago. It is known only to three people on this planet, other than myself, but when the Croans came looking for it I naturally denied knowing anything about it."

"I thought you might."

Qu laughed. "Nobody fools you for long."

"So now we have a choice," said Andrew.

"You have a choice, use it or not. I brought you two here because I trust you, and because you were giving evidence for me, Jelani and the others."

"And yet you brought us here in the dark."

"An essential part of the protocol, Andrew. Now, take your time, but you must either use the tunnel now or give up the opportunity forever. I should warn you though, I can't be sure if you'll return to your home planet, or any planet."

Andrew stared into the tunnel. The light was very enticing. It spoke to him of happy families, of cheerful evenings in front of a blazing fire, of being loved and cared for. And as he looked into it it swept his mind away to some unimaginably remote but beautiful distance. He looked at Belzic.

"Take it, Andrew. I'll come with you."

Belzic turned to Qu. "It's been a real privilege, ma'am."

"And you, dear Belzic." She held out her hand, but Belzic stepped back a pace and gave his stiff little bow.

Andrew now looked at Qu but was tongue-tied. Eventually he said, hesitantly, "Is all this some kind of magic, ma'am?"

"You mean, is the tunnel real? I'm told that when the portal isn't showing you could drill into that wall and all you'd ever find is rock. If I was to define it I'd say it sits in a borderland between what is real and what is pure fantasy. There are, I was told, a number of tunnels all over Groob, but this is the only one that operates on call. Now, off you go before it disappears."

Andrew in his turn gave a bow, and then, staying close beside Belzic, he walked into the tunnel.

CHAPTER 81

The funeral

The characteristic dry heat of the fire season had given way to a misty drizzle. It drifted in from the sea and found its way up the various terraces that Kraab was built on. The cemetery for Kraab and its environs was a little north of the city, and being chosen for the view rather than a convenient access, sat on the brow of the highest hill east of the desert. The staff from Dream Hunters, wrapped up against the wet, gathered around the box that contained the mortal remains of Hamul. Jelani, weeping, stood close to Aleb, and next to Aleb, Qu stood with Rain. Next to Rain was Umus, talking with a cluster of technicians, sales people and clerks. It would be the last time the Dream Hunter Company staff would all be together.

"No, I don't think he suffered in the end," said Umus. "Yes, we weren't very happy that the only people to care for him were a couple of army nurses, but he was locked away in his own world, even smiling a bit, so they said."

Qu, meanwhile, raised her eyes from the coffin and looked out over the ocean. Numilis, big and full, had risen, and cast a watery glow through the mist.

"They'll be on their way," she said.

"Do you think they'll be back, ma'am? They alarmed me when they talked about hunting for portals, but of course you put them off the scent."

"They won't be back, but not because I put them off the scent."

"Ma'am?"

"Euse knew I was bluffing. Nothing was said, but I could tell she knew."

"Ma'am, I was wondering …"

"What I am planning to do next?"

"I know there are companies queueing up to have you on their payroll."

"No, Rain, I've finished with big companies." Qu paused, and looked once more down into the hole in the ground, and then at the box containing Hamul. Life was short. "Rain, Rain, how would you like to go into business with me? Perhaps just the two of us …?"

"Ma'am, I'd love that."

"Only on condition that you stop calling me ma'am, or Qu for that matter. You must use my personal name."

"Oh yes, yes, I'd be very happy to meet that condition."

And spontaneously, the two turned away from the burial site and embraced. Rain began to cry.

"It's all right, Rain, I know, I know."

"Ma'am, we've found each other at last."

Qu too was finally crying. "Do you know Rain, I've never really let myself cry, not since I was a very little girl. But you've done it for me. Rain, I love you so much!"

Rain continued to cling, but she looked over Qu's shoulder. "Listen, the birds are coming back."

Qu turned to watch as thousands upon thousands of cawing birds headed inland towards the Great Desert and the far mountains beyond.

Ω

Finding home

"Belzic, where have you got to? I can't find you!"

The words echoed, not once, but endlessly along the passage ahead of him. The enticing light that had led the two of them into the portal had faded to a dim red glow, and the walls that had looked like shining glass were no longer smooth, but covered with cracks. There were now, he noticed, various side passages, mostly in complete darkness, and although the way ahead was still obvious it was no longer straight, but dipping and turning.

"Belzic!" he called again, and listened to the echoes running ahead.

There was another problem. Andrew was tired, unnaturally so, and the fatigue seemed to grow with every step.

"Belzic, I can't continue. I'll wait for you here." Andrew sat down where he was, and in another moment he was lying on his back, looking up at the domed ceiling, which was very slowly tipping and turning. Little creatures, very strange creatures, were crawling in and out of the widening cracks.

A terrible anguish drove Belzic further and further into the shadows, until he was enveloped in absolute darkness. He could hear his name being called, but the sound was infinitely remote, and somehow his calls in reply did not belong to him. The darkness took away all distinctions; and who he was, along with who he had ever been, all melted away. There was no more Belzic, and in time the darkness itself melted away. Without darkness, or light, or space itself, time was no more. There was nothing. Except, somehow, a presence. "I am nothing," Belzic whispered, and then, because the presence engulfed him more and more, "I am everything."

You have found me again.

"The transition is the hard part—but now I remember …everything."

Belzic basked for a little time in the consciousness that he was everything, and nothing. He was God, he was Belzic, he was nobody, he was everybody, he was the love that somehow incorporated them all.

"My God, my God …the words mean nothing," said Belzic.

The words mean nothing.

"Why do people not see, not understand?"

They wall themselves off from me, and therefore from themselves.

Belzic was silent a little longer.

"What will happen to Andrew? I suppose he will carry on."

He will continue as before.

"He walls himself off with words," said Belzic after reflecting on the matter. "On Earth he has a little group of followers and he paints beautiful word pictures for them."

There was no response to that, and Belzic too was silent once more, but presently, since the darkness had returned, he stood up , trying hard to confront the Presence that was everywhere and nowhere.

"What should I do now? Should I keep living in this world, any world?"

That, Belzic, is entirely your choice. Do not put responsibility onto me.

"Everything I did was always my choice, my responsibility. I can see that now."

Belzic was silent for that last time, and then he gave a little gasp, in which astonishment mingled with pleasure. The darkness lifted as light filtered in through a thousand cracks in the walls, the floor and the ceiling. The place where Belzic had been standing was now an empty stone slab that was cracking and crumbling into dust.

The noise intensified, and became a roaring like an angry sea. Little balls of light raced down passageways, always to encounter luminous shards from the collapsing roof, and explode into rainbows. Then the sound diminished as darkness once more descended over the entire portal. Finally, nothingness.

Ω

Andrew floated slowly into consciousness. He thought he could hear his mother calling him from a great distance. "Dodo! Dodo!" It was how she had named him in his early childhood, a name he barely remembered in his waking life. He tried to move, to respond in some way, but it was all too hard. He was still lying on his back, trying to understand what had happened. There had been a ceiling above him, domed and glassy. That had gone, and was replaced by sky. Early morning or late evening. A bird was singing nearby, and there was a sound of running water.

"My God, look who's here!"

"Andrew, what happened? Are you all right?"

"Easy, everyone, don't crowd him!"

He was surrounded by people he somehow knew, but could not name.

"Andrew, what happened? Where have you been?"

"We've been so worried."

"Were you lost in the woods?"

"You've been gone for days!"

"We had the police looking for you."

Andrew tried to raise his head, to take in what was happening. His memory of Groob was fading fast.

"Elizabeth, can he stand? See if he can stand."

Andrew rose to his feet, and suddenly everyone around him had a familiar face, was indeed an old friend.

"Yes, that's right, I was lost," he said. Then he frowned. "There should be a tunnel somewhere. Isn't there a tunnel, or a portal, or something? And where is Belzic?"

"Andrew, you're dreaming. Wake up! Help me with him, Jack."

"Goodness, look at you! You're filthy. Come on, lean on me. We'll get you home and clean you up."

EPILOGUE

Euse finished her debriefing, handing over all the information that hadn't yet been delivered. All, that is, except for the last energy survey, which she thoughtfully mislaid among her own private files. She next took a high speed travelator to the nearest health and fashion centre, and chose the latest, lightest, priciest exoskeleton on offer. Off went the old service uniform, while an assistant brought in a selection of dresses.

"No, no, no! None of those," said Euse. "I want to wow them! Get me something spicy! Order it in, if necessary, only make the order urgent!

Just the same, she left the centre in a moderately 'spicy' outfit, including jewellery that glowed enough to enhance her presence, and her confidence. Her next mission was to choose a wedding card, and she settled on one of the big, jolly, optimistic kind. She wrote: *To my old fellow pirates, Grice and Schyl. Behave yourselves, go happy, and no more fighting! Life is too short for all that nonsense.*

Next, she took a walk through the Hallway of Encounters, and looked out greedily over some of the most fabulous sights Cronalink has to offer: the hexagonal building facades, and the big green 'Stairway to Heaven' on the horizon. *I've been away too long.*

"Happy going, Euse."

It was a man she knew vaguely, but now was not the time.

"Always," she said dismissively, suddenly conscious that the pay she had collected from the mission would keep her in luxury for a long time to come.

There was someone else. Ess! There would be no more neutralising 'master' addresses from Ess. It was time to deal with the man.

And there indeed was Ess, coming towards her.

"Happy going, Ess."

"Only if it can be with you."

Euse reached out an arm, caught hold of her one time technical assistant. "Of course it can!"

The two headed for the nearest bunker. They took an express lift, tabbed one of the vacant cells, and hurried towards it. Euse felt almost giddy with excitement as she looked around. The room contained two large circular pads, a plunge pool, and a great many cupboards and hooks. She sat on the edge of one of the pads and tested its springiness. Ess sat opposite on the other pad. There was a long pause.

"I hear you are getting an award as well as a promotion, Essie boy," said Euse. "Well deserved, of course."

"And you too, master, get an award for saving planet Earth from that comet."

"I am now your mistress, not your master, Essie boy."

"Of course, you put the comet there in the first place."

"Ess, don't you dare say that to anyone!"

"Although of course it was great to be able to study the earthlings under threat, master … I mean, mistress."

"Enough of that! I want to see what you look like under your exoskeleton."

Ess began to strip. Euse came up close to help.

Later, a sleepy Ess twisted his mobile neck towards his lover. "We could make a lot of money if we went back, mistress. Or back to Trilfarne."

"We already have a lot of money. At least, I have. Besides, I gave my word."

"It was all a wee bit risky, wasn't it. Especially that last planet."

"No, Essie boy, and especially not that last planet. Guriang was the quintessential politician, easily manipulated by the scent of power, or money. Between us we had more than enough knowledge and technology to keep him in his place."

Euse reached out a tentacle, wrapped it firmly around her lover's neck, and drew it in hard against her body. Ess gave a strangulated gasp, and yielded.

"Enough talking, Essie boy. Enough talking."

Ω

5d28 lexin C: Exelyn

Exelyn, how are you, old colleague, old rogue? You can see that, in spite of all predictions, I have come through the three planet mission alive and more or less unscathed, and am now safely back on Cronalink. No thanks to our old mate and leader Euse, who scared the tits off all of us. We now regard her as the most dangerous woman in the world.

Exelyn, I have a proposition which I can tell you about in detail when we meet, but briefly, it's to do with the energy which we suspected all along was coming from that 4th planet in the Groobian system. No, I won't say any more, except that the artefacts still mostly buried on that planet would be well worth examining. Say nothing of this!

Apart from myself, there are two of the Duvra crew who would like to talk to you—and after that last mission you can be sure we are looking for investment opportunities! And there is a lot of money, repeat, lot of money, to be made.

Best regards to you, and that lovely family of yours, Groose.

Groose completed his letter and looked up.

"Erg, have a read, tell me what you think. And you, Cherg. Exelyn is the one we want, though I can't contact him directly at the moment."

Erg stood over Groose and looked at the monitor. "Sure, Groose, we need to do something. The rest are doing well, especially Euse and her toy boy. But you, Groose, did a ton of work. I did too really, when it came to all the exploration we did."

"You more than the rest of us, Erg," said Groose. "And your work on portals wasn't even acknowledged, thanks to Euse!"

"So what do we do, Groose? Another big trip?"

"We wait for Exelyn. I have a feeling he'd be interested in what we know about those portals."

Groose smiled, and the low sun caught the side of his face as he led the others into his hexagonal cell. He produced a bottle and glasses.

"Let's all drink to our next venture!"

The End??

The four seasons form a dance: they are the nurseries for ideas that take root, grow and blossom like young saplings taking their chances, to thrive or perish. Either way they are eventually passed over, deceased and forgotten, or invisible because too familiar; and all attention is on the new round, which is forever different and forever the same: water, earth, air and fire. There is only the dance.

And each character in the dance carries on, but to no particular end, for there is none. Nor are there any goals, other than the illusory dreams of the dancers. And yet, by a mystery inherent in the very nature of every world, there are endings, and beginnings, and there is, just sometimes, what the dancers might call resolution.

ALSO BY BEVAN KNIGHT

The Wishing Tree

"Readers will find this a fantasy thriller to mesmerise them and leave them longing for more." —*Jennifer Weiss for Pacific Book Review*

"A wonderful meld of science fiction and fantasy." —*David Reyes for the Book Commentary*

"Daring adventure, sharp betrayal, and soft romance combine in a well—written fantasy and science fiction tale where things are never exactly as they seem"—*John E Roper for US Review of Books*

Earthlight

"The trials and struggles of every character felt realistic ... with visceral descriptions of scenes and settings that really transported me to that near future"—*best selling author K C Finn.*

"An enthralling science fiction adventure"—*the Book Lighthouse*

"From the stellar writing to the impeccable world—building, Knight offers a delightful entry that reads perfectly as a standalone novel" —*Christian Fernandez for the Book Commentary*

"Explores how humanity might be viewed by another civilisation" —*January Magazine (January 26, 2022)*